ALSO BY DICK ELDER

Which Way is West
You and Your Horse
Lovers & Liars
It Sure Beats Working
The Way Out

Lucky Numbers

DICK ELDER

iUniverse LLC
Bloomington

LUCKY NUMBERS

iUniverse books may be ordered through booksellers or by contacting:

iUniverse LLC
1663 Liberty Drive
Bloomington, IN 47403
www.iuniverse.com
1-800-Authors (1-800-288-4677)

ISBN: 978-1-4917-3196-3 (sc)
ISBN: 978-1-4917-3197-0 (hc)
ISBN: 978-1-4917-3195-6 (e)

Library of Congress Control Number: 2014906739

Printed in the United States of America.

iUniverse rev. date: 04/16/2014

"Money often costs too much."
Ralph Waldo Emerson

"The waste of money cures itself,
for soon there is no more to waste"
M. W. Harrison

Dedication

To the millions of gamblers who never won a lottery and,
To those who won, but squandered every cent and,
To the few who used their winnings wisely...
This book is especially for you!

Prologue

There was nothing unusual about Edward Noble or his wife Sandy, or their twin daughters Patricia and Beverly. They were a typical middle-income family living in "The Knolls," a subdivision of new cookie-cutter stucco homes in Peoria, Arizona. The Knolls offered five styles and the Nobles bought the three bedroom model in 2001 for $230,000. That was the year that Ed became manager of a Safeway store at a salary of $75,000 a year. Sandy earned around $30,000 as the office manager for a group of dentists

At the time they moved into their new house, Ed was thirty-four, Sandy, a year younger, and the twins had their twelfth birthday shortly afterwards. Ed and Sandy had met while attending Arizona State University. They graduated in 1989 and married in 1990. Nothing unusual or particularly exciting about any of that. Just a loving couple with two children, a nice new home, good jobs, living their version of the American Dream. As far as they were concerned, things were about as good as they could be. The Nobles were a happy, well-adjusted family. That is, until six numbers changed everything.

Chapter 1

Peoria, Arizona was a desert community of 100,000 northwest of Phoenix when Ed bought his home. At the time, the best supermarket in Peoria was the Safeway. Now, in 2005, other supermarkets had been built and competition was keen. A manager had to be clever and resourceful if he wanted to stay on top and keep his job, and Ed was exactly that.

Late on this particular afternoon, he stopped briefly at the door to say good-night to the four cashiers.

"Ain't you gonna buy a ticket, Ed?" Verna called from her check stand. "It's the last day."

"Geeze, that's right." Ed walked back to her station. "Let me have three and the machine can pick the numbers."

Verna ran off the Lottery tickets and handed them to him.

"Thanks for reminding me," he said. "This one pays around two hundred million and I never miss the big ones," he added with a laugh. "Of course, I never win them either, but like they say, 'You can't win if you don't play.' Right?"

"I guess so," Verna said with a smile. Her own tickets were in her purse.

Ed paid and said, "Goodnight, now. See you tomorrow."

The evening stock boy came hurrying down an aisle. "Hey, Mr. Noble, have you got a minute?"

Ed turned around. "What's up, Barry?"

The boy held up a sheaf of stock records. "I need to ask you about some of this."

"Okay." Ed sighed as he laid the raffle tickets next to the cash register and reached for the pages the boy handed him.

Fifteen minutes later, Ed was at last on his way. Arriving home around six, he stopped briefly in the kitchen to give his wife a peck on the cheek. Then he went to his bedroom, where he kicked off his shoes, took off his shirt and tie, and threw the shirt in a laundry hamper. He slipped out of his pants, carefully attached a pants hanger and hung them on his side of the walk-in closet. The tie he placed on a tie rack. He slipped into a worn and severely faded pair of Levi's, pulled a tee shirt over his head, put on an old pair of loafers and went down to the kitchen.

"Are you going to have a drink tonight?" Sandy asked.

Ed gazed at her and thought, *Even after ten years and having twins, she's as beautiful and sexy as ever*—tall and slim with baby-blue eyes, dark blonde hair, beautiful face and a lovely figure. *I sure got lucky.* Ed blinked and said, "Drink, sure. How 'bout you? What would you like?"

"Vodka and tonic," she replied. She opened the refrigerator, pulled out a lime and cut off a wedge. "Here, squeeze this in it."

The liquor was kept in the cabinet above the refrigerator. When Sandy wanted to get something out of that cabinet, she had to use the step-stool to enhance her 5'-8" height. Ed's 6'-3" made it easy for him to reach it. He took down a bottle of Smirnoff vodka and a bottle of Early Times bourbon and made the two cocktails. Handing Sandy hers, he said, "There you go, Pilcher." He had started calling her by her last name when they were students. Ed thought it was definitely a term of endearment.

The twins were watching television when Ed entered the living room. Patricia, tall for her age, and slim, had stretched her long legs along the sofa. A brighter blonde than her mom, Pat was already getting attention from the boys in her class. Beverly, too, was—in Ed's view—an equal beauty, a bit shorter and a little huskier than her twin, but with flaming red hair that caught people's eye.

"Good evening ladies," he said, dropping into the armchair nearest the couch. "How are my double bubble girls doing today?" The girls looked at him briefly and said in unison, "Fine."

"Anything interesting or exciting you'd like to tell me?" Both girls gave him another glance, shrugged, and turned their attention back to the program.

"Well," he said, rattling the ice in his glass, half in exasperation. "That was a very nice conversation. Thanks a lot for giving me your undivided attention and for bringing me up to speed on everything you did today."

Pat jumped up and gave Ed a hug. "We'll talk during dinner, Daddy. Don't get all pissy—"

"Hey, that's not a term that nice young ladies use—"

Pat broke in, "All the kids say it. There's nothing wrong with it. It's not like a dirty word or anything like that."

"Okay, let's just say that I don't like you saying it." He stood up. "So just don't say it anymore."

Pat rolled her eyes. "Okay, okay." Flopping back down on the couch, she gave Bev a look which her sister returned with a dismissive shake of her head.

Back in the kitchen, Ed stepped behind Sandy, put his arms around her petite waist and whispered in her ear, "Something smells pretty damn good. It's either you or whatever you're cooking."

Sandy eased around and faced him. He kissed her lips, inhaled deeply and said, "It's you...definitely you. You smell good enough to eat." He kissed her again.

She put a finger over his mouth. "Shush, the girls will hear you."

Ed laughed. "So what? I'm sure they heard you the other night when you let go with that, what was it, a yelp?"

"Hey, I couldn't help it. You hit the jackpot and it blew me away." Her cheeks took on a slight glow. "Anyway, when they asked me what happened, I told them that there was a spider in our bed and I screamed when it bit me."

Ed gave Sandy a pat on the behind. "Good one," he chuckled. "I'm going to watch the news." He picked up his drink and headed for the den.

Later that evening, Sandy was in the bathroom brushing her teeth when Ed walked in. He picked up his toothbrush then suddenly laid it down and walked out of the room. Sandy looked after him, then followed him into the bedroom.

"What's the matter?" she asked.

"Nothing. I just remembered that I bought some Lottery tickets today and I left them in my pants. I was just going to get them. The drawing is tonight." Ed walked into the closet, stuck his hand in the pants pocket and was surprised to find it empty. He checked the other pockets and his sport coat. "Damn, what the hell did I do with those tickets?" Suddenly he remembered. He called the store and asked Verna to look next to the register for the tickets. She had them.

Sandy asked, "Why all the fuss about raffle tickets, for gosh sake? I don't understand why you waste your money buying them. It's not like you're going to win."

"You never know," he said.

"You never know? You don't know that they've sold millions of those damn tickets and your chances of winning are like one in umpteen million?"

"Yeah, I know and I don't buy them all the time, just when there's a super big jackpot. This one's around two hundred million."

"You want to win something? Next time, instead of buying raffle tickets, how 'bout buying me a dozen roses? The odds are much better that you'll get lucky getting that thing you like so much."

Ed and Sandy were sitting on the love seat in the den watching the ten o'clock news. At the end of the newscast the scene switched to a live shot of the Lottery drawing. "The results of the Lottery, right after the break."

Ed jumped up. "I should have asked Verna to give me the numbers."

Sandy shook her head and rolled her eyes. "Geeze, Ed, relax. You can check 'em tomorrow. I'm going to get the girls' lunches ready." She stood and walked into the kitchen.

Ed had a pen in his hand and picked up a magazine from the coffee table ready to record the numbers as the announcer called them out. The numbers were printed on ping pong balls that were shot down a cute from a whirling mass in a glass jar. "Our first number is seven," said the announcer somberly. Another ball popped out and rolled down the rack. "Number fifty-one. Next, number thirteen. That's seven, fifty-one and thirteen." The next ball joined the others. "Number thirty six and now here comes the last white ball, fifty-seven." The announcer's voice built the tension. "And the red ball...here it comes, number 44. And there you have it. The winning number worth two hundred and four million dollars is seven, fifty-one, thirteen, thirty-six, fifty-seven, and the Lottery ball, forty-four. Congratulations to the winner."

Ed walked into the kitchen and said, "They did the drawing."

"Oh, did the boy not win the big jackpot?" Sandy said with mock indulgence. "Don't cry. Here, come to Mama." She put down the plastic wrap and spread her arms.

He walked into them. "I might have won." He nuzzled her neck. Sandy held him until they both broke down laughing. "Like I told you before, you'll do a lot better if you stop buying those stupid raffle tickets and just bring me a dozen roses. I've got your prize right here and all you have to do is hand me the roses to collect your winnings."

"How about a consolation prize then?"

Sandy stepped back and waggled a finger in his face. "Sorry, no prize for losers."

The next morning when Sandy was in the den straightening up, she picked up the magazine from the coffee table and noticed the numbers Ed had written on the back cover. She found the morning newspaper in the kitchen. In a box on the front page were the winning lottery numbers. She checked the winning numbers in the paper with those Ed had listed. She called Ed at work. "Did you check your raffle tickets yet?"

"No, not yet. I've been busy."

"I've got the paper here and the numbers are listed on the front page. Read me the numbers on your first ticket."

"Thought you didn't believe in—"

"You never know, right?" she said facetiously.

Ed chuckled. "That's what I always say. Okay, here you go." He recited the numbers.

Sandy let loose a raspberry. "Sorry. That is a loser. What's the next one?" She noticed Beverly had left her lunch bag. "Damn," she said, thinking about having to drive to the school to drop it off.

"Honey?" Ed asked.

"Oh, sorry. Okay. Go."

Ed picked up the next ticket and said, "Seven, fifty-one, thirteen, thirty-six, fifty-seven and the red ball, forty-four."

Sandy sucked in her breath. "Whoa, whoa, whoa. Hold it. Say those numbers again, slowly."

Ed felt his heart jump into his throat. "What? Are those the numbers?"

"Read 'em again. I want to write 'em down." The room seemed to be spinning a little.

"Seven, fifty-one, thirteen, thirty-six, fifty-seven and the red ball, forty-four."

Sandy gasped and reached for a chair, the pen clattering to the floor.

Ed screamed, "Sandy—what the hell—talk to me!"

No, that can't be, she thought. "Just a sec," she said. She took another very careful look. *What the...* She checked again, saying each number aloud, "Seven, fifty-one, thirteen, thirty-six, fifty-seven and the red, forty-four. Right?"

"Right."

"Oh, my God!" she screamed. "You won it!" She dropped the phone and went dancing around the room, yelling, "We're rich, we're rich!" She picked up the phone. Her hands were shaking and her breath was coming in bursts. She could feel the veins in her neck pulsing. For a moment, she thought she might faint.

Ed was shouting, too. "Talk to me. Did I win it, really?"

Sandy swallowed, took a couple of deep breaths and gasped, "Yes, yes. You won the God damn lottery. We are frigin' millionaires! Can you believe it? We must be dreaming." She continued to babble hysterically. Suddenly, she paused. "What do you think we'll end up with after taxes?"

"Hell, I don't know—but it'll be a lot, that's for sure..."

Ed was silent so long Sandy asked, "Ed?'"

"This is just... I don't know what to..." His voice drifted off again.

"Talk to me, honey," Sandy begged. "Are you alright?"

Ed laughed. "Alright? You gotta be kidding. But listen, Pilcher, for now don't say anything to anybody, you understand? Don't tell the kids, your mother, nobody. We need to think about how we're going to handle this. I don't want to make the same mistake most winners make."

"What mistake?"

"I'm coming home and we'll talk about it, so stay put and don't tell anyone. I mean it, don't tell a God damn soul about it. I'll be there in ten minutes." He hung up.

Sandy heard the garage door open and was waiting for Ed to drive in and get out of the car so she could greet him with a kiss. Maybe more.

He was sporting a huge grin and holding a large bouquet of red roses as Sandy ran into his waiting arms. "You did it, you son of a gun," she squealed. She cast an eye on the roses, "Hell, you don't need the roses this time. You won the blow job."

"Wait. Where are the girls?"

"At school, of course." She grabbed his hand and pulled him through the kitchen and up the stairs to their bedroom. "Give me those," she insisted. She took the bouquet and laid it on her dressing table. "Now, get out of those clothes and get ready to collect your prize," she said while pulling off her tee shirt and unhooking her bra. As she watched him undress she admired him—his athletic frame, his face still as handsome as when they'd married, the pale blue eyes that seemed to dance when he became excited, and the shock of wavy brown hair that topped it off. She remembered the first time she saw him when they were in college. It wasn't just his height that made him stand out from the group of men he was with. She had made it a point to meet him and once she did, they became inseparable.

Ed was virtually tearing off his clothes, but his words brought her back to the present. "Hey, Pilcher, you're in this too. Don't you get a prize as well?"

"Sure, why not? Tell you what. We'll give each other the prize at the same time. Can you go for that?"

An hour later, fresh from the shower, they sat at the kitchen table drinking coffee and beginning to process reality. Sandy said, "So you said you didn't want me to tell anyone about winning. Why's that?"

He cupped the mug in his hands and studied it for a moment. "I'll tell you why. I've read that a large percentage of big jackpot winners end up broke within a couple of years."

"Really?" She leaned back in her chair. "Why would that happen?"

"A lot of reasons. They just go nuts and start throwing it around, buying all kinds of stuff they don't need—big houses, fancy cars, boats, airplanes, big parties—just throwing money around. And people take advantage of them, relatives come out of the woodwork looking for loans, charities and churches are after them for donations. There's no end to it."

"I guess I never paid much attention to any of it—no reason to, actually."

He nodded. "Anyway, they've tracked most of the big winners and have found out that, like I said, most of those people end up broke. There was one guy who actually won twice and pissed the money away both times.

The problem is they get taken in. Most of them aren't very smart about money, investing and, you know, managing finances and the first thing you know, boom, it's all gone." He gazed at her, lifting his eyebrows. "That is definitely not going to happen to us."

"No, certainly not. We know how to manage money, we've been doing it for years, which are why we had the down payment for this house." Sandy added, "Am I right or what?"

"You're exactly right, my sexy little wife. This family is not going to fall into that trap. We'll make some gifts. I think that's the right thing to do—maybe a million or so. We'll set up some kind of a trust fund for the girls' college costs and another trust for them so if something happens to us, they'll be safe but they won't get a ton of money dumped on them all at once. I'm going to talk to our tax guy about all this as soon as I can."

Sandy refilled her cup and held the pot up to Ed, who shook his head. "People will find out about it when you cash in your ticket, won't they?"

"I guess so," he replied. "I don't imagine you can avoid it since the IRS will probably be right there to get our name and all the information."

Sandy returned to the table and sat down. "What if you wore some kind of a disguise when you turn in the ticket?"

"I don't know. I would still have to give them my real name and show identification, wouldn't I?"

"I suppose so. But at least, if there are TV cameras, people won't know what you look like and when you go out on the street they won't be hounding you."

"We need to do some research on this before I go in. The main thing is, we have to handle it right because if we don't, things could go south in a hurry." Ed paused for a long moment and smiled at his wife. "Are you with me on this?"

"Absolutely. This is a fantastic thing. We've simply got to deal with it in a mature and responsible way." She took hold of his hand and gave it a squeeze. "And we will."

Chapter 2

In Arizona, the winner of a lottery has six months to claim his prize, but after claiming it, the winner has only sixty days to state whether he wants a lump sum settlement or the full amount paid out as an annuity over a number of years. A winner can remain anonymous for a while but eventually, by law, the name must be revealed. Ed and Sandy took advantage of that rule and were able to remain anonymous for a couple of months.

They told no one, not even the girls, about winning. Even though both of them were practically bursting with the news, Ed remained on the job at Safeway and Sandy kept her job with the dental group. Quietly, Ed contacted his good friend and attorney, Aaron Feldman, whom he swore to secrecy. Feldman's assignment was to form an advisory group consisting of himself, a money manager, an estate planner, and a certified public accountant who specialized in taxation and related topics. Ed and Sandy met with the various individuals as Feldman submitted their names. It took close to a month for them to settle on the members, but once the selection process was over, the committee was formed and a meeting was held. Kip Garvan, the CPA, advised the Nobles to take the lump sum rather than the annuity. He explained in detail why he thought this would be the best choice. Manny Franklin, the estate planner agreed, stating that it would be much easier that way for him to set up some trusts and other tax saving devices, especially gifts to the two girls. The money manager, Carl Griffin, said he would wait and see what the others developed before offering any specific investment advice, but meanwhile he would set up a plan for what to do initially with the money after it was paid out.

Ed and Sandy were satisfied that they were going about the business of handling their huge windfall in an intelligent way that would insure that they would not fall victim to squandering their fortune or being hijacked by unscrupulous con artists.

It was Feldman who actually received the check on Ed's behalf. An agent from the IRS and another from the Arizona State Treasurer's Office were there to receive their respective share of the loot. What remained was a little over eighty-eight million dollars. It was immediately given to the money manager, Griffin, who had prearranged where it would go to insure its safety. Now, all that remained was for Ed and Sandy Noble to enjoy being millionaires.

The first order of business was to tell the twins, close family, friends, and their employers, to whom they also gave a month's notice. It took only a week of phone calls from long-lost and many-times-removed relatives, charities they'd never heard of, and one persistent annuity salesman parking himself at their front door, for Ed to realize, with Sandy agreeing, that it would be in their best interests to move away from Peoria and from Arizona as well. They decided on southern California, someplace along the central coast and a home near the ocean. Someplace where people didn't know them and how rich they were. Someplace where no one would hound them for loans or offer them schemes that would "make them even more money." No, they'd be out of harm's way. They would buy a nice home, maybe a couple of nice cars, send the girls to a nice private school, and then live a nice life by limiting their spending to a very respectable yet quite generous $300,000 a year. That's what they decided.

All of this information was given to the twins one evening after dinner.

"So you see," Ed said, "what your mother and I are trying to do is not end up like most winners who, in a matter of just a few years, end up with nothing. The trust funds and other things we are setting up will insure that the money will last longer than Mom and I and be a wonderful thing for you two and your children."

Sandy added, "I hope you girls appreciate and understand what we're telling you." Sandy looked into Beverly's eyes and wasn't sure what, if anything, was registering. "Bev," she said, "Do you have some questions you'd like to ask us?"

Beverly gave her mother a wide-eyed look. "No, not really. I think I understand all that stuff and that it's for our own good."

"And the good of the family," Pat exclaimed. "But, it's like going to change the way we live, right? I mean, like we're rich. We can afford just about anything... I mean eighty-eight mil—that's like a huge amount of money, I mean, who even has that much?"

Impatient, Sandy asked, "What's your point?"

Pat spread her arms, taking in the room. "We don't have to live like this anymore."

Ed jumped in, "And what's wrong with this? This is a really nice place—a lot better than most people have."

"No, Daddy, I don't mean that. What I'm talking about is that we can afford to live in like a really big house—a fancy place, you know like some of those people in Scottsdale."

"And we could have some really cool cars, too," Beverly added.

Ed broke in with a definite edge in his voice. "Listen, you two, it's not like that. That's what some of those idiots did who ended up with nothing. But, okay, I'll tell you what we've decided to do. We are going to move away from here to some place where people won't know we've won a lot of money, and—"

"Where are we going to move to?" Pat broke in, excitement building in her voice. "Oh, please say it's California. Please!"

"Near the ocean," Beverly added.

Sandy and Ed broke out in laughter. "How'd you guess?" Sandy sputtered.

"Really?" Pat jumped up from her chair, ran behind her father and wrapped her arms around him.

Beverly watched for a second and hugged her mother. "This is so cool," she cried. "Where are you thinking—or have you already found someplace? C'mon, tell us all about it."

"Just settle down, girls," Sandy said. "Your father and I are thinking about an area on the coast north of Los Angeles—an area called Malibu."

The name caught Pat midway into flopping down on the sofa. She turned open-mouthed to Sandy, then grinned at her sister.

"Malibu!" The girls shouted in unison.

"That's where all the big movie stars live," Beverly squealed. "It's the coolest place in the world!"

Ed raised his hands for quiet. "Hey, you two, chill. We're going to go out there and look around. Nothing has been decided yet. We have a real estate agent looking at properties for us and she did find a home on the beach that's for sale but it's terribly expensive."

Pat jumped in, "So what? I mean, how much could it be? We've got millions, so it doesn't really matter what it costs, does it?"

"Well, that's not the point," Ed said. "We don't want to be taken advantage of, do we? Anyway, we're going out there next week and meet with the realtor. She has other places to show us while we're there."

"And," Sandy added, "we'll have a chance to look around and see what's available and make sure that we buy a place that we'll all enjoy—that's the main thing."

Chapter 3

The home they bought was on the beach, just steps away from the water's edge on the west side of Malibu Road and just a little north of Puerco Canyon Road. Ed wasn't exactly crazy about it because the houses along the beach were so close together. "You can darn near reach out and touch the house next door," he complained. However, Sandy and the twins loved it and that was that.

It was big—not the largest house on that stretch of the beach—but over 5,000 square feet of living area. Ed "darn near choked" when he learned the $4,750,000 price. The realtor's commission was more than Ed had paid for his new home in Peoria.

"I know it's crazy extravagant," Sandy declared, "but we certainly can afford it. Besides, you know it's a great investment. These houses are never going to be cheaper." That was certainly true. Houses on the beach in Malibu were prime real estate and historically, a solid investment.

Ed fought it, but knew he was in a losing battle. Sandy and the girls pushed hard and eventually got their way. Furnishing a home of this size was a monumental task, as Sandy quickly learned. She told Ed she needed help—a decorator who was familiar with houses such as theirs, someone who "knew what she was doing." After shopping around and making inquiries, Sandy decided on a high-end furniture store in Santa Barbara. She and Ed drove to Shackleford's, the best and most expensive store on the central coast. They met the store's chief designer, Keisha Burkhardt, an impeccably dressed woman in her forties who showed Ed and Sandy the store's inventory of fine furniture, rugs and accessories. Ed saw a beautiful dining room set and asked the price. $27,000, Ms. Burkhardt told him.

Ed's eyes widened. "You're kidding, right?"

Keisha gave him a straight-faced glower. "Kidding?" she said somewhat disdainfully. "Why would I be kidding? You asked how much it was and I told you."

Taken aback, Ed replied, "Hey, relax, sister. I guess I'll just have to get acclimated to the price of things out here."

Keisha snapped back, "I certainly am not your sister, and if you find these prices out of your comfort zone, I can suggest some other stores that may be able to accommodate your needs somewhat better than we."

Sandy, her own feathers ruffled, exclaimed, "Miss Burkhardt, we just bought a home on the beach for close to five million dollars and," she paused and shot Keisha a ferocious look, "we paid cash for it. The home is rather large and we need to furnish and decorate it from top to bottom. If you are unable to handle this project and, I should add, handle it very well, then it may be that you and Shackleford's are not going to work out for us." She proffered a generous smile. "Now, would you prefer we seek another store and a different decorator?"

Keisha, choking down her arrogant demeanor, went to work putting a household full of high quality furniture, all very tastefully arranged, together with lamps, rugs, carpeting, draperies, wall hangings and accessories of every description. Sandy was surprised when the bill for the items and Keisha's services came to nearly $500,000. When she told Ed about the cost, he cautioned her to put the brakes on her spending as the cost of buying the home and furnishing it was way more than he had anticipated. Now it was time, he told her, to start living somewhat more frugally. She was sure he really didn't exactly mean frugal, but *sensibly,* as they had agreed.

Small wonder that Sandy was rather surprised when, within a few weeks of Ed's admonishing her for spending so much decorating the house, he drove home in a very sporty and extravagantly expensive Aston-Martin DB9 convertible. It was the most beautiful car she had ever seen. Nonetheless, when he took her for a short drive, she couldn't resist commenting, "Aren't you the guy who recently gave me hell for spending all that money with Keisha?"

Ed was not in the least put off. "This car is an investment. I can probably drive it for the rest of my life, that's how well it is made. And like you said about the house, it won't lose much value over time."

Sandy gave him a doubtful look. "Do you mind telling me how much it cost?"

"Under two hundred thousand."

"Are you kidding me? That's crazy, especially after your lecture about being frugal."

"Look, Pilcher, I know it's super extravagant but I'll probably drive it for the next ten years. When you amortize it over that time period, keeping in mind that these cars don't lose their value like most other cars, it's really a pretty good investment. Plus," he added, slapping the steering wheel with both hands, "I'm driving one of the world's greatest cars." Ed flashed a huge smile, his eyes sparkling with *bonhomie.*

"Really? And you expect me to believe that load of crap? Meanwhile, I'm driving a three year old Toyota. I guess you should have bought two of these cars, seeing as how they're such great value."

Ed bristled. "Hey, did I give you any shit when you spent a ton of money furnishing the house?"

"As a matter of fact, yes—you did." Sandy pushed open the door, got out of the car and strode into the house.

Ed stepped out of the car thinking, *I could have handled that better.*

Sandy was in the kitchen reaching for bottle of beer in the refrigerator. Ed came up behind her and put his arms around her waist, pulling her to him. "I'm sorry, honey."

Sandy turned holding the beer in her hand. "You want one?"

"Sure."

She retrieved it, pushed the door closed with her hip and carried the bottles to the island counter. "You see," she said, twisting the caps off and handing Ed his, "this is the very thing we promised each other we would not do."

Ed took a sip. "You're right. We're going nuts just like most of the other big winners have."

Sandy pulled out a long-legged stool and sat down at the counter. "Come over here and let's see if we can get ourselves back on track."

Ed sat next to her and took a drag from the bottle. "From now on, before we make any large purchase," he tapped his lip as he thought, "say anything over a thousand bucks, we consult about it and decide if it's really something we should spend money on."

"There you go. That's a darn good idea. I vote yes on that."

Ed drained the bottle. "Okay then. Here's our first vote. I move that we buy you a new car. Maybe an SUV would be handy to have. Would you want an SUV? I mean two convertibles would be kind of silly, right?"

"Sure. An SUV would be great. What kind?"

"How about a Lexus or a Mercedes? We'll drive into LA tomorrow and look around. What do you say?"

Sandy put out her hand and shook his. "It's a deal." She stood, bent over and kissed him generously on the mouth. "Now we're cooking."

Chapter 4

They bought a Lexus. They kept the Toyota for the twins to use and insisted the girls pay for the gas and minor upkeep out of their allowances, which were generous but not over the top. They hired a housekeeping company that sent a four-girl team to clean every week. At first, Ed tried to maintain the pool himself, but when the water started turning green and algae was beginning to grow around the water line, he figured it made sense to hire a pool service. Sandy thought having fresh cut flowers brought in every week would add a nice touch and since the monthly bill was only five hundred dollars, it fell below the thousand dollar criteria for holding a meeting to approve the service.

The twins were definitely not very happy about having to drive a Toyota. The evening that subject came up was something of a firestorm.

"The kids at school all drive cool cars and that old Toyota is like seriously not cool," Bev insisted. "Why would you want us to be laughed at?"

"Ridiculed," Pat added. "Toyotas suck. Like nobody in Malibu drives a Toyota except like maybe the maids or gardeners...you know, *workers.*"

Both Sandy and Ed jumped in the middle of that remark. Sandy held up a hand. "Let me handle this, Ed." She faced the girls. She hadn't been this angry in a long time. "Listen, you two prima donnas, what's going on with you? All of a sudden you're turning into debutantes. Just because your father won a lot of money and we suddenly became rich—that makes you special? I don't think so."

"But, Mom—" Pat began to protest.

"No buts, young lady." Sandy glared at her. "Consider this: the reason we're rich is because of your father's dumb luck. He didn't invent something or run an investment firm or have any kind of a job that paid him a huge salary. No! He was a supermarket manager, that's all. You two are the daughters of a *worker*, you understand?"

Pat flinched.

Sandy pressed on. "Your father is a great guy, an honest, hard-working, intelligent man, but he didn't make his money like most of the people around here who earned it. No, he was just lucky. So don't you two get on your high horse like you're somebody special. You're the exact same girls who lived at the Knolls in Peoria. Nothing more. You should thank God that all this good fortune came our way and you should be thinking, like Dad and I have been, about what good things you can do with money instead of thinking only of yourselves."

Sandy sat back in her chair and glared at Bev and Pat, who sat with mouths open, speechless.

Ed, too, said nothing but gave Sandy an admiring smile, then he reached over and patted her shoulder. He shifted his gaze to the twins. "So what's the bottom line? You two will share the Toyota or simply ride your bikes. I frankly don't care which you choose to do except that when you drive the car you'll make darn sure there's no drinking, no horseplay going on and whoever is driving is paying attention to the road—which means, no cell phone use, period."

Both girls started talking at once but Ed cut them off. "Just shut it. When you go to college, and if you have demonstrated that you have been responsible drivers, that you have studied hard and got good grades, I'll get you each a car…a nice, cool car that you'll be proud to drive. So let's agree right now that there will be no more discussion about cars until after you finish your freshman year at college."

Sandy nodded her agreement. "That makes perfect sense to me. Keep in mind what's important and don't get caught up in all the nonsense some of your classmates think is cool."

Ed said, "When you are older and look back on all of this, you'll be thankful you had responsible parents who stuck to their principles and made sure that you did, too."

The girls stood and were about to leave when Sandy said, "Wait a minute, sit down." The girls gave each other a roll of the eyes and sat. "I just want to say something about your education. You are attending Malibu High. Are you aware that your school is one of the top high schools in California? It's rated number 184 of the top 1,200 hundred high schools in America."

Ed looked up. "Is that right? That's pretty darn good."

Sandy continued. "Not only is it a top school but did you know that, like you two, over half of your senior classmates have a 3.0 or higher GPA?"

The twins looked at each other. Beverly said, "No, I didn't know that, although there's a lot of really smart kids in our class taking advanced placement courses. I know one girl has like a perfect 4.0. Can you believe it?"

Pat asked, "Who's that?"

"Emily Bernstein. And that goofy guy, Nathan."

"Okay, there you go," Sandy said. "The point is, you can get an outstanding education at Malibu and that will open doors for you at Pepperdine or whatever college you want to go to. You won't have to rely on luck—you'll have your great education to give you all the opportunities you could want."

Malibu High was located on a 35 acre campus near the famous Zuma Beach. The senior class of 175 students, of which 85% were white, were mostly serious students compared to the general student population throughout the United States. The girls had been good students while attending school in Peoria and Sandy was determined that they should continue with good study habits at Malibu regardless of their new-found wealth and the distractions it could bring.

Ed stood. "Your mother has obviously given your education a lot of thought and study so I hope you appreciate it."

Pat pushed back her chair. "Look, we know what's going on. And you're not going to get an argument from us."

Bev nodded. "Don't worry. I guess we got like caught up in the whole being super rich thing. You'll have to admit, that's some pretty heavy stuff to deal with, especially when you live in a place like this and go to school with a lot of very rich kids."

Ed said, "Well, remember this; the kids aren't rich. It's their parents. Right?"

"Right," the girls said in unison.

Chapter 5

Life began to settle into a loose routine. Obviously, having no jobs gave Ed and Sandy a wide open agenda. The big question confronting them was "What shall we do today?" Ed thought they needed some sort of regular routine that would give their lives some purpose. He was feeling guilty about not having anything he *had* to do. For now, his only responsibility was to keep in touch with his committee of advisors and this he did at least once a week.

Every Friday, he called Aaron Feldman first and told the lawyer what was going on. Next, he filled in Kip Garvan on what large purchases they had made so the accountant could update the balances. Then he chatted with Carl Griffin about investments. And finally, even though there might not be much new to report to the estate planner, Ed called Manny. Manny had set up several trusts for the girls that would insure money for college through a master's program, should they opt to pursue an advanced degree. He advised Ed that the cost for each girl attending Pepperdine University would be about $45,000 a school year, of which $34,000 would go for tuition and the balance for housing and living expenses if the girls didn't live at home. Ed reminded Manny that Pepperdine was located in Malibu and it would be a terrible waste of money to have them live on campus when their home was a 20 minute drive away.

Regardless, Manny wanted Ed to provide a million dollars for their college education and another million dollars each for a managed trust that would insure that the girls would be independent after college. Each trust would, of course be managed to maximize greatest return and therefore be a source of revenue for the girls.

Ed laughed. "You talk about millions of dollars the way I used to talk about hundreds. Anyway, go ahead and set it up. Let me know what you need and I'll have Kip send the checks."

As it turned out, after graduating from Malibu High in May 2007, the twins announced they wanted to go to UC Santa Barbara. Beverly's GPA was a solid 3.8 and Pat's a 3.5 When they discussed their decision with their parents, they insisted that the choice had nothing to do with living at home if they went to Pepperdine; rather it was about the curriculum and other aspects of school life that they found more appealing. Additionally, Santa Barbara was only seventy miles from Malibu which would allow them to make frequent visits home.

At that, Ed laughed wryly. "You mean it will be easier to bring your dirty laundry home for the housekeepers to wash, right?"

The twins ignored Ed's shot at humor. "We want to try it for our freshman year, at least," Bev said, adding that they could always transfer to Pepperdine if UC failed to meet their expectations.

It was a very well prepared presentation and at the close of the twins' remarks—actually they were more like a couple of well thought-out speeches—both Ed and Sandy gave the girls a hearty round of applause.

"All right then," Sandy said. "Your dad and I will go with you to Santa Barbara and check it out. It sounds like you've given your college education some serious thought and I'm proud of you for having done that. On the other hand, if your dissertation was nothing more than blowing smoke to cover the real reason you picked UC, and that reason is to get away from us and be on your own to do whatever ill-advised young ladies do, then I want you to know that you will be living back here!"

Pat turned to Ed. "Daddy, we really have checked it out, I mean like really, really, carefully and this is not some lame scheme to get out of the house. Come on. UC Santa Barbara is a very good college and we think it's like the right choice for us, at least for our freshman year. After that, well, you know, we'll see how things turn out."

Beverly nodded.

So in September the twins left Malibu to take up residence in Santa Barbara. In this case, "residence" turned out to be a very lovely and nearly new two bedroom condominium.

With the girls gone, the subject of how Ed and Sandy should productively spend their daytime hours was discussed daily without achieving any satisfactory resolution. Sandy suggested they go to a gym and work out at least three or four times a week. Ed thought they should buy a small sailboat and take sailing lessons. Sandy wasn't particularly enthusiastic about sailing but said she would try it. They found a gym they liked and signed up for a six week course with a private trainer on Monday, Tuesday and Thursday mornings. Ed researched sailing opportunities and found a school in Marina del Rey, about 30 miles from their home. The school provided the boats and excellent instruction but after just three weeks, Sandy decided that sailing wasn't her thing, although she encouraged Ed to continue. In fact, he absolutely fell in love with sailing—couldn't get enough of it. He quit going to the gym, opting instead to spend his days sailing. Within a few months, Ed was as comfortable piloting a boat as driving a car.

One morning during breakfast on the patio, Ed looked longingly out to sea where a sailboat, it appeared to be a ketch, was sailing south about a quarter mile out. "Look at that, will you?" He drew Sandy's attention to the horizon. "That guy is sailing along, not a care in the world. Just enjoying a morning sail on a calm sea. That's what I love to do. I don't understand how you cannot enjoy sailing."

She laid her coffee cup down and shrugged. "What's not to understand? I don't enjoy it." She thought for a moment. "Okay, a few hours of sailing at cocktail time, that's okay, but to spend day after day like you do, forget it! It's boring. I'd much rather be at the gym or playing tennis—"

Ed broke in. "You're playing tennis? I didn't know that. When did you start?"

"I don't know—about a month ago. I was talking to that guy down the beach, he lives in the house with the little observation dome on the roof—you know the one?"

Ed nodded. "Yeah, I know where it is. So, what about this guy?"

"I was walking on the beach and he came down from his house and asked if I lived around here and I told him yes and pointed out our house. He told me his name, Barton—Bart something, I forget his last name. He invited me up to his house to meet his wife and have a cup of coffee. So we walked up to his house and he called for his wife but she wasn't home after all. We had coffee and he told me he played tennis and when I told him I'd never played he asked if I would like to learn. I said sure and asked him if there was a place nearby where I could take lessons. I thought it'd be fun, something to do plus good exercise."

Ed unclenched his jaw and said, "So this guy, whose wife was not home, suggests you take tennis lessons? Really? I mean, why would he care if you played tennis?"

Sandy became a little irritated. "He said it was a fun sport and he would be happy to teach me. I guess he doesn't work and was looking for something to do. It's no big deal. He's a very nice guy and it turns out I enjoy playing tennis." She raised her eyebrows and stared at him for a long moment. "You have a problem with that? You enjoy sailing. And no, he's not hitting on me, if that's what you think."

"I wasn't thinking that at all," Ed lied. "Tell you what. Invite him and his wife over for a drink, maybe they'd be fun to do stuff with. Hey, they might enjoy going for a sail."

Sandy relaxed. "Okay. Sure. I'll invite them over for cocktails and then maybe the four of us could go out to dinner."

"Good. That's good. Do that." Ed picked up his coffee cup and sipped. "It's cold." He went into the house and came back with a fresh cup. "You want some?" he asked, holding up his cup.

"No, thanks, I've had enough." She stood.

Ed stopped her. "Wait a sec. There's something we need to discuss. It's about the thousand dollar rule."

Sandy sat. "Okay. You want to buy something that costs more than a thousand?"

"That's right. It's not that expensive, only fifty-eight thousand. If it wasn't for the recession, this boat would be selling for a heck of a lot more."

Sandy's eyebrows shot up.

Ed's enthusiasm was building. "It's a used Pearson thirty-six foot sloop in beautiful condition. It's in a slip up at the Channel Islands Marina, just north of Port Hueneme." Sandy gave him a questioning look. "It's near Oxnard."

Sandy laughed. "Geeze, I was prepared for something expensive like that damn car. Fifty-eight thousand and you want my okay? Okay, you got it. Go buy the boat, but you better have a professional check it over first."

Ed walked to the edge of the patio and threw his coffee on the sand. He gazed out to sea. The sailboat he'd seen before was just speck on the water. He turned back to the house and began to laugh. "I was thinking about what you just said," he explained. "You said, 'only fifty-eight thousand?'"

Sandy gestured with her hands. "So?"

"So, it took you two years at your job with the dentists to make fifty-eight thousand. Two years and now we think that's not very much money. Is that not funny? I mean, how quickly you've adjusted to being a millionaire?"

Sandy didn't laugh. "It's happening to us whether we realize it or not," she said seriously. "We're becoming the very people we said we'd never be. And look at us now. We're talking about buying a boat for more than fifty thousand dollars with no more thought about it than when we used to discuss whether to spend a hundred on a new vacuum cleaner."

"But back then we had a combined income of around a hundred grand and now..." He held his arms in front of him and spread them. "And now we have millions, so theoretically, it's the same thing." He stopped short and shook his head. "Jesus, I sound like an idiot." He strode to the house then stopped and turned back to her, a grin cracking across his face. "I'm still buying the boat."

Ed actually expected the recession to get worse, and he was right. He called his advisory group to a phone conference and they spent an entire afternoon talking about strategies for dealing with, for one thing, the plummeting stock market. Kip suggested that perhaps Ed should sell a significant portion of his investments and wait out the recession and when things began to improve get back into the market. Carl and Manny took a contrary view. They told Ed he might sell off some of the losers but keep the good companies even if they lost some of their current value. They both advised that when the market looked like it had hit bottom, Ed should get back in and buy. Aaron agreed, saying, "Never bet against the U. S. stock market. In the long run, it's always been a winner." And that's exactly what Ed did.

Sandy continued playing tennis with Bart. He was, she thought, a good looking guy, about her height with a bit of a gut but what the heck, she thought, he's someone to talk to and do things with. They played tennis almost every morning. She was getting better at the game and was able to return most of the shots. After playing, they would go into the club house and have something to drink. At first it was iced tea or a soda. Then it was a beer. She developed a taste for Irish ale and sometimes had as many as three. She and Bart would have lunch and then go to Bart's house and sit on his beach-front patio. They engaged in banal conversation and drank ale or a cocktail. She enjoyed a Manhattan and Bart's were especially good. She knew now that Bart and his wife had separated, but since Ed hadn't brought up the subject, she put off mentioning it.

Frequently, it would be dinner time before Sandy returned home from Bart's and she'd be more than a little intoxicated. She'd sit in front of the television and fall asleep in a chair. Fortunately, Mrs. Weir, the woman she had hired to cook dinners, would have the meal prepared and ready to serve so that when Ed came home from a day of sailing, a good dinner would be waiting.

Ed bought the 1980 Pearson P39 yacht for $57,500 after Brad, his sailing instructor, had given the boat a very thorough going over. The boat was, as advertised, in excellent condition. The former owners had taken a great deal of pride in it and kept everything shipshape. Brad was particularly impressed with the equipment, all top of the line. He explained to Ed that the boat was yawl rigged, providing a proper sail plan for a variety of weather conditions.

When they took the boat out for sea trials, they found it very easy to handle, even for one man. The addition of a Lewmar bow thruster simplified dockage and maneuverability. Speed was a very respectable 7 knots. They learned that with a good blow, the boat could make over 12 knots.

Ed realized he was spending far too much time with his boat and Sandy was spending far too much time with Bart. But whenever he stayed home to spend time with Sandy, he wished he was out on the water. Just the simple act of having a conversation with her had become difficult and Ed worried that they were drifting further and further apart.

One evening at dinner, after seeing Sandy fill her wine glass for the third time, he said, "You know, I'm sorry, but I just have to tell you that I think things are getting out of hand."

Sandy's eyebrows rose. "Like what?"

Ed winced at the slight slur in her words. "Well, for one thing, you're drinking way too much. You're actually turning into a drunk. That's right. Oh, don't give me that look. I'm not kidding around. You are becoming a drunk. I can hardly remember the last time I saw you stone-cold sober at dinner time."

Sandy jumped up, her face beet-red, and glared at him. "You're full of shit!" she yelled and ran out of the room.

Ed looked after her but decided not to say or do any more, at least not tonight. "Jesus," he whispered, "what is happening to us?"

That night Ed slept in one of the guest bedrooms. The next morning, he got up around daybreak, made coffee and strolled down the beach. The morning sun was low in the sky, casting weird shadows on the sand. He looked to his left to see what structure was producing this odd shadow and realized that he was standing in front of Bart's home. He turned and quickly walked home.

Ed had planned on sailing, but decided to stay home so that he and Sandy could have a serious talk about the direction their marriage was taking. Around ten o'clock Sandy walked into the kitchen looking rather ragged and unkempt. She obviously wasn't expecting to see Ed.

"Good morning," he said with a cheery lilt. He poured a cup of coffee and handed it to her. "Can I make you some breakfast? How about some eggs and bacon? Would you like that?"

Sandy cleared her throat and then cleared it again. "Ah, sure. Thanks. Just one egg though—scrambled." She sat at the table and sipped her coffee while Ed busied himself making her breakfast. "You didn't sleep in our bed last night, did you?" she remarked.

"No, I thought it would be better to let you sleep alone, given your dramatic exit last night."

Sandy sipped her coffee "Did you eat already?" she asked.

"I had something a couple hours ago," he replied, without turning from the range. "I walked down the beach around sunrise. It was very pretty. I walked past your friend's house. Thought I might stop in and say hello but it was pretty early so I didn't do it." Ed faced Sandy who showed surprise.

"So you actually didn't see Bart?"

"No." He plated the eggs and bacon and placed the dish in front of her, then he refilled her coffee cup and asked, "Want some toast with that?"

Sandy shook her head. "No, thanks. This will be plenty." She picked up her fork and began eating, then laid her fork on the plate and gave Ed an intense look. "I'm sorry about what I said last night. You didn't deserve that. I know you were trying to help me and God knows I probably can use some help." She picked up her fork again, then laid it back down. "I don't know how the drinking thing started. I guess I was bored or something and Bart was always willing to accommodate me. Maybe he's thinking that I'll be drunk one of these days and he'll get me in bed and..." She couldn't look him in the eye.

"Exactly what I've been worrying about," he said. "I'd hate for that to happen. You're not that kind of girl." He paused. "And you and I have always been close. We've always been able to talk things out, but now it's different. It's like suddenly we've become strangers—hell, we haven't had sex in weeks."

Sandy cast her eyes down.

He went on. "You know I love you and I'd be devastated if... you know...something happened that wrecked our marriage." He became more animated as he spoke, reaching for her hands and holding them tightly. "I don't think you'd be very happy with yourself if you let..." He couldn't bear to say it aloud.

Sandy returned his earnest gaze. "That's not going to happen. C'mon, you know me better than that. Besides, Bart hasn't made a move on me. He just wants a tennis partner and someone to talk to."

"What about his wife? Doesn't he talk to her?"

"They're separated. She's living in a condo in Beverly Hills. I'm sorry. I should have told you that."

Regardless of her good intentions to stop the drinking and spend more time with Ed, Sandy nonetheless still played tennis with Bart—almost every day when Ed was sailing. Within a month, her relationship with her husband was back to what it had been before their talk. Sandy spent more time with Bart and started drinking again in the afternoons, coming home more than just a little tipsy. Sometimes, she'd come home and fall into bed and the lovely dinner for two the cook had prepared was enjoyed only by Ed. She fretted about Ed frequently staying on his boat overnight while she would be the one eating alone. She realized that life on the water was much more serene for Ed than spending time with her. Subconsciously, Sandy hated what was happening to their marriage, and yet she didn't seem to have the energy or desire to do something about it.

When on the odd occasion the two of them were together for a meal, Sandy very rarely encouraged conversation. They might discuss the children, or household matters, but little else. By the time the meal was over, Sandy would have consumed a bottle of wine and conversation would become pointless. Later, she would struggle into bed and fall into a restless sleep. She might wake in the night and out of habit, reach out to touch Ed but he wasn't there.

Sandy was not unaware of what was happening but felt powerless to change the course of events. She knew she was drinking too much, maybe seeing Bart too much as well. Some days she would make up her mind to change the direction of her life, and so she would stay at home or drive to LA and go shopping. She ended up buying things she didn't need or, for that matter, didn't want. More often than not, she would leave her purchases in the back of her car where they would remain for weeks. When she did finally remove them, she would throw the parcels in a closet and there they remained.

Sandy made an effort to avoid Bart, but he persisted in coming to her house, knowing that Ed wouldn't be there and that Sandy would offer coffee and then he would invite her to lunch where the meal would be preceded by a Bloody Mary or two and a bottle of good wine with lunch followed by some port or something stronger. It became habitual—a ritual that was repeated almost every day. By the time Bart brought her back home, she wasn't just tipsy. She was staggering drunk.

One afternoon in early May, after tennis and lunch followed by some even more serious drinking than usual, Sandy was so intoxicated that Bart had to carry her to the car. When they arrived at her home, he carried her into her bedroom, laying her carefully on the bed. He laid a light blanket over her and turned to leave but then looked back at her snoring softly into the pillow. Bart, feeling no pain from his share of the afternoon's imbibing, decided that he should make her more comfortable. He began to undress her and in the process she awoke.

"Hey, what are you doing?" she asked, grabbing her tennis dress before he could raise it over her hips.

"I'm taking off your clothes so you'll be more comfortable. Is that okay?"

She giggled, "No, no. You just want to see me nude, don't you?"

Bart stumbled for an answer but failed.

Her words slurred, she muttered, "You want to see me nude, I know you do." She shook her head as if to clear it and mumbled, "Forget it. Go home." Her head fell back on the pillow and she was asleep.

Bart looked at her for moment then pulled the skirt up and slipped her panties down her legs. Quickly he tore off his clothes and slipped into bed beside her. Without preamble, he rolled on top of her, fumbling around, trying to enter her.

Sandy blinked, suddenly awake and momentarily shocked sober. "Hey, wait. What the hell? Get off of me! No!" But he was already inside her. Her mind screamed, *Oh, my God!* She attempted to push him off, but he was intent on completion. And he was much stronger than she was.

It was over in a few short minutes. Sandy stared at his back as Bart got out of bed and began dressing. She sat up, pulling the sheet up to her neck, her head spinning but her mind suddenly clear.

"What the hell was that?" she screamed. "Wham, bam and I don't even get a thank-you-ma'am?"

Bart turned around and stared at her. "What?"

"You heard me. That's your idea of making love?" she spat, her tone thick with sarcasm. "No wonder your wife left you." Her voice became harsh and forceful. "What just happened was cruel of you and a big mistake that will never be repeated. You understand—never again will you do that to me. Now, get the hell out of here, and don't come back. I never want to see you again."

Bart moved toward her. "Sandy, what are you talking about? What happened? I don't understand."

Sandy shot him a chilling look. "Exactly. You don't understand. You're an idiot!" She reached for the night stand, opened the drawer and pulled out a Glock pistol. She pointed it at him. "Are you going to get out or do I call the police and report a rape and murder?"

Bart didn't need more encouragement. "You're crazy," he shouted as he ran from the room.

Sandy heard the front door slam. She put the pistol back in the drawer and fell back on the pillow. Aloud, she babbled, "Why the hell didn't I stop him? That was stupid, stupid, stupid!" She began to cry. "I've got to get a hold of my life. This is crazy!" She got out of bed, took a shower, put on a pair of shorts and a tee shirt. Her brain was going ninety miles an hour trying to process one thought after another. She made a pot of extra strong coffee and when it was ready, she poured it into a mug that was inscribed *Have a nice day*. The twins had given it to her years ago as a Mother's Day present.

"Have a nice day," Sandy mouthed, then began to cry. *What kind of a mother am I? A drunk with lots of money and nothing to do except drink and commit adultery.* "Adultery," she said in a loud voice. "What in the world was I thinking?" She shuddered. "God, why did I let that happen? I hate Bart. The bastard took advantage of me." She sipped the coffee. *Ed said I'd end up in bed with Bart. He was right. What am I going to tell him? Maybe I shouldn't tell him…it'll never happen again, that's for sure. Jesus, why did I do that? 'What's done is done and cannot be undone.' Who said that? It doesn't matter who said it, it's true. Now I've got to live with it. But I've got to stop drinking starting right now. I need something to do to keep me busy. I need a job. A job! Sure, that's it. I need a job. As soon as I get myself straightened out, I'll look for a job.*

Sandy heard the back door open and jumped up thinking it would be Ed, but as soon as she heard talking, she knew it was the housekeepers. They were surprised to see Sandy home.

"Good afternoon, Mrs. Noble," they said in unison. One of the girls added, "We'll be cleaning today. Is that okay?"

"Sure, go ahead. I'll get out of your way." She picked up the newspaper the girls had brought in and went out to the patio. She sat in a lounger and watched the ocean for several minutes, then opened the paper and began reading the Help Wanted ads.

Chapter 6

Ed was maneuvering his boat out of the Channel Islands harbor into the open sea. A few days earlier, he had a painter change the boat's name from *Seacrest* to *Pilcher*. He had it in mind to insist that Sandy go with him for a little sail on Sunday. He planned to surprise her with cocktails at sunset followed by a lovely dinner prepared by him on the boat. He wanted it to be a romantic afternoon and evening and he imagined them having make-up sex while spending the night together being rocked by gentle waves. He was desperate to regain that great relationship they had enjoyed before moving to California. He missed the old Sandy, his best friend.

He had a good supply of champagne, wine and liquor on board but decided to remove all of it except one bottle of excellent champagne, and replace it with soft drinks, fruit juice and non-alcoholic beverages. He sure didn't want her getting tipsy and falling overboard or worse yet, getting into an argument about—what else—her drinking problem. Anyway, that was the plan and Ed was determined to pull it off. It wasn't just about the two of them. He was thinking about the twins coming home for summer vacation in just a few weeks. He and Sandy had to be responsible parents and that meant loving parents. Sober parents. The kind of parents they'd been when they lived in Arizona.

Ed brought the boat about and under full sail, headed back to the dock, arriving around three o'clock. After securing everything, he got into his car, lowered the top and took off for home. He was surprised to find that Sandy's car was not in the garage. He took a shower, shaved and feeling tired, got into bed, their bed, and quickly fell asleep.

Ed awoke to the sound of the garage door opening. He jumped out of bed, straightened the bedding and pulled on a pair of shorts and a tee shirt. He was just slipping his feet into Birkenstocks when Sandy entered the room. She was dressed in a smartly tailored suit and looked very professional and, he had to admit, very pretty.

"Hey. What's going on?" Sandy cast a surprised eye around the room then turned back to Ed. "You're home early."

"I came back because I need to talk to you. Actually, to invite you on a date." He looked at her, letting his eyes travel from her head to her shoes and back again. "You look very pretty, and that's a very sharp outfit you're wearing. You look like a lawyer or something. Very professional."

Sandy acknowledged the accolade with a tilt of her head and a smile. "Thank you for noticing." She walked up to him and surprised him by putting her arms around his neck. "Yes," she said. "I needed to look professional. You know why?"

"Haven't a clue. Are you going to tell me?"

"I went to Santa Monica for a job interview—office manager for a group of five doctors."

Ed stepped back and gave her an incredulous look. "What are you talking about? A job interview?"

"That's right. I came to the conclusion that I had to find something to do...to give my life some purpose, to keep me from spending the afternoons drinking. It seems like it could be a good job and I think they are interested in me. Anyway, let's hope so."

Ed sat down on the edge of the bed. He just shook his head as he looked up at her. He wasn't sure if he heard her right and if he did, what this meant. "Help me understand this. You applied for a job at a doctor's office so that you would have something to do? So you wouldn't spend the afternoons drinking and getting drunk... Right?"

Sandy smiled broadly. "That's right. I need something to do—a job. The girls will be coming home from school pretty soon and there is no way that I would let them see me wasting my life away playing tennis with some idiot and coming home sloshed every afternoon." She sat down next to Ed and took hold of his hands. "Okay. I'm going to tell you something, something that happened yesterday afternoon." She cast an eye around the room then focused, looking deeply into his eyes. "Yesterday afternoon I was so woozy that I almost fell down leaving the club. Bart had to almost carry me to the car."

"Almost. What do you mean?"

"Okay, he carried me to the car. I guess he was afraid I'd fall down in the parking lot. Anyway, we got to the house and he carried me in here and laid me on the bed." She paused and studied Ed's face, trying to gauge his reaction. Ed's gaze was intense but he said nothing. "The next thing I remember was him fooling around with my tennis dress—he was trying to pull it over my head. I looked at him and asked him what he was doing and he told me he was going to take off my clothes so I'd be more comfortable."

Ed gasped. "He was trying to undress you?"

"Yes, but wait a minute. Let me finish. I pushed him back and pulled my skirt down. He was trying to tell me that he wasn't going to do anything and suddenly it seemed like I was sober. I told him to get the hell out and that I never wanted to see him again."

"And?"

"And he left."

Ed stood and glared down at her. "What did I tell you? I knew something like this would happen but you wouldn't listen, would you? You're lucky you were able to stop him before he had your clothes off and was having sex with you. Jesus, Sandy! Damn it!" Ed walked out of the room but Sandy caught up with him before he reached the garage door.

"Wait a minute. Where are you going?" Sandy wailed.

"I don't know. For a drive. I've got to get out of here." He reached for the door knob but she grabbed his arm and pulled it away.

"Ed, you know I would not have let him do anything. I threw him out of the house. I called him an idiot and every other name I could think of. Come on, don't run out. Sit down with me and let's talk."

Ed looked at her, watched the tears forming in the corners of her eyes, and with a sigh and sag of his shoulders, said, "Okay, okay. Let's talk and see if we can sort this out." He took her hand and walked her into the living room. They sat on a love seat as Sandy, no longer able to hold it in, burst into tears. Ed put an arm around her and pulled her into him. He held her close until her crying subsided.

In a voice so low he could hardly understand her words, she said, "I'm so sorry for letting myself get into this mess. It was too easy. All this money, no job, no friends to do things with or just to talk to. You left me, too, to go sailing." She pulled back and looked into his face. "No, I'm not saying it's your fault. You needed something to do, too, and you found it. But sailing isn't for me and then Bart and tennis—it was something to do. I should have had better control of myself but I didn't and, well, getting drunk was one way..."

"Yeah, I know, but drinking is never the answer to a problem. But obviously, what happened yesterday with Bart was an epiphany for you. You decided on a course of action and you had the guts to do it. I'm proud of you for doing that."

"Getting a job, going to work will definitely keep me occupied and out of trouble, right?"

"I hope so. Although, if you feel the need to work and given the fact that you don't need the money, perhaps working for some charitable organization would be more fulfilling and accomplish the same thing. Helping people out can be very rewarding. It's good for your self-esteem—makes you feel not so guilty about having all this money while so many people are struggling just to feed their families. And there's your other job, the one you already have— being a good mother to our girls. That certainly is a worthwhile cause. And you know, you might not consider it exactly a job," he added with a smile, "but you do have a role as my wife."

Sandy nodded to acknowledge every comment Ed made. "Let's see what happens with this job. Maybe I won't even get it. I hadn't thought about the charity thing—that could be a better way to go and you could get involved too. Instead of making money, we can get rid of some we already have."

Ed stood and pulled her up. "There you go. Our advisory group is flying in from Phoenix on Friday for a meeting. Come to the meeting and we'll talk to them about it. I'll bet they'll have some good ideas."

"Okay. Sure, that's a good idea."

Ed's face suddenly lit up. "Oh, I almost forgot to tell you about what I have planned for this Sunday. It's a surprise actually so all I can say is, you and I have a date. Okay?"

"Sounds exciting. I'll be looking forward to it."

"Good." Ed leaned into her and kissed her lips. "You know I love you and want you to be happy."

"I know. And I love you. You're a great guy, a darn good father and my pal."

"And your one and only lover. Don't forget that."

Sandy choked a little but cleared her throat. "No, I won't ever forget that."

Chapter 7

The doctors hired another applicant. Ed was pleased with the outcome even though she told him she viewed the rejection as a personal put-down. He really didn't want her working full time. His preference would be for her to work at something that didn't require her to be committed to formal office hours. Working with some sort of charitable organization would give her the flexibility he felt she should have.

When they met on Friday with the advisors and had covered the business part of meeting, Ed raised the question about Sandy finding a position with a charitable organization. Aaron put forward the idea of Ed and Sandy forming a charitable trust. They would have complete control over how the money would be spent and they could choose the recipients, be they established charities or individuals. Other members of the advisory group agreed that this would be a good plan as it would give both Ed and Sandy as much or as little involvement as they wished. Aaron said he would start the paperwork at once. Carl said he would work on trust funding, how distributions would be made and so on.

On the drive back to Malibu, Sandy was excited about the prospect of finally doing something substantial and worthwhile with their millions. "I think we should go back to our original plan of living on $300,000 a year and set aside maybe a half million for giving away."

Ed turned his head toward her momentarily and smiled. "That's all? We should average somewhere around five percent on the eighty million we've invested. So, that means we should be earning around four million a year. I don't know what the taxes would be on that but we should end up with at least half of it. Hell, we could budget five hundred thousand to live on, give away around a million and a half and still not really deplete our principal."

Sandy whistled. "Whew, that's amazing! You know, I never even thought about all the money we're making on investments." Now animated, she turned toward Ed. "Do you realize how much more fun giving away money and helping people will be than playing tennis and drinking all afternoon? I'm going to love this." She turned toward the window and watched the landscape whiz by. "You know what else? I'm going to get the girls involved in this when they get home." A minute later she added, "Here's an idea that just popped into my head. The girls could start a scholarship program. You know, set up requirements for need and grades and such, then review applications, interview the students, and choose who to give the money to."

Ed banged the steering wheel. "Damn, Pilcher, that's an excellent idea. And the girls would get so much out of it—life experience and a feeling of accomplishment. Good. I love it!"

Sandy said, "Let's drive to Santa Barbara on Saturday and tell the girls what we have planned for them over the summer." She reflected on that thought then said, "Maybe we won't tell them what we want them to do. Maybe we should just tell them about the plan and see if they volunteer to be a part of it."

Sandy called Beverly and told her that she and Ed would be picking them up around noon on Saturday.

Beverly asked, "Where are we going?"

Sandy replied, "We're taking you and Patty to lunch. There's something we need to talk about. Also, we want to know how school is going and what you two have been doing both in and out of school. You haven't called or sent us an email in a week."

"I'm sorry, Mom, but you how it is...we get busy. As for this Saturday, I'll have to check and see what's on my schedule and let you know. I'll have Pat email you, too."

"No, no." Sandy's tone became stern. "We will be there Saturday at noon and we're taking you two to lunch. Whatever you have planned for Saturday afternoon, cancel it. This is important."

"Mother, I can't—"

"Yes, you can, so just do what you need to do and be ready at noon. Is Patty there? I want to talk to her."

"No. I don't know where she is, but I'll tell her to call you when she gets back, okay?"

"Okay. Now, listen, honey, I think you two will be very pleased with what Dad and I have in mind for you. It's a good thing we plan to do and we want you girls involved."

With a hint of frustration in her voice, Beverly replied, "Okay, okay. I've got the picture. Is there anything else?"

"No, unless there's something you want to talk about."

"No, nothing of importance. Oh, where do you want to eat? We'll meet you there."

"How about Barclay's? It's near the Barnes and Noble book store on State Street. But we'll pick you up at the condo around noon. Dad will probably want to see how you girls furnished the condo and—"

"Hey, you don't have to bother driving up here. We'll just meet you at Barclay's, okay?"

"Beverly," Sandy said firmly, "I said, Dad will want to see your place, so we will pick you up there at noon. End of discussion. Now, anything else you want to talk about?"

"No, I guess it can wait 'til Saturday," Beverly said in a subdued voice.

"Don't forget to tell Patty to call me as soon as you see her, okay?"

"Okay. Love you, Mom."

"I love you too, honey. Bye bye."

An hour later, Pat called and wanted to know why all the secrecy and why Sandy couldn't just tell her over the phone.

"Listen, Patty, we need your input and that's all I'm going to say right now. You'll find out all about it at lunch Saturday."

"Bev said that you didn't want us to meet you at the restaurant, that you were going to pick us up at the condo. I think it'd be a lot easier if we just met you there."

"Patricia, I'm not going through all that again. We will pick you up at noon Saturday at the condo." Sandy realized why she was getting uncomfortable. "Why do I get the impression that you two really don't want us to come up to the condo? What's going on?"

"Nothing's going on. Just trying to save you the trouble of driving up here, that's all. No problem. We'll be here at noon. See you then. Love ya, Mom. Goodbye."

Sandy told Ed about her conversations with the girls and added, "I don't know, but I get the feeling something's going on with them. They sure didn't want us to see the condo. At least, that's the impression I got. What do you suppose is going on up there?"

Ed made a wry mouth and scratched his head. "Maybe nothing, maybe all kinds of stuff—who knows? But we'll know more on Saturday."

Sandy placed her hands on her hips and faced Ed. "You know what? I think I'll just take a little drive up there tomorrow and have a look-see. I've got a key."

"We're going there on Saturday anyway. If you don't find anything bad or dangerous, and they find out you've been there," Ed raised his eyebrows, "they're going to get really pissed off that you walked in, unannounced to spy on them. That would not be a good way to start off our meeting with them Saturday—you know, with them felling threatened or whatever."

"Don't worry. I'll go when they're in class, take a quick look around and leave. They won't even know I was there."

Chapter 8

The next day, Sandy drove to Santa Barbara. She slowed down to a crawl as she drove past the girls' condo and scanned the building. The girls' Toyota wasn't there, so she drove to the next street, turned in and parked. She climbed the condo steps to unit 7. Seeing no one, she took a key from her purse, unlocked the door and stepped in.

Ed and Sandy had purchased the condo for the girls a few weeks before the fall semester had started. It was a two year old condominium with a nice sized living room, a small dining area, and a compact kitchen with first class appliances, and it was only eight miles from the campus. The girls had fallen in love with it, promising Ed that when they left school, be it in a year or whenever, they were sure to be able to sell it for at least what they paid for it—not that the cost had anything to do with the decision. The girls wanted it, so Ed bought it and that was that. One glance revealed to even the most casual visitor that the furnishings hadn't come from a second hand store. No indeed! Sandy brought in her decorator, the same Keisha Burkhardt from Shackleford's, to attend to furnishing the place. The cost was over the top but the place looked terrific. Once again, the girls and Sandy had won the discussion and Ed had written the check.

Sandy walked from the living room toward the bedrooms. She stopped short when the bedroom door opened and a young man stepped out. Sandy cried out. The boy jumped back, staring at her wide-eyed and open-mouthed. They both started to yell.

"Who are you—what are you doing here?" Sandy screamed.

"I'm a friend of Beverly's. Who are you?" the boy stammered.

"Never mind who I am. I own this condo. Now, what are you doing here?"

"I just told ya. I'm Bev's friend. I was just—"

Sandy strode toward him, pushed him aside and entered the bedroom. She looked around thinking that Beverly might be there. She saw that the bed was unmade and there was a pair of men's blue jeans, a shirt and a baseball cap lying on a chair. She turned and walked back into the hallway and saw the young man with a bulging backpack slung over one shoulder, hurrying toward the front door.

"Hold on," she yelled. "Just stay right there." She walked toward him and in an elevated voice asked, "Now, just what the heck are you doing here?"

"Hey, lady, I'm not a robber or anything like that. I told you, I'm a friend of Beverly and she invited me to...ah..."

Sandy cut him off. "She invited you to do what? Stay with her or maybe have sex with her, is that the idea?"

"No, ma'am. No, nothing like that. We went out last night and came back late and she said I could crash here until—"

"Really? Tell me the truth. Have you been *crashing here,* as in living here?"

"No, I told you it was just last night." He moved to the door and opened it. "I gotta go to class. I'm late already. You ask Bev about it."

"You're darn tootin' I'll ask Bev about it. What's your name?"

Over his shoulder he barked, "Kevin," and shot out the door, slamming it shut behind him.

Sandy ran to the door, jerked it open and watched as Kevin ran down the steps to a parked Jeep across the street. As he was getting in, Sandy pulled a notepad and pen from her purse and jotted down the license plate number just as the Jeep roared into life and took off.

Sandy decided to have a good look around. In the bedroom, she found other articles of men's clothing in the closet and in one of the dresser drawers. She walked through the rest of the apartment, then sat down on a stool at the kitchen counter. She tried her best but in the end, could not hold back the tears.

Ed had worked on his boat but didn't go sailing that day, returning home a little after three. Sandy met him at the door. Ed could sense that something had gone wrong and by the time she related everything, he knew he was facing the terror, the disappointment, the event that sooner or later, every father of a daughter will face.

"I need a drink," Sandy said, moving toward the bar.

Amazed, Ed noticed that she hadn't already been drinking. "No, you don't." He took the bottle out of her unresisting hand. "You don't *need a* drink. What you need right now is a clear head and a strategy, so sit down and let's talk about this."

They discussed a number of scenarios for the meeting on Saturday in light of Sandy's encounter. Ed summed it up. "So, we know the kid will tell the girls what happened at the condo and even though you didn't tell him who you are other than the owner, the girls will know it was you. Okay, then. It's likely that Beverly will call you this evening and give you a song and dance that she hopes you will buy and you are going to go along with it, right?"

Sandy crossed her legs and sighed, "I said I would try to stay cool and pretend that whatever story she tells me, I'll accept, but I will say that if the boy is staying there, he has got to go and at once." She uncrossed her legs, stood and began pacing back and forth. "Here's the way I really feel about it. If they are planning to turn that condo into a party palace or have kids staying there or, God forbid, allow drugs in there, that will be the end of the condo and it's dorm living for them." Ed sensed that Sandy was working up a fury that needed to put out.

"Okay, okay. Take it easy. Sit down. I fully support you with that, but as I said before, for now and on Saturday, I don't want to get into all that. We have got to keep those girls talking to us and trusting us not to make too many demands of them—controlling their lives. Kids nowadays just don't operate under the same rules we did."

Sandy stopped her pacing and stood in front of him, hands on hips. "That's a load of crap and you know it. Good parents set rules and make sure, through intimidation if necessary, to enforce them. It's the lazy parents who let kids do as they damn please and by God, we are not going to become lazy parents just because it's easier."

"Honey, that's all well and good," he said gently. "But you know it's not realistic. Just how do you keep the girls from having sex, huh? How did your parents keep you from having sex when you were in college?"

Sandy fell back in her chair, saying nothing.

Ed leaned forward, hands on his knees and in a quiet voice, earnestly said, "We had sex on our third date in your dorm room during your sophomore year. And did you turn out badly? Hell, it happens and our girls will no doubt be subject to the same pressures as you were." He grimaced. "Only more so now. The fact is that half the girls have had sex while still in high school.

Sandy stood up and walked into the kitchen. Over her shoulder she said, "I'm going to make some coffee. You want some?"

As she measured the grounds and filled the pot, her mind was recalling something Ed had said, "And did you turn out badly?" When he'd said that, the events that played out in her bed with Bart had flashed across her mind. Now she mentally answered Ed's question: *Yes, I did turn out badly. It was a terrible experience but that doesn't change anything. I still committed adultery.* Her eyes suddenly filled with tears and in a moment she was sobbing uncontrollably.

Ed jumped up and went to her, wrapped her in his arms and whispered in her ear. "Hey, Pilcher, what's going on? Come on. It's not the end of the world, you know."

"Maybe it is," Sandy moaned. She pushed back, tore a paper towel from the roll and wiped her tear-streaked face. "I'm sorry, honey, it just overwhelmed me for a second. Sorry. I'm okay now." The pot beeped, and she poured two cups. Handing him one, she said, "Let's sit down and finish the plan for Saturday."

"Okay, but please don't let this situation get to you. It's all part of living with two daughters. Things are going to happen that we don't like but they are going to happen anyway and the best we can do is take on each one and do the best we can for the girls."

Sandy sipped her coffee. "You're right. It's all we can do. Okay, so moving on, I'm not going to get upset with Beverly regardless of what she tells me. And I will be cool, just focusing on the charity topic Saturday because, as I will tell her, it's more important than anything else right now. So, that's the plan, right?"

Ed nodded, "Right."

Just as Ed and Sandy were sitting down to a lovely dinner of grilled quail in a sumptuous sauce prepared by Mrs. Weir, Ed's cell phone rang. He took the phone from his pocket. "Hello."

"Hi, Dad. It's Pat." Anger seemed to radiate through the phone.

Ed placed the phone against his chest and glanced at Sandy. "Patty," he mouthed.

Sandy reached for the phone but Ed whispered, "Wait a minute." He put the phone to his ear and asked, "What's up?"

"Really? You don't know what's up? Like you don't know that Mom was here at the condo this morning and saw Bev's friend, Kevin?"

Ed cleared his throat. "Well, yes, I know about it. What I don't know is why he was there and basically what's going on. Would you care to enlighten me or should I get that information from Beverly?"

"Look, Dad, first of all, Bev is not here right now, but Kevin told us that Mom was here and saw...well, whatever she saw. I mean, actually there was nothing to see except Kevin getting ready to leave for class."

"I don't mean to sound like an old geezer or something, but don't you think the parents of freshmen girls—living alone in a lovely condo that their loving parents bought for them—would be interested and maybe even concerned if they suddenly found out that some guy was staying there and maybe, and I'm just sayin', maybe sharing a bed with one of their daughters?"

Pat didn't reply for a long moment. "What? Geeze! Wait a minute. Nobody is like sharing a bed. What are you talking about? This is crazy for you to assume we're having some kind of an orgy here. That's totally wrong."

"Okay," Ed replied in a quiet voice. "Then all is right with the world. Think no more about it. Bev and that boy—"

"His name is Kevin, and he's a good guy. Seriously!"

" I'll put Mom on the phone. I want you to tell her what you just told me." Ed handed the phone to Sandy and whispered, "Just listen to what she has to say and be cool."

Sandy spoke, "Hi, darling. How are you?"

"I'm okay but I gotta tell ya that Bev is really pissed that you came spying on us. Really, Mom, that was not very cool. Bev was going to tell you about Kevin on Saturday but now..."

"Well, I'm sorry she is upset. I thought I was just being a responsible parent who wanted to understand why her daughter didn't want her parents to see her home. Maybe it was spying. Call it what you want, but I'm just saying—"

Pat said, "Yeah, I know, but like I told Dad, I don't think she and Kevin did anything other than just, you know, like make out. I know all the kids are doing it, like *doing it,* but we're not going to be pressured and that's all I have to say about it."

"But that boy was there," Sandy pointed out.

"Okay, like he probably shouldn't be sleeping over and if that's a big whoop for you then we won't allow it any more, okay?"

"Alright, honey," Sandy said, relief in her voice. "I appreciate you being very open and frank with me and I'm relieved that you girls are taking a sensible attitude toward, ah, what you will and will not do with boys.

"Sure. So, we're good, right?"

"Yes, absolutely, we're good. Bye, darling. See you Saturday."

The twins had their place in showroom condition when Ed and Sandy arrived. They walked Ed through the condo, pointing out all the cool decorating things they had done. He was impressed. The place looked great and he said so. Following the tour of the condo, they all piled into Sandy's SUV and drove to the restaurant.

After ordering lunch, Ed looked around the table. "I'm a very lucky guy and I'm not talking about the Lottery thing. I'm a lucky guy because I have a lovely, loving wife who also happens to be a loving and most capable mother. Of course you know that. But in addition, I am the father of two very smart...and I'm talking about intelligent and beautiful young ladies who, not too long ago were just girls. Unlike most of the girls attending college these days, my daughters," he lowered his voice to a stage whisper, "I won't mention any names to protect their privacy..." Sandy smiled and the girls giggled. "Anyway, these two lovely ladies are about to embark on a mission. This will be code named, *Mission Possible.*"

"Geeze, Dad," Pat said, "C'mon. Quit the screwing around and get to the point—you do have one, don't you?"

Bev turned to Pat, held up her hand and she and Pat did a fist bump.

Sandy laughed and said to Ed, "Okay, I've got it." She turned her attention to the twins. "We think it's time we quite fiddling around with life and do something worthwhile with some of our money and we need you to help us accomplish this 'Mission Possible.' It's possible because we have the money to do this thing but you two are the ones who can make it happen." She explained what she wanted the girls to do in connection with her plan to help motivated high school kids get into first class colleges.

When Sandy had finished detailing what part the girls would play, Beverly said, "So we do the research, interviews and all that other stuff and then we, not you, decide which kids will get the money?"

"Not money," Sandy corrected. "The grant will be a scholarship."

Beverly looked at Pat. "Do you think we can do this, I mean, do it right?"

Pat replied, "Probably, but we need to talk about this. Once we start this thing we have to stay with it until it's done, you know, until we've picked the kids and all that, right? This is a big deal with a lot of money involved." Pat looked at Sandy then Ed. "You guys actually think we can handle this?"

Ed said, "Of course, but you're going to have help. Besides your mother and me, we will have a whole team working on it. It's going to be a part of our charitable foundation but not the only thing we'll be doing. We've got big plans and I'm talking about giving away millions of dollars a year, basically the money earned from our investments."

Hearing this, the twins' eyes widened and Pat let a low whistle escape from her lips. "Okay." She turned to Beverly. "You down with this?"

"I guess so."

"You're not sure?" Sandy asked. "That's okay. I want you girls to talk about this over the next week and read the material that we have put together. It will answer most of your questions and give you more insight into how this is going to work. This is a great opportunity but only if you are willing to give it your best effort. If you have questions or suggestions, let us know. If we can't come up with answers, we'll have someone who knows call you."

Sandy picked up her napkin and wiped her lips, then asked Ed, "Anything you want to add?"

Ed pushed back his chair and stood. "No, I think the girls got the idea." He looked at them and smiled. "And I think they'll do a great job." Suddenly his smile collapsed and his face became somber. He sat down as the girls were preparing to stand. "Wait a minute. Sit down. There is one more thing. We've been dancing around it but I want to ask, Beverly, would you care to tell us what's the deal with you and Kevin?"

Sandy face displayed surprise. "Do we want to get into that now?" she asked.

"Only if Bev feels comfortable talking about it." He looked at Beverly. "Do you?"

"What? There's nothing to talk about." She shrugged. "He's a friend. I let him crash the other night after we got in late." She glanced at Pat. "It's no biggie."

Ed put his elbows on the table and laid his chin on tented fingers. "If I asked you not to do that again...you know, have boys spend the night in the condo, would you be inclined to honor that request?"

Bev stared at her father for a long moment before replying. "This a request, not an order?"

"That's right. I'm not telling you what to do. I'm suggesting that it would be in your best interests to ask Kevin, or any boy who may be visiting you, to leave at whatever time you determine is appropriate. People who come to your place have to know there are rules and you two need to tell them what the rules are. You set the rules, then you stick to them. On the other hand if you don't want any rules and you let things get out of hand, then there may be consequences."

"Like what?" Pat asked.

"Like moving out of the condo and living in a dorm."

"Wait a minute," Bev said. "So, it's a threat after all? Fine." She pushed her chair back and stood. In a loud voice that turned nearby heads, she said, "We'll make up some rules and send them to you for approval. How's that? And we'll post them just inside the door so that everyone who comes over knows what they are. Will that make you happy?"

Ed glared at Bev and was about to speak when Sandy rose and quietly said, "Okay. I think this conference is over and I prefer it to end it on a positive note. Dad and I both know that there will be lots of temptations, but I feel like you know what's going on and will use good judgment. You are here to get an excellent education, so that should be your focus. But I'm not so naïve as to think you are not going to take advantage of the rest of college life. Just be careful and use your good sense and it will be alright." She glanced at Ed then turned to the girls, "Having some basic rules is, I think, a good idea. As for posting them in the house, that's up to you two." Sandy pushed her chair under the table. "Let's go."

Chapter 9

Sunday morning found Ed pouring freshly squeezed orange juice into a couple of glasses when Sandy walked into the kitchen. She gazed at the clock on the microwave. "How long have you been up?"

"About an hour or so," Ed replied. "I took a little stroll down the beach and watched the sun come up—beautiful." He handed her a glass. "Want me to fix you some breakfast?"

"I can do it." She took a sip, laid the glass down, opened the refrigerator door, peered inside and asked, "Want some eggs and fried ham?"

Ed joined her to scan the refrigerator shelves. "Is that what you're going to have?"

Sandy pulled out the remains of a baked ham and placed it on a cutting board. She took a long slicing knife from the rack. "So it would seem," she said with a smile. "Bring the eggs. Do you want fried ham or not?"

Ed brought the eggs to the counter and reached in the cabinet underneath for a small mixing bowl. "Okay. Cut me a slice—not too thick." He opened the egg carton and asked, "How do you want your eggs? I'm having scrambled." He cracked a couple of eggs into the bowl.

"Scrambled's fine. Two, please."

Ed cracked two more eggs, got a carton of half and half, poured a little into the bowl along with some salt and pepper. He began furiously beating the mixture with a wire whip while Sandy placed two slices of ham into a large skillet.

Ed stood beside her and poured the egg mixture into a frying pan. As if by some unspoken word, he turned to look at Sandy just as she turned to look at him. Ed smiled broadly. "This is like old times in Peoria on a Sunday morning, isn't it? You and me cooking breakfast, waiting for the twins to wake up."

Sandy laughed. "Funny, that was what I was just about to say. You're right. It's like we were back in Peoria." She put her arms around his neck, pulled him down and placed an open-mouth kiss on his lips. Stepping back with a frown, she asked, "Do you think we'll ever get that old feeling, that comfortable feeling we had...you know, like it used to be before the money?"

Ed smiled and kissed her forehead. "Sure we will. In fact, I think it's coming back right now and will be with us all day today during our special Sunday date." Glancing at the pans, he stirred the eggs. "I think you'd better turn the ham over before it burns or this breakfast will be like the old days when the twins were learning to cook."

Top down, the wind whipping her hair about, Sandy kept an eye on the road ahead as Ed piloted the Aston-Martin north toward the Channel Islands marina. "You're going kind of fast, aren't you? What's the hurry?"

Ed checked the speedometer, noted it read 95 and eased up on the gas. "This car is so smooth that a hundred feels like fifty in any other car." The car slowed to seventy. "That better?"

"Much. I'm guessing this, but even though you can afford it, I don't think you want to get a bunch of tickets for speeding, do you?"

"No," he replied through a laugh. "I really should watch my speed. This car is a cop magnet."

"That's right." Sandy took a furtive peek at the speedometer then returned her gaze to the road ahead. Presently she said, "I was just thinking about the twins. Do you think it went okay yesterday? That rules thing you suggested to Bev got her ticked off. I thought we had decided to be cool about my visit to the condo. What happened?"

Ed glanced her way. "Hell, I don't know. I got carried away. Guess I should have kept my trap shut. I'll call her and make sure we're okay. If she gets mad at me she might do something stupid just to show me that she'll make her own decisions...thank you very much."

Sandy rubbed her thumb across her lips but didn't reply for a long moment. "Okay, let's not talk about the kids any more today. You said we were going on a date, right?"

"Right!"

"Okay. Starting right now until we go home, we're just a couple of lovebirds on a date and we're out to have fun. So, what have you got planned?"

When they reached the marina, Ed parked the car and taking Sandy's hand, walked down the line of boats to where his Pearson was birthed. He led her down the slip gangway to the stern.

"Take a look. Notice anything?"

The new name shone in fresh, dark blue letters. Sandy read it aloud, "*Pilcher.*" She turned and planted a solid kiss on Ed's smiling lips. "You son-of-a-gun," she shrieked. "You named your boat after me. That was sweet. Thank you, thank you. I love it." She climbed on board and yelled, "Come on, Skipper. Let's take *Pilcher* out for a spin."

Ed jumped into the cockpit and gave Sandy a hug. "You like it, Pilcher?"

"I love it and you know why?"

"No, tell me."

"It means you love me. Men never name their yachts after a woman unless they really love them." She did a little dance and let out a whoop. "He loves me," she shouted into the wind.

Ed gave her a long and tender kiss. "You got that right." He pulled a key from his pocket and started the engine. After letting it warm up for a couple of minutes, he jumped back on to the dock and untied the bow and stern lines then hopped back on board, took hold of the wheel, advanced the throttle and eased the boat out of the slip.

Sandy, sitting on the port side bench, watched with admiration as Ed skillfully piloted the boat out of the harbor.

He looked at her and smiled. "Okay, what I'm going to do now is set everything up for navigation then I'll set a course, put it on autopilot and then we'll rig the ship for sailing."

"Like running up the sails," Sandy added, remembering some of the things she learned when she and Ed first went to sailing school.

"On this boat, it's *rolling* out sail. Check this out. This boat has some really cool navigation stuff." Ed turned on the Icom VHF, the Standard VHF with AIS, the two Garmin GPS receivers, depth sounder, and radar. He explained the function of each as he went through the checklist. "We also have a Raymarine wind recorder and autopilot plus a Garmin chart recorder. Like I said, the owners of this boat knew what they were doing and they really tricked it out. The main, jib and mizzen are like new. They installed lazy jacks on the main plus twin-stay roller furling. This boat is a dream to sail. I can't believe I got it so cheap. The navigation stuff and the sails alone must have cost what we paid for the boat."

Sandy laughed. "Okay. Enough already. I'm convinced you got a great deal." She got up and made her way into the salon, galley and master stateroom, taking in the elegant woodwork and other custom appointments. Returning to the cockpit, she said, "It really is a beautiful yacht. They certainly took good care of it. How old is this boat anyway?"

Ed laughed. "You're not going to believe it, but this boat is almost thirty years old."

"Are you kidding me?"

"Nope. It was built in 1980. You do the math."

"Gee, that's amazing...I mean, it looks like it could be almost new."

"That's the thing about these kinds of boats. The real sailing enthusiast takes more pride in his boat than anything else he owns. His car might look like hell or his house might be messy, but his boat—ah, that's another story. As you can see, the couple that owned this boat really cared for it for all the years they had it. I'm told they never let it look anything but perfect. On top of that, the guy was a nut for keeping the mechanics and equipment up to date." Ed swept his arm in an arc taking in all of the electronic gadgetry on the forward wall of the cockpit. "Look at all this stuff. Sailing this boat is like flying an airplane."

Out on the open sea with sails rigged and a course set on the autopilot for a heading that would carry them south toward San Diego, Ed went into the galley and reappeared with the lunch the caterers had brought on board that morning. With a flourish, he laid a plate on her lap and handed her utensils wrapped in a linen napkin. "Here you go. A gourmet lunch fit for the Queen herself."

"Wow, this is pretty special," Sandy muttered as she scanned the artfully plated fare. "What the heck is this stuff?"

"Hell, I don't know. I just told them I wanted a very special lunch for a very special lady and this, plus some other stuff that also really looks delicious, is what they put on the boat this morning." He handed her a basket of assorted rolls. "Have one of these."

Sandy took a spoonful and chewed slowly. Dabbing her mouth with the soft napkin, she said, "Mmmm. It's obviously all kinds of seafood and rice. The sauce is marvelous."

They sat at the fold-out table in the cockpit and ate in silence for a while. When they finished, Ed took the plates back to the galley and returned with a tray of assorted petits fours. "How about these babies for dessert?" He held the tray out for her selection. "Want some coffee or tea with them?"

They sailed south, keeping within three to five miles of the coast. Sandy insisted that they should always be able to see land...*just in case*. She was enjoying the light deck work Ed had her perform. He kept up a running commentary on what they were doing and why. She humored him by being attentive and following his instructions. She had to admit, at least to herself, that sailing a boat like this one was fun and something of a challenge as well. She could appreciate why Ed loved it so much. But as the hours slipped by with the autopilot and other electronics doing most of the work, Sandy remembered why she hadn't embraced sailing as Ed had. After a while, it just got boring. When Ed brought the boat about and set a course for the Channel Islands Marina, Sandy was pleased that Ed's plan for their date didn't include a long sail that ended up spending the night at a mooring at some marina in San Diego or Mexico. She knew the long sail back the next day would not be that much fun—for her!

It was almost six o'clock when Ed piloted the boat into the marina and tied up. Sandy jumped out of the cockpit onto the dock and wobbled around a bit. Ed trotted up to her and grabbed her around the waist. "Easy does it, sailor," he said. "It'll take you a minute to get used to dry land." He hopped back on board. "I've got a few things to take care of and then we'll think about dinner." After shutting down the electronics, he ducked down and went into the cabin.

"Where are we going to eat?" Sandy called to him from dockside.

Ed shouted through an open porthole, "It's not very far from here."

Sandy came back on board and found Ed in the salon. He was setting up the mahogany drop leaf dining table. "Whatcha doin'?"

"Setting up for dinner."

"We're eating here?"

"That's right." He gave her a smile and added, "I know, I know, you didn't see that much food in the ice box but magically..." He looked at his watch. "In just about ten minutes, your dinner will magically appear. Right now, I'm going into the galley and make a bottle of really good champagne appear. There's just one bottle so we're only going to have a few glasses to celebrate the fact that..." He threw his arms around Sandy and laughed, "We're going to celebrate the fact that we're not going to get wasted. We'll enjoy the wine and a great dinner and the best part is, you will be able to remember it tomorrow morning."

Sandy had to laugh, even though she wasn't quite sure if she should feel insulted at the insinuation about her recent and, perhaps, ongoing drinking problem. She decided to let it go. "Okay, smart-ass. I know what you're doing and the old Sandy would be pissed but the new and, I should add, reformed Sandy accepts it as, as what—humor?"

"Exactly." He kissed her. He kissed her again, deeply. Releasing the kiss, he continued to hold her very tight and whispered in her ear, "I love you, baby. You know that, right?"

"I know you do," Sandy whispered.

"I want things between us to be like they used to be. You were my best friend and buddy then and I want that feeling, that comfortable feeling you were talking about, I want it back."

Sandy looked into his eyes and murmured, "And so do I."

The moment ended when they heard voices and footsteps. "It's the caterers," Ed exclaimed, "and right on time." He hurried aft to the cockpit and guided the two women, dressed in starched chefs' jackets and white slacks, into the salon.

Sandy walked in and greeted the women.

One of them said, "Did you enjoy the lunch we fixed for you?"

"You bet," Sandy said. "It was delicious."

"Good. We'll have you all set up in fifteen minutes," the caterer said, "You two go out on deck, have a cocktail and enjoy the sunset."

Ed went into the galley, removed the bottle of champagne from the ice box, grabbed a couple of glasses and led Sandy up on deck. They sat on deck chairs with a small round table between them. Ed popped the cork, poured the wine, they touched glasses, and Ed said, "Here's looking at you, kid."

Sandy laughed. "Ah, Bogie, you're too funny." They clinked glasses again and drank. Sandy smacked her lips. "Mmmm, that is really good. You know, this is the first drink I've had in–"

"Quite a while," he interjected. "Good for you. Enjoy it."

The dinner was, as Sandy put it, incredible. She also said that a great wine would have been nice, to which Ed had replied, "I agree, but the Pellegrino made it possible for us to enjoy the rest of the evening," which he had stated was also incredible. After dinner and a long stroll along the docks, they had returned to the boat ready for the next thing Ed had planned. And that *next thing* carried them away into the night only to be repeated when they awoke in the morning.

They walked hand in hand to a little café nearby and ordered breakfast. Sandy could see and feel Ed's euphoria. It seemed as if their marriage was back to where it used to be—like it had been in Peoria.

Sandy smiled and kept up the light-hearted banter. However, her demeanor did not reflect her innermost thoughts—thoughts of that afternoon with Bart. She had committed adultery; she had unwittingly cheated on her husband. Nothing could change what happened. She would have to live with that lie for the rest of her life. But could she?

Chapter 10

Sandy looked at Ed. He was smiling and she knew why. Sunday had been the perfect day...just what he had hoped it would be. Still Sandy fretted as they sped north along the highway toward Malibu. She might have shared that same euphoria had it not been for that intruding memory of her infidelity. Her cell phone rang. She retrieved it from her purse—it was Pat.

"Hi, honey."

"Hi, Mom. I need to talk to you and Dad."

"What's going on? You sound funny."

"It's about Bev. She—"

Sandy sucked in air sharply. "What about her?"

"She didn't come back last night."

Sandy's voice rose. "What are you talking about? She didn't come home from where?"

Ed found a pull-out, stopped the car and turned off the engine. "Who is that?"

"It's Pat. Okay, honey," she said into the phone. "I'm going to turn on the speaker. Dad and I are in the car but he just parked. Now, tell us what is the problem with Beverly."

Ed leaned in toward the phone as Pat told them that Beverly and Kevin had left Saturday morning in Kevin's Jeep. Bev told Pat that they were going to take a trip over the weekend to some place in Mexico. Pat couldn't remember exactly where they said they were going but she thought it probably was near the border. Bev told her that they'd be back Sunday evening. Bev called Pat Saturday night around seven o'clock and said they were staying at a nice hotel with a pool. Pat couldn't remember the name of the hotel but it was "something Guadalupe."

Ed yelled into the phone, "You can't remember the name of the town or the name of the hotel? Think!"

In a small voice Pat answered, "I'm sorry, Daddy, but I was on a date and we were having dinner when Bev called...it was noisy and..."

Sandy put her hand on Ed's arm. "Okay, honey. Don't worry about it. Maybe it will come to you after a while," she said, struggling to keep her voice calm. "So, go on with rest of it."

Pat told them that around nine Sunday morning, Bev had called again and said she and Kevin were taking the Jeep out to see some little village their waiter at the hotel had told them about and they were going to spend the day "Jeeping around" and then head back home in the late afternoon. Bev told Pat that it had taken them about 5 hours to drive down so she thought they'd be back at the condo by nine or so.

"When they weren't back by nine, I tried calling her," Pat said, "but no answer. I thought, well, okay, maybe they got a late start and decided not to drive all the way home and to just hole up someplace and come back in the morning. But they're not here, she doesn't answer her phone and so I think we need to do something right away." Pat sounded close to tears.

Ed rubbed his face, trying to think. "Listen, Pat, we're about twenty minutes away from home." He checked the dashboard clock. "We'll be home by ten o'clock. As soon as we get there, we'll call you. Okay? Meanwhile, if you hear from her, call us." He added, "Listen, Google a map for northern Mexico and see if any of the towns rings a bell. If Bev said it was a five hour drive, then it's got to be some place near the border like Tijuana or someplace on the Baja Peninsula. Okay? Will you do that?"

"Sure. I'll get right on it. And you'll call me just as soon as you get home?"

"Okay, we gotta get going. Talk to you later."

Sandy took a breath, about to say something but the call had been disconnected.

Ed started the car and roared off the pull-out and onto the highway. "This is bad," he yelled over the rushing wind. "Damn it. If I get my hands on that Kevin, I wring his friggin' neck."

Sandy glanced at the speedometer. "Hey, you're going a hundred and twenty. Slow down or you'll get us killed."

As soon as they were in the house, Ed phoned Pat. As he dialed, he said to Sandy, "See if you can find a map of the south coast and northern Mexico." Into the phone he said, "Okay, Patty, we're home. Any word?"

"No. I tried calling her a little while ago but no answer. What do you think we should do...call the police?"

"Yeah, but I think we'd better wait until we can figure out where they are; otherwise it'll be a needle in a haystack kind o' thing."

Pat was silent for a moment then brightly exclaimed, "Hey, I got an idea. How 'bout I call Kevin's folks and see if they've heard from him?"

"You have their number?"

"No, but I know their house is on the Silverado golf course—it's near Napa. Kevin's always talking about it. Should I call them?"

"Sure, call them up right away and then call me back and let me know what they say or better still, ask them to call me."

"Okay." Pat hung up.

Sandy walked in the kitchen holding a road map. She opened it and spread it on the table. "So, what did Pat say?"

Ed gave her the gist of their conversation and then bent over the map. With his finger he traced the route from Santa Barbara to San Diego then south to the Mexican border. "Okay, since Bev told Pat that it took them five hours, my guess is they would have gone to one of the three closest towns, Tijuana, Mexicali or Ensenada."

"Or maybe someplace near but not in those towns."

"Well, Bev did say they were staying at a nice hotel with a pool so I'm guessing it probably was in or close to a town." Ed studied the map as Sandy gazed over his shoulder. "Okay, for starters, get on Google and look up hotels and resorts in those three towns and see if any of them have Guadalupe in their name. Pat's going to call me after she talks to Kevin's folks."

"Oh, that was a good idea," Sandy said. "Did she come up with that?"

Ed smiled slightly. "Yes. Her idea." His phone rang.

It was Pat. "Kevin's parents haven't heard from him in a week. They did say he doesn't call them very often but when I told them what's going on, they got pretty excited. Mr. Kendall said he would try to contact Kevin and then he'd call you so I better get off. Call me right after you talk to him, okay?"

"I will." He looked up to see Sandy waving a legal pad at him. "I think we're in luck. There's a very nice resort about thirteen miles from Ensenada called," she consulted the pad, *Posada Inn Mission de Guadalupe.* I have the phone number. Should I call them and see what they know?"

"Sure. Kevin's dad told Pat he'd call Kevin right away and find out what's going on. Pat said he sounded concerned."

"Well, he sure as hell should be." Sandy picked up her pad and headed back to the office.

"Yes." Ed's phone rang again. "Hello, yes, this is Edward Noble, Patricia's father. Sorry, would you repeat that? Okay, Carl Kendall—got it."

The two men talked for a quarter of an hour. Carl hadn't reached Kevin but since they might still be in Mexico, and perhaps some distance from a cell tower that could be the reason. On the other hand, Carl wasn't ruling out an accident or perhaps foul play. "It is Mexico, for Christ's sake! There's a bunch of lunatics down there running around dealing drugs, shooting people, what have you. So, we shouldn't rule out that scenario."

"Let's not get carried away with worst case scenarios." Ed added, "At least not for now. I'm thinking maybe they were exploring around and got lost trying to find their way back to civilization and ran out of gas. Regardless, I'm going to charter a helicopter and fly down there and make some inquiries. My wife is talking right now to the folks at the hotel where we think the kids were staying to see if they can shed any light on this. Anyway, I'll have the helicopter to have a look around while I'm down there."

"I'd like to go with you," Carl said.

"Can you get on a plane and fly down to LAX right away? That's where I plan to pick up the chopper and pilot."

"I'll check on it and call you back. By the way," Carl said, "Do you have any idea what it will cost to rent a chopper?"

"Actually, no. I've never rented one before. But I don't care what it costs—we need to get moving on this thing and a helicopter is the best for getting down there fast and for searching from the sky. Don't worry about it, I'll pay for it."

"I rented one a couple years ago to look at a property. It was a small one and it cost about $500 an hour." For emphasis he repeated, "That's $500 an *hour* and I can't remember if that included the fee for the pilot."

"Like I said, Carl, I can handle it. If you want to go, it's not going to cost any more for another passenger. Right now I need you to check flights to Los Angeles and get back to me right away, okay?"

"Okay."

Sandy walked in, clearly agitated. "I just talked to the hotel manager who told me that a Mr. and Mrs. Noble registered on Saturday afternoon using a credit card issued to Beverly Noble. He told me that they checked out yesterday morning." Sandy began shaking and then burst into tears. "Oh God," she wailed, "what if they're out in the middle of nowhere or worse, they've been grabbed by some drug people?"

Ed put his arms around her and held her tightly for a long moment. "Listen, we're going to find them. They probably are either got lost or ran out of gas or—"

"Or worse," Sandy groaned. "Some gangsters see these American kids in their fancy Jeep fooling around out in the desert and grab 'em. Maybe they're just after the Jeep but then they think they might be able to get some money out of their parents. Hell, that's happened many times." She took a deep breath and looked at Ed with beseeching eyes. "What are we going to do?"

Ed filled her in on his conversation with Carl. "The next thing I'll do," he went on, "is call the FBI and report the incident and see what they can do. Then I'll call the police in Ensenada and enlist their help. Maybe they'll refer me to the Federal Police or some other agency down there that would deal with this kind of thing."

"That sounds like a good start," Sandy said, starting to brighten. "Should I pack some clothes for both of us?"

"Yes, do that. Better pack enough for about a week."

Ed located an air-charter company and made arrangements to rent a Robinson R-44 helicopter. He was told that the aircraft would be available with an experienced pilot for whatever length of time was needed. The plane could seat three passengers, had a range of 550 miles and flew at 215 miles an hour. The trip to Ensenada would take about an hour and a half. The cost with pilot would be $850 an hour plus fuel and other costs incurred by the pilot such as food, overnight lodgings, tie down or hanger costs. Ed told the agent that they might need the plane for a week or more. In that case, the agent told him, there would be some adjustment to the rate. Ed gave the agent his credit information and credit card number and the agent asked Ed to hold while he confirmed the information.

Sandy came back in and asked, "What do you want me to pack for you?"

Ed looked up from the phone. "What? Oh, I'll do it. I'm on hold waiting for the helicopter guy to check my credit." Ed's phone buzzed with another call. It was Carl. "I'm talking to the chopper people. I'll call you right back."

The agent came back on line. "Okay, Mr. Noble, you're all set. Your plane is at LAX but it just came back from a trip and will require servicing. I'm pretty sure it will be ready to fly by noon. The pilot will call you when he is ready to go but I suggest you be at the General Aviation helipad a little before noon."

"Excellent, thank you." Ed hung up, then checked incoming calls, found Carl's number and called. Carl and his wife, Sherry, would not be able to get to the Los Angeles airport until 4:40.

"I'm sorry, but the plane holds only three passengers and my wife is going, so that leaves one seat. The other problem is, I don't want to wait that long. The chopper will be ready to go at noon and we need to leave so that we still have daylight to do some searching before it gets dark."

Carl said, "Well, what should we do then?"

"Fly to Ensenada or if that doesn't work, fly to Tijuana or Mexicali, rent a car and drive to Ensenada. Call me when you arrive and we'll tell you where to meet us. Can you do that?"

Carl said, "Okay, we'll work something out. Maybe we'll just go ahead and drive down there. I'll let you know."

"We've just got to get moving on this. Anyway, we'll see you down there but in the meantime, if we locate them, I'll call you right away. How's that?"

"Fine. And Ed, thanks a lot. Good luck."

Ed called the FBI local station agent and gave him the particulars. The agent promised to call the Mexican Federal Police and get them going on the case. He reviewed the details Ed had given him and asked, "Anything else you can think of?"

"No, but I've rented a helicopter. We're going down there and fly around and see if we can spot the Jeep. If we don't, we'll stay there and keep trying. I'll call you if anything develops that you should know about."

"Very well. Better check in with me every day. My name is Burke, Tom Burke. If I have any news, I'll call you."

In the bedroom, Sandy was closing her suitcase. Ed said, "We need to be at LAX by noon so we gotta get a move on." He dropped clothes and toiletries into his suitcase while giving Sandy an account of his conversation with the FBI and Carl. "The chopper's gonna be expensive as hell," Ed said, "but I don't care what it costs. We've got to get down there and find those kids."

"I'm ready whenever you are," Sandy said. "I guess we'd better take the Lexus, right?"

"Yes. And why don't you call the cook and the housekeeper lady? Tell them we'll be gone for a while but will call them when we get back."

"I'll do it right now," Sandy said over her shoulder as she hurried to the office.

At LAX, Ed drove over to the General Aviation office. He asked the Fixed Base operator if he had heard anything from the R-44. Just then the radio came alive with a call from the pilot who stated he would be landing in five minutes. Ed was told where to park his car. Then he and Sandy, with bags in hand, watched as the helicopter hovered for a moment then set down on the apron.

The pilot opened the door and yelled, "You Edward Noble?"

"Yes," Ed yelled.

The pilot jumped down and, ducking low under the idling rotor blades, came over to meet them. "I'm Ben Turner. You folks ready?" he asked.

"Absolutely," Ed said.

"Okay, then, we can go right now." Ben picked up the two suitcases and said, "Follow me."

He helped them board the aircraft and made sure Ed, sitting up front, and Sandy, behind the pilot's seat, were securely buckled in. Handing each of them a headset with earphones and microphone, he said, "You need these to communicate with me and with anyone I contact by radio. They're voice-activated." After stowing the two suitcases, he closed the door, climbed into his seat, buckled his harness and said into his mic, "Just a couple things you need to know." He gave the usual safety talk and added, "I know you're on urgent business, so I'll skip the usual invitation to relax. But I've been flying helicopters since the Viet Nam war, and I mention it so you know that I've had a little experience flying these birds. Since this trip, I was told, may turn out to be a search and rescue type mission, you'll be glad to know I've flown these kinds of missions many times."

He did a quick pre-flight check. "I'm going to fly over the water, just off the coast most of the way to Ensenada. On the way, I want you to give me whatever details you have about this mission so I can be thinking about the best way to handle it from the air." Ed nodded. "Okay then," Ben said. "Here we go."

Having received clearance to take off, Ben pulled the collective, the engine roared, the plane shook. He moved the cyclic and the craft rose. Ben headed out to sea then turned south. He adjusted the collective, the plane sped up. "We're going to cruise at around 200 miles an hour," he said into his mic, "and we'll stay at around 4,000 feet over the water. We've already spoken to the authorities down there and we're cleared to take a look around Ensenada and the northern part of the peninsula for any signs of that Jeep or the missing couple. I was informed during the briefing that the Mexican Federal Police have already initiated a search mission for your kids."

Ed reached back and patted Sandy's knee. "Things are happening already, so stay positive. Okay?"

Sandy smiled weakly. "We're going to find them, right?"

Ed yelled into his mic, "You bet we are."

Chapter 11

Nearing Mexican air space, Ben called air traffic control. The ATC gave him instructions in English which the pilot acknowledged then asked for permission to do a low-level search of the northern peninsula. He was told to stand by and a few minutes later the radio crackled. ATC gave Ben permission to fly a search pattern around northern Baja at an altitude of 500 to 1,500 feet, depending on terrain. Ben acknowledged and told the ATC that he would advise when he was in position to commence the search.

"Okay, folks, if you look out around eleven o'clock, you can see Ensenada," Ben said. "I think our best bet is to begin looking at the area to the east of the city on the south side of town." They flew over the harbor then Ben turned inland. He dropped down to 1,400 feet and slowed the plane considerably. They were flying over an area corrugated with ridges that Ben said were between 600 and 1300 feet high.

"You can see the city just ends where these high ridges begin," Ben said. He turned east until they saw a road which wound between and over some of the lower ridges. "That's Highway 3. The Posada Inn Mission de Guadalupe is on this highway. I'm going to follow it since they would have used it to get out into the country." Ben slowed the chopper to 60 mph and dropped down to 800 feet. "Okay. Mrs. Noble, you keep a sharp eye out your port side and Ed, you do the same on your starboard side. Use the binoculars. They're under your seats. I'll concentrate on what's going on in front of us and be on the lookout for other traffic, although ATC here said we shouldn't encounter very much."

Ben maintained a course over Highway 3. Ten minutes later, Sandy said, "Is that a village ahead and to the left of the road?"

Ben checked the chart. "I'm pretty sure it's Ojos Negros." He turned the plane north. Below were symmetrical squares and rectangles of cultivated land. Soon they were over the village.

"I doubt they would have made a trip up here," Ed said. "My daughter told her sister that a waiter at the hotel told them to go see something but she couldn't remember what or where it was."

Ben turned to Ed. "Did anyone ask the waiter where he told them to go?"

Sandy broke in. "Yes, I told the manager of the hotel about that conversation and he asked the waiters who were working Saturday evening about it. All of the them, I think he said there were five, remembered the pretty American girl with the red hair but the one who waited on them claimed he didn't give them any advice on where to go or what to see. Of course, he could be lying." Sandy pursed her lips. "Probably is lying."

Ed spoke. "Sandy, did you tell the manager to lean on that waiter?"

"No. I just asked him to try to get more information and that we'd be down there sometime today."

Ed said, "So, what do you think, Ben? Should we abandon the search for now and get to the hotel and question that waiter? I can throw enough money at him to make him want to tell us what he told the kids."

They flew southwest, keeping the road in sight. About 15 miles east of the coast, they spotted the hotel. There was nothing but flat vacant land behind the building and Ben set the chopper down there. "You guys go ahead and see what you can find out. I'll stay here with the bird." He shut down the engine and when the rotor stopped spinning he opened the door, got out and helped Ed and Sandy. "You've got my cell number," he told Ed. "Do you have international dialing on your phone?" Ed said he didn't think so. "Well, you better get it. Meanwhile if you need to call, you can use my phone."

Ed took Sandy's hand and they trotted over to the back of the hotel where then found a door that led down a long hall to the lobby. At the front desk, Sandy asked to speak to Mr. Carlos Estrada. In less than a minute Mr. Estrada appeared. He shook their hands.

In excellent English, he said, "I am very pleased to meet you, although these are not the best circumstances. The police have already been here and talked to me. Obviously, you haven't heard from your daughter but you can count on me and the staff to assist you in every way."

"Thank you very much," Sandy said.

"Now, I want you to know that I've spoken again to the waiter who served your daughter and the young man. He insists that he didn't speak to them about where they might go or anything else that was unrelated to the meal." Mr. Estrada raised his arms, palms up. "Of course that may not be the truth. I didn't press him further, although I did say that you would be happy to reward him should he be able to remember anything that might shed light on the whereabouts of your daughter. I can enhance that with the threat of his being dismissed if he isn't, how you say...forth...ah..."

"Forthcoming?"

"Yes, exactly so. Thank you." He led them to his office off of the lobby, offered them a seat and asked if he could get them anything to drink or eat.

"No, thanks, we want to keep moving while there is still light enough to look around. Our helicopter pilot is waiting behind the hotel."

"Ah, I thought I heard a helicopter close by. Very well then, I'll have the waiter come to my office and I'll arrange for rooms for you two and your pilot. May I do that?"

"That would be great," Ed said.

Estrada picked up the phone and briefly spoke in Spanish. "The waiter will be here in a minute or two," he said. "His name is Luis. His English is such that you can speak to him directly." At the sound of a light knock, the manager said, "Ah. Here he is now." He invited Luis to enter and then introduced him to Ed and Sandy, who shook his hand.

"Now then," Estrada said to Luis, "Señor Noble must not waste time searching for his daughter. So, no nonsense. If you have any idea where they might have gone, you must tell us now."

Luis turned frightened eyes towards the Nobles. Ed reached in his pocket and took out three one-hundred dollar bills and laid them on the desk. "You can have these if you will tell me if you suggested a place they should visit. Understand?"

"Yes, sir," Luis replied.

"And when we find my daughter and her friend, I will give you five hundred more as a reward."

Luis looked at Estrada in bewilderment.

"*Como un recompense. Así que, ¿comprende qué el señor le está ofreciendo?*" Estrada asked.

"Si. Comprendo," Luis said. He faced the Nobles. "I am not wanting to have trouble but I was, how say...*asustado?*"

Estrada inserted, "Afraid."

"Yes, afraid...but I understand is necessary because maybe peoples go lost and maybe bad things happen." The young waiter took a deep breath. "So, I tell you. They ask me what is good thing to see. I tell them drive north on number 3 road and go to Palm Valley. I say, for lunch, the Hacienda Hotel is nice place and then if have time the 3 road would be good for Jeep...many turns through canyons, pretty to see. I tell them to go to Tecate to enter U.S. then go west on 94 to coast. I myself have traveled this way many times to see my brother in San Diego." Luis glanced at Mr. Estrada who encouraged him with a nod.

Estrada opened a map of the Baja Peninsula. "Here is the route that Luis just described." Ed and Sandy stepped to the desk and followed as Estrada traced his finger along route 3 from Ensenada to the U.S. border at Tecate. "It is," he said, "an interesting and scenic ride, especially after you get into the hills. As you can see, there are many twists and turns so I would think it would have been a trip that might have appealed to them." He asked Luis, "¿Sabe cuántas kilometros es ése?"

"I believe is maybe one hundred-thirty."

Estrada translated. "That would be about eighty miles."

Ed turned to Luis and shook his hand then patted him on the shoulder. "Okay, my friend, this is exactly what we needed. Thank you very much." He picked up the three one-hundred dollar bills and handed them over. "When we find them, you'll get five more of these." To Mr. Estrada he said, "Okay, we're going to take off but we'll be back tonight, hopefully with the kids. Thanks a lot for your help. Come on, Sandy. Let's get going."

Sandy offered her thanks and hurried after Ed.

Back in the air, Ed briefed Ben on what they learned. Ben followed the highway east for a few minutes then spoke into his mic. "There's that hotel the kid told you about. Shall I drop down there? You can go in and see if your kids actually stopped there for lunch." He flew lower, checked out the dirt landing strip behind the buildings and put the chopper down about a hundred feet from the rear of the hotel. He shut down the engine and the three of them climbed out.

Ed asked the clerk at the desk if he could speak to the restaurant manager. The young man asked Ed to follow him. Sandy and Ben followed behind. The plaque on the door read, *Frederico Silva, Jefe de Servicio Gastronómico.*

Sandy asked the clerk, "Does Mr. Silva speak English?"

"I do not know, but I would be pleased to interpret for you." He knocked and opened the door. Silva sat behind a small desk. He looked up expectantly, then stood.

"Señor Silva, estas personas tienen un poco de preguntas para usted. Puedo interpretar el lo que dicen si usted desea."

"Ello." Silva extended his hand to each of his visitors. "What question you have of me? Please to speak slow, I understand English but small. Roberto to help. He speak the English good."

In slow, precise English, Ed asked if he remembered seeing a young man and red-headed woman in his restaurant for lunch on Sunday.

Silva's face lit up. *"Si, si.* Sure I see. I take to table the boy and girl with hair red. Pretty girl and, ah how say, much to laugh. Sure, they here, eat."

"Do you recall the time that they left?" Ed asked.

Silva gave Roberto a questioning look.

Roberto said, *"¿A qué hora partieron?"*

"A la uno y media." Silva replied.

Roberto added, "One-thirty."

"Good," Ed said reaching in his pocket and handing Silva and Roberto each a fifty dollar bill. "Gracias. You have been a great help. Many thanks." To Sandy and Ben he said, "Okay, let's roll."

The three of them trotted to the chopper and in minutes they were once again flying low and slow above Highway 3. As they headed toward Palm Valley they crossed over a large plantation of what appeared to be fruit trees and then they saw a town with many buildings. Ben looked at his chart. "It's called Heroes Del Desierto." He dropped down to 500 hundred feet and hovered. "Use the binocs and look around. That Jeep could be near or even in one of those houses or large buildings. I'll move around a bit, you guys scan each sector as I pass over it."

Sandy saw a Jeep next to what looked like a large warehouse. "Fly over to your left. You see the big building...that's it straight ahead...yes, right there. You see the Jeep on the right side?"

Ben dropped down another 100 feet and hovered. "That's a Jeep alright, although it doesn't look very new. The kid's got a pretty new one, right?"

Ed quizzed Sandy. "What do you think? Could that be the one?"

"No," she said. "I remember it being tan with black fenders and a black roof, but I just saw it that one time at the condo."

"Okay, keep looking." People were coming out of buildings and looking up at the helicopter. "We're attracting a lot of attention," Ben said as he moved the plane to another location to let Ed and Sandy scan.

After another fifteen minutes of flying over the town with half the population staring up at them, Ben said, "Okay, we'll follow the road up to the area around Palm Valley then we have to zip over to the airport and get fuel."

Ed said, "Where's the airport?"

"It's near Tijuana," Ben replied.

"It'll probably be too dark to see anything after that. Can you radio somebody and find out if the Federal police have any news?" Ed asked.

Sandy said, "We should tell them what we learned today."

"Yeah, you're right. I need to call the FBI agent I talked to this morning and do that. Maybe he could contact the Mexican police."

Ben came on. "There you go. I'll radio the LA FBO and set up a radio relay with the FBI guy. What's his name?"

Ed pulled a slip of paper from his shirt pocket. "Tom Burke."

Sandy scanned the terrain below and to the north through her binoculars, following the road with her eyes. At this point the highway wound its way through the foothills forming what looked like an inverted U. Just ahead, a road seemed to go to the center of the U leading up to a small group of buildings. "Ben, look to your left, that road there."

"I see it. Looks like a little ranch at the end of it."

"Go over there and let's have a look," Sandy said.

Ben dropped the plane to 500 feet, flew over the buildings then hovered close to what looked like a small home. Immediately, three men burst out of the back door. They looked up. Each of them was holding a weapon.

Sandy screamed.

Ben quickly pulled the collective, the engine roared, the craft gained speed and altitude as he swung the chopper over the house and away.

Ed shouted, "Jesus, they had guns...did you see that?"

At 2,000 feet, Ben throttled back. "Hell, yes. I wasn't about to hang around and be a target. I don't know, but it's possible that your kids could be in that house."

"Oh my God," Sandy wailed into her mic.

"I'm heading for the airport at Tijuana. It looks like it's about thirty miles from here so we'll be there in ten minutes. We'll get fuel and I'll try to raise the police." He scanned his gauges then flipped through some pages in a small book. He worked several dials on one of the radios and contacted Tijuana ATC.

Ben identified his aircraft, received permission to land and advised that he needed to speak to Federal Police as quickly as possible. He was given clearance to land on helipad 3, part of the "Old Airport" complex which, in addition to the military, houses offices of the Federal Police and Federal Investigation Agency.

When they were on the ground, they were met by a uniformed officer and a man in civilian clothes who identified himself as Andres Hierra, the Federal Investigation Agency (AFI) agent in charge. The policeman was Captain Cesar Ruiz of the Federal Police (PF). The two escorted Ed and Sandy into the office of Captain Ruiz in the Old Terminal building. Ben arranged for a fuel truck and remained with the plane.

Captain Ruiz told Ed that they had been keeping an eye on their helicopter all afternoon. Agent Hierra said, "We noticed that rather abrupt departure from what looked like a hovering attitude when you were flying near the eastern top of Route 3. We checked that area and saw there was a house set back from the north side of the highway, and we determined that was where you were. Correct?"

"Yes, sir. We did hover over that house to see if the missing Jeep was there and then some men came out with what looked like rifles. I think they took some shots at us but our pilot got us out of there pretty quick—"

Sandy jumped in. "As soon as the men came running out, he really reacted and got us away from there. It was scary."

"And then we flew directly here," Ed said.

Hierra nodded. "After we determined what was happening, we sent a chopper with six men to the site. They were on their way just before you arrived here. I'm waiting to hear from them. Also, a PF team in armored vehicles was dispatched from Mexicali."

Sandy asked, "They won't storm the house, will they? I mean the kids might be in there and—"

"No, no," the agent reassured her. "The teams know how to handle these situations. Unfortunately, tourists are abducted and held for ransom with some frequency but we have had some good success in getting their release. Unfortunately, it frequently takes money to get it done."

Ed said, "We'll pay the money...whatever they want. The main thing is that we get them back unharmed."

"Yes, of course," the captain said. "We will assist in every way,"

A knock on the door and a uniformed man stepped in the room. He looked around for a moment then, after a nod from the captain, said in Spanish, "The AFI team reports that they are at the target and after getting no response from inside the house, they entered the house but it was deserted. However, they did find a Jeep with a California license plate."

Agent Hierra jumped up from his chair. "¡Cague!" He quickly conveyed the news to the Nobles. "I'm sorry. I wanted to catch them before they ran so that I could offer a deal. Too bad." He said to the captain, "*Tendré el equipo busque la zona, ver si pueden verlos.*"

"*Haré lo mismo con el equipo de suelo,*" the captain replied. He turned to Ed and Sandy. "He will inform his team to search from the air and I will have my team do a ground search." He stood and took both of Sandy's hands in his. "Señora. You don't worry. We will find them."

Sandy was on the verge of tears. "Yes," she said. "I'm sure you will."

Hierra returned and said, "They found a note in the Jeep. It's in Spanish. I'll translate it for you." He read from the sheet of paper in his hand.

"*To the parents of Beverly Noble and Kevin Kendall. We have your children. They are unharmed and will remain so if you follow our directions perfectly. Beverly has told us her parents won much money in a lottery and so it would be easy for you to pay us a great amount. Soon she will call you and tell you what you must do. Be assured if you bring the police into it, and something bad happens to us, you will never see the boy or Beverly again. Beverly says she loves you and we are certain that you love her as well and do not want a bad thing to happen to her. We are ready to do bad things to her and we will if you don't follow our orders with perfection. Beverly and the boy will sign this so you understand they are with us.*"

Hierra raised his eyes and met Sandy's. He showed her the paper. "Is that her signature?"

Sandy gazed at the page through building tears. "I don't know...I suppose...yes, it probably is."

Hierra nodded and handed the page to Ed. "I think we can be reasonably sure they have them. The only sensible thing you can do is wait for the call and follow their instructions. Go back to the Posada Hotel and do not call us or anyone else. Just wait for your daughter to call you and then do whatever she tells you. Be assured we will be on the case but we will not do anything that may jeopardize your daughter or the boy. They will probably get your money but I don't think they will hurt the hostages. And in the end..." he gave the Nobles a smile that chilled Sandy to the bone. "In the end, we will find the bastards and try to get your money back, before we kill them." Hierra cocked his head to one side and spread his arms. "It will be an accident, of course—a matter of," he paused and gave them that cold smile again, "self-defense, something like that."

Chapter 12

Before leaving the office of Captain Ruiz, Ed was able to call Agent Burke who had been in constant contact with both the Federal Police and the Federal Investigation Agency throughout the day. Ed brought him up to speed on what he and Sandy had discovered. He put the phone on speaker and asked Captain Ruiz to give Burke a translation of the letter from the kidnappers. Burke and Ruiz then had a brief discussion about protocols and what they planned to do from now until Ed heard from the kidnappers.

"It's possible, I suppose, that the waiter is hooked up with the bad guys," Burke said. "Maybe they pay him to suggest places for likely customers—like the Noble girl—to go, and then they set up a road block or something and jump them."

"Hierra and I also believe that is possible," Ruiz said. "We have seen this kind of situation before but never has anyone from that hotel been involved. But Hierra told me he was going to put that waiter under surveillance and see if he is working as a setup man. We'll see. Also, the mobile unit I sent over there is still searching and may turn up a lead."

"Before any other consideration, you know, like capturing the bad guys, we need to get those kids to safety. We agree on that, right?"

Ruiz smiled at the phone. "Of course. Listen, Señor, always in this situation we worry about getting the hostages out first, then we do what we have to do with the, ah, as you say, bad guys. I will call you with any news throughout the night."

Ed asked Burke, "So, anything else I need to do?"

"No, get to your hotel and wait for them to call or get a message to you. For now, just follow their orders. They'll want cash so make sure you have it available. It would be a good idea to get it right away. Better call your bank and ask them to transfer a large sum of money to a bank in Ensenada. By the way, I do know you won a lot of money and chances are the bandits know it too. Better be ready to pay a million, maybe more."

"Sure. I'll take care of it. Thanks. Good bye." The call was disconnected.

Ed thanked Ruiz, took Sandy's hand and they went outside where Ben was waiting. "Is the chopper ready to go?"

Ben nodded. "I talked to the hotel guy and he gave me permission to land behind the hotel. He said he would post armed guards to keep an eye on it all night."

Over dinner, the three discussed the plan for the next day while Ed and Sandy waited to be contacted. Ben would have the plane ready to go as soon Ed received instructions from the kidnappers. Meanwhile, Ed would confirm that a million dollars had been deposited in Scotiabank Inverlat, a large bank in downtown Ensenada.

Ed was awakened a little after 6:00 AM by the ringing phone. It was Carlos Estrada, the hotel manager.

"I'm sorry to call so early, señor, but something has happened."

Sandy sat up, and Ed mouthed *hotel manager* to her.

Estrada's voice was breathless. "Can you come down to my office at once? No, wait. I will come to your room. I'll give you a few minutes."

Ed was about to speak when he heard the phone click off. He quickly got out of bed and as he hurried into the bathroom, he told Sandy, "Estrada wants to talk to us. He's coming up."

"Up here, to our room?"

"Yes."

"Oh!" Sandy jumped out of bed and pulled a robe from the closet.

When Ed came out of the bathroom, she ran in and closed the door.

Ed opened the hall door to Estrada's light knock and let him in.

Glancing around the room, the manager asked, "Where is your wife?"

"In the bathroom."

Estrada glanced at the bathroom door then turned to Ed. "Something terrible has happened," he murmured.

Ed felt his heart contract. "What?"

Sandy came out and confronted the two of them. "What's going on?" she demanded.

"Oh, señora, señor, perhaps you should seat yourselves for I have some terrible news."

"Oh, my God," Sandy moaned. "It's Beverly...something has happened to Beverly!"

Ed grabbed her under the arms and held her as her knees buckled. Then he eased her into a chair.

Estrada looked dismayed. "No, no. I am so sorry. Of course that is what you would think... but I have no news of your daughter. What I came here to tell you is that sometime in the night, the two men I had posted to watch the aircraft were murdered."

Ed and Sandy both gasped. Ed said, "What? What in the hell are you talking about?" Sandy just shook her head in disbelief, buried her face in her hands and began to sob.

Estrada looked at her with regret. Turning to Ed, he said in a low voice, "Both of the men had their throats cut and were dragged into the bushes by the pool. One of the gardeners found them this morning. But that's not all, the helicopter was damaged. They shattered most of the instruments and cut wires and, and—"

"Jesus! You've called the police, right?"

"Of course. I expect them any moment now. But there is another element to all of this—"

Ed took hold of Estrada's shoulders and hissed, "What? What do you mean?"

Estrada's cell phone rang. He pulled it from his pocket. "¿Qué es? Estoy ocupado ahora."

The caller replied in Spanish, "This is Captain Ruiz. Are you with the Nobles now?"

"Yes, I'm in their room, 427. I just told them about the murders and what happened to the helicopter. I called their pilot and told him what happened. I expect he checked the plane and will be here soon."

"I'm coming up," Ruiz said and hung up.

Ed urged Estrada, "So, what is that other element you were about to tell me."

Sandy had stopped crying. "What else?" she asked.

Estrada reached inside his jacket and took out an envelope which he handed to Ed. "Here, it is addressed to you."

Ed opened the envelope and pulled out a single sheet of yellow lined paper. The writing was in Spanish and written in pencil.

There was a knock and Estrada opened the door.

"Ah, Capitán Ruiz and Señor Turner. Come in."

Sandy and Ed stared wide-eyed at Ben. Ed said, "What the hell happened?"

Ben's expression was grim. "They wrecked the chopper—busted up instruments and controls, cut wires and cables. Pretty much ruined it. You heard about the guards?"

"Yes." Ed's posture showed his growing despair. "This is getting crazy."

Sandy snatched the letter from Ed's hand. "Let me see that." She glanced at the page. "It's in Spanish." She handed the page to Estrada. "Read it to us in English."

Estrada scanned the page and began to read aloud.

> *To the parents of Beverly Noble. We have your daughter and the boy. Now they are not harmed but for sure they will be if you do not pay attention to what we tell you to do. Your daughter told us you would be able to pay us a large amount of money. I asked her how much and she said you could pay a million dollars. So, that is what you must pay if you want to see these two again. How you will get the money to us is a problem you must solve. I know you have talked to the PF and the AFI so that makes things more difficult. But I tell you this, if we are killed, your daughter and the boy also will die, you can be certain of that. So tell the Federales and the others to keep out of it. They must allow you to deliver the money. When we have the money and have moved to a safe place, then we will set them free and let you know where you can find them. These are the rules. We don't change them for any reason. Understand! Remember, we don't live, they don't live. I will tell you also that the death of your daughter will not be pleasant. We will have much pleasure and your daughter will have much pain before she is killed.*

*So, it is up to you now to save her from that. You will hear
from us soon. Be ready with a good plan.*

Sandy fell upon the couch sobbing hysterically. Ed stood dazed, feeling sick to his stomach. The others, with eyes cast down, didn't speak.

Captain Ruiz broke the silence. "Very well then. Let's not waste valuable time. The sooner we get them the ransom, the better are the chances of the children surviving. Unfortunately your aircraft has been disabled. That was stupid of them. How did they expect you to deliver the money? *Los idiotas!*" Ruiz looked at Ben. "But we can arrange for another, a small civilian helicopter like yours. Keeping your plane on the radar would not be a problem and a small civilian fixed wing, flying high with high-powered scanners, could keep you in sight even if you were on the ground, and not be detected by esos imbéciles."

"But, Capitán, you do not know how...ah... *sofisticados*. I don't know the English word."

"*Comprendo.*" Ruiz said. "They could be very sophisticated which will make the job more difficult or they may be a gang of *tarados* in which case it should be easier to take them out. And now, Señor Estrada, I need to talk to Señor Noble, so if you will excuse us—"

"Of course." Estrada turned to Ed. "If there is anything you need or I can help you with, please do not hesitate to call me." He nodded to Sandy and departed.

Speaking to Ed, Ruiz said, "The fellow who wrote the note doesn't appear to be stupid. The spelling was good so we have to assume he has had some education and may be able to stay ahead of us."

Ed nodded.

Ruiz continued, "The plan I would suggest is that when you hear from them, you tell them that you will rent a helicopter and fly to a remote place. You will tell them that the police no doubt will be following your every move, probably by radar but you don't think the police will be near you when you hide the money. You say that you have told the police to stay out of it for the safety of your children and they agreed to leave you alone to do whatever you need to do. Señor Noble, are you understanding this?"

"Yes. We land the chopper then take off on foot and conceal the money somehow—bury the money in the forest or something—and take measurements and so on so that we can tell them how to find the money."

"Exactly so." He handed Ed a cell phone. "I have this for you to use. It has international calling and has the same number as your old phone. Make sure when you next hear from the bandits, you give them this number." Ruiz addressed Sandy. "Try not to worry, señora. We will get the children back safely—be assured of it." At the door, he stopped to say, "I will not call you on the cell phone as long as you are in the hotel. I will use your room phone or leave a message with the hotel operator." Turning to Ben, he said, "Come with me and we will get you a helicopter." The two men departed, leaving Ed and Sandy feeling suddenly adrift.

The room phone rang. It was Carl Kendall. "I've been trying to reach you for hours—"

Ed put his hand over the mouthpiece and in a hushed voice said to Sandy, "It's Kevin's dad." Into the phone he said, "Where are you?"

"Sherry and I are here in the hotel. Shall we come up to your room?"

"Sure. It's room 427. We need to talk."

Chapter 13

When Ed had finished telling the Kendalls everything that had happened since Ed and Carl had last spoken, Kevin's parents sat in stunned silence for several minutes.

"And so," Sherry finally said in a trembling voice, "you haven't heard anything more from those villains other than the note they left in your plane?"

Ed nodded. "We're just waiting for them to make the next move. Right now I have no way to contact them." He was pounding one fist into the palm of the other hand. "Which is making me crazy...I mean this waiting..."

Carl said, "May I see that note?"

Sandy had taken a seat on the couch next to Sherry. "It's in Spanish," she said, "and Captain Ruiz took it with him so that their crime lab can check it for fingerprints and any other clues. The part that terrified me the most was what they said they'd do to Beverly if things didn't go right." She couldn't hold back a sob.

Sherry put her arms around Sandy. Doing her best to hold off her own tears, Sherry whispered, "We will get them back, honey. I'm sure we will. I don't think those people will harm them...I mean without the kids, they have no bargaining power. I'll just bet they've pulled this stunt before and know how to handle hostages to make sure they'll get their pay-off."

The phone rang and the four of them jumped. Ed ran to the room phone and grabbed it. "This is Edward Noble."

It was the hotel operator. "A boy brought a letter addressed to you. Would you like me to send it up with a bellman?"

"Is the boy still there?"

"No, sir. He gave the doorman the letter and ran off."

Ed sighed. "Damn. Okay, I'll be right down. Thank you." Ed told the others about the letter. "I'll be right back," he said as he hurried out the door.

Carl said to Sandy, "What about the million dollars? Does Ed have that kind of cash?"

"Don't worry. He's already made arrangements to have it sent to a bank here in Ensenada."

Carl sat at the desk, put his elbows on the desktop and put his head in his hands. "You read about stuff like this but you never imagine it's going to happen to you. It's such a hopeless feeling. Those bastards can call the shots. They can get the money and still..." He couldn't verbalize the rest of that thought.

Ed returned somewhat breathless, holding a large manila envelope. He walked over to the table and sat down. The others joined him. Ed tore open the envelope and pulled out several sheets of yellow ruled paper. Again, the writing was in pencil. "Damn, it's in Spanish. I need to have Estrada come up here and read it."

"Let me see it," Carl said, reaching for the pages in Ed's hand. "I can read Spanish." He shuffled through the pages, one of which contained a map-like sketch. Carl examined it then handed it to Ed. "Does any of that look familiar to you?"

Ed examined the map and read the labels. "No, not really."

Sandy got up and looked at the map over Ed's shoulder.

Carl was scanning the letter. "It's pretty well written. Whoever wrote it certainly isn't illiterate. Let's see. Okay." He began to read.

*"To the family of Beverly: Change of plans now. I will
tell what is necessary for you to do. You must rent a
helicopter. I told those idiots not to touch your ship but
they did. Stupid..."*

Carl looked up from the page and said, "I don't know the word,
but it probably means something like assholes. Anyway, I guess he's
not too happy with some of his gang." He resumed reading.

*"It should be no problem to rent one. You must do this
quietly. Your pilot would be very well to do this job. I
make a map. Look at it. Fly south to San Felipe—after
go west to the Parque Nacional Sierra De San Pedro
Martir, (your pilot will find it on his chart). Look for the
observatory on top of 2.7 meter mountain."*

Carl did the calculation on his phone and said, "That's about
9,200 feet."

*"Is a round white building with some blue trimmings.
Will be easy to see from the air. East of observatory is
Vallecitos meadow, a large open space good for landing.
I have learned that parents of the boy have come to
Ensenada and are with you now no doubt. That is good."*

Carl turned the page over.

*"The million dollars shall be in $100 U.S. money. Use 4
strong boxes and put $250,000 in each and close with
much strong tape. Carry boxes down the road toward
entrance to the park. You will see a small chapel built*

of wood with a large cross over the door. In the back of the chapel on the left side are some large rocks. Pull the rocks away. You will see an opening under the building. Push the boxes in there and put the rocks back as they were before.

After we get the money without any problem, we will hire a driver who is not of our team and knows nothing of this. He has no understanding of English. When we are sure the area is not being covered by police, he will drive the children to the observatory. There is a good road. They can call you and wait for you there where they will be safe and warm. The boy's parents will drive to the park. It should take 4 hours to drive from Ensenada. They pick up the children and bring them to you. You and Mrs. must stay in your hotel room while other families drive to observatory. If anything goes wrong, the children die and none of you will leave Mexico alive. You understand?"

Carl looked at the others. "That's it."

Ed, Sandy and Sherry were viewing the map which made the logistics of the plan plain enough.

Sandy spoke. "My God. Why would they make it so damn complicated? How are we ever going to do all of that?"

Carl was working his iPhone. "I just Googled what a million dollars in hundreds would weigh and it comes to twenty-two pounds. I thought it'd be a lot more than that."

"Me, too," Ed said.

Carl turned to Sandy. "Look, it sounds complicated but actually it's not. Those bozos figured out a pretty good plan. If you break it down it's fairly simple, that is, what we have to do. It may not be that simple for them but then again, they've probably worked out the logistics and think they can pull it off, provided we do everything they told us to do and do it as they imagine we will."

Ed said, "Carl's right. Basically, after we get the money and pack it up in four boxes like they want, Sandy and I fly to this place here," He put his finger on the map next to a box with the letter 'O' in the middle."

Carl added, "Observatory in Spanish is *observatorio*. It's on the highest point in that National Park so your pilot shouldn't have any trouble finding it. And the flat area, what he called the *Vallecitos pradera*, little valley meadow, is just below."

Ed picked it up from there. "So, we land the plane in the meadow, follow the road toward the entrance to the park, find the chapel and put the boxes underneath and scoot back to the plane. We'll take along some hand-held radios so we can keep in touch with Ben. If he sees anything that looks like trouble I want him to get the hell out of there."

"And what happens to us then?" Sandy asked.

Ed gave her a blank look. "I guess we wait it out until it's safe for Ben to pick us up."

Carl said, "The bad guys aren't going to be there when you make the drop. They're not stupid, at least not the head guy. No, they're gonna wait, maybe for days, until they are damn sure it's safe to go into the park and get the money. I doubt they'll have access to a chopper so they'll need to drive into the park and that's where it'll get tricky for them."

Sherry said, "If it was me, I'd get some guy to act like a tourist, to go in there and get the money."

"You know, that's a pretty good scheme and I'll bet it would work," Ed said. "I'm sure lots of Mexicans go there to camp or visit the observatory."

"Anyway, what's the plan for right now?" Sherry asked.

"I'm going to call Ben right now and see if he's been able to get a hold of another chopper. I'll tell him where we're going so he can get whatever charts he needs. Once he has one ready to go, I'll have him fly over here and land behind the hotel. I don't think the crooks will want to destroy this one. While he's doing all that, I'll get in touch with the bank and see if the money has been sent down. Once we get the cash, we can figure out what size boxes we'll need, get them, load the money and take off for the observatory. Carl, you make sure your car is gassed up and ready to go as soon as we get the word."

"Hey," Carl said, "I just looked up how high ten thousand hundred dollars bills would be and the answer is—anyone care to guess?" The others just looked at him without speaking. "Well, ten thousand hundred dollar bills in a stack would be forty-three inches tall."

"That's all?" Ed exclaimed. He picked up the phone and asked the operator to have Mr. Estrada call him as soon as possible. Then he called Ben on his cell phone. "What's the deal with getting a chopper?"

"I've got one lined out. They're pre-flighting it now and will fly it here in about an hour."

"Where's here?"

"Oh, I'm at the airport in Tijuana in the building where we were before."

"Have you talked to anyone?"

"No," Ben replied, "I'm sure they are keeping tabs on me but for now they're being cool."

Ed bit his lip, thought a moment and said, "What do ya think? Should we tell them what's going on but ask them to stay put or...?"

"Listen, for all I know, one of the bad guys might have me in his sights right now. So I'm going to stay out in the open until the chopper gets here. Don't worry, the cops will be tracking the chopper from the second I lift off. The bandits probably know that and have figured out how to handle it."

"Yeah, you're right. All we can do is stick to their instructions and deliver the goods as they want it. Nothing else we can do."

"Okay. I'll call you back when I'm on my way to the hotel."

Ed closed the call, found the number of the bank and called. Cipriano Gomez, the bank manager, said the money hadn't arrived but he thought it would be in his hands within the hour. Because of the urgency, Ed had told his personal banker to charter a plane and fly the cash to Ensenada. An armored truck would meet the plane and bring the money directly to the bank. Ed asked Gomez to have the money put up in four stout cardboard boxes and call when it was ready.

As soon as Ed put his phone in his pocket, he was bombarded with questions from everyone speaking at once. "Okay, okay, take it easy. Here are the details in a nutshell." Ed filled them in on his various conversations, ending with, "Ben has a small helicopter rented and they are flying it to him now. He's pretty sure the cops are keeping an eye on him but they are leaving him alone. As soon as the bank has the money, they'll bring it here and we fly it to the park, put it under the chapel and hopefully get back on the chopper and fly back here. That's it. Then we wait for them to take the kids up to the observatory."

"Who knows how long that will be? And the cops may get impatient and try to do something without consulting us, which could put the kids in jeopardy," Sandy said, again trying to hold back tears.

Ed sat beside her and held her tightly. "It's going to be alright. We'll do everything they told us to do exactly the way they want it. That's all we can do for now. So, hang in there, Pilcher, we've got work to do and we don't want to screw it up, right?"

Ed's cell phone rang. He quickly pulled it from his pocket. "Hello, this is Edward Noble."

"Good day, sir. Cipriano Gomez with Scotiabank Inverlat. The one-million U.S. dollars has arrived. I have had it put in four boxes, as you directed. Each box has two-hundred and fifty thousand dollars in one-hundred dollar bills stacked in two rows. So you know, I will tell you that each box is six inches by six inches by 12 inches high and weighs approximately six pounds. We have an armored carrier ready to deliver the boxes to you. I assume you want them delivered to your hotel, yes?"

"Ah, let me think about it. I'll call you right back." To the others, Ed said, "It's the bank. They have the money ready to go. They'll send it over in an armored truck. Trouble is, I'm a little worried about that being too obvious and kind of makes us a target."

Sherry had an idea. "Okay, what about this? Have the bank make up four other boxes like the ones with the money and send them over here in the armored truck. Have the guards bring the boxes up to this room. You sign for them and—"

Carl jumped in. "What the hell are you talking about?"

Sherry snapped, "Will you let me finish, please?" She turned back to Ed. "Now, tell the bank guy you want him to give the money to someone he trusts with his life—"

"Okay, I know exactly where you're going with this. Correct me if I'm wrong." Ed redialed and got the bank manager on the line. "Sorry for the delay, señor. Is there a person in your office in whom you have complete trust? Preferably a woman?"

"I am sorry, sir. I do not understand. There are several women here in whom I have complete trust. What is it you wish me to do?"

Ed relayed Sherry's plan, then he added, "While the empty boxes are on their way over here, have the woman put the money in the trunk of her personal car, drive to the hotel and park in the car park behind the hotel. It's near the swimming pool. Have her lock her car, go to the hotel lounge, order a white wine and pretend she is waiting for someone to join her. For example, have her keep checking her watch or pretend she is talking to someone on her cell phone. You understand?"

"Yes sir. I have just the person who could play this role. Her name is Florentina Paz. She is a woman of great character. She has been employed here for many years. Her car is in our garage within the building and so we can make the preparations in private. When should she leave the bank?"

"I'll call you. Meanwhile, perhaps you should ask the lady if she is willing to do this job. You may tell her that if all goes well, and I see no reason why it wouldn't, she will receive a thousand dollar gift from me."

"Oh sir, that is not necessary...no, no."

"Yes, I think it is. I would want to do something for you as well. But for now, I'd like you to put this plan in motion. Send the armored truck as soon as you can. I'll call you when we are ready for the lady to drive over here. And thank you very much for your help in this."

Sandy put her arms around Ed's neck and kissed him. "That was so clever. What a great idea—"

Ed interjected, "Hey, give Sherry the credit. As soon as she started telling me her idea, I knew at once what she had in mind."

Sherry piped up, "You handled it just perfectly. That was exactly what I had in mind but the idea of using a woman in her own car...well, that was genius. Good for you."

Chapter 14

In a small house off the Boulevard Rosedo G. Castro in the city of Los Mochis in the Mexican state of Sinaloa, Flaco Guzman and Lalo Medina sat at the kitchen table drinking tequila. Lime skins were piled high in a bowl and acrid cigarette smoke hung like smog in the dingy room. Their conversation was in Spanish.

Flaco, hearing the front door open, jumped up and pulled the pistol from his waistband. "Chuy?" he called out.

Chuy Aguilar ambled into the kitchen carrying a case of beer. He looked at Flaco. "Put that gun away, you *tarado*. What's with you anyway?" Chuy started putting the beer in the refrigerator, the clanking bottles echoing in the nearly empty space. He looked over his shoulder. "Flaco, I said put the fucking gun away before you kill someone."

Flaco stuck the pistol back in his pants.

Lalo laughed. "Don't rag on him, Chuy. The poor bastard is already so jumpy—"

Flaco glared at Lalo. "Shut up, you skinny *chimba*."

Chuy brought four beers to the table and sat down. "Where's Gordo?" Gordo—Ramon Delgado— was the fourth member of Chuy's gang.

Flaco and Lalo looked at each other nervously.

"He's in the bedroom with the gringos," Flaco said. "We told him to leave them alone, but...well, you know Gordo."

Chuy bellowed at the closed door, "Hey, *pinche*, get your fat ass out here. We have business to do."

A dreadful scream emanated from the bedroom.

Chuy slammed his chair back and strode to the door. Flinging it open, he yelled, "God damn you, Gordo, I told you to leave the girl alone. Get off of her and take the tape off her mouth."

Gordo reluctantly disengaged himself from Beverly, untied her arms and ripped off the tape.

She screamed again as the tape tore at her skin and began to cry hysterically, her eyes wide in terror. "Please, please no more. My father will give you the money, I promise he will." She pulled the filthy sheet over her naked body and looked over at Kevin who lay unconscious on the floor.

Chuy said in textbook English, "I am sorry for this. It was not my intention to let harm come to you or your friend, but," he glanced toward the kitchen, "what am I to do when these morons get drunk. I must not offend them, you understand. I am boss, but these are dangerous men so I don't press them. It will be over soon for you and you will be home. Okay?"

Beverly didn't reply. She drew her knees up to her chin and began to shake uncontrollably.

In Spanish he berated Gordo and pushed him out of the room, locking the door behind him. The two other men laughed heartily when Gordo returned to the table.

Lalo punched Gordo on the arm. "So, fatso, you like that red haired cunt? Remember, if anything happens to her and we don't get the payoff, I'm going to cut off your balls, eh?"

"And I will help him," added Flaco.

Chuy pounded his fist on the table. "Enough bullshit. Let's get down to business. Hector called me and said that he's in the park with his family and has set up a tent in the Vallecitos about a half a kilometer from the road. He said he has a good view of the whole valley and if a helicopter lands he will be able to spot it."

Lalo said, "Ah, that's good. But I worry he might try to shortchange us on the money. He's on his own—if he decides to run for it, then what?"

"Don't be stupid," Gordo said, "We promised him fifty thousand American dollars. That's more money than he could make in all of his life. No, he'll bring us the money."

Chuy agreed. "Hector will do his job. He knows that he's a dead man, and his family, too, if he doesn't follow orders exactly as we told him. Anyway, just in case there are any PF or AFI cops checking cars at the gate, he knows what to do."

Gordo lit a cigarette, blew smoke out of his nose and said, "Listen, Chuy, you should call and tell them that if any cops are checking cars going out the park gate, the deal is off and we kill," he thrust his head toward the bedroom door, "the two of them."

Chuy looked at Flaco and Lalo. "What do you think? The cops could be hidden out on the road to the park and jump Hector."

Lalo said, "What? You think the cops are going to stop every tourist that comes out of the park? I don't think so."

Chuy scoffed, "You also didn't *think* before you messed up the helicopter and killed those two guys. So now, thanks to you, we have murder hanging over our heads."

Lalo jumped up. "You said to go over there and see what they were doing. If they didn't have that fucking helicopter, they never would have spotted us in the first place. So I did the right thing. We didn't need them flying around looking for us."

Flaco motioned for calm. "Sit down and take it easy. It's all past and done with, so forget it." He addressed Chuy. "I think you should talk to them today. Let them know that it's up to them to handle the cops. Make them understand that if we don't get the money without interference from anyone, they will never see their children again."

"I'll take the pickup to Topolobampo and call the father. I've got his cell phone number. When he answers, I'll talk in English, tell him not to talk, just listen. I want this to go fast so I can get the hell out of there and come back here." He looked at Gordo intently.

Gordo hissed, "What? You got something to say to me?"

"That's right. I've got something to say to all of you, but especially to you." He raised his voice, almost to a shout. "Leave the girl alone and the boy as well! If something happens to them and we cannot deliver them after the payoff, what do you think will happen the next time we snatch some gringo?"

In a quiet voice, Flaco muttered, "They won't trust us to return the hostage—"

"That's right," Chuy said. "and there won't be any payoff. So no more messing with the girl. Let her take a shower and give her some clean clothes from her suitcase and something to eat—the boy also."

Lalo added, "Chuy is right. Once we have all gone our separate ways, then Hector's wife will drive them to the observatory. It's a good plan and we don't want to screw it up." He leaned in to Chuy. "You have that fancy phone. Does it not send messages? Why don't you just send him the message from your phone instead of going all the way to Topolobampo?"

"Are you stupid?" Chuy replied. "The cops will trace the message to this phone and they'll be down here like a swarm of bees."

"I am not stupid," Lalo hissed. "Do not call me stupid again..." He half rose from his seat.

"Cool down, for God's sake. It's just an expression—I know you're not stupid, okay?" Chuy turned to Gordo. "Remember, stay away from the girl. You scared the shit out of her and probably hurt her, and we can't have any more of that. And what about the boy? What the hell did you do to him?"

"He gave me some lip and I hit him a couple of times. That's all."

Chuy pushed his chair back and stood. "Lalo," he said. "I'm putting you in charge of our guests. Come with me."

The two men went in the bedroom. Beverly was lying in a fetal position, her knees pulled up to her chest. She was whimpering quietly. Her eyes widened at the entrance of the men.

In a quiet voice, Chuy said, "Listen, chica. I am very sorry about what happened with Ramon...the fat one. It won't happen again. Eduardo here will take you to the bathroom. Have a shower and clean yourself. He will bring your suitcase so you can put on clean clothes, okay? When you have finished, the boy can also have a wash. We will bring you some food and something to drink. Would you like a Coca Cola or a beer? Whatever you want, okay?"

Beverly averted her eyes and simply shook her head.

In Spanish, Chuy said to Lalo, "Okay, take care of her. I've got to get going." He looked over at Kevin who was still lying exactly as he had been earlier. Chuy patted Beverly's shoulder. She flinched, and he stepped back. In English he said, "Okay, get out of the bed now and go with Eduardo and wash."

Clutching the sheet around her, she got off the bed. Eduardo took hold of her arm and helped her wobble to the bathroom.

Chuy knelt down by Kevin. "God damn it," he growled. Then he yelled, "Gordo, get in here."

Gordo popped his head in the doorway. "What's this?"

Chuy looked up from the boy. "This, you dumb ass, is a dead man. You fucking killed him."

Chapter 15

Carl and Sherry had gone to their room down the hall and Ed and Sandy were in their suite nibbling the remains of a room service lunch when the armored truck guards delivered arrived. Ed signed the Acknowledgement of Receipt and the guards departed. The delivery was accomplished without incident. Ed called the bank and was immediately put through to Señor Gomez.

"Señor Noble," Gomez said, "We are ready here. The four boxes are in the, ah, how say?"

"Trunk of the car?"

"Yes. I could not recall that word. So, the items are in the trunk of Señorita Florentina Paz. She is ready to leave at your command. Her English is good."

"Excellent." Ed thought a moment. "What make of car is she driving? What color is it? Oh, and what does the señorita look like?"

"She is driving an older model Fiat sedan. It is dark green. She is standing here in my office now. Let me observe: Florentina of medium height, she has short black hair, and she is wearing a blue skirt, a white shirt and a scarf of many colors around her neck. She has a small silver watch on her left wrist and—"

Ed interjected, "That's fine. Please put her on the phone for her instructions."

"Hello, señor. This is Florentina. I am ready for instructions."

"First of all, thank you very much for taking on this very important assignment."

"My pleasure, señor."

"Now, there has been a change of plan. You will not go in the hotel. Park in the lot by the pool but remain in your car. Keep the motor running and the door locked. An American man will come to your car and say, 'My name is Ben. I need a ride.' He is a tall man with brown hair. He will be wearing a black cap and a brown leather jacket."

Florentina repeated the line, albeit with a heavy Spanish accent. "'My name is Ben. I need a ride.' Do I have it correct?"

"Yes. 'My name is Ben, I need a ride.' He will say it just like that. If anyone else comes to your car, or if you are not sure, drive away very quickly and call me. If you are sure it is our man, unlock the passenger door. He will get in your car and direct you to drive to the place where he has parked his helicopter. You will give him the four boxes which he will put inside the plane. You should leave at once and return quickly to the bank. Is that clear?"

"Si, señor. I understand."

"Leave now but first, give me your cell phone number." They exchanged numbers and Ed told her again to call if anything unexpected happened. Gomez came back on the line.

Ed thanked the bank manager for his help and rang off. "Okay, Ben, time for you to go. She's on the way." Ed described the girl and the car she was driving. "As soon as she leaves, fire up the chopper and wait for Sandy and me. Don't forget. You must say it exactly as I told the girl: 'My name is Ben, I need a ride.' Got it? Oh, and be sure and give her this." Ed handed Ben a thick envelope.

Ben smiled as he slipped it into his jacket and put on the cap. "Don't worry, I've got it. See you at the egg beater."

"Should I take the pistol?" Sandy asked.

Ed thought for a moment and shook his head. "Ahhh, maybe not. It's liable to cause more trouble than we can handle. Ben has a hand gun and I'm sure he knows how to use it—"

"You're right," Sandy said. "I'm not going to take it."

"C'mon then," Ed said, "We'll skip the elevator and go down the stairs and wait in the hall by the back door."

Ben waited behind some bushes between the pool and the parking lot. Five minutes later, he saw the green Fiat pull in and park at the end closest to the pool. He looked around, and seeing no one, he moved quickly to the car, tapped on the window and said, "My name is Ben, I need a ride."

Florentina reached over and unlocked the passenger door. Her hand was shaking.

Ben got in. "It's okay," he reassured her. "It will be over in a few minutes. Let's go." He directed her along an unpaved service road that ran parallel to the hotel just outside a high hedge screening the pool area. He had her pull up close to the helicopter. "Okay, this is good."

They both got out. Ben unlocked the cockpit door while Florentina opened the trunk. Then she handed him the boxes, one at a time, and he set them securely in the luggage space. "Okay. You handled this perfectly, and Mr. Noble wants you have this." He reached into his jacket pocket and gave her the envelope.

"Oh no, señor, is not necessary. I require nothing more." She tried to hand the envelope back to him but he pushed her hand aside.

"There is not time for discussion. Now, get in your car and drive directly back to the bank. Do you understand? *¿Comprende, usted?*"

"*Si, señor. Comprendo.*" She got in the car and drove off.

Ben turned back to the plane and climbed in. As soon as he fired up the engine, he saw Ed and Sandy exit the hotel and run toward him. When they were in and buckled up, Ben took off.

"Okay, boys and girls," he shouted into his mic, "here we go. We'll take a south by southeast heading, sort of following Route 1 which will be on your right. When we cross a river they call Arroyo Colonet, we'll turn east and fly over the park. The mountains are pretty high so I'll stay up until we get close to the observatory, which should stand out like a sore thumb. Then we'll circle around and lose some altitude until we spot that open Vallecito area which is just east of the observatory. We'll look for the road that goes from the park entrance to the observatory and put her down close to that so you won't have to walk very far—but I have no idea how far it will be to the shrine."

"Maybe we'll be able to spot it from the air," Sandy said.

Ben replied, "We'll just have to wait and see, but the Google maps and other info I got from the internet show it in the trees and not too far from the entrance. Here's the thing, I don't think it'd be a good idea to spend too much time goofing around before we land. Don't want to attract a lot of attention or make us a target."

"Oh, my God," Sandy groaned. "You don't think they'd try to shoot us down, do you?"

Ed reached back to pat her knee. "I don't think they'd even consider doing that after they have made all these preparations. Besides, if they shot us down they might never get the money. Ben's right. Best to play it safe. So let's just stick to the plan. Get in and get out as quick as we can."

They were in the air about an hour when they spotted the river. Ben made the necessary course adjustment for the observatory and checked the instrument panel chronometer. "It's almost three o'clock. I don't want to be flying in these mountains in the dark. As soon as we land, you each put two boxes in your pack. We'll double-check the walkie-talkies before you leave. Now keep your eyes open. Use the binocs and try to spot that round white building."

Near the road leading to the observatory and just inside the line of trees surrounding the open area known as the Vallecito Meadow, Hector was waiting. As instructed, his wife and two children were staying inside their tent which Hector had pitched about a quarter mile to the south of where he was waiting. His cell phone rang.

It was Chuy. "The boy is dead," he said. "Never mind how. We have a change in plans."

Hector gripped the phone more tightly. Dead. What did this mean for him?

"I have not been able to reach the girl's father," Chuy said. "When he comes in the helicopter, you will run to it with your hands up."

"My hands up?" Hector swallowed hard. There was not supposed to be any contact with the Americans.

"*Si.* Exactly. Hands up, high. You tell them in English to give you the money. They should not take it to the *capilla.* You can do that, no?

"Si, si."

Then, you will call me and give your phone to the *gringo.* I also will tell him to give you the money."

"*Muy bien.*" Hector's palms were beginning to perspire.

"I will have the girl talk to her father. She will tell him that he is to give the money to you. Do you understand what I am telling you?"

"*Si, comprendo.*"

"And later, find a good place to bury the boxes so they will be safe until you leave the park. Now, are you sure you know what you are to do?

"*Si,* Chuy."

"Good boy, Hector. Make sure you don't fuck it up." The connection went dead.

Hector heard a faint whooshing sound that quickly became louder. He looked up at the observatory dome and watched as a helicopter came in low and just to the north of the building. He stepped back into the trees, not wanting to alert those in the plane that someone was watching. The aircraft flew low over the meadow, then, gaining altitude, it flew east above the road that led to the entrance to the park. This puzzled Hector who had pulled out his phone and was about to call Chuy when the sound of the chopper became louder and soon after, it reappeared. It hovered just north of the road on the east side of the meadow then landed. Both doors opened and three people got out.

Hector held his arms up and trotted toward the plane. "*Hola, hola, amigos,*" he shouted. "I have some news for you."

When he was within fifty feet of the helicopter, Ben reached inside his jacket and pulled out an automatic pistol. "Okay. Hold it right there and keep your hands up...way up, *comprende?*"

Hector stood still, hands in the air. "I talk some English, okay? The girl is very fine, no problem. You to give me money. I give to boss. The girl will be for you at... ah..." He pointed to the observatory building on the top of the hill. "No problem. I call boss now. Girl to talk to you, good?"

Sandy had not taken her eyes off of the man. She couldn't believe what he was saying. She took hold of Ed's arm. "What the hell is going on? We give this guy the money? And Bev is going to talk to us?" She addressed Ben. "Is this guy for real? You think he's with the gang?"

Ben handed Ed the pistol. "Walk up a little closer. There. That's close enough. I'm going to frisk this guy. If he tries anything... anything, don't hesitate. Shoot him!"

Hector started to lower his arms. Ben yelled, "Hands up, *sabe?* Turn around." Ben made a circular motion with his hand. Hector turned around and Ben gave him a proper frisking. "He's clean," Ben said, taking the pistol from Ed. "Now," he said to Hector, "What's all this about talking to the girl?"

"I call on phone now, you talk, good?" Hector pulled a cell phone from his pocket, punched in a number and immediately someone answered. In Spanish he said a few words then handed the phone to Ben who handed it over to Ed.

"This Edward Noble. Who am I talking to?"

Ed almost dropped to his knees when he heard his daughter's voice.

"Daddy? They want you to give the money to the man there. His name is Hector. I am to tell you that I'm okay." She paused a moment. A voice in the background said something Ed couldn't make out. In a voice choked with emotion, she added, "And so is Kevin. Oh, Daddy, please hurry. I can't stand this much more. They—"

Ed almost shouted, "Bev, Bev! What's going on? Are they hurting you?"

A man answered. "She is not hurt. She is fine and will remain so and we will deliver her as we promised as soon as the money is in our hands and we have gone far away. So, señor, give Hector the four boxes which must hold one million U. S. dollars and once we are gone, someone will deliver your daughter. Do not talk to the police about Hector or what you are doing. Tell only that you put the money under the chapel and returned to Ensenada. And tell them they must not do anything that would interfere with our receiving the money. You understand? Remember if we do not get the money, your daughter is killed. Now, give Hector the boxes and get in your plane and go. *Adios.*"

Ed handed the phone to Hector.

Sandy grabbed Ed's sleeve. "What did Bev say? Is she alright?"

Ed put his arm around her. "She's okay. She just wants this to be over with." He looked at Ben and in a quiet voice said, "Okay, give him the money."

Ben unlocked the luggage door, pulled out the boxes and put them on the ground. "There you are," he said.

"*Gracias.*" Hector scooped up the four boxes and trotted off toward the trees.

"Now what?" Sandy asked Ed.

"We get in the chopper and get the hell out of here. Let's go."

When they were buckled up and helmets and headphones were on, Ben started the engine, let it run for a few minutes then reached for the collective and cyclic and took off, heading northwest toward Ensenada. Into his mic, he said, "Well, that was one crazy adventure. What the hell are those guys thinking about anyway? They give you a detailed plan and now this?"

Ed said, "I get it. They gave us all that crap about putting the money under the chapel. Then, before the police could adjust to a new scenario, they pull the Hector thing. Maybe they're not so dumb after all."

Sandy spoke. "I'm just worried about Bev. Once they have the money and get away, what's their incentive to return her?"

Ed sighed. "Look, honey, we'll just have to hope they got at least a shred of honor—"

Ben inadvertently let out a guffaw which he quickly stifled. "Sorry." He looked back at Sandy who appeared to be on the verge of tears. "No, I didn't mean to imply you couldn't trust them. No. I think the other lady was right when she said that they needed to return the hostages if they were ever to pull a trick like this again."

Ed joined in with, "That's right, honey. They have no reason not to return her, especially since they plan to leave her with someone else while they make their getaway. She wouldn't have any idea where they were going."

Sandy remained silent all the way back to the hotel.

Hector retrieved the shovel he had hidden, dug a hole and put the four boxes in it. It was the only way he could be sure the boxes would be safe. Besides, Chuy said to bury them. After carefully covering up the boxes and scattering bits of twigs and stones over it he walked west, more or less parallel to the observatory road. He counted the paces from the burial spot to the meadow, took out his pocket knife and marked a tree—it would tell him where to begin counting his paces when he returned to dig up the boxes. Then he returned to his wife and children at the tent.

"It went well," he told them. "We will stay here for maybe two more days then pack up and leave. When we get home, I will put the product away in a safe place and when the boss comes to pick it up–"

Hector glanced at the children who had been listening to this conversation and told them, "You two go on out and gather some wood so we can cook our evening meal." The children ran outside. Hector said to his wife, "So when they pick up the money, they are to open a box and give me fifty thousand American dollars—can you believe it, Magda?" The pitch of his voice heightened with excitement. "We are going to be rich. Fifty thousand dollars!" He paused a moment, his brow wrinkling. "How much is that?"

Magda pulled a pen and a scrap of paper from her purse. She jotted down some figures, did the multiplication and gasped. "*Madre de Dios*, it is about 640,000 pesos. My God, it is a fortune!" She stood, grabbed Hector and the two of them danced around and around, finally collapsing in a couple of camp chairs.

"This calls for a drink, no?"

Magda jumped up, reached into a camp cooler and pulled out a bottle of tequila. She filled two plastic cups, handed one to Hector and through a laugh squealed, "*Salud!*"

Hector raised his cup, kissed her hard and cried, "*Salud!*" His phone rang.

"Did it go well?" Chuy asked.

"Yes, very well. They gave me the boxes and then they flew away. No problem."

"Do not tell me what you did with them, but you did as we planned, no?"

"Yes, yes. When shall we go?"

"I think tomorrow after it is dark. Handle the cargo as we discussed. Be sure you don't leave anything behind. Nothing. Check your cook fire. It must be completely out. Cover it with dirt to be sure. Call me before you are ready to go. *Adios.*"

Hector pocketed the cell phone and gave Magda a fierce hug. "We are rich, my girl, rich! Soon we will move away from the stinking city and enjoy life like the Americans."

Chapter 16

Immediately upon entering their room, Sandy dropped down on the couch, stretched out her legs, and lay back against the cushion, her arms crossed over her chest. "I'm whipped." She sighed deeply. "I've got a bad feeling, Ed. Really. I don't think we're going to see that happy ending we've been wishing for."

Ed sat down beside her and kissed her softly on the cheek. "Come on. Don't talk like that. We have every reason to believe they'll let her go once they have the money and are on their way, probably out of Mexico."

Sandy unfolded her arms and sat up. She looked deeply into his eyes. "Every reason? And what reason would that be?"

Ed looked at her curiously. "What? What do you mean?

"You said we had every reason to believe she would be returned. I'm asking you, what reason are you talking about? We don't know a damn thing about these people." Her tone sharpened. "No, I'm wrong. Of course we know about them, don't we? We know they shot at us from that house in the hills. We know they took—" she inhaled deeply. "They took Beverly and Kevin. And we are pretty certain that when they say they'll kill them if they don't get away with the money, they will do just that. These are some evil men, so how can you say we have every reason to believe them? Hell, what about today and the switch with that Hector guy? They change their minds every day. I'm sorry, but I don't trust them for a minute and our daughter is with them right now. Our daughter, Ed. With evil men who would love to rape her." Sandy ran her hands through her hair and wailed, "Maybe they already have. Good Lord." She covered her face with her hands and wept.

Ed sat in stunned silence. Despite his attempts to reassure her—and himself—Sandy had it right. Trust those guys? That was like putting your trust in... He let the thought go. "I've got to call Carl and Sherry and tell them what happened and I need to call Captain Ruiz and tell him to keep hands off until we get the kids back." He pulled a handkerchief from his back pocket and gave it to her. "Come on, honey, you need to pull yourself together."

Sandy blotted the tears and blew her nose. "I know, I know. I'll be alright. Go ahead and make your calls. Just meeting that guy Hector made me feel dirty." She shuddered, but kept herself from more crying. "I'm going to take a hot shower." She arose and went into the bedroom.

Ed called the Kendalls and told them what happened. Carl was incredulous. He couldn't believe the kidnappers had changed everything at the last minute.

"So what happens now?" he wanted to know.

"We'll have to just sit tight until we hear something from them. I don't know what else we can do. It might be days. That guy of theirs has to make it out of the park and take the money to them. But we have no idea where they are hiding. Plus, Hector may stay in the park for a while figuring if he leaves too soon someone will suspect something or, geeze, I don't know. I'm sure they have a plan for getting the money out of the park but—"

"Yeah, I'm sure they do," Carl said. "We'll just have to tough it out. Say, you said you talked to Beverly. What about Kevin? Did they put him on the phone?"

"No, I'm sorry. It was just Beverly on the phone, and only for a few seconds before a man started talking. That reminds me. I'd better talk to Ruiz and tell him what that guy said about not trying anything. I'll call you back."

Ed called the captain at Federal Police headquarters and told him exactly what Chuy had told him to say. Ed said nothing about giving Hector the money. He told Ruiz that he and Sandy put the money under the chapel as they had been instructed. He reminded Ruiz not to interfere in any way that would jeopardize the lives of the captives. Ed said, "Once we have those kids safely back home in the USA, then you can do whatever the hell you want. But for now, I don't care about the money or catching those guys. All I want are those two children alive and unharmed. So tell me, Captain, are you with me on this?"

"Absolutely, Señor Noble. The PF and the AFI have been alerted. There may be surveillance, you understand, but it will be very discreet with no moves against these men until your daughter and the young man are safely away. You have my word on it."

"Thank you, Captain. You can be sure there will be a very generous donation given to...let's say, the charity of your choosing once this is over."

"Thank you, Señor Noble. Of course that is not necessary, but will be much appreciated by the widows and children of police killed in the line of duty."

Later that afternoon, Hector decided to move his family and pitch their tent in one of the park's improved campgrounds. He thought they would be less exposed. Besides, he wasn't sure if camping out in the Vallecitos meadow was legal. No sense taking chances, he explained to his wife. They packed up everything except the shovel, which he hid in the trees close by, and then they moved to a campsite just south of the road and near the park entrance. No other campers occupied the other sites nearby. Hector and his family pitched their tent, the kids gathered wood, and Magda began preparing the evening meal. As the sun set, a cold wind blew through their camp, the temperature dropping rapidly. They ate quickly, the children bundled in warm coats. Then they put out the campfire, retired to the tent and crawled into their sleeping bags. Magda and Hector shared a double sleeping bag.

She snuggled up to him and whispered, "We are going to be very rich, no?"

"Yes. Very soon. We will buy a little farm in the country. Would you like that?"

"Yes, yes. Perfect. The children will love it and they can run and play with no worries...we could have some chickens, no?"

"Of course, my pet." Hector turned to her and pressed his body against hers. He began to caress her breast.

She caught his hand and laughed softly. "Wait, *querido*. Wait until the children are asleep."

Hector awoke at dawn. He eased out of the sleeping bag, quickly dressed and quietly left the tent. He had put hot coffee in a Thermos the night before. He took that and some tortillas and put them in his car. After unhitching the flatbed trailer, he drove toward the meadow. As soon as he exited the trees, he turned left and slowly drove along the tree line to the place where he had left the shovel. He picked up the shovel and walked back to the marked tree, turned and walked east twenty-three paces.

Hector looked at the site for a full minute, trying to visualize how the place had looked the day before. He had been careful not to leave any sign that the ground had been disturbed but now he wished he had made some sort of a mark. He remembered that there was a large pine tree just to the left of the spot and so he started digging there. But the ground felt solid as he punched the shovel deeper. This was not the right place. He decided to keep poking around until he found a soft patch of recently disturbed earth and dig there. He poked his shovel into the ground for a half hour and wasn't able to locate the burial place.

Hector was sweating profusely despite the chill morning air. As panic slowly began to grip him, he thought, *What the hell?* He walked out of the trees, found the marked tree and carefully counted twenty-three steps which took him back to within a few feet of where he had been before. He picked up the shovel and walked an ever widening circle, punching the ground with the shovel—searching for a soft spot.

Dear God, how can this be? If I don't leave here with the money, Chuy and the rest of them will kill me. He fell to his knees and placed his hands over his face. *I've got to go back and get Magda and the children to help me search. It has to be here...somewhere. Those boxes didn't jump out of their grave and fly away. They must be here...but where?* He heard the crack of a branch breaking and looked over his shoulder. A cougar stood silently with one front foot held up as if poised to spring. Hector couldn't restrain the scream that was building in his throat and when it emanated from his mouth, the cougar jumped back then turned and ran off. At once a chorus of animal and bird voices echoed through the forest. A condor flew out of the trees and across the meadow while smaller birds seemed to be flying in every direction.

With his hands covering his head, Hector ran out of the trees to his car and got in. He was breathing hard. He could feel sweat rolling down his back. Calming down after a few minutes, he poured some coffee from the Thermos, pinched a cigarette from the pack and lit it. Inhaling deeply, he let the smoke slowly exit his mouth and nose. He took another drag on the cigarette followed by a gulp of tepid coffee.

"I've got to think this through," he said aloud. "I must be making a mistake. Maybe the tree with the mark is not the tree I marked. He was about to get out of the car when a beautiful mule deer doe tip-toed out of the trees and scanned the meadow. She took a few steps, put her head down to eat then abruptly raised it and looked toward the road. A minute later, a car appeared and the deer ran off. Hector followed the car with his eyes as it crossed the meadow and headed up the road to the observatory.

He started his car and drove back to the campsite. When he arrived, he told Magda what had taken place. They rounded up their children, and drove back to the meadow. They were, Magda vowed, not going to leave until those four magic boxes were safely in their hands.

Wednesday morning, Captain Ruiz had just concluded a meeting with Agent Hierra and Carlos Estrada, the manager of the Posada Inn. He had asked Estrada to bring the employment file of the waiter, Luis Aguilar.

Previously, all of the hotel's employees had been questioned in an effort to gain as much information as possible about Luis. One bit of information resulted in a follow up and subsequent surveillance of the home of Luis' parents, Jorge and Adona Aguilar, in the city of Los Mochis, Sinaloa. Another AFI agent was assigned to tail Luis, noting where he went and who he talked to. When Luis left work late each evening to go to his boarding house in a poor section of Ensenada, another agent kept tabs on him. The AFI even had a man on board the ferry that Luis boarded to travel to his parents' home on the two days he had off from work each week. As Hierra told Ruiz, "We have that boy well covered."

The agent in Los Mochis, Esteban Romero, whose nickname was Bonito, had bugged the Aguilar home and was now set up in an empty storefront at Plaza Valertina, a small strip mall on the corner of Boulevard Rosedo G. Castro and Fortuna Street. He rented space using a fictitious name and paid a month's rent in cash. He set up the equipment then wandered the streets and parks of Los Mochis—his ears open and his mouth shut.

At 10:15 on Tuesday morning, Romero received a call from Agent Torres, stationed at La Paz, who told him that Luis had boarded the boat. Torres said that he would maintain surveillance as Luis might have a contact on the boat. The two agreed to meet at Romero's rented store after Luis arrived at his parent's home.

Six hours later, the ferry docked at Topolobampo. Luis hurried down the gangway and trotted over to a black Ford pickup. The driver pushed open the passenger side door, Luis got in, and the truck pulled away from the dock and sped off to the northeast.

Agent Torres pulled out his phone and called.

On the second ring an abrupt voice answered, "Romero."

"It's Torres. Our man got in a 2002 Ford F-150, crew cab, black, Sinaloa plate, VFS-67-40. I'm still waiting to unload my car."

"Very well. I'll head down the highway and try to pick them up and if I do see them, I'll tail them. You drive over to the store in Plaza Valertina I told you about. You have the combination to the padlock. Go to the back room and check the bugs. See if there is anything interesting on the tape. I'll let you know if I see them."

The black pickup sped up the highway toward Los Mochis.

"So, Luis," Chuy said, "what's going on at the hotel? Have the Federales been poking their noses around some more?"

"They questioned me yesterday for an hour but I just keep telling them the same story over and over again."

"Which was...?"

"That the red haired lady and her friend wanted to know where to go in their Jeep and I told them about going to the Hacienda for lunch then Palm Valley then north to the border at Tecate. The agents made me repeat it again and again but I kept the exact same story every time. They asked where I lived and I gave the address of my boarding house." Luis looked out at the passing scenery for a moment then added, "I think they might have searched my place when I was at work—I'm not positive but I'm pretty sure."

"Was there anything at your place that could connect you with us or with Los Mochis?"

"No, nothing. I told you that I am always careful about that. If I write something down from you, I always tear it up and throw it away before I go home. You don't have to worry about me being careless."

Chuy smiled and tapped the wheel with the palm of his left hand. "That is why you are still alive, no?"

"But listen, Chuy, you promised me ten thousand American dollars and I want to know, am I going to get it today?"

With a note of agitation, Chuy replied, "No, you're not going to get paid today. We haven't got the money yet. I mean, the gringo paid the money—it is in our possession so to speak but it is not here. We haven't seen it yet. If all goes as we planned, the money should be here tomorrow evening, on the last ferry." He gave Luis an intense look. "That's if all goes right which, as you know, things don't always go as planned. But don't worry, I am telling you that when we get our hands on the money, you will be paid at once. Okay?"

When they arrived in the neighborhood where Luis' parents lived, Chuy said, "I will slow down and you jump out."

"My home is a kilometer from here," Luis complained.

"It's less than that. You can walk it. I'm not so stupid that I would pull up in front of your house. The cops probably know where you come on your days off and are watching. They're not stupid." Chuy slowed and looked in his rear view mirror then checked the road ahead. No cars, no pedestrians. "Okay, get out."

Agent Torres drove by the Plaza Valertina and parked his car on a side road a block away. He walked back to the store, entered a number in the padlock and went inside. For more than ten minutes he watched from behind a Venetian blind to see if anyone showed interest in the store front. When he was satisfied, he walked into an adjoining room where Agent Romero had set up his listening and recording devices. Torres listened for several minutes to the live sounds originating from the many mics Romero had planted throughout the house. He could hear the Aguilars talking in the background over the sounds of what Torres assumed was a TV program. He called Romero and asked if he had spotted the pickup.

"I picked them up just about a mile from town but lost them in traffic. You at the store?"

"Yes. I checked the bugs, nothing there. I did get a picture of the guy that picked Luis up at the dock. It's kind of fuzzy but maybe the lab can make something of it. I sent it to them for an ID."

"Okay, I'll see you later."

Torres turned up the speaker volume, lit a cigarette and relaxed in a chair.

"Hello, I'm home," Luis' voice came from the speaker. Torres sat up and checked the recording device to make sure it was working. He heard Luis' parents greet their son and engage him in conversation. Later, he imagined they were at the table eating dinner and still talking but saying nothing of importance, at least not to Torres. He heard a noise and got up to check it out. It was Romero.

"Hey, Bonito, what's up?"

"We are," Romero replied through a smile. They shook hands. "And how are you doing, my friend. Long time no see."

"I was undercover on a job for almost four months. Not much fun, I can tell you."

Romero gave a knowing nod. "Yeah, I know. Looks like you lost a lot of weight since I last saw you."

Torres laughed. "I guess so." All at once he became serious. "Our boy is having dinner with his parents. I've been listening but nothing but family talk. It's being recorded."

The two men walked into the other room and stared at the speaker broadcasting the conversation going on in the Aguilar home. They heard the father say, "They questioned you some more but you told them nothing, is that so?" A voice they presumed was Luis' said, "I just told you..." Then they heard Luis' father say, "Why don't you just go over there and see what is going on for yourself? See if that girl and boy are still alive—you know, in case those miserable whores try to pull a fast one on you, you'll have something to tell the parents and maybe even the Federales. Chuy said he'd pay you ten thousand, but you said the gringo is a big time millionaire. Don't you think he would be happy to pay much more if you made it possible for him to get his daughter back, eh?" There was a pause then the father said, "What do you think, Adona?"

"Chuy and that bunch are crazy people," the mother added. "I think your father is right, Luis. You would be much safer working with the police and the parents and since they were willing to pay Chuy a lot of money, they would do the same for you if you make it possible for the police to arrest the gang and rescue the boy and girl."

There was a long pause. The two agents looked at each other. "Jesus, this could be a break if we could turn that kid and…"

Luis voice came over the speaker. "I've been thinking about doing that but I was afraid for you. If the police botch it, Chuy would come after you and me without a doubt."

The father said, "You need to talk to that PF agent who questioned you. You can be sure he will be very interested in what you have to say, no?"

The conversation continued for some time, Romero and Torres listening eagerly.

"Do the right thing, Luis!" Romero yelled at the speaker. "Just do it, you son of a bitch."

When, in the end, the family agreed that they would take the early ferry to La Paz the next morning and contact the police, the agents were so excited they could hardly contain themselves. Romero called AFI headquarters and asked for Hierra.

At Hierra's greeting, Romero blurted out, "You're not going to believe this but…" and he gave the details of the overheard and recorded conversation.

Hierra said, "Damn, that's great. Good work, Esteban. Very well then, I'll fly down in the morning with a few men. You and Torres get on that ferry but don't reveal yourselves. When he and his parents get off the boat, we'll nab them, take them to the airport where we'll get the address of the house where the children are. Then we will fly them up to the office. Meanwhile, I want you to case the house and then come up with a plan for getting those hostages out. If it means killing the felons, I'm okay with that but—"

Romero broke in. "I know. Make sure the boy and girl are not hurt or killed. But it's going to be tricky."

"I know, but you've pulled off some pretty good tricks in the past. Let's hope you have one more up your sleeve."

Romero put the phone back in his pocket and stood silently gazing out the window.

Torres gave him a moment, then said, "So, Bonito. What did the chief have to say?"

"Basically, he said make sure the hostages don't get hurt. But I am afraid we know that if the gang believes that we're closing in and they're going to have to shoot it out, the first bullets will go into the heads of the girl and her boyfriend."

Chapter 17

Less than a mile away, Chuy and "the boys" were once again having the same conversation they had been having all day—why hadn't Hector answered his phone?

Chuy and Lalo tried to calm the other two down suggesting that Hectors' phone wasn't working. Lalo reminded them that Hector had to drive to La Paz, get his car onto the boat and wait for it to leave. "It takes the ferry six hours to cross. When he gets here, he'll go to his uncle's house, stash the money like we told him and then go home. In the morning, he'll get the money and hook up with Chuy and that's that."

Chuy added, "In case you forgot, the reason for this screwing around is to make it hard for the cops to know what's going on. But I tell you again, Hector is not the kind of guy who will try to screw us. He knows we would kill him and his family if he tried. So quit bugging me about it. We know where the money is and I know Hector will get it to us."

"What about this Luis boy?" Gordo asked. "You and he are cousins, no? His last name, is the same as yours."

"*Si.* His father, Jorge, is my father's brother. He's a good man. No way is he or Luis going to do anything other than what we tell them to do. In case you have forgotten, it was Luis who set us up with those college kids we nabbed before. That wasn't a million-dollar deal like this one but one hundred thousand kept us in tequila and women for a couple of years." He looked around the table and saw that tempers were cooling down. With a broad smile, he leaned back in his chair and added, "So let's just cool it and not do anything stupid. When we get the money and have gone our separate ways, we can each start a new life, no?"

Gordo raised his glass to salute Chuy. "And that doesn't mean working for a living." He let out a large guffaw and gulped the tequila.

On Thursday at 5 AM, Luis and his parents boarded the ferry. Six hours later they disembarked at La Paz. As they drove off the boat, a uniformed policeman blew his whistle and motioned for them to pull out of the line of cars and stop. The policeman came to the driver's side door and, through the open window, asked, "Señor Aguilar?"

Jorge nodded.

The policeman pointed and said, "Drive over there and park."

Adona sputtered, "What is all this? We have done nothing wrong."

Luis touched his mother's shoulder. "It's okay, Mama. They do these random checks for drugs all the time. Don't worry."

Jorge parked as directed by the policeman, who then told them to follow him into the police station. Once inside, they were escorted into a small, windowless room and told to take seats at a large table. Immediately, three men, dressed in suits and ties, entered and took seats opposite the family.

The eldest of the three spoke. "I am Special Agent Andres Hierra of the AFI. These men are also AFI agents." Hierra smiled disarmingly at the Aguilars as he clasped his hands together and laid them on the table. "First of all, I want to assure you that none of you are in any kind of trouble—with the law, that is. We simply are here to help you with what we believe is a problem you may be having." He paused and let that statement sink in.

Luis and his parents looked at each other. Luis shook his head slightly, as if in non-comprehension.

Hierra continued. "Let me explain why we think you came to La Paz. It is your desire to have the police help you get out of a dangerous situation and give you protection from some very bad men who intend to harm you if they find out you have spoken to us." He looked at each of them in turn. Focusing then on Luis, he said, "You and I have spoken before and you have also spoken to the American whose daughter and her friend were abducted last Sunday. You know the American is a very rich man. You probably also know that these villains have demanded a million U.S. dollars for their safe return. Am I correct so far?"

In a small voice Luis replied, "Yes, sir."

Hierra continued to engage the waiter. "Very well then. We know you were the set-up guy for this little caper. You were the one who told the girl and her friend where to," Hierra made quotation marks with his fingers, "'find some good places to go' with their Jeep. Yes?"

"Yes, sir," Luis replied. "Chuy promised to pay me ten thousand American dollars if I would suggest where they should go." He hurriedly added, "But I swear, I haven't received a single peso from him."

"And why is that?"

Luis answered, "Because Chuy said they haven't got the money yet."

"That's interesting because Señor Noble himself took a million dollars by helicopter to the Parque Nacional, and hid it in the place where your man Chuy told him."

"I know that, sir. But the man Chuy has waiting there hasn't brought it out yet. Chuy told me that."

One of the agents whispered to Hierra and Hierra said, "Very well. We are going to take all of you to our headquarters in Tijuana and we'll put you up in a safe place until the girl and boy have been released and we have dealt with Chuy and his friends. However, what I need to know now is, where are they holding the Noble girl and her boyfriend and where will we find Chuy and his pals?"

Luis looked at his father who said, "It is done now. We have no choice. If the police don't capture that bunch, you know what is in store for us." He ran a finger across his throat.

Luis nodded. "I know, Papa, but I don't know where they are. They are somewhere in the city, I'm pretty sure of that, but I've never been there and Chuy has never told me. I do know that it's not the house he usually lives in because I've been there and the only people there were his sister and her husband."

"Very well then," Hierra said, "give me that address." One of the agents wrote it down. "Okay, time to go." Hierra led the way out to two unmarked SUVs.

En route, Hierra called Romero and gave him the information Luis had disclosed. "I don't think it would be wise to lean on Chuys sister or her husband as they would tip off Chuy and the children would suffer. For sure, they would move to another location."

"You're right, Chief. We'll just have to see what develops. If the guy you say picked up the money in the park brings it to Los Mochis tonight, he'd have to take the ferry. Why don't you put some men on that? See who gets off the ferry and where they go. Also, what about the picture Torres took of the guy in the black Ford pickup? Can you push the lab to enhance it and get a copy to us?"

"Okay. Will do. I'll call you when we get to Tijuana."

Hector, his wife and two children spent Thursday morning poking the ground with sharp-pointed sticks looking without success for the money boxes. They drove back to their campsite for lunch, Hector and Magda picking at their food. The two children had grown tired and frustrated with this odd game and were cranky and whining. The boy accused Hector of making up the whole story about buried treasure. After lunch, Magda sent the kids into the tent to lie down. In minutes, both were asleep.

"I suppose I better call Chuy and tell him I can't find the boxes."

Magda snickered. "What are you saying? Sure, you call him. He will say, 'Don't worry Amigo, just keep looking, you'll find it.'" She snorted through her nose. "Or will he say, 'You idiot, you think I believe such a story? You are a dead man if you don't arrive with those boxes.'"

Hector slumped, put his head in his hands and cried, "You are right, that's exactly how it will go down." He jumped up. "Come on. Wake up the children and let us try again."

He collected his thoughts, then punched in the redial and heard the phone ring. Chuy answered on the second ring.

"Where the hell have you been? We've been waiting for you to call for hours. You were supposed to have checked in with us this morning. We are getting nervous, and you don't want that, do you?"

Hector fumbled his prepared reply. "We were out in the woods, playing with the children. Ah, my phone must have fallen out of my pocket and we had to go back and find it. I'm sorry, Chuy. It was an accident, you understand, I—"

"Just shut the fuck up!" Chuy barked. "You are coming out tonight with the boxes in time to get on the eight o'clock ferry."

"Yes, the eight o'clock ferry."

"New plan. I will be waiting for you in the pickup. You know that one, the black Ford?"

"Yes."

"When you get your car off the boat, follow me. When I stop, pull up in front of me. We'll transfer the boxes there. Understand?"

"Yes, I understand."

"When you are ready to leave the park, call me and just say, 'leaving now,' and hang up. Got it?"

Hector was sweating. He started shaking. He took a deep breath and replied, "Got it." He was tempted to say more but Chuy ended the call. Hector put the phone in his pocket and dropped to his knees. "Dear Mother of God, what am I going to do? I've got to find that money."

"We are ready to go look some more," Magda told Hector, her hands on the shoulders of her unhappy children. They all got in the car and drove back to the meadow.

Hector said, "We need to change the place where we've been searching. It can't be the right place or we would have found it by now. I'm going to go back to where the helicopter landed and start from there."

When they reached the meadow, Hector turned south and stopped. "Wait in the car while I check something. I'll be right back." He crossed the road and walked the short distance to the place where the helicopter had landed. He could still see the faint remains of the marks the skids had made in the tall grass. He turned back and trotted south as he done when he left the plane with the four boxes. He stopped and concentrated on what he had done that day. He played the scene in his mind. *What did I do? I took out my knife and sliced a patch of bark off of the old pine at the edge of the grass.*

Hector stood, eyes closed. He had the mental picture clearly in the forefront of his mind. *And what did I do next?* Suddenly he remembered that after he marked the tree, he turned and looked back at the gringos who were standing by the plane watching him.

"Hector, you idiot!" he shouted slapping his forehead with the palm of his hand. "Of course. They were watching me."

Hector turned and ran back to the car. "Magda, I know why we haven't been able to find it. I was looking in the wrong place. The gringos were watching me, so I ran further down and hid in the trees and waited for the helicopter to leave. Then I went back for the shovel and I marked another tree with the knife...I carved an X. Then I walked back into the trees and buried the boxes."

Magda jumped out of the car, opened the back door, and said to the children, "Are you ready to play a new game? Then come with me. We are looking for a large tree with an X carved into it." She made an X with two fingers. "You see. It looks like this. Now let's see who will be the first to find it."

Thursday morning found Torres at the police station trying to find out if they had a rap sheet on Chuy whose name, he now knew was, Jesus Aguilar. Fortunately, they had one. Torres studied Chuys record and then examined the accompanying mug shot. *Could that be the guy who was driving the black pickup? Probably not.* But just in case, Torres made a copy and stuck it in his pocket.

When he returned to the store in the Plaza Valertina, Romero filled him in on his conversation with Hierra. Torres showed Romero the rap sheet and photo and said, "So, what's the plan, Bonito?"

"Wait a minute," Romero said, "I just got your photo from the lab." He thumbed through his photos and stopped. "Here it is." He enlarged it and they both studied it closely next to the mug shot. "What do you think?" Romero asked.

Torres placed a forefinger over his mouth and mumbled, "I don't know. Maybe. Of course the mug shot was taken, let's see, okay it says it was taken in 2007 when he was hauled in for questioning about a young couple that had been snatched. Ha," he looked up, his eyes narrowing. "That's interesting. Another kidnapping?"

Romero nodded. "Maybe more than a coincidence, eh? There definitely is a similarity between to two photos, I can see that, but the fact that he was suspected of being involved in a snatch makes me want to talk to this guy. What did he give for an address?"

Torres scanned the rap sheet, located the address and read it. "Shit," Torres growled. "Officer's note says, 'Address checked, no such.'"

"Hmmm. Okay. We've got nothing better to go on except the pic you took and the address of his sister. What say we scope out where she lives? It's possible he may be holed up at a house somewhere in the general area."

They set the GPS and headed to the sister's house on Calle de Maizo. At the first cross street, Avenida Aquiles Serdan, they turned left and slowly cruised west past the sister's house.

Romero craned his neck to take a look behind them. "Let's park up the street and wait a while. See if anyone shows up." They turned around and drove back to Avenida Aquiles Serdan. There were many parked cars on both sides of the street but Romero found an opening about a hundred yards west of Chuy's sister's house. They pulled in, turned off the engine and hunkered down to wait.

At a house two blocks north and a mile west, Chuy and the others sat at the kitchen table downing tequila. They had not heard from Hector and all of them were in an argumentative mood. Fed up with his mates, Chuy got out of his chair and walked into the bedroom. Beverly was in bed feigning sleep. Chuy gave her a gentle shake. "Wake up, chica." Beverly opened her eyes but didn't move. Chuy gazed at her for a long moment then lightly let his fingers caress her hair as he whispered, "It won't be long now." He exited the room and quietly closed the door.

They all looked at Chuy as he came into the kitchen. "She's sleeping but she should have some food and something to drink. In fact we all should. When it gets dark, Gordo and Flaco, you go to the Cantina Rosario and eat. When you come back, Lalo and I will go."

"I'm sick of that place. The food is crap," Gordo complained. "We'll drive over to Francisco's. The food is much better there."

"No!" Chuy exclaimed. "Just walk over to Rosario's, eat something and come right back. We might hear from Hector."

Gordo exploded. "Now what? You gonna tell us where we can eat. Fuck you!"

Chuy gave Gordo a cold stare but didn't make a move. "Okay, *Señor Delgado*," he said, his tone mocking, "you and *Señor Guzman* eat wherever you wish."

Beverly knocked on the bedroom door. "I've got to go to the bathroom, *el baño*," she cried through the door. Chuy escorted her down the hall to the bathroom. He closed the door and remained outside. When she knocked again, he led her back to the bedroom.

"I'm really hungry," she said. "Won't you please get me something decent to eat...like a hamburger and maybe a salad or..." She shrugged. "Something that isn't so hot it burns my mouth and gives me a stomach ache."

"Of course, we can do that. A couple of the boys are going to dinner at a nice restaurant. I'll have them bring back a proper dinner for you and maybe some milk to sooth your stomach."

"Thank you," she said. Then she asked hopefully, "Did you get the money yet?"

"No," Chuy replied, "but I think we'll have it tomorrow and then you can go home."

"Oh God, I hope so."

Chuy turned to leave but Beverly stopped him with a timid question. "You told me that Kevin would be back soon, so where is he?" With downcast eyes, she asked, "He's okay, right?"

"No, no, *chica*. He's fine. We just thought it would be better if the two of you were not held in the same place in case something happened. You understand. It was a precaution. Besides, we wanted him to see a doctor, as I told you. You will see him soon." He took hold of her hands, brought them to his lips and kissed each. If he felt her fighting not to pull them away, he didn't show it. "Don't worry, *chica linda*. Now, let me see about your dinner." He closed the door and locked it.

"Gordo," he called. "You and Flaco should go eat now. Order a dinner for the girl, no spicy stuff. Maybe a steak, eh? Some vegetables and milk. Be sure to bring some milk. And don't take too long. Here, for her dinner." He reached in his pocket, pulled out a wad of bills and counted off 330 pesos. "A nice steak, potato, vegetables and milk. Don't forget the milk. Okay? Go."

As Gordo walked to the back door he handed Flaco the keys to the pickup. "Here, you drive."

Romero was awake but had his eyes closed. He popped them open when a flash of light pierced his eyelids. He looked up and saw car headlights reflected in the rear view mirror. He tapped Torres arm. "Car coming. Get down!"

The men slid down and waited. They heard the vehicle pass but remained still for a moment, then they sat up and saw a black pickup traveling down the road.

"That's a Ford!" Torres exclaimed. He pulled a notepad from his shirt pocket and flipped the pages. "We're looking for Sinaloa plate VFU-67-40."

"Okay, we'll tail it, see if it matches up." Romero started the engine and pulled out with the lights off. "Get that glass in the glove box."

Torres found the small binoculars and looked down the road. "Too dark—can't make out the number. Get a little closer. Okay, that's good. VFU6740." He looked at his notepad. "That's it."

Romero pulled over and parked. "Call it in. Let's see who owns it." Romero turned on the lights and pulled out. The pickup, now some distance ahead, made a right turn. Romero followed.

Torres thanked the dispatcher and signed off. "The pickup is registered to Eldora Vargas." They stared at each other for a moment. In unison they cried, "Chuy's sister."

Keeping a safe distance, Romero followed the truck to a restaurant. He did not follow it into the parking lot but rather continued past, making the block and parking in the street. Torres got out and walked to the lot, found the Ford and peered in. Seeing nothing of value inside and only some bags of ready-mix concrete partially covered by a canvas tarp in the bed, he returned to Romero and reported.

The two men discussed their options, all the while keeping an eye on the pickup. Romero said, "When they come out, we'll follow them and see where they go, identify the place and ask Hierra what he wants to do." He cast an eye toward the restaurant entrance. "Okay, there they are."

Flaco and Gordo, holding a carry-out bag, walked to their truck. After taking a long look around, Flaco got behind the wheel while Gordo slid into the passenger seat. They headed out of the lot. The agents watched as the pickup turned at the first crossroad, then Romero pulled out, made a U-turn and began the tail. His phone rang.

Romero checked the I.D. It was Hierra. "I was just about to call you."

"What's going on? Anything new?"

"All kinds of stuff going on," Romero replied. "In fact, right now we're tailing that pickup Torres photographed. Ran the plates and the truck is registered to that Chuy guy's sister. So, yes, I'd say this is hot."

"Damn, Esteban, that's great. Good work!"

"We've got a hunch that it's going to lead us to Chuy and his boys and maybe the kids, too. Now my question for you is, once we give you the address, maybe we snoop around a bit, see if we can see anything—"

Hierra broke in. "No, don't do that. Can't take a chance on you being spotted. For now, just see where they go and then call me. I'm going over to Ruiz' office and see what ideas he has. This case is as much his baby as it is ours and I don't want to step on any toes."

"Okay. I'll call you when our bird lands." Romero clicked off and gave Torres a synopsis of the conversation.

They left the main streets and were traveling down a quiet side street. Romero slipped into an open parking space and turned off the lights. "I'll just let them get a little further ahead, then I'll follow with lights off."

Torres nodded. "Good. You can sure see their tail lights for a hell of a ways. Besides, there's not another car on the road."

They pulled out again and followed the truck while Torres jotted down the names of the streets on which they were traveling. The pickup made a left turn on Calle San Philippe. Romero waited before making the turn. He slowly edged into the intersection and saw the tail lights of the pickup brighten for a moment as the truck braked to turn into a driveway.

Romero quickly turned right and parked. Torres jumped out and stepped behind a large tree. He watched the two men get out of the truck and walk toward the house, climb the steps and enter. He motioned to Romero to join him.

"They went inside. Now what?" Torres asked.

Romero called Hierra. "Those two guys we were following led us to their house. They went inside. Torres will give you the details."

Torres read from his notes giving the route to the house. "I don't have a house number yet but it's on Nayarit, the fifth house from the corner of Calle San Philippe, on the north side."

"Very well. Don't get too close but keep your eyes on the house. Meanwhile we'll have a SWAT unit and a squad of PF out there to contain the area. They've already been put on alert and are ready to go. Hold on, I'm giving the location to Ruiz so he can give them orders."

Romero tapped Torres' shoulder. He thrust his chin in the direction of the house. "Look," he whispered, "Someone is getting in the truck." He thought for a moment then said, "You stay here. I'm going to follow him."

"Maybe he's going to get something to eat like the other two."

Romero looked again and saw the pickup lights come on. "Okay. I'm going to tail him. As soon as he turns the corner, I'll take off."

Hierra's voice came over the phone. "Torres, you still there?"

"Yes, sir. One man came out of the house, got in the truck and is driving this way. Romero is going to follow while I stay here and watch the house."

"Very well, I'll alert the PF. Give me the plate number on that pickup." Torres read off the number then Hierra said, "Okay, the teams are on the move. They have your number and will contact you when they are in place."

"What do you want me to do?"

"Just stay where you are and keep the squad informed if anything changes." He gave Torres the leader's number. There was a long moment of silence. Then in a strained voice Hierra added, "Let's hope they can pull it off without losing those kids."

Chapter 18

"Yes, yes, I'll call you the minute we hear anything. Please, Patty just stay right there. There is nothing you can do down here that will..." Sandy paused to let Patty vent a little more. "Don't worry sweetheart, I promise. The very minute we have any news, I'll call you right away, okay? I love you too, bye." Sandy laid the phone down and looked sadly at Ed. "She is really having a hard time with this. She wants to come down here."

Ed said, "You did the right thing, telling her to stay put. We don't need someone else to worry about." He stood and moved his head from side to side to stretch his neck muscles. "Damn, this waiting is the worst. You would think those guys would have had their money by now."

"We're dealing with thugs," Sandy said. "You don't know what they will or will not do. But I know this much—the longer it takes before he calls, the worse our chances are of seeing Bev again." She rubbed her forehead with the back of her hand. "I've got a splitting headache and it won't go away. Just saying her name makes me frantic."

"I know," Ed said. "I feel the same way but there's really is nothing more we can do. We gave the police a description of that Hector guy. Now it's up to the police to find the kids and get them away safely, or it's up to the crooks to call to tell us the kids are on their way to the observatory." Ed released a long breath and took one of Sandy's hands in his, giving it a squeeze. "But I got to say, this suspense is killing me."

Chuy took the sack of food Gordo had brought back from the restaurant and walked to the kitchen where he picked up a plate, a fork and knife and entered Beverly's bedroom.

Gordo and Flaco sat on the couch in the living room drinking beer and watching TV. Flaco asked Gordo, "Did you remind Lalo to pick up some beer on his way back?"

"Yeah, I told him."

"Good," Flaco said. "This waiting is making me *loco*."

Beverly was sitting in a chair by the window which had been nailed shut. She looked up when Chuy entered and stood when she saw the take-out bag.

"Look what I have for you, *chica*." He opened a large Styrofoam box and showed her the contents. He put the plate and utensils on the dresser and transferred the food to the plate. "And look at this." He took a quart of milk from the bag and opened it. He held up the plate to show her the steak. "Does this not look good? It's still warm. Come, eat."

Beverly stood in front of the dresser and hungrily attacked the food. She actually couldn't remember when they'd last given her any food. It felt like days. Maybe it was days.

Chuy sat in the chair and watched her. He gave her a large smile. "Is good, no?"

Chewing with gusto, Beverly stared at him for a moment. Then she nodded.

Lalo pulled into the parking lot next to Francisco's Cantina.

Romero reported to the squad leader. "When he comes out, I'm going to nab him. If it's the boss, Chuy, then that could help you. The rest of them might be less formidable without their leader. If it's just one of the gang, at least you'll have one less gun to contend with."

"Okay, go ahead and take him. See if you can get him to tell you how many are in the house and if the hostages are also in the house. Once we know that, then I'll have a better idea about how to proceed. You copy that?"

"Yes, sir. Got it. You're just going to sit tight until you hear from me, right?"

"Right." The squad leader signed off.

"Where the hell is that damn Lalo?" Gordo groused. He stood to look out the picture window behind the couch. As he sat back down, he said, "How about that Chuy? The dumb shit is in there with the girl, probably cutting the steak for her."

Flaco chuckled. "I think he's in love with her. Maybe they're making love right now, hmm?" Flaco goaded Gordo. "How was it when you gave it to her?"

"Are you kidding? That dumb *puta* doesn't know her ass from a doorknob about it. I'd rather fuck a goat!"

Flaco laughed. "I'm sure you would...a Billy goat, ha, ha, ha!" He punched Gordo on the arm.

"Shut up, you asshole." Gordo jumped up and fiddled with the TV, then stopped at a soccer game.

Romero hid behind some shrubbery that lined the walkway to the parking lot. When Lalo walked past, Romero stepped behind him and, pressing the gun into Lalo's back, said, "Just walk quietly to your truck, keep your hands at your side and I won't kill you. Try anything and you're dead."

Lalo gasped. "Who are you?" he asked, his voice unsteady.

"I'll ask the questions and your answers better be good if you expect to live much longer. Now, hands behind your back."

Lalo swung around, right hand ready to throw a punch, but Romero hit him hard on the side of head with his pistol and Lalo dropped like a stone. Romero cuffed him, and dragged him across the gravel to his car, parked two spaces away. Once he had his prisoner in the back seat and hooked up to the restraints, he called the squad leader.

"Got our man. He's restrained in my car. I'm in Francisco's parking lot right now but I'm going to find someplace where I can discuss some things with him." The squad leader congratulated him. Romero continued, "When I get the intel on how many are in the house and where the hostages are, I'll call you. Give me a little while, but from the look of this guy, I don't think he'll be hard to crack. Meanwhile, arrange for a tow truck to haul his pickup to the station and have the lab guys check it out."

"Will do. Oh, we did a little high-powered surveillance. All we see is two guys watching TV in the front room. The front door opens right into that room, so that's a possibility. There are lights on in other rooms but shades are down so we can't confirm additional inhabitants."

Romero parked in a wooded area at the end of a dirt side street. He pulled the barely conscious Lalo from the back seat and marched him into the trees. Tying him to a large tree, he said calmly and quietly, "Okay, my friend, this can all be over in a minute or it could take an hour. Either way, before we leave here you are going to tell me where you and Chuy and the rest of your friends are living, how many guys are in the house, and where we will find the American girl and the boy that you assholes snatched last Sunday."

He put his hand on Lalo's throat and squeezed. Lalo reflexively tried to inhale, without much success.

Romero smiled at him. "Okay, you can give me that information right now and we are done. I'll take you to the police station where you will be safe and that's the end of it. You understand that in the end you will answer my questions. It's just a matter of how much suffering you can take."

He was right. It didn't take long.

Romero reported to Hierra. "There are two men called Flaco and Gordo, plus the Noble girl and Chuy in the house. The girl is locked in a bedroom off of the kitchen. When this guy left the house to go eat, Chuy was also in the living room. He said he didn't think Chuy was going anywhere because he was going to give the girl the food Gordo brought from the cantina."

"Wait a minute," Hierra said, "What about the boy?"

"He's dead, Chief. This guy claims the big guy, Gordo, accidentally killed him. They did something with the kid's body—he wasn't sure what."

"Oh, hell. I was hoping to—"

"I know, but nothing we can do about that now. I think we can get the girl out, though. This Lalo guy told me that Chuy has been taking care of her. He thinks Chuy is in love with her, those were his words. I asked him if he thought Chuy would kill her if the cops stormed the house and killed the other two guys. He said he didn't think so. Then he said again that he thinks Chuy is in love with her."

Hierra sighed. "Hmm, that's interesting. Very well, stand by while I discuss this with Ruiz."

Romero called Torres. "What's going on over at the house?"

"Nothing. What about the guy you tailed?"

Romero gave him the details of what he called his "chat" with Lalo. "The local guys have him now. Have you had any contact with the PF?"

"Yes. They let me know they were in place and ready to move on the house when they get the order from Ruiz. There are four of them in front of me, just around the corner. They're in full armor and carrying AKs."

"Okay. Listen, you stay the hell out of it, understand? Once they have the place secure, you go find the girl and stay with her until they send someone to take care of her. I'm on my way there now. See you in a few minutes."

Torres rocked back on his heels and watched as more shadows dressed in black took up positions nearer the house. He jumped when he felt something press against his back. He craned his head around and saw a SWAT team member dressed in black. "Take it easy," Torres murmured as he slowly stood with hands in the air. "I'm AFI."

Beverly had managed to choke down about half her dinner. It had been so long since she ate any kind of a decent meal that her stomach could only tolerate so much. She cast an eye at Chuy who sat smiling in the chair by the window. "I can't eat any more—I'm full. There's still half a steak left. Do you want it?"

"Sure," Chuy replied. He rose from the chair and took the fork and knife she offered him.

Chuy leaned down and kissed her cheek. "Thank you," he whispered in her ear. "I am pleased that you enjoyed the dinner."

Beverly stiffened and pulled back. "Yes, it was very good. Thank you again." She walked toward the door.

"What are you doing?" Chuy asked.

"I need to go to the bathroom. I'll come right back."

"No, I'd better take you there. You don't want those monkeys staring at you, do you?" Chuy took her hand and led her to the bathroom. "When you are ready, you know what to do."

Chuy went back to the bedroom and began to eat. Just as he raised the fork to his mouth, he heard a loud explosion. He moved to the bedroom door and looked across the kitchen to the living room. Smoke was drifting into the kitchen. He heard Gordo yell and then he heard the staccato sounds of automatic weapons. He reached for his pistol tucked in his pants, withdrew it just as black clad figures entered the kitchen, automatic weapons aimed at him. He brought the pistol around and was about to drop it and put his hands up when a burst of bullets hit him. He was dead before he hit the floor.

Beverly was washing her hands when the gunfire erupted. She screamed and ran into the shower stall where she closed the curtain and crouched, making herself as small as she could. She heard the door burst open and two men dressed in black charged into the room, guns raised. She tried to hold it in but a sob escaped as the two men stood looking in the shower stall with guns pointed at her.

"It's the girl!" one of the men yelled, lowering his weapon. "Go get the AFI guy."

Romero had joined Torres just as the action started. They watched as the squad shot a smoke grenade through the living room window, then a half dozen men burst into the house. They heard the gunshots and then silence. The two of them ran to the house, holding their badges up for the officers to see. They entered the house and were immediately taken to the bathroom. They stood in front of the shower stall and motioned for the SWAT officer to move away.

Romero spoke in English. "Beverly? You are safe now. I am Agent Romero and this is Agent Torres. We are with the Federal Investigation Agency. We are going to take you to your parents." He took her arm gently and led her to the kitchen. "Do you have anything here that you want to take along?"

"Just my suitcase." She pointed to the bedroom. "It's in there." It was then she saw a body covered with a sheet. She let out a gasp. "Is that Chuy?" she asked in a halting voice.

Romano answered kindly, "We think so but we need you to identify him. Do you think you can do that?"

"Oh my God, is he dead?"

Romero nodded.

"And you want me to look at him?"

"I know it's not something you want to do, but you are the only one who can tell us who that person is."

Beverly felt her stomach contract. "Okay. I'm pretty sure it has to be him because he was in the bedroom with me just before I went to the bathroom."

"The other two men that were in the living room," Torres said. "Do you know their names?"

"Two?" Beverly asked. "No, there should be three others." She looked around nervously, as though someone could still be hiding in the house. "Their names are Gordo, Flaco and Lalo."

"That's right, but we apprehended Lalo when he went out to eat. If this is Chuy here, the other two are Gordo and Flaco. Correct?"

"Yes."

"Those are their nicknames. Do you know their Christian names?"

Beverly considered the question for a moment. "Chuy called Lalo, Eduardo. I don't remember any others."

Two coroner's men appeared with a stretcher. As they loaded Chuy's body, Romero said, "Wait a minute please. The girl needs to identify the body." In English he said to Beverly, "Just take a quick look—just at his face, and tell us who he is."

She stood next to the stretcher and closed her eyes as one of the coroner's men lifted the sheet to reveal the head. She popped her eyes open for a spit second and then shut them tightly.

Romero took her arm and turned her away while the body was being removed. "Do you know the name of the man you just looked at?" he asked.

She choked back a sob and with her eyes lowered she whispered, "It's Chuy. He was kind to me. He liked me. He wouldn't let anything bad happen to me. When Gordo—" She drew in a sharp breath. "When Gordo attacked me, Chuy made him stop." She looked up at the two agents. "It was Gordo who killed Kevin, you know. He was a mean bastard." She swallowed hard. "They all were, except Chuy. He was bad, too, but not like the others."

"Just one more question before we go. Do you know what they did with the money your father gave them?"

Beverly's face showed surprise. "They didn't get it yet, that's what Chuy told me. He said a man, they called him Hector, was someplace where the money was delivered and this man was supposed to bring the money to them tonight. I heard that name, Hector, a lot but they were speaking Spanish so I didn't know what they were talking about."

A woman in a police uniform walked in and identified herself to Romero who in turn introduced her to Beverly. "This is Paula and she will be with you until you are united with your parents. A police helicopter will take you there in the morning." He addressed Paula. "Her suitcase is in the bedroom. She wants to take it." He turned to Beverly, took both her hands in his and said, "You have been very much on our minds these past days and I cannot begin to tell you how relieved we are that we were able to find you alive and unharmed. Good luck to you and please," he gave her a wry smile, "be very careful if you ever come back to Mexico again."

Carrying the small suitcase, Paula took Beverly's arm and started to walk toward the front door which now was battered and hanging lopsided from one hinge. Beverly looked back at the two agents and gave them a weak smile. To Paula she said, "Don't worry. I'll never come back here. This one time was enough for me."

Chapter 19

At 6 AM Friday, the ringing phone was like a charge of electricity that caused both Ed and Sandy to jump as if they had been shocked. Wide-eyed, they exchanged glances as Sandy bawled, "Oh, my God."

Ed grabbed the cell phone. His voice was small and tentative. "Hello, this is Edward Noble."

"Ah, Señor Noble, this is Captain Ruiz and I have good news for you."

Ed could barely breathe. His heart was racing. He looked at Sandy who returned his excited look with one of her own. "You do? What is it?"

"Your daughter is at this very moment in our custody and is being flown to our office at the Ensenada airport. Is that not the very best of news?"

Ed nearly dropped the phone as he shouted, "They have Bev! She's on her way here right now!"

Sandy jumped up, threw her arms around him. "Oh God," she moaned. "Oh, darling, I can't believe it. Is she okay?"

"Captain, is our daughter all right...she isn't hurt or anything, is she?"

"I haven't seen her, but the agents who interviewed her say that she seems to be fine, although I'm sure the effect of this ordeal will probably reveal itself in time."

Ed lowered the phone. "He says she's fine." He asked Ruiz, "Do you want us to drive over to the airport now?"

"That will not be necessary," Ruiz said. "I've sent a car for you. The agents will drive you to the airport. Just one thing—after you've had a few minutes to talk to her, we really do need to debrief her. I would like to put this questioning off for a day but I'm afraid if we don't find out what she knows and act on it right away, it may be very difficult to find out what happened to your million dollars and we are quite anxious to be able to locate it and return it to you."

"I understand."

"Agent Hierra and I will see you in Ensenada."

Suddenly Ed realized there was another critical piece of information he wanted. Stopping Ruiz before he could hang up, Ed said, "Wait a minute. What about the boy, Kevin? Where is he right now?"

"I am going to call Señor Kendall now and tell him about his son."

"What are you going to tell him?"

There was a pause. In a subdued voice the captain said, "I am sorry. The boy was killed." He hastened to add, "But not during our raid. No, he was killed several days ago by one of the kidnappers. We haven't been able to recover the body. It's one of the things we need to talk to your daughter about."

Ed's euphoria seemed to evaporate as his mind absorbed Ruiz' words. "Thank you, Captain. We'll see you later."

Sandy became alarmed when she saw Ed's bleak expression. "Now what? What did he say? Something is wrong. I can see it on your face."

"It's Kevin." He gently eased Sandy into a chair. "He was killed by one of the gang a few days ago. The police haven't located the body. It's one of the things they need to talk to Bev about."

Sandy put her hand over her mouth to stifle a cry. Ed dropped to his knees and wrapped his arms around her. As he held her tightly, he murmured, "I don't know how the Kendalls are going to handle this but, whatever happens, we have to help them through it."

Captain Ruiz called Carl and told him what had happened to Kevin. "Thank you, sir," Carl whispered. "I appreciate the call." Carl replaced the phone on its cradle and looked at his wife. Words wouldn't come. Tears welled up as he tried to choke off a sob.

Sherry suddenly lost her breath. "It's Kevin—something has happened!" She jumped out of the chair and grabbed Carl by the shoulders. His body was trembling with uncontrollable weeping. She shook him. "Carl, what is it? What did he tell you?"

Carl pulled loose from her grasp and collapsed into a chair. He held his head in his hands as he muttered, "He's dead. They killed him. Kevin is gone."

Sherry gazed open-mouth at her husband who suddenly became a blur. She looked up. The room was spinning, spinning, spin...Her knees buckled and the world went dark as she fell to the floor.

Sandy and Ed waited for their ride to the airport. Their excitement about seeing Beverly was muted by the news of Kevin's death. Suddenly, Sandy exclaimed, "Oh, my gosh, I forgot to call Patty. Give me your phone." Sandy entered the number and immediately heard Pat's anxious voice.

"Dad?"

"No, it's me." Sandy's voice rose with excitement. "They found her...the police have Beverly. They are flying her up to Ensenada now."

"Oh my God," Pat breathed in relief. "Is she alright?"

"They say she's fine. We're waiting for a car to take us to the airport now. I'll call you when we see her and you can talk to her, okay?"

"Oh my God, this is incredible, this is so fantastic." Patty's voice rose. "And she's okay, right?"

"That's what they told us."

Patty broke in. "What did Dad have to say?"

"Here, you talk to him." Sandy handed the phone to Ed.

"Hello, honey. Is this great or what? I mean that they found her and apparently unharmed. We couldn't have had better news."

Pat was so excited she could hardly contain her emotions. "What about Kevin? Is he okay, too?"

Feeling ridiculously unprepared, Ed suddenly didn't know how to respond. He looked at Sandy and mouthed, *Kevin.*

Sandy shook her head and put a finger to her lips. "We 'haven't heard,'" she whispered.

Ed spoke into the phone, "Ah, we didn't hear anything about Kevin. Maybe they're de-briefing him before they bring him here...I don't know."

"Please call me as soon as you hear about him, okay?"

"Sure, honey. Listen, we've got to go now but we'll call you as soon as we see Bev. Love you, bye."

A light knock brought Sandy to the door. A man showing his official ID and police badge introduced himself.

"Are you ready to leave for the airport now?"

Ed asked Sandy, "What about Carl and Sherry, shouldn't we stop and see how they're doing?"

Sandy thought for a moment. "No, we don't even know if they have been told anything yet. Let's wait until we get back with Bev. Maybe she'll be able to tell them what happened."

Ed said, "I'll call Ben on the way to the airport and that FBI agent, Burke. Let them know what's going on." He addressed the policeman, "Okay, we are ready to go."

They were packing the car and trailer when Magda said, "I put the four boxes in the big cooler in the back of the trunk and then stuffed all the dirty clothes in there."

"The park ranger has seen us camping like any family. I don't think he suspects anything. Besides, Chuy told me we'd be safe because the gringo father told the police that if anything goes wrong, the girl will be killed. I don't think anyone will bother us."

"I don't care, I'm still going to walk over to the Capilla San Pedro and pray for our safe return home. I'm taking the children. You should come as well."

"I'll say a prayer here. I don't want to leave the car, you know, with all of our *things* in it."

"Yes," Magda said, "That is a good idea. You stay, but," she pointed a finger, "Don't forget to pray, and Hector, pray hard."

Chapter 20

In the small offices of the Federal Police at the Ensenada Heliport, Ed paced the floor nervously while Sandy sat in a chair fidgeting with the small cross she wore around her neck. The agent who had driven them there asked if they would like some coffee or a cold drink. They thanked him but declined.

The pulsating whoosh of the rotors alerted them to the arrival of the police helicopter. "Okay if we go outside?" Ed asked the agent.

"Of course," the agent replied, pushing open a door to the helipad. "But stay close to the building until it lands and the pilot has shut down the engine."

The helicopter lightly set down. When the large rotor blades had stopped turning, the door opened and steps dropped to the tarmac. A uniformed woman stepped down and offered her hand to a girl with red hair who hurried down the steps. Seeing Sandy and Ed, Beverly broke free and ran toward them.

Ed and Sandy met her halfway. There was laughter and crying and hugging and kissing and everyone talking at once.

Captain Ruiz and Agent Hierra watched, beaming. Ruiz turned to Hierra and exclaimed, "Well, Andres, it appears that this time, all the work and worry paid off, no?"

"Most of it, certainly. I have to say that this is a very rewarding scene. It's unfortunate that it doesn't happen more often. And the boy...I wish he were here as well."

A shadow crossed Ruiz' face as he nodded. "True. But I think one of the things that made this case work as well as it did was the cooperation between your service and mine. It was exceptional, although much of the credit has to go to your man, Romero. He cracked this case. I tell you, that operation in Los Mochis was outstanding. I say *bravo*, my friend."

Hierra smiled broadly as he watched the scene playing out in front of him. "You are right, Cesar. Romero and Torres certainly deserve credit for this picture." He motioned toward the Nobles. "But come, we have work to do. We must find out what this girl knows, especially where the money is and what happened to the boy."

The Nobles were escorted to a private room where they spent a half hour without interruption from the police. They talked very little about the kidnapping, except to receive assurances from Bev that she was truly okay. They concentrated on just being together and enjoying the happiness of the moment. Beverly called Pat and that conversation would have lasted for hours had not Sandy asked Bev to end it and call back after the interview.

Captain Ruiz knocked on the door and entered with Agent Hierra, who said, "I am so sorry to break into your homecoming, señorita, but we have some questions that need immediate answers. If you want your parents to stay with you while we talk, we have no objection."

Beverly turned to her mother. "I'd like you to stay if you can handle what you may hear."

Sandy gasped. "What we...?"

"Mom, some stuff happened." Bev touched her mother's arm. "You know, like Kevin and other things. You probably should hear it all now so I don't have to go through it again later. Okay?"

Ed took Sandy's hand. "Come on. She's right. We need hear this. We don't want to be wondering about what she went through. I sure there was some rough stuff..."

Captain Ruiz called in an officer who carried a portable recorder which he placed on a small table. Then the officer pinned a small lapel mic onto Beverly's collar and pulled up a chair. He asked her to say something and as she spoke he made some adjustments to the equipment. When all was ready, he nodded.

Hierra made the usual identifying statement and then, sitting across from the couch where Beverly and her parents sat, he began. "We will start with you and your friend Kevin Kendall eating breakfast at the Posada Inn last Sunday. What did you ask your table waiter, Luis Aguilar?

Beverly cleared her throat, started to speak then cleared her throat again. In a small voice she replied, "We the waiter if he could suggest a place where we could do some fun Jeeping. He gave us a route and told us that the Hacienda Hotel would be a good place to stop for lunch and then to continue on Route 3 through the Palm Valley and then on to Tecate where we could enter the U.S."

"Very good," Hierra said. "So you went to lunch, yes?"

Beverly sipped some water from the bottle she was holding. "Yes, we had lunch there, and afterwards, we continued on Route 3 which was very scenic and then it curved to the right and the road became pretty steep and I remember saying to Kevin that this couldn't be the right road to Tecate and he said that he'd seen a sign a few miles back that said '3.' We hadn't gone very far when we saw a car in the middle of the road, I mean it was turned sideways and pretty much blocked the road. Three men got out of the car and they were all carrying big guns."

Sandy reached for Beverly's hand and gave it a squeeze. Ed closed his eyes and took a deep breath. Beverly continued, an obvious tremor in her voice.

"Kevin jammed on the brakes, I about went through the windshield. He said to hang on, he was going to turn around and get the hell out of there. As he started to turn, at least two shots, maybe more, I don't know—I heard something hit the car. Then the men ran toward us with their guns pointed at us and I screamed and Kevin..." She started to cry. "Kevin, he jumped out of the car with his hands up."

Sandy put her arms around her and whispered, "It's okay, darling. It's over now and no one can hurt you."

"I know, but poor Kevin." Sandy handed her a tissue and Beverly blotted her eyes. "I'm sorry," she said to Hierra.

"I know this is hard for you. Just take your time."

She took a deep breath and continued, "That man Gordo ran up to Kevin and hit him on the side of the head with his gun and Kevin fell down and just lay on the road. I think he was unconscious. Another man, Chuy, he was the boss, yelled at Gordo. I couldn't understand what he was saying but he was really, really mad. Anyway, Gordo grabbed Kevin's legs and started to drag him to the car and Chuy told him to stop and pick Kevin up. I mean, I didn't know exactly what he was saying 'cause it was in Spanish but that's what he must have told Gordo because Gordo and another man, Lalo, picked Kevin up and put him in the back."

"Excuse me, let me interrupt you. I was wondering, could you describe the car they were driving?" Hierra asked.

"It wasn't like a regular car, I don't know why I said 'car.' It was a pickup truck, a black pickup truck and they put Kevin in the back—the open part. Gordo got in back with him. They put me inside the truck, in the front seat. Chuy got in and Lalo went back to the Jeep and drove it."

Hierra held up his hand. "For the record, how is it you knew the names of these three men? Had you ever seen them before?"

Beverly shook her head. "I didn't know their names then but I learned them afterward, you know, when..." Her voice trailed off, then she grew alert again. "There was another guy in the gang, too. They called him Flaco. I guess... Agent Romero told me, these were all nicknames, you know. That's what they called each other."

Hierra nodded. "Kevin was in the back of the truck, you were up front next to Chuy, the driver, and Lalo was driving the Jeep. Where did you go?"

"We went about a mile or so up the hill then turned left and down a long drive to a house. We got out of the car...truck. Chuy had a hold of my arm—." Beverly pulled up her sleeve to show a purple bruise. Ed grunted. Beverly continued. "Gordo pulled Kevin to the back and helped him down...he was awake but pretty shaky. Chuy said something and Gordo helped Kevin into the house. They put us in a bedroom and shut the door." Beverly sighed and took another sip of water from the bottle. "I asked Kevin if he was okay and he said he had a terrible headache. I told him to lie down on the bed and I laid down next to him. I think we just both drifted off to sleep because the next thing I knew, guns were being fired and I could hear the sounds of a helicopter."

Sandy said, "That was us, darling. We were looking for you. When we flew over the house, some men came running out and shot at us."

"You found us that quick?" Beverly exclaimed. "Oh my God, we had no idea it was you guys."

Hierra broke in, "Please continue. When the police came to that house, you, of course, were gone. Where did the men take you and Kevin?"

Beverly thought for a moment. "There was a big argument about the Jeep. I don't know exactly what was being said but the word 'Jeep' was clear enough. I guess they wanted to take it but Chuy said no. Later, I found out the Chuy told them that it was too dangerous, that the police would be looking for that Jeep. Anyway, they didn't take it. We left in the pickup. I was in front, Chuy was driving, Kevin and Flaco were in the back seat and Gordo and Lalo were in the... ah..."

"Bed of the truck. It's called the 'bed.'" Ed told her.

Beverly smiled at her father. "Yes, I knew that. I just forgot." She shook her head as if to clear it. "Thanks. We drove a long time. Kevin was saying how much his head hurt and Chuy, who knew English, told him he would take him to a doctor when we got there. I asked him where we were going and he said I shouldn't ask questions."

"And at some point, did you get on a boat?"

"Yeah. They had me and Kevin get in the bed. There were some bags of stuff under a canvas cover and they told us to get under it and be very quiet...no talking. So we did. I know now that they drove onto a ferry and we crossed the water. It took a long time. Anyway, after that we drove someplace to a house. We went in through the back door to a kitchen. There was a bedroom off of the kitchen and they locked us in there with our stuff."

Hierra asked Beverly, "Would you like to take a short break now?"

"No," she said, sitting up straighter and squaring her shoulders. She glanced at her parents, on either side. "I'm fine. Let's get it over with. I want to go home."

"Of course. I'm sorry but you understand this is quite necessary."

"I know." She sipped more water and continued. "The next day Chuy came in with some Mexican food and a couple bottles of water. The food was terrible...it was so spicy hot. Anyway, he took me and then Kevin to the bathroom and back to the bedroom. He told Kevin he was sorry that Gordo had hit him and he asked if Kevin still had a headache. Kevin said yes and it was getting worse. Chuy said, when he came back, he would take Kevin to see a doctor and then he left.

"We could hear the men talking and laughing. I guess they were eating. Anyway, Kevin was looking pretty bad. He was like all pale and sweaty...he was hurting real bad. All of a sudden the door opened and Gordo came in." Beverly gulped and took her mother's hand. "He looked at me and then Kevin..." Her voice grew thin with suppressed tears. "Then he... then he told Kevin to lie on the floor and he grabbed my arm and threw me on the bed and ripped off my shirt. He had some rope and he tied my hands behind my back. I was yelling like crazy and Kevin came over and tried to wrestle Gordo away from me, but Gordo hit him in the head with his fists over and over and Kevin fell down by the wall. He didn't move." Beverly choked back a sob. "He didn't move." She spoke as though she couldn't believe her own words. "I'm so sorry!"

Sandy put her arms around her and held her tightly. "It wasn't your fault, honey. It wasn't. Do you want to stop now for a while?"

Beverly drew in a breath and said, "No, Mom. Let's just get it over...all of it."

In quiet voice, Hierra said, "Can you describe this man, Gordo?"

"Yes. He must have been over six feet tall. He was fat, I don't know, like maybe two hundred and fifty pounds, something like that. He had huge arms, really huge and he stunk bad. Anyway, he looked at Kevin and saw he was out cold. I was screaming and crying. He pulled out a roll of gray tape and taped my mouth shut.

Then he..." Beverly gave her mother a fleeting look then turned back to Hierra. Speaking very fast, she blurted out, "Then he pulled off my shorts and pushed his fingers into me. He laughed and said something in Spanish then opened his pants and took out his thing and was about to rape me, I guess, when Chuy came busting in and yelled at him to get off of me. He made Gordo untie me and take the tape off of my mouth. Chuy told him to get out and Gordo said something, maybe he was swearing. Anyway, he left."

"Thank you, Beverly. I know this is very difficult. You're doing fine." Hierra's voice was soothing. Beverly nodded.

"Chuy spoke pretty good English. He said he was sorry for what happened and that it would not happen again. I think underneath, Chuy was a good man. Anyway he sure took care of me from that time on."

"It is a good thing that he did, no?" Hierra commented. "Now, what about Kevin? You say he was lying on the floor while all this was going on. What happened after Gordo left the room?"

"Chuy saw Kevin was still unconscious and asked me what happened and I told him. Chuy had one of guys get me some clean clothes out of my suitcase and take me to the bathroom so I could take a shower. When he brought me back to the bedroom, Kevin was gone."

"Did Chuy tell you where they took Kevin?"

"He said they took him to a doctor who would take care of him...that's what they told me but," she swallowed hard. Her voice came out high and trembling. "I was pretty sure Kevin was dead." She looked at her mother. "What could I do? All I could do was pray they'd get their money and turn me loose." Sandy patted Beverly's hand. "It was too late to help Kevin. Besides, I was like on the verge of losing it myself."

"You're a very brave girl, Bev," Ed said.

"I think we have everything we need," Hierra said. He nodded to the man at the recorder who turned off the device and removed the mic from Beverly's collar.

Beverly looked bewildered. "Don't you want to know what happened after that?"

"No, I know what happened after that. I have two agents who are responsible for your rescue. I think you met them after the police had secured the house. They really did some amazing detective work and I'm going to arrange for you and your parents to meet them before you leave for home." Hierra paused and thought for a moment. "Ah, just one more item. The ransom money. According to the man called Lalo, the money your father gave to someone who identified himself as Hector, was never delivered to Chuy. Do you know anything about that?"

"I heard that name Hector a lot. Chuy told me that the money was going to be delivered soon, maybe the next day but he told me they didn't have it yet but as soon as they got the money, I would be taken to a safe place where my parents could come and get me. He said that many times and I believed him. I think he liked me and wanted to be sure I was going to be okay. To tell you the truth, I'm sorry they killed him. Like I said, he was basically a nice person. He was just involved in a bad business."

Chapter 21

Friday evening, with the family inside the car, Hector pulled out his cell phone and called Chuy.

"Yes?"

Hector knew at once that it was not Chuy's voice, but he thought, *maybe it's one of the other guys.* Without hesitation, he said, "Leaving now," ended the call and drove out of the park. When they reached the ferry, a uniformed guard stopped them. Hector lowered the driver's side window. "Good evening."

"Good evening," the guard replied. He poked his head into the car, saw Magda and the two children on the back seat then looked at the tent and other camping equipment on the trailer. "Been camping?"

"Yes. It was very nice. The children had a wonderful time."

The guard backed away from the car. Have a pleasant crossing. Goodnight."

Hector nodded, rolled up the window, drove on the ferry and parked. Aside from a trip to the lavatory, the family remained in the car for the entire trip. When they off-loaded at Topolobampo, Hector drove into the parking lot, looking for Chuy. He said to Magda, "What the hell? You would think he would have parked some place where I could quickly find him." He continued searching, going up and down the lines of parked cars. "He's not here. Now what?"

Magda looked around. "No, here he would have seen us driving around but perhaps he's waiting just outside the docks, further up the road. Drive out and let's look there."

Hector exited the parking area, turned right and slowly drove north on the highway to Los Mochis. Several cars passed him heading north and one car passed going south but no pickup. Hector pulled into a turnout and stopped.

"What do you think?" he asked Magda.

"I don't know. With all that money he's been waiting for, you would think he would have been here early." Magda checked the time. "It's been at least a half hour since we got off the boat. Something must have gone wrong. Do you think he tried to call you while we were on the water?"

Hector checked missed calls. "No, unless there is no service out there. I'm going to take a chance and call him. I don't know what else to do." He pressed *recent calls* and listened to the ringing. One ring, two, three, four, five. No answer. Hector became very nervous, his voice began to shake, and his heart began to race. "Dear Jesus, what should I do? You know he'll kill us if I don't deliver the money. But where the hell is he?"

Magda placed her hand on Hector's arm. "Don't panic. Something has gone wrong and he couldn't leave the house. Maybe the police have grabbed him. Anyway, we can't stay on the side of this highway anymore. Let's go home. Unless something has happened to him, you know he will call you."

"And if he doesn't?"

"We will worry about that when it happens. Now, let's go."

When they arrived at their home in Los Mochis, Magda woke the sleeping children and led them into the house. Hector unhitched the trailer then drove the car into the garage. He decided to leave the money where it was, thinking it would be safer there than in the house. He walked inside and turned on the kitchen lights. He needed some coffee and a large slug of Tequila.

Magda came out of the children's bedroom and quickly turned off the lights. "What is the matter with you? You don't need to tell everyone we are here."

"I was going to make some coffee and..."

"Never mind. I'll make it." She fumbled around in the dark but eventually had the coffee machine brewing. "I think you should try Chuy again."

Hector called but there was no answer. "Shit, something is definitely wrong."

"It's almost three o'clock. They're probably all sleeping."

"Don't be stupid. If you were them, would you be sleeping if you hadn't heard from the guy you hired to bring you a million American dollars?" Without waiting for her to reply, he added, "I'm going over there, not right to the house but close enough to see what's going on. If the cops did find him, I sure don't want to be left hanging."

Magda asked, "Why do you think they would tell the cops anything about you or where the money might be?"

"To save their hides, why not? Anyway, I'm not taking any chances of getting involved with the police." He took a few gulps of the hot coffee and went to the kitchen door.

Magda ran up to him. "You be very careful—very, very careful. If you think the cops may be there or close by, stay away. We need you, so don't do anything foolish."

Hector gave Magda a kiss and departed.

He drove to Avenida Aquiles Serdan and parked a block away from Chuy's rented house. He started to get out of the car but then stopped. He thought, *If the cops have found the place and raided it, they probably left some men to guard it. I'd better just drive past, take a quick look and move on.* And that is what he did. He drove down the street and as he came close to the house, he saw two police cars. He looked at the house and saw yellow tape stretched all around it. He didn't need to see any more. He drove to the corner, made a left turn and sped off. He turned on Boulevard Rosendo G. Castro, found an all-night coffee shop and went in. Suddenly ravenous, he ordered three eggs with green chilies, flour tortillas and coffee.

As he waited for his order, he pondered his options: *There is no doubt, the cops have Chuy and the rest of them. I wonder what happened to the boy and girl. Not my concern. If the cops have them, it will probably be on the news and in the papers. The kidnapping must have been big news since last Monday. But what do we do if the cops have all of them? They probably will sing if the cops make them a deal and that's when everyone will be looking for me and the money.*

The young waiter brought the food, refilled the coffee mug and left. Hector began eating, quickly at first but slowing down as he thought more about his predicament. *I have a million American dollars...a million! How can I keep it? There's no way I can keep it. Those bastards will rat on me. The police are probably at my house now. I've got to think this through. How can I keep it and get away with it?* He tore off a piece of the tortilla and dipped it the coffee. He ate it then washed it down with a slug of coffee, burning his mouth. He gulped some water. *What if I was to turn myself in? Would I get a reward? No, they'd throw me in jail with the rest of them. I better get home and talk this over with Magda. Maybe she'll have a good idea.*

Hector finished his meal, picked up the check and paid it. He drove home, being careful not to speed, and when he got close to home he drove by slowly and checked the house for any activity. The house was dark and quiet. He pulled into the garage, locked the garage door and entered the house.

Magda was sitting in the living room. She jumped up when Hector came in. "What did you see?"

"The cops got them. I saw the house. There's that yellow tape they use all around it. They got them for sure."

"What about the money? What are we going to do with it?"

"The boys will rat me out, you can be sure of that. So, this morning I will call the Federales and make a deal. I'll tell them where to find the money if they will not charge me with anything. I will tell them that we were threatened. I'll say that we had no part in taking the boy and girl and if we didn't follow their orders, we would be killed."

"Actually," Magda added, "that's not far from the truth. You were worried from the start that they would kill all of us if you didn't bring them the money, right?"

"That's true enough. And maybe even kill us after I gave them the money. The question is, will the cops believe it?"

Hector remained in the living room and slept in his chair. He awoke Saturday with the first morning light and checked the time, 6:12. He turned on the TV and found a local news station.

The news anchor was talking to the weather girl who had just made the weather forecast. The camera returned to the reporter.

"Once again," he announced, "here's the latest on the story we broke an hour ago. The young American girl, who was traveling in the Baja with a male companion and taken hostage near Palm Valley last Sunday, was rescued unharmed by agents of the AFI and a team composed of local police and members of the PF in Los Mochis, Sinaloa. One of the gang members was apprehended by an AFI agent as he came out of a Los Mochis restaurant—he is now in police custody. Shortly after his capture, a SWAT team forcibly entered a home in which other members of the gang were hiding.

During the ensuing gun battle, three gang members were killed. One officer was slightly injured in the melee."

In the background, still photographs showed Chuy's rented house and the yellow crime scene tape.

"The million dollar ransom was allegedly delivered by the parents of the kidnapped girl, to a man known only as Hector. Details of where and when that took place have not been released. While the girl was rescued unharmed, the boy was not. We are told that one of the gang killed the boy prior to the police raid. The boy's body has not yet been recovered."

Hector switched off the TV and hurried to his car. He drove the main road to a gas station. He got out of his car, ran to a pay phone and dialed zero. He asked the operator to connect him with an AFI agent, telling her it was an emergency. She asked what sort of an emergency and he told her it had to do with the kidnapping case. Hector waited for several minutes. A voice came on the line.

"This is Agent Torres. You have information about the kidnapping?"

"Yes, sir. I know where to find Hector and I know where the money is."

"You do? Well, that's very interesting. Tell me more, but first, what is your name?"

Hector raised his voice. "Never mind my name. Do you want to find the money or not?"

"Okay, my friend, take it easy. Of course we want to find the money. What is it you want me to do?"

"This man Hector, I heard on the news this morning, is supposed to have the money. I know this man. He told me to call you and tell you that he and his family—a wife and two small children—they had nothing to do with the kidnapping of the Americans. He said they had already been taken when a man they call Chuy, his real name is Jesus Aguilar, came to Hector's house and said he had a job for them that would pay fifty thousand American. Hector asked what kind of a job it was and Chuy said it would be fun for the family. All they had to do was go to the park where the big observatory is west of San Felipe and camp out for a few days."

"That's all, just go camping for a few days?" Torres asked.

"No, no. Chuy said a man would come in a helicopter and land in the park near the campgrounds. Hector was to run to the helicopter and tell them he was Hector and the gringo would give Hector four boxes."

Torres asked, "And what was Hector supposed to do with these boxes?"

"He was told to hide them and after a few days bring them Los Mochis and give them to Chuy."

There was a long pause. Torres asked, "Did this man Chuy tell Hector what was in the boxes?"

Hector said, "*Si.* Money. American dollars."

Torres asked in apparent disbelief, "And that's it? He was to hide the money for a few days then bring it to Chuy? Is that right?"

"That's it. But when Hector came back to Los Mochis with the money and went to Chuy's house, the cops were already there and then he heard on the news this morning what had happened."

Hector became nervous. He suspected that Torres was keeping him talking so that they could trace the call. Hector said, "I'll call you back. What is your number?"

Torres gave him a phone number. Hector hung up, got in his car and raced off. He drove a long distance taking a circuitous route before using another pay phone.

Torres answered on the first ring. "Torres here."

"It's Hector's friend again."

"So what does Hector want? I don't think he would be in trouble. If he was forced to take the job because Chuy threatened to kill his family and if he's willing to give back all of the money—all of it—chances are the American father would give him a reward, a large one. You tell Hector to call me and I'll meet with him and tell him I don't think he's in any danger, particularly since three of the gang are dead and the other one's in jail."

"Okay. I'll tell him to call you." Hector hung up, jumped in his car and took off. His cell phone rang. "¿Bueno?"

"It's me," Magda said. "The police are here. Lalo told them where we live. You better come home. They want to talk to you."

"Tell them I have been talking to an AFI agent. His name is Torres. I am going to meet with him. I've already told him what you and I talked about, you know, being threatened, Chuy saying he would kill us if we didn't do the job. The agent said if that is the case, I have nothing to worry about—maybe even get a reward from the girl's father. You tell them that."

"*Muy bien.*" Magda hung up.

Hector found another pay phone and called Torres. He changed the tone of his voice a little when Torres answered. "This is Hector. Where shall we meet?"

"I am at the AFI office downtown? You know where it is?"

"Yes. I'll be there in twenty minutes."

Torres looked across the desk at Romero. "Our man is coming here. He said he'd be here in twenty minutes."

"I've got a tail on him right now just in case he changes his mind."

"I don't think he will," Torres said. "He's got to know that there's no way he can keep that money. The first time he spent some of those Yankee dollars, we'd be on him. It's all in hundred dollar bills—not easy to spend without raising eyebrows."

Romero stood and stretched. "If he can convince us that he really was coerced into getting that money from Noble, he may be out of the woods." They both laughed at the unintended pun. "When I asked Lalo how they recruited Hector and his family, he said Chuy got him lined out. He also said that when Chuy and Hector talked on the phone, Chuy would always remind Hector what would happen to him and his family if the money wasn't delivered and on time. Hector may be telling the truth about that. We'll see if he sticks to that story."

A uniformed officer escorted Hector in. Torres got up and put out his hand. "I'm Agent Torres. This is Agent Romero." Hector released Torres' hand and shook hands with Romero.

Romero pointed to a chair. "Have a seat...ah...what is your last name?"

"Morales, Hector Morales."

"Thank you, Señor Morales. Now in your own words, tell us how it was that you got involved with Jesus Aguilar, whom you call Chuy. Take your time and try to remember every little detail. I must tell you that we will record, for the record, everything you say, so be careful and think before you speak. Good?"

"Yes, good."

Hector gave the two agents a detailed account of what took place from the time Chuy first approached him. Hector's primary theme throughout was that once he took the job he knew Chuy would kill him if he didn't follow orders. "And my poor wife and lovely little children also," he said. "Mother of God, what could I do? I never should have taken the job but it was too tempting. Besides, once Chuy told me the plan, how could I say no? Do you think a man like that is going to take no for an answer? He knew he had me hooked."

When Hector had finished, Torres, speaking in English to Romero, said, "What do you think, Bonito? Do we charge him with aiding and abetting a criminal activity? Or is he a victim of coercion, intimidation, etc., etc.?"

Romero replied, "Good question. I'll call Hierra and see what he thinks." Romero turned to Hector and in Spanish said, "Well, my friend, you have told us a very convincing story. If it is true, then I think you may not be charged with helping a known felon commit a crime—a very serious crime. However, it is not up me to decide. Personally, I think you may be okay, that is if you tell us where you hid the money and the entire million dollars is there. Can you take us to the money now?"

Hector stood. "Yes, sir. I'll show you where I hid the money. It's not far from here."

Romero noted the surprise on Torres' face, mirroring his own. He said, "It's not far from where?"

"Come with me," Hector said, "I'll show you. It's all there. You will see, the four boxes have not been opened." Hector led them to his car, opened the trunk and began throwing out the clothes and other things Magda had packed in there. Finally, the cooler was exposed. Hector pulled it out and laid it on the ground. "There it is."

Torres lifted the lid and saw the four sealed boxes. He immediately closed the lid and laughed. "Are you kidding me? You have been driving all over town with a million dollars in the trunk of your car? Man, you've got some balls, I'll say that."

Romero called for a policeman to take Hector to a holding room, telling Hector that he was not under arrest but simply being detained until it was decided by higher authorities whether or not to hold him. Romero couldn't hold back a huge smile. "This is one for the books," he said to Torres. He pointed a finger at the cooler. "It's a cool place for a cool million." He picked up the cooler and carried it to his office.

Torres was still chuckling as Romero placed a call to Hierra.

Chapter 22

Romero gave Hierra the particulars of his interview with Hector Morales. "That's his story. It sounds credible to me. Plus, we have the money, all four boxes and they are still sealed."

"Sealed? You haven't checked the contents?"

"No. I'm not going to open them. You need to tell me what we should do with them."

"Stay right there, and I'll call you back in ten minutes."

Romero hung up and said to Torres, "He's going to call me back. I think he was surprised we didn't open the boxes and check the contents."

"It's pretty obvious, no? If any of the money was missing our asses would be on the line. I don't want any part of that. The sooner we turn those boxes over to somebody, the better I'll like it."

The phone rang. "Romero."

Hierra said, "Listen, Esteban, here's what we want you and Torres to do."

Ed, Sandy and Beverly were driven to their hotel and escorted to their suite by two agents who saw them inside, inquired if there was anything more they could do and departed.

Sandy let out a cry of astonishment when she saw what was waiting for them in the suite—baskets of flowers, chocolates, and snacks of every description. There were silver buckets of champagne and bottles of wine. Two large bowls of fresh fruit were on the table.

Beverly put her hand to her mouth in surprise. "Wow! Where'd all this come from?

Ed picked up the ringing room phone. "Hello."

"Señor Noble, this is Carlos Estrada. Welcome back. We heard the wonderful news that your daughter had been rescued and we were so pleased to see her as you came in the hotel. I know you and your wife must be, how say? Overjoyed, yes?"

Ed took a deep breath. "Yes, of course we are. We want to thank you and your staff for all the wonderful things you have done for us, and for the gifts in our room. That was very thoughtful."

"Thank you, señor. It was our pleasure, but I will not keep you. We can speak later, if you wish. Good bye."

Beverly was grazing her way through the fruit and snacks. "This is sooo good," she muttered. She was trying to talk and eat at the same time. "The food they gave me was gross. Chuy got me a steak that last night and that was a little better..." A sudden flash of Chuy lying dead in the doorway made her gag.

Sandy noticed. "What's the matter, darling? Something go down the wrong pipe?"

Beverly ran to the kitchen sink to spit out the contents of her mouth. She could feel her heart throbbing. She took a couple of deep breaths then turned toward her mother. Clearing her throat, she said, "I'm okay. I got a piece of apple stuck in my throat. I'm fine." She looked around and asked, "Are there two bedrooms?"

"Yes. Are you tired, honey?" Sandy asked.

"Kinda. I'd like to lie down in a clean bed for a change. That place was filthy." Involuntarily she shuddered.

Sandy took her hand and led her to a bedroom. "Isn't this nice? And you have your own bathroom. Go ahead and lie down for a while. We aren't leaving for home until tomorrow morning. Dad's got to take care of some things before we go." Sandy turned to leave the room but returned immediately to give Beverly a long hug. "It's so good to have you back, darling." She clung tightly to the young woman. "I just hate to think about what you had to go through but at least you're back with us again and that's all that matters now."

Beverly eased back from her mothers' embrace and, with eyes glistening from emerging tears, she said, "Kevin's not coming back. What am I going to say to his parents? I mean, they're gonna want to know what happened, right? I can't tell them the truth...it would gross them out and..." A low moan escaped her lips. "I can hardly stand to think about it?" She gazed sadly at Sandy. "The memory of this will never ever go away."

Sandy held her close and whispered, "Shhh, darling. In time it will fade, you'll see." She led Beverly to the bed and pulled back the covers. "Lie down for a while and try to get some sleep. We'll talk some more later."

Sandy returned to the living room and gave Ed an enormous hug. Ed said, "Is she okay?"

"Not entirely. How could she be? She was just talking about Kevin and worrying about what she's going to tell Carl and Sherry."

"Carl and Sherry," Ed said. "What will we say? Nothing we say or anyone else says is going to make a difference, is it? Their only child is dead and that can't change, not with words or..." Ed released Sandy and went to the house phone, picked up and asked for the Kendalls' room.

"Hello." It was Sherry.

"Sherry, it's Ed. We just got back and we'd like to see you and Carl. We are so sorry."

Sherry's voice was thick with tears. "Thank you. "Is Bev with you?"

"Yes, the police flew her up. She's resting now but I think she'll be okay—eventually. Right now her nerves are a little shattered and..." He was at a loss for more words.

"Of course they are. Why wouldn't they be? She's been through so much and then Kevin..."

"Right. Anyway, Sandy and I would like to come over if..."

"Oh, Ed, not right now, please. Maybe later we can get together. We want to see Bev and talk to her but, you know, it's too soon. We don't want to upset her."

"What are your plans?" Ed asked.

Sherry didn't answer immediately. "We are driving home tomorrow morning. We need to get out of here." Clearing her throat, she said abruptly, "We'll talk later. Bye."

Beverly was awakened by the phone ringing in the other room. She heard the murmur of her father's voice. She got out of bed and went into the bathroom, splashed some cold water on her face and gazed at her image in the mirror. The tousled mop of red hair, the red-rimmed eyes and the sallow complexion caused her to grimace. "What a wreck," she muttered. She walked into the living room just as Ed hung up the phone.

Ed gave her a quick hug and kissed her forehead. "Were you able to get a little sleep?" he asked gently.

"I guess."

"Good." He glanced at the phone. "That was Agent Hierra. He's coming up with the two detectives that led the investigation."

Beverly brightened. "Oh! I need to comb my hair and wash my face so I don't gross them out. I'll be right back."

"I doubt the sight of you would 'gross out' anyone, honey, but okay." Ed chuckled a little at this sign of normalcy returning.

Ed admitted Hierra, along with Romero and Torres who were holding small suitcases. He offered them refreshments, waving his hand in the direction of all the food and drink and adding, "As you can see, the hotel has provided us with plenty."

Sandy had been napping but heard the talking and came into the living room. "Ah, Agent Hierra, how nice to see you again." She ran her fingers through her hair in an attempt to improve her look.

Hierra introduced Romero and Torres. "These two fellows are the pair I told you about, the ones who broke the case and made it possible to get Beverly out safely." There were handshakes and polite exchanges, then Hierra said to his men, "Show the señor what you have brought him."

The men opened their suitcases and brought out the four boxes.

Ed and Sandy gawked. "Are you kidding me?" Ed exclaimed. "They're still sealed. You haven't opened them?"

"No, sir. We thought we would give you the pleasure," Romero said. He reached in his pocket and handed Ed a pocket knife.

Ed went to work on the first box. He cut through the tape and opened the box, and there it was—bundles of crisp one-hundred dollar bills. Ed opened the other three boxes. All the money they had given to Hector was there. "Where did you find it? Who had it?" Ed asked.

Just then, Beverly came into the room, saw Torres and Romero and ran to them, giving each a generous hug and kiss on the cheek. "These are the guys who saved me."

The men laughed. Torres quipped, "Maybe you saved yourself, eh? We just made it possible for you to do so."

Romero added, "This man," he tapped Torres on the shoulder, "gave us the break we needed to get Chuy and his gang." He looked at Hierra. "You remember that picture he took of Chuy in the pickup? That gave us our first solid lead."

Beverly applauded and the rest joined in.

Ed picked up a box worth $250,000 and said to Hierra, "Is there any way I can give this to you guys?"

The three agents laughed. Hierra said, "I wish there were but, no. The taking of a reward for something we are paid to do would be most improper and probably put us in jail as well. As Captain Ruiz suggested, a donation to the organization that helps the families of fallen police would be allowed and very much appreciated."

Beverly held up her hand, wanting to speak. Hierra acknowledged with a nod. "What about that guy Hector, Chuy was always talking about? Did he actually have the money?"

Romero and Torres laughed. Romero said, "It's really a funny story." He gave them the details of Hector's confession, and laughed when he reached the part when Hector opened the cooler. "Imagine that idiot traveling around town all morning with a million dollars in the trunk of his car...in an ordinary Styrofoam cooler."

Torres said, "That's what I call a cool million."

"What's going to happen to Hector and his family?" Ed wanted to know. "From what you just said, it sounds like he didn't do anything wrong. It seems like he was an unwilling participant."

"That's not up to us to decide. But, I agree. He was just protecting himself and his family, no?" Hierra said.

"I'd appreciate it if you would keep me informed about what happens to him," Ed said. "After all, he did return the money. I suppose he could have tried to get away with keeping it, but he didn't, did he?"

After the agents left, the Nobles stood silently looking at each other and smiling. Ed glanced at the four open boxes of money and then in a quiet voice said to Beverly, "That's the million dollars I gave them to save your life. But if they had demanded every cent we have, I would have gladly given it to them to get you back."

Chapter 23

Ed found out from the front desk clerk that most of the downtown banks were open on Saturday but many would be closing at 3:00. He called Cipriano Gomez to arrange to deposit the ransom money, and Gomez promised to send a bank guard at once to pick it up.

"What is it that you wish me to do with the deposit?" the manager asked.

"Please open a checking account. I want to make some payments in pesos rather than dollars. Can you take care of it for me?" Ed asked.

"Of course, Señor Noble. You will need to complete some paperwork. I will send my assistant, Señorita Paz, to assist you."

"Thank you. I certainly appreciate everything you have done for us."

Gomez replied, "And I am very pleased that your money has been returned to you. How very fortunate, no?"

"Yes, sir, that is certainly fortunate, but the safe return of our daughter is the real blessing."

"*Sin duda,*" Gomez let slip. "That is, without a doubt your daughter's return is indeed a blessing. God has taken care of her, no?"

Ed smiled, picturing the faces of all who helped with the rescue. "God and some very clever AFI agents."

"Exactly. The guards and Florentina Paz should be at your hotel in thirty minutes time. If there is anything else I can assist you with, please let me know."

Ed called Ben. "Are they sending a plane down to take us back to LA?"

"Yes, sir," Ben replied. "They are sending an Embraer Phenom 100. It should be in Tijuana by no later than 9:00 tomorrow morning."

"A Phenom 100? What kind of a plane is that?" Ed asked.

Ben said, "It's a four passenger, twin engine small business jet—a really nice aircraft, and fast." As an afterthought he added, "Four seats, just right for the four of us."

Sandy called Sherry around five and asked if she and Carl would like to join them for dinner. "We'll have it brought up to our room and you'll have a chance to talk to Beverly. She really does want to talk to you and Carl. What do you say?"

"I don't know, Sandy..." Sherry's voice trailed off.

"Come on, you guys need to eat something. It'll be low key. If you want to talk about it you can, but if not, it's your decision. You have a long trip ahead of you tomorrow. We'll have a nice dinner and you can leave whenever you want, okay?"

Sherry sighed. "Let me talk to Carl. I'll call you back."

Beverly was in the room listening to her mother's side of the conversation. She picked up some grapes and popped one in her mouth. She chewed and muttered, "These are really good. You want some?"

Sandy shook her head.

"What did she say? Are they going to come over for dinner?"

"I don't know, honey. She said she'd call back. I guess she wants to talk to Carl first."

After eating a few more grapes in silence, Beverly said, "I'm gonna go down there and talk with them. They need to talk. It's gonna be hard for them—and for me, too, but they need to hear it from me and until they do, they can't, you know, like they can't start healing. It'll just keep buggin' 'em—wondering what Kevin went through, how he died—and that's not good." She opened the door and asked, "What room are they in?"

Sandy shook her head. "Are you sure you want to do this? Maybe it'd be better to wait a while."

"When am I going to see them? It's not like I'm going up to Napa. No, I'm gonna do this now. What's the room number?"

Reluctantly, Sandy said, "406."

Ed walked in from the bedroom just as the door closed. He looked around. "Did Bev just go out?"

Sandy grimaced. "Yes, she insisted on talking to Carl and Sherry."

"Is that a good idea?"

Sandy held out her hands, palms up and murmured, "Hell, I don't know."

The bank guards and Florentina Paz arrived. Sandy invited them to help themselves to the array of fruit and snacks while Ed completed the required documents. The guards declined politely and left to collect the money from Estrada, who had locked it in the hotel safe.

Ed asked Señorita Paz to open a couple of special accounts in addition to a general account. "I want you to set up an account for the benefit of Hector and Magda Morales. They live in Los Mochis, Sinaloa. AFI Agent Esteban Romero can provide an address and other information about them. I'd like the first payment of $2,000-" he paused and asked, "How many pesos would that be?"

Paz entered some numbers in a small calculator and replied, "That would be about 26,000 pesos."

"All right," Ed said. "Pay out 26,000 pesos each month starting on the first of next month and continue sending them that amount each month for five years. Also, open an account...call it Noble

Mexican Charities. Deposit $200,000 in that account. Call Captain Ruiz, he's with the PF, and tell him you have $100,000 to be disbursed to charitable funds that provide help to the widows and children of slain policemen. Have him give you, in writing, the names of the organization or organizations he thinks would be appropriate beneficiaries. After you receive his written request, send bank checks to those organizations he named. Do the same thing with Agent Hierra of the AFI."

Paz finished writing her notes and said, "That is very generous of you, señor. And I want to thank you for the gift your pilot gave me last week. That was not necessary. I was—"

Ed cut her off. "You did a personal service for us and there was an element of risk to it, so think of it as a token of our appreciation."

When everything was in order, Señorita Paz addressed Ed and Sandy. "On behalf of Señor Gomez and the bank, we wish to thank you for allowing us to handle this very delicate transaction. We are happy that your daughter is back with you and we are very sorry that her trip to Mexico was so, so ah..."

Sandy offered, "Traumatic?"

"Yes, that is the word. I do hope your next visit to our country will be much more pleasant."

"Thank you very much," Ed said. He doubted a "next visit" would take place any time soon.

An hour later, Beverly returned. With red-rimmed eyes and a rasping voice, she said, "They're coming over in about an hour. They'll have dinner with us."

The flight to Los Angeles took less than an hour. The Nobles thanked Ben for all his help, Sandy gave him a hug and said goodbye. Ed shook his hand and gave him an envelope. "Just a little something for going beyond your job description. We probably couldn't have done it without you."

On the drive home, Sandy and Beverly sat in the back seat holding hands. Sandy said, "I am so proud of you, darling. I don't know what you said to the Kendalls, but you must have done a great job because they just couldn't say enough about you."

Beverly smiled and then her smile weakened and faded. "I had to lie to them a little. I don't know if that was right but I just couldn't tell them the truth. It would have killed them. So I made up a little story. Kevin was a hero, he tried to save me—which is true in a way, but I didn't tell them all the other stuff...no..." She wiped a tear with the back of her hand.

Sandy wrapped Beverly in her arms and whispered. "You did the right thing. Now, try to get your mind off of it, okay?"

Chapter 24

The following Tuesday, in Los Mochis, Magda answered the ringing phone. "¿Bueno?"

"Is this the Morales residence?"

"Yes. Who is this, please?"

"My name is Florentina Paz. I'm with the Scotiabank Inverlat in Ensenada. Are you Magdalena Morales and is your husband, Hector?"

Magda hesitated. "What is this all about? We have no dealings with a bank in Ensenada."

"Yes, I know, but you do now. But first I need to talk to Hector Morales."

"Just a minute I will get him." Magda ran to the garage. "There is a lady on the phone from a bank in Ensenada. Come talk to her."

"What are you talking about?" Hector barked.

Magda grabbed his hand and pulled him along. "You must talk to the lady. It may be about the money."

Hector ran to the phone. "Hello, this is Hector Morales. You wish to talk to me?"

"Yes, sir," Paz replied. "I have some good news for you but first, just to be sure you are the right Hector Morales, what is your birth date?"

"August 19, 1974," Hector quickly replied.

"And I need your wife's maiden name."

"Benevidez. She is Magdalena Morales de Benevidez."

"Good. Do you know of an American man by the name of Edward Noble?"

"I do not know him, that is, I saw him one time. I am the one he gave the money to—"

"Yes, I know what you did. Señor Noble wanted to reward you for returning all of the ransom money and he has asked me to set up a trust account for you."

"A trust?"

"It is a special account for you, from which you will be paid 26,000 pesos a month for the next five years. I need to come to your home tomorrow as there are some forms you and your wife must sign. Will you be home tomorrow?"

Hector was too stunned to speak.

Paz asked again. "Señor, I said, will you and your wife be at home tomorrow to sign some papers?"

Finally, he found his voice. "Yes, yes! We will be here. At what time will you arrive?"

"I should be at your home by 1:00 tomorrow afternoon. Is that a good time for you?"

"Any time will be good. Thank you so much. We will see you tomorrow." Hector hung up and his face blossomed into a huge smile. "The gringo Noble is giving us 26,000 pesos a month for five years—five years! We are rich! The bank lady is coming tomorrow with the papers." He threw his arms around Magda and the two of them danced around the floor, laughing and crying and kissing and yelling until they fell exhausted on the couch.

Magda became serious. "We should go to the church right now and light a candle to thank God and the saints for sending us this miracle."

Hector touched Magda gently on her cheek. "And do you not think we should also thank Señor Noble and say a prayer for him as well?"

Chapter 25

Life for the Noble family didn't quite return to the way it had been only a week earlier. None of them seemed able to let the incident go. In addition, for almost a week, their home was surrounded by reporters, photographers, and a host of curiosity seekers. TV trucks from local and national news organizations clogged the road, much to the consternation of their neighbors. None of the Nobles dared venture out of the house until eventually, as with all hot news stories, the media decided it was time to focus their attention elsewhere.

Beverly went back to college but her notoriety prevented her from having any peace. Virtually everyone on the U.C. Santa Barbara campus was aware of the kidnapping. How could they not be? It had occupied huge segments of both local and national news. Her fellow students, with their incessant pursuit of sensual stories, were an ever-present intrusion on Beverly's privacy. Any thought of laying the kidnapping to rest, any chance of healing, was out of the question.

When summer vacation began, she and Pat left the condo and returned to Malibu. Bev was a wreck, but being away from all the prying eyes and ears, helped Bev find some peace. It calmed her nerves to spend time with her sister and mother or go sailing with Ed.

She particularly enjoyed sailing and proved an apt student and Ed, to Beverly's surprise, turned out to be an excellent instructor.

They had fun sailing together and when she returned from a sail, she would give Sandy and Pat a blow by blow description of everything she and Ed did during the day, including what new sailing skills she had acquired.

Pat, too, had been affected by everyone's snooping. She was determined to enroll in a different school in the fall and she persuaded Bev that neither of them would get any peace at U.C.S.B. After many family discussions, it was decided that the twins would apply to a college in the east where they hoped to be left alone. That decision was heavily influenced by the twins who, having never experienced it, thought it would be a great adventure to live in New York City or Boston or "someplace like that."

By June, applications had been sent to Columbia, Princeton, Seton Hall, Barnard and Vassar. They were invited for interviews only at Vassar since they had applied, just for the fun of it, when they were seniors at Malibu High School. Their applications were too late for the other colleges.

Ed chartered a jet and they flew east. They were accepted for enrollment at Vassar.

During their summer hiatus, the twins were inseparable. Beverly wanted to be on the boat with Ed and would have accompanied him on every outing had not Pat insisted they do something else once in a while.

With her parents and sister pressing her, Bev agreed to see a psychologist twice a week. Dr. Millstein was a character right out of a 1940s movie. He was an old—although not nearly so old as he looked—gray-bearded, soft-spoken, Jewish grandfather type. His specialty was child psychology and he was very good at it. By the time the twins were due to leave for Vassar in late August, Beverly had the most horrific dreams, the ones of Gordo tying her up and attacking her, under reasonable control. She still had dreams that shattered her nights—Gordo hitting Kevin with his gun or Gordo knocking Kevin out or Chuy lying dead on the floor. But little by little, the nightmares diminished in intensity. Dr. Millstein patiently allowed Beverly to articulate her fears and deal with them as something that certainly had been real but that was now a memory which, like most frightening memories, would eventually fade from the forefront of her consciousness.

In the fall, housed in a college dormitory, the girls joined 2,400 very savvy and mostly very wealthy students as sophomores at the prestigious college. The large campus was located in the Hudson Valley, three miles from Poughkeepsie and just seventy-five miles from New York City. Ed wrote a check for $104,000 to cover the cost of tuition, housing and other fees for their sophomore year. He also agreed to buy them a car. He contacted a dealer in Poughkeepsie and purchased a 2007 BMW sedan for $28,000. It was the all-wheel drive that clinched the deal. The girls had never experienced winter driving in snow and ice.

Ed fretted about spending so much money. After all, before winning the lottery, he had a history of self-imposed frugality. One mitigating event, however, cheered him. He sold the Santa Barbara condo for only $50,000 *less* than he had paid for it.

Chapter 26

With the twins back in school and the dreadful memories slowly waning, Sandy worked to bring her marriage back to the closeness she felt that Sunday before Mexico. As she put it, "before the money pushed us to Malibu." Sadly, those few minutes of imagined infidelity gnawed at her conscience.

An incident during the past summer gave her some comfort, and she blessed her smart daughter for providing some reassuring insight.

She and Bev had been walking on the beach one morning in July, letting the waves wash over their feet, when they heard someone behind them yell, "Hey, wait a minute!"

They turned and saw a man jogging toward them. He waved.

Bev had asked, "Do you know that guy?"

Sandy's eyes narrowed behind her sunglasses. "No, not really. He lives over there." Sandy thrust her chin in the direction of Bart's house. "Just keep walking." They continued to walk in the water. Soon, the man caught up with them.

Bart kept pace with them. "Hey, Sandy. Long time no see."

Sandy turned her head in his direction but said nothing.

Beverly finally spoke. "So, Mom, you gonna introduce us or what?"

Sandy stopped and turned. With little enthusiasm she muttered, "This is my daughter, Beverly."

Hearing nothing further, Bart said, "And I'm Bart—Bart Maddox. I live just over there in the house with the little observation tower."

Beverly looked at the house then turned her attention to Bart. *He's a nice looking man, in fact very nice looking. Why is Mom being all weird?* She blinked and offered her hand which Bart shook. "Pleased to meet you," she said.

Sandy began walking. "C'mon, Bev," she said over her shoulder. Bev jogged to catch up.

Bart kept pace with them. Sandy removed her sunglasses and gave Bart an icy scowl. "Go away, Bart. Bev and I were having an important conversation and I'd rather not have it interrupted."

Beverly gasped at her mother's rudeness.

Bart, taken aback, stopped momentarily then, realizing who Beverly was, he caught up to them again and said, "I'm sorry, Sandy, honest to God, but I just want to say that all the while you folks were in Mexico, I prayed for Beverly's safe return...honest to God, I went to church and lit a candle for her and you know what a lousy Catholic I am, but I prayed for you," he said to Beverly. "And I'm so glad you are back home and safe."

"Thank you, Mr. Maddox. That was real nice of you."

"Okay, Bart," Sandy said sternly. "You've told her, so now just go away." She took hold of Beverly's hand, turned around and headed for home at a brisk pace.

Beverly looked back and saw Bart standing, hands on hips, looking in their direction. "So, what the heck was that all about?" she asked.

Sandy didn't reply for a full minute then she stopped and looked squarely at her daughter. "It was about nothing, nothing at all except I don't like that man." She paused, then added, "He did a very bad thing and...and that's it." She turned and resumed walking toward the house.

Beverly followed her. "What do you mean, 'he did a bad thing'? What bad thing?"

Sandy's reply was gruff. "I don't want to talk about it. Besides, it's none of your business."

Tears began to build in Beverly's eyes as she looked at Sandy in bewilderment.

Sandy quickly gathered Beverly in her arms. "Oh, sweetheart," she murmured, "I'm so sorry. I didn't mean that. Of course it's your business, but it was such a horrid thing I've done and with everything you've been through, I can't burden you with yet something else—not now anyway. Please, don't ask me anything more just now." She hugged Beverly even more tightly and kissed her forehead and cheeks. "Just promise me you won't say anything about this to your father or Patty. Okay?"

"You had an affair with that guy, didn't you, and now you're regretting it. Hey, Mom, it's okay, I get it. Things like that happen all the time. Relax, I won't say a word to anybody."

Sandy relaxed her grip and took a step back. "No, honey, I did not have an affair with Bart or any other man—ever. That's the truth. I love your father and I've always been faithful to him."

Beverly gave her mother a puzzled look. "Now, I don't get it. So you never had an affair—"

"That's right but there was one time—" Sandy groaned as the memory of that moment flashed across her mind. "Just one time when I was drunk, I mean falling down drunk, and Bart got me." She hastened to add, "Although being drunk is no excuse. I was barely aware of what was happening until it was too late." She shook her head. "It was all over in two minutes. When I realized what had just happened I told him to get out and never ever try to see me again." Sandy swallowed. "I remember that day so vividly. That's the day I decided to quit drinking and get a job so I'd have something to do. Actually it was after that when your dad and I decided to devote time and money to doing charity work."

Beverly said, "So, you see, there was some good to come out of it."

Sandy said dryly, "You're too kind, but yes, I guess so."

"Mom, listen. What happened to you is like what happens all the time at college. Date rape. Girls get drunk and the first thing you know, some guy is doing it to 'em."

Sandy gave her a small smile. "That's what it was, for sure."

They arrived at the house and sat down at the kitchen table.

"You should tell Dad. He'd understand it was a mistake. I mean, you weren't looking to get laid." Beverly put her hand to her mouth and muttered, "Whoops, that just popped out, sorry."

That remark broke the tension and Sandy let loose a resounding laugh. "It's okay, honey, I use that word too."

Beverly seemed at a loss for what to say next. She looked at Sandy. "Okay, as long as we are making confessions today, I guess you deserve one too. Kevin and me, we had sex—quite a few times actually. I lied to you. We did it at the condo before we went to Mexico. Pat knew about it. You know we tell each other everything, but I made her swear she wouldn't say anything to you guys."

Sandy laid both palms on the table and gave Beverly a sweet smile. "Honey, we were pretty sure you and Kevin were sleeping together. It came as something of a surprise but we weren't exactly shocked. Do you think I was a virgin when your dad and I got married?" She straightened up and laughed. "You don't have to answer that." She laughed again. "If you could see the look on your face!"

Beverly giggled and then said more seriously, "You know, in one of my sociology classes or maybe it was a Human Behavior course, I can't remember, we read studies about extramarital affairs and it turns out that fifty to sixty percent of husbands and forty-five to fifty-five percent of wives had sex with someone who wasn't their spouse. I mean, like that's a lot of married people hooking up, so when you think about your deal, it doesn't seem so bad, does it?"

Sandy reached for Beverly's hands. She leaned in and whispered, "What other people do, and what other people think about what other people do, doesn't change my perspective on what happened that terrible afternoon. The bottom line is, willingly or not, I committed adultery and that is a sin."

Although Beverly clearly didn't agree, she wisely hadn't commented.

Chapter 27

Sherry Kendall had kept in touch with Sandy, but her messages were full of self-recrimination. She never should have done this, or allowed that, or, or, or. All the imagined reasons why her son was now dead—not at the hands of a foreign assassin, but because she and Carl had failed the boy in so many ways. Sandy tried hard to convince her otherwise. It was nonsense, and Sandy told her so. She reminded Sherry that they had absolutely nothing to do with Kevin's murder, nor could they have done anything to save their boy. Fate and circumstance had done the job and the only thing they could do at the time was stand by helplessly and observe the outcome.

In one of her emails to Sherry, Sandy wrote, 'Did you remind Kevin that Mexico was a dangerous place? Of course you did. Had Beverly asked, we would have said the same. Regardless, it would not have deterred them from going there and once there, neither you nor we could possibly have had any influence over what took place. That is what you must tell yourselves because that is the truth—that is the reality.'

Sandy discussed the exchange of emails with Ed one evening. "After all," she explained, "what could I say? Things like this happen and the only one to blame, if one feels the need to assign blame, it would be Kevin for going down there in the first place."

Ed's reply was thoughtful. "Or Beverly. For all we know, she talked him into the trip."

"What?" Sandy was incredulous. "Bev talked Kevin into going...?"

"Why not? Patty told me that Bev was the one who ran that relationship, so it's possible—in fact it's likely it was her idea. Of course, that's something I'll never ask her," he added emphatically.

Stifling a sigh, Sandy glanced into the dining room. "Mrs. Weir has dinner on the table. Ready to eat?"

Ed headed for the bathroom. "I'll be right there."

The dinner Mrs. Weir had placed before them was, as usual, very tasty, well-balanced, and different. Sandy took a bite of the veal and exclaimed, "How does she come up with all these incredible meals?"

Ed chuckled. "Why don't you ask her—better still, find out how she does it. You never know, you may have to do all the cooking some day."

"Not as long as you have anything to say about it or we go broke, whichever comes first."

"By the way," Ed said, "what do you hear from the Kendalls? You're still staying in touch with them aren't you?"

"Funny you mention that. I was talking to Sherry this morning. I meant to tell you. She invited us to come up to Napa and stay with them for a long weekend."

"What did you tell her?" Ed asked.

"I said I'd talk to you about it, which is what I'm actually doing now. Would you like to go up there? She said their home is close to the fifteenth hole on the Silverado golf course. I guess Carl is a big-time golfer."

Ed got up from the table to answer the house phone. It was Carl Kendall. "Carl—hey, this is really weird. Sandy and I were just talking about you two, no kidding. How are you and Sherry doing?"

"We're doing a lot better, thanks. So, you were talking about us? What about?"

"Sandy told me that Sherry had invited us to your place for a visit. Do you know about that?"

"Sure, I know about it. Are you going to do it?"

"Probably. Do you have room to put up all four of us?"

Carl laughed. "And then some. This house has five bedrooms. We sure would love to have you and Sandy and the girls spend some time with us and you can assure Beverly that Mexico will not be part of any conversation, unless she wants to talk about it."

Ed said, "That's fine. We'll set something up, okay?"

"Good." Carl paused a moment then said, "The reason I called today is to talk to you about all the expense you went to, part of which was on our behalf. I know it must have cost you a fortune for the helicopter and all the other expenses, and we sure would feel lot more comfortable if you would allow us to pay at least some part of it."

Ed wasn't sure what to say but he quickly made up his mind. "Listen, Carl, you don't owe me anything. If you remember, I told you right from the start, even before we left for Mexico, that I would take care of it—the chopper and the rest of it. You remember that?"

"Yeah, but—"

"No, no buts. I told you not to worry about the cost, that I could handle it. I don't want to sound like a jerk, but really, my lifestyle won't change because of what I spent on that deal. Besides, I got the entire million back. I never thought that would happen, did you?"

"That certainly was unexpected. Anyway, we do want to show our appreciation and you folks need to let us do something."

"Come on, there's nothing you need to do except get on with your lives and stay in touch with us. That would make us happy."

Sandy, overheard the last comment. "Is that Carl?" she mouthed. Ed nodded.

Sandy whispered, "Invite them down to spend a long weekend with us."

"Carl, you want to do something for us?"

"That's what I've been saying."

"How about this? Come down to Malibu and spend some time with us. We can talk about what happened or we don't need to. You can set the agenda about that. Regardless, it would be great seeing you two again and just spend a little time together."

Carl said, "That does sound nice. Thanks. Tell you what. I'll talk about it with Sherry and call you back. But, one way or another, you and I are going to get straight."

"Fine, whatever. Meanwhile, talk to Sherry and tell us when you can come down."

"All right. Thanks again. So long."

Sandy asked, "Are they going to come down?"

"Carl's going to talk to Sherry and let us know."

Ed walked back to the table, picked up his coffee cup and desert plate and rinsed them off in the pot sink.

"I'll get those," Sandy said.

Ed opened the dishwasher drawer. "It's okay. I've got it." He turned, leaned against the counter and gave his wife a wide smile.

Sandy looked up from a copy of *Cosmopolitan* she was leafing through and returned the smile. "What?"

"Nothing. Can't I admire a pretty woman, even if she is my wife?"

"Of course. Nothing wrong with that." She stood and lifted her blouse, exposing her breasts. "Here, have a good look. Okay, that's enough, unless you want to take it to the next level."

Pat answered her cell phone. "Hi, Mom, what up?"

"'What up?' Really? You're at Vassar, for gosh sake. You shouldn't talk like that. What's your next line? 'Yo, I be g'ttin' down wid da sistahs in da hood'?"

Pat exploded in laughter. Catching her breath, she exclaimed, "Yo mama. Wah-it-be?" More raucous laughter. "You crack me up."

"Okay, hot stuff. I was just trying to get back to my roots. Seriously, though, you get in the habit of talking like that and it will just pop out sometime when you might want to demonstrate that you're a serious Vassar grad."

"Okay, okay. I get the picture. I'll put on my Vassar cap and gown and we'll have like a serious talk about...what?"

"And that's another thing you should stop...saying 'like' all the time. That doesn't make any sense and it certainly isn't good English. And saying 'goes' when you mean 'said' is another thing you should—"

"Okay, let's get on with what you really called about."

"Well, first of all, is Bev with you?"

"No, she's in class and I'm on my way to one."

"Okay. Tell me how she is doing, emotionally. Is she still having nightmares?"

Pat thought about it for a moment. "I guess she's doing better, but yeah, she's having trouble sleeping and she still wakes up in the middle of the night screaming. It's not every night, you know, but—"

"Is she still talking to Dr. Millstein?"

"Yes. She calls him two, three times a week."

"Do you think she's getting any better?"

"I guess. But here's one of the problems." Pat sat down on a nearby bench. "As you can imagine, guys from around here and from schools in the City come over here trolling for girls—the younger ones, know what I mean?"

Sandy let out a sigh. "Yes, I'm afraid I do. They think the young girls will be easy. Believe me, it's not just at Vassar."

Pat replied, "I'm sure. Anyway, a couple of guys from NYU were talking to Bev and me last Saturday at the Student Union. They didn't believe, like—sorry, we were twins or even sisters. They asked our names. I was going to give 'em some phony name but Bev blurted out her name and mine—"

"And the cat was out of the bag," Sandy finished.

"Right. At first I guess our names didn't mean anything special to them but later on, this one guy, Mark, he all of a sudden goes—oops, says that he knew he'd heard Bev's name before and asks her if she was the girl who got kidnapped by the Mexicans."

Sandy moaned. "Oh hell. Then what?"

"Bev jumped up and says to me, 'Let's go.' So, we go, leaving those guys wondering, what did we do?"

Sandy thought about it for a moment then asked, "Do any of your classmates know about it?"

"I suppose, but at least nobody has ever said anything to me about it. Bev complains about it all the time. It really bugs her."

Sandy said, "It's old news but I imagine some of the kids would like to hear about it first-hand from Bev."

"I'm sure they would. They sure did at Santa Barbara, and Bev hated it." Pat looked at her watch. "Hey, Mom, I gotta get to class. I'll call you later, okay?"

"Sure. Tell Bev I'd like to talk to her. Love you."

"Love you too, Mom. Bye."

Of course Beverly's classmates and others were interested once the word got out that the Beverly Noble at Vassar was the same Beverly Noble who had been kidnapped last May by a bunch of Mexican bandits. They knew the story, at least the TV and newspaper versions of it, and they could—and did—go online to get old news reports. They knew her boyfriend had been killed. They were eager to learn more, and who was best able to tell them the real story, all the sleazy and sexy details? Who indeed?

At the end of each class, Beverly began to hurry to her next class, or, if she was between classes, she would flee to her dorm room. She tried wearing disguises, even had her hair dyed black but not many were fooled. It was too late. Some of the girls wanted to befriend her and Bev did accept the friendship of a few. But inevitably, the conversation would drift to her adventure in Mexico. Within a short time her new friends would ask, *What was it like? Did they try to, you know, like do anything? What really happened to your boyfriend—what did they do to him? Have they ever found his body? What was he like? Were you sleeping with him?* And on and on.

It was three in the morning and Pat was sitting on the side of Bev's bed holding her hand and cooing, "It's okay—it was a dream, that's all. C'mon, relax, you're okay."

"I can't handle it," Bev moaned. "This sucks. I'm out of here. I'm not kidding, Patty, I'm going home. They just won't leave me alone. They don't give a crap about me—all they really want to know is what those creeps did to me. Did they rape me? What was it like? Between that and my dreams of Gordo sticking his filthy fat fingers in my pussy or beating up Kevin and killing him—" She threw her head back hard against the headboard and screamed, "I give up! They win, okay?" Her head dropped down. She sucked in several deep breaths and whispered, "They win. They beat me." She slowly raised her head and focused on Pat who sat speechless, mouth open, horrified. She had never before seen her sister so defeated.

After a while, Bev spoke. "I'm sorry, baby. I hate to lay all this on you." She reached for Pat's hand. "Being here is a waste of time. You understand, right? I can't study or get anything done. I can't sleep. I'm tired all the time." She took hold of Pat's other hand and softly but emphatically said, "I'm sorry, but I gotta go home."

Chapter 28

Sherry called Sandy to accept the invitation to visit. Sandy was pleased. "Ed and I share something with you, something no one else in the whole world can possibly know or understand. Besides that, we should be friends. We'd like to maybe take a trip with you or have you take a ride on Ed's boat or just hang out with us here. We live right on the beach, there are great restaurants and things to do and see. It will be fun."

"Okay, I'll make a deal with you. We'll come down for a couple of days, if you and Ed and the girls, if they want to, absolutely promise to come up here for that visit Carl talked with Ed about." Sherry said.

"You've got yourself a deal."

"Okay. How about we arrive next Friday afternoon?"

"Perfect. We'll probably go sailing so pack accordingly. See you then."

Sandy walked through the front hall to Ed's office. "Okay. They're coming down this Friday afternoon. We left the departure date open. I told her we might go sailing."

Ed swiveled his chair to face her. "By the way, did you talk to the twins today?"

Sandy sat down in the large leather chair next to the bookcase. "I talked to Pat this morning. I asked her to have Bev call me but she hasn't called yet. When I do talk to her, I get the feeling that something is bugging her. I mean, you know, besides the usual bad dreams."

"Like what?"

"I'm not sure. Pat tells me Bev isn't making any friends and some of the kids are bugging her about what happened in Mexico, which Pat says makes Bev crazy."

Ed said, "I can sure understand that."

Sandy tilted her head back and looked up at the ceiling. "And...I don't know." She lowered her head and looked at Ed. "I know Bev is having problems but she doesn't say anything about them to me."

"I'm sure she tells Pat." Ed stood and stretched. "I'll call Beverly tomorrow. Right now, I'm going to take a little walk on the beach. Want to come along?"

Beverly looked up from the computer screen. "I've got a reservation for Sunday morning at 10:25 from LaGuardia." She checked the screen. "Just one stop in Chicago. It gets into LA at 2:48. Do you want to drive me to the airport? It's about eighty miles. Maybe I should take a cab."

Pat leaned over Bev's shoulder and looked at the screen. "No cab. We have a GPS so I guess we can find it okay. Sunday morning... shouldn't be very much traffic. But we have to leave pretty early to get to the airport by nine."

Bev brought up Google and typed in, driving time Poughkeepsie to LaGuardia Airport. "Okay, it's an hour and a half." She then checked a route map. "Most of the trip will be on the Taconic Parkway and a couple other parkways so that shouldn't be too bad. What do ya think?"

Pat said, "You better print the map just in case." She sprawled out on the bed. When she heard the printer stop, she asked, "Did you tell Mom and Dad you dropped out and are coming home?"

"No, not yet."

"Well, it's Thursday. When are you gonna tell 'em?"

"Here's what I intend to do: When we stop in Chicago, I'll call them up and tell them I'm coming home and would they please pick me up. They'll go crazy but they can't do anything about it by then. That's what I'm going to do and you are not going to say one damn thing about it when they call you."

"For sure, they'll be calling me." Pat snorted. "You can bet on that, and what am I supposed to tell them?" She looked thoughtfully at Bev. "Do you know how tired I am of covering for you? I love you—you know that—but you gotta stop asking me to lie to Mom and Dad all the time." She buried her face in the pillow.

Bev lay down on the bed next to Pat. She turned on her side and said, "I'm sorry to drag you into this, but when I get home I'll explain everything to them and say that I made you promise you wouldn't say anything. I promise." Bev rolled onto her back, put her hands behind her head and stared at the ceiling. She spoke softly. "I'm going to tell you something that I haven't told anyone." She paused, licked her lips and rolled her head from side to side. "No one knows this...no one."

She took a breath and exhaled slowly. "Kevin didn't want to go down to Mexico. He wanted to go someplace in the desert where he could race around in the sand. That's what he really wanted to do. I talked him out of it...I mean, I said I didn't want to do that, the desert thing. I insisted we go someplace in the Baja and get a room and make out all weekend. Anyway, he still didn't want to go but I kept buggin' him. I looked up hotels on the internet and made a reservation at that hotel outside of Ensenada. Anyway, he gave in and we went down there." She drew her arm across her face. "I guess you could say I'm to blame for him getting beat up and killed."

Pat sat up. "Oh, my God! So that's what it is. That's why you're having such a hard time getting over it. You feel responsible for Kevin's death, don't you?"

"Of course. How else could I feel? I killed him and there's no way that'll ever change."

It was Friday afternoon and Sherry called to give Sandy their ETA.

"Okay. See you in a little bit." Sandy hung up and popped her head into Ed's office. "That was Sherry. She said they should be here around 4:15."

Ed glanced at the clock on his desk. "I'd better change my clothes." He looked at Sandy. "Is that what you're wearing?"

She blinked and looked down at her blouse and slacks. "Yes. Something wrong with it?"

Ed laughed and planted a kiss on her lips. "You look too cute, Pilcher, and you'll make Sherry jealous. You wouldn't want to do that, would you?" Chuckling, he turned and walked out of the room.

Sandy sat at the desk and dialed Beverly's cell phone. After five rings the call went to voicemail. "Honey, it's Mom. Where the heck are you and why don't you return my calls? Is something wrong? Please call me when you get this. I'm worried about you. Love you." She laid the handset in its cradle and tried to hold back emerging tears. What was going on with that girl? She picked up the phone and dialed Pat.

"Is that you, Dad?"

"No, it's me. Listen, I just tried calling your sister for the umpteenth time today and she doesn't answer and she hasn't returned any of my calls. What's going on?"

Pat hesitated, trying hard to think up a good answer. "She's in her room sleeping. She was up most of the night until I finally convinced her to take those pills Dr. Millstein gave her. They knocked her out and I don't think I should wake her. She really needs the rest."

Sandy's voice betrayed her concern. "Listen to me, young lady. I want to know exactly what is going on with her. You're not fooling me, you know. Now, you tell me, has something happened to Beverly? And no bull this time!"

Pat became flustered and stammered, "Nothing real bad, Mom, really. Okay, she's talking about quitting school and going home. Just talking about it, but I'm thinking that maybe that's what she's gonna do. There's a lot of pressure on her here with people bugging her about the kidnapping and all. It's getting her down and she feels like she needs to get away from it."

"Ah, so, that's it. Okay, and what are you advising her to do?"

"You know, I can understand it. She's not happy here. We talk about it all the time. She said that she's going to make up her mind about leaving and call you Sunday with her decision. So, just leave her alone for a couple of days and I promise that she'll call you Sunday. Okay?"

"God, Patty, I feel so helpless here. I wish you hadn't gone so far away." After a thoughtful pause, Sandy said, "Alright, we will wait to hear from her on Sunday, but I'm telling you, if she doesn't call and tell us truthfully what her situation is, we'll charter a plane and come out there. I'm not kidding. This is serious and could impact her recovery. I'm counting on you to give her good advice and not let her do anything rash or stupid...you know what I mean? And Patty, call me as often as you can so I can stay up to speed, okay?"

"Okay, Mom. Don't worry. It's going to be alright. It may be a little rough for a while, but I'm sure everything will work out and she'll be okay."

"I hope so," Sandy whispered. "Okay, darling. Love you, bye-bye." The clock read 4:10. *Damn, they'll be here in a few minutes. I wish they weren't coming now.* She hurried to the kitchen. "Mrs. Weir," she said, "I think we'll eat at seven. Is that okay with you?"

"Whenever you like. It's all set to go and I'm just making the dessert now—crème brûlée."

"Sounds great. Thank you." She walked into the master bedroom just as Ed was coming out. "Well, you look pretty dapper." She sniffed. "What's that you've got on?"

"I don't know. Something in a fancy bottle. I think you bought it for me."

Sandy took hold of Ed's arm. "I just had a long and very disturbing talk with Pat."

"Oh. About Bev?"

Sandy nodded.

"And what did Pat say?" The doorbell rang. "Crap. Here they are. Okay, you can tell me later." Ed hurried to the front door and opened it. "Hi, come on in. Great to see you again."

Sandy returned Sherry's hug and kiss on her cheek. "So good to see you. Welcome to our home."

Carl and Ed shook hands and exchanged greetings. Carl turned to Sandy who gave him a hug. "Thanks a lot for inviting us," he said.

Sandy gestured toward the stairs. "Come on. Let's go up and I'll show you to your room and afterward, if you like, we'll take a little stroll on the beach."

Sherry's attention was fixed on the expanse of glass opposite the entry. "You really are right on the ocean. This is fantastic."

After getting the Kendalls settled in and inviting them for cocktails in the den, Ed and Sandy slipped away to Ed's office downstairs. Ed took hold of Sandy's arm, his look severe. "Alright, tell me quickly before they come down, what was your conversation with Pat about?"

Sandy sat down in the leather chair and Ed rolled his desk chair close. In the span of five minutes, Sandy gave Ed a synopsis of her conversation, ending with, "And that's about it."

Ed shook his head in dismay. "Oh, man," he moaned. "And now we've got these guys to deal with. Christ!"

"I know, it couldn't be a worse time but we have to, you know, not let them see. We need to show them a positive attitude. I don't know how long they are staying but I'm guessing it won't be more than two or three days and after that—"

"We'll fly to New York and see what needs to be done. If she wants to drop out of school and come home, we'll just have to let her do it and then when she's here do whatever we can to pull her out of her doldrums. Maybe daily sessions with the shrink would help."

Sherry and Carl peeked in the office doorway. "Oh, there you are," Sherry said. "Is this a good time?"

"You bet," Ed said, as he and Sandy jumped up, full of smiles, and escorted their guests to the bar in the den.

Chapter 29

Pat called Sandy Saturday morning and told her that Beverly had a better night and was still considering her options but would definitely call home Sunday morning with her decision. After spending fifteen minutes talking to Sandy and another five with Ed, Pat hung up. She gave Bev a thumbs up, saying, "Okay. How did I do? I think they're cool."

"You did good. Thank you." Bev smiled at Pat. "Now, let's take the car to town and buy a bunch of boxes and tape and I'll pack up my stuff and we can take it down to FedEx and ship it this afternoon."

"Oh, I almost forgot. Mom told me that Kevin's folks are visiting," Pat said.

"What? What do you mean? They're at our house now?"

"Yeah. They invited them down for a visit about a week ago and they showed up yesterday afternoon."

"Crap!" Bev exploded into a tirade of swear words. "This sucks. Damn it, just what I need! Did she say when they were leaving?"

"Not exactly. All she said was that she didn't think they would stay more than a few days. They could be gone by the time you get there tomorrow afternoon."

Bev slumped down in a chair. "Why the hell doesn't anything ever go right for me anymore?"

Pat knelt beside her sister. "Come on. Don't get all pissy about it. Mom and Dad will know you're coming home after you call them tomorrow morning. I'm sure they'll tell the Kendalls and they'll split. They probably won't want to be around when you get there. So, don't worry about it."

"Yeah, I suppose." For Bev, the relief she'd felt about making the decision to go home was marred by the specter of seeing the Kendalls again. "It's just that everything I do anymore ends up—"

Pat grabbed Bev's hand and pulled her up. "Get over it, okay? Get dressed and let's get going."

Ed and Sandy were sitting at the table in the breakfast room drinking coffee. They had been talking about Beverly when Carl and Sherry stepped into the kitchen.

Sandy looked up and gave them a cheery greeting. "Good morning. How are you this morning?"

"Great," Carl replied. "That bed is really comfortable."

"Come in and have a seat. How about some coffee and breakfast?" Ed asked. "What would you like?"

The Kendalls placed their breakfast order. Sandy stood at the range preparing fried eggs and sausage patties then brought the loaded plates to the table. Ed filled glasses of orange juice and made toast. "What else can I get you?" he asked.

Carl said, "Nothing at all. This is great."

Sherry said, "That dinner last night was fabulous. Your cook is really talented. Does she fix your meals every day?"

"Gosh no. Just dinner five nights a week," Sandy said.

The conversation rolled along affably with small talk until Sherry asked, "What do you hear from Beverly? Is she enjoying Vassar?" She intercepted a glance between Ed and Sandy, and said, "Oh, I'm sorry. If you'd rather not get into any of—"

Sandy jumped in. "No, no. It's okay." She looked at Ed who simply rolled his hands as if to say, go ahead. "The truth is, she isn't doing very well. She is constantly plagued by nightmares that keep her awake most of the night and leave her exhausted."

Carl shook his head in dismay while Sherry made little clucking sounds.

Ed said, "As you can imagine, this makes attending classes and studying darn near impossible. On top of that, and we heard this from Pat, people are bugging Bev about the kidnapping. They want to know all the details."

Sherry nodded. "I understand that. We get that, too." She sighed.

Sandy patted her arm. "Yes, us, too, but not so much anymore." She sipped her coffee. "It's worse for Bev—other kids can be so insensitive. So she is thinking about leaving school. We haven't talked to her in several days but Pat tells me what's going on." Sandy thought about leaving it at that but continued. "I think it was a mistake letting the girls go to school back east."

Ed added, "They can't seem to get away from the notoriety, no matter how far they go. Pat told me that Beverly even dyed her hair black so that people wouldn't recognize her, but I guess that's something she should have done before she started school. Anyway, it's a lousy situation, that's for sure."

Sherry asked, "Is she getting any help, like seeing a doctor, a psychologist or..."

"Yes," Sandy said, "She was seeing an excellent psychiatrist before she left for school and now she calls him frequently, but maybe that's not the same as talking one on one."

Carl asked, "What do you think will happen?"

"I'm not sure. She promised she would call us tomorrow morning with her decision about whether she'd stay in school or come home." Sandy stood and picked up some of the dirty dishes. "Anyway, Ed and I talked it over. I'm going to tell her to come home."

The others pushed back their chairs and brought dishes to the sink.

Sherry put her arms around Sandy and hugged her. "I'm so sorry she's having such a hard time coping with this. But, you know, it was a horrendous experience and it's certainly understandable that she can't just put it behind her. We lost a son." She swallowed hard. "But there's finality to that. He's gone. Nothing we can do except grieve." Sherry stepped back, but held on to Sandy's shoulders. "It's different for Beverly. Hopefully, given time, the horror of it will fade."

"God, I hope so." Sandy murmured.

Ed tried to brighten the mood by suggesting that perhaps the cure for lifting all their spirits would be a pleasant sail on his boat.

"That would be fun. We're looking forward to seeing your boat." Carl said.

Ed nodded and Sandy said, "It's a really nice boat and Ed is an excellent skipper. Let's pack a picnic and go, what do you say?"

Sunday morning, Pat and Bev left for LaGuardia at 7:15. As Pat had predicted, the traffic was light as they cruised down the Taconic Parkway at seventy miles an hour. Pat turned the radio volume down. "I've been thinking about what you said yesterday about like it's your fault that Kevin is dead."

Bev looked over at her. "What?"

"I'm just saying, you think it's your fault he was killed because you made him go down to Mexico instead of going someplace in the States."

Bev folded her arms across her chest. "Well, that's right. That's what I believe because that's what happened."

"No, you're wrong!" Pat gripped the wheel more tightly. "Let's say he'd won the argument and you ended up like going someplace in the desert where he could race his Jeep around. And let's say, he rolled the Jeep over and got himself killed. The way you talk, that would be your fault too, because you didn't stop him from going there and screwing around with the Jeep." Pat scowled. "Like I've been saying, stuff happens sometimes and you have no control over it. I mean, you guys could have gone to a movie and some idiot with an assault rifle comes in...you know, like that deal in Colorado and he kills Kevin and a bunch of other people." Pat signaled for a lane change. "Just because you picked the movie to go to, does that make you responsible for Kevin getting killed?" She moved to the left to pass a semi.

Bev shook her head. "It's not the same, Patty. This thing is way different. It's..." She looked out of the window and watched the cars on the other side of the parkway. "It's not the same." Pat started to speak but Bev spoke over her, "Look. Let it go. It doesn't matter what you think or Dr. Millstein thinks or what anybody thinks. I know how I feel about it and that's not going to change just by people telling me something different." She looked at Pat. "Let's just drop it for now, okay?"

Pat reached over and patted Bev's knee. "Okay, baby. I'm just trying to help."

"I know." Bev turned the volume up on the radio and sat back with her head against the headrest.

Pat's tone brightened as she said, "I'll be coming home during the Christmas break and we can do some fun things while I'm there. And after school ends in May, I'm going to leave."

Bev rolled her head to the side to look at Pat. She wrinkled her brow. "Going to leave? You mean not go back in the fall?"

"That's right. Here's what I think we should do, and don't get all negative about it. I think we should both enroll at Pepperdine and live at home with Mom and Dad. Hmmm? What do ya think?

Life would be a whole lot easier for everybody and you would be in a friendly environment where you wouldn't have any hassle."

Beverly smiled. "Yeah, that would be a good idea except I know you love the whole Vassar thing and—"

Pat blew air rudely through her closed lips. "I don't give a crap about Vassar! Where the hell did you get that idea? Besides, you and I have always been together and I want to keep it that way, if you don't mind." She pointed. "Oh, look. There's the exit for the airport." She took the off-ramp and followed the signs to Departures, pulling up in front of the American Airlines area. "Okay, end of the line." She got out and opened the trunk. Bev came around and grabbed one of the two suitcases while Pat took hold of the other. Then they set the suitcases down and hugged. "I'm going to miss you," Pat whispered.

"Me, too," Bev replied, gulping back tears.

"Call me when you get home and like every day, okay? I need to know how you're doing and what's going on." Pat brushed away the tears. "I love you, sweetie, so, you know, take care and work hard at getting better."

Bev blinked as tears began to form. "I love you too—you know that, right? And, don't worry, I'm gonna be okay. I just need a little peace and quiet and a lot of rest."

Pat waved at a skycap. "You got five dollars to give to the guy?"

The porter arrived, took hold of the two suitcases and said, "This way, miss."

One more fierce hug and Bev disappeared into the terminal.

Bev sat in First Class, seat 3A. When the rest of the passengers were on board, she took out her cell phone and saw a text from Pat—*have a good trip...love you.* She looked at her watch, 10:30. The cabin attendant, a tall, exceptionally attractive woman, probably in her early forties Bev guessed, was securing the cabin door. She motioned to the attendant who was standing up front preparing to give the departure speech.

"Is there something you need?" the attendant asked.

Bev noticed her name badge, *Missy*. "How long does it take to get to our first stop?"

Missy gave Beverly a sweet smile. "We will stop in Chicago in a little over two hours."

"Thank you." Bev made a quick calculation and determined she would be in Chicago about 10:00 California time. *I'll call them from there.* She sent Sandy a text. *I've decided to quit school and come home. I am on a plane now. When we stop in Chicago, I'll call you. My flight gets into LAX at 2:12 your time. I'm on AA flt 7703. Will you pick me up? Or order a car to pick me up? Either way is fine. Love you. Talk to you soon.* Bev read her message twice, and sent it.

After Sunday breakfast, the Kendalls went upstairs to their room, packed their bags, thanked Ed and Sandy for their hospitality, and walked to their car.

Eyeing Carl's car, Ed asked, "How do you like the Mercedes?"

"It's a great car,' Carl replied. "I've been driving them for quite a while. Sherry has one too—a convertible."

Sherry added, "I love that car." She gave Ed a hug. "That boat ride and the rest of it yesterday, it was just a delightful day. Thank you so much for everything and please remember our deal. You'll be paying us a visit soon, right?"

"Right," Ed and Sandy said in unison.

"When you talk to Beverly, tell her we always think about her. She is in our prayers every day. I mean it. Every day." She hugged Sandy and Ed.

Sandy said, "I'll tell her and we'll look forward to seeing you in Napa."

Carl shook Ed's hand then added a manly hug. He hugged Sandy and whispered, "It'll be alright. Give Bev a little time."

Ed and Sandy waved goodbye as their guests backed out of the drive and headed north. Ed took hold of Sandy's hand as they walked back in the house. "That went well, don't you think?"

"It turned out a lot better than I thought it might. I was afraid they'd want to rehash everything and we'd all end up in tears. But it turned out okay. I admire their ability to move on. And they really did like being on the boat. That was nice."

Ed looked at his watch. "It's almost nine, which would be noon in New York. I thought Pat told you Bev would call us this morning."

"She probably was thinking about the three-hour time difference and didn't want to call too early." Sandy reached for her cell phone. "Oh—I have a text from Bev. Oh! Ed!" She held the phone out to him.

When the plane reached cruising altitude, the flight attendant worked the first class cabin taking drink orders. When she came to Beverly she asked. "May I get you something to drink?"

Beverly looked at her and smiled. "Yes, please. I'll have a vodka and orange juice."

Missy blinked in surprise. "You want vodka at," she looked at her watch, "Eleven o'clock? May I ask your age?"

"I'm nineteen, but so what? What does it matter up here?"

"Well, it does matter. You have to be twenty-one. I can bring you an orange juice but sorry, no vodka."

Beverly scowled and in a gruff voice said, "Fine, whatever. Wait a minute, make it black coffee."

When Missy had completed her beverage service, she returned to Bev's row and asked, "May I sit here with you for a minute?"

Bev looked at her warily. "I guess."

Missy sat down and offered Bev a warm smile. "You're going to LA. Do you live there?"

"No, I live in Malibu. It's west of—"

"I know where it is, been there many times. In fact I lived with a guy who had a home on the beach. Yeah, I guess you could say I know Malibu very well."

Bev's interest was piqued. "Our house is on the beach just a little ways north of Puerco Canyon Road. Know where that is?"

"Sure do," Missy replied.

Bev put her hand out. "I'm Beverly Nob...ah...Jones."

Missy shook Bev's hand. "Pleased to meet you, Beverly." She was quiet for a long moment then she turned back to Bev. "Look, I'll be honest with you. When a young girl like you wants to drink vodka before lunch and it looks to me like she may be in the middle of something that maybe she can't handle, well, it makes me curious. You know why?"

Bev shook her head.

"Because that was me. That's right. When I was your age and for the next, I don't know how long, but it was a long time, my head was up my...you know what. I was one lost little girl and getting into all kinds of bad situations. So when I see a girl like you do things or say things or just have that certain 'look,' I just want to reach out and give her a hug or something. But I sure as hell don't want to give her vodka for breakfast."

Bev cracked a smile. "So you think I've got a problem?"

"I know you have one. I happen to know from the passenger manifest that your last name isn't Jones, it's Noble. You just told me where you live in Malibu and I know that area has nothing but multi-million dollar homes. I also read the papers and watch the news." Her gaze travelled to Bev's head. "And I can see that you dyed your hair, but the roots are showing me a little red."

Bev's eyes expanded and her jaw dropped.

Missy leaned in close and in a whisper said, "You are the girl who was kidnapped down in Mexico last spring."

Even on a plane, I can't get away. Bev raised her voice and said, "So, what about it?"

"Shhh. I have a pretty good idea what's going on with you and I'm begging you not to let yourself go off the deep end. I'm sure it's a terrible ordeal you experienced and you're entitled to let it distract you, maybe continue to scare you, but in the end, it's up to you to put it way, way back in your mind and get on with a normal life. Listen, I know. I've been there, not exactly the same thing that happened to you but something very similar and as I said, it took me years, but I'm doing pretty good now." Missy looked up and saw a call light flash. "I gotta go. Maybe we can have another chat later in the flight, okay?" She patted Bev's knee and got up.

Bev looked after her. *Wow, did I just dream that? How did she figure it out so fast? And she didn't ask me any questions. She seems to understand. I need to talk to her some more.*

Missy walked by several more times and each time, she would give Bev a wink. When they landed and the Chicago passengers disembarked, Bev called home.

"Beverly? Is that you?"

"Yes, it's me and I'm fine." She took a deep breath and plunged in, her words tumbling out in a wild cascade. "Did you get my text? Everything just got to be too much and I knew I'd go crazy if I stayed there with people bugging me about Mexico and wanting to know everything." She shuddered. "And it was weird, Mom. They wanted to be my friend because they thought somehow it would make them famous, and—"

Sandy broke in. "Hush. It's okay, sweetheart. We understand. Wait a sec, I'm going to have Dad get on another phone." She covered the mouthpiece with her hand and called, "Ed, pick up the phone, it's Bev."

"Beverly, hi, honey. How you doing?"

"I'm fine, Dad. I was just telling Mom that—"

"Don't worry about it. We'll have plenty of time to talk about it when you get here. So relax, enjoy the flight. Are you in first class?"

"Yes."

"Good. Anyway, I'll drop Mom off at baggage to pick you up. Just go down and get your bags and Mom will meet you there."

Sandy added, "If the plane is going to be late or anything, send me a text. And call me when you get off the plane, okay?"

"Okay. I'll see you soon. Gotta go now. Bye."

Sandy said, "Love you." Then she realized Bev had already disconnected the call.

On the second leg of the trip, Missy returned and sat next to Bev. They talked for ten minutes and would have talked longer but Missy had work to do. When Bev deplaned at LAX, Missy gave her a hug and handed her a card. "If you ever want to talk about anything at all, call me."

"Thanks a lot. I will call you."

Feeling nervous, wondering how things would go, Bev headed down the long hallway then down the stairs to meet Sandy in baggage claim.

Chapter 30

On the drive to Malibu from the airport, Beverly was less than effusive. Her answers, even to simple questions, were abrupt and lacked warmth. Sandy sensed that Bev was upset with them.

Looking in the rear view mirror at his unhappy daughter, Ed asked, "Beverly, what is wrong? Are you mad at us? Did we do or say something to upset you?"

Sandy, who was sitting in the back seat with Bev, said, "Darling, look at me. If you'd rather not talk at all, that's fine. We won't talk. I just want you to know that we're fine with you leaving school and coming home. In fact, we're glad you came home since things weren't going very well at school."

Ed made a lane change, then glanced again at Bev. "We know you've got issues you need to come to terms with and we're here to help. Tomorrow you can call Dr. Millstein and arrange to start seeing him again. If he can't help you, you're perfectly free to see someone else. The main thing is to just relax and get plenty of rest and not worry about anything." He smiled at her. No response. "Because," he said firmly, "there is nothing you need to worry about."

Bev focused on her father's eyes through the mirror. "And what about the Kendalls? Pat told me they were down here. Are they still here?"

Sandy stroked Bev's arm. "No, honey. They left this morning. The last thing Sherry said to me before they left was that I'm to tell you that you are in her prayers every single day."

"They're not mad at me for going down there with Kevin?"

The question surprised Sandy. "What? Mad at you? Why would they be mad at you?"

Bev shook her head. "I just thought...Oh, never mind, it doesn't matter."

"Honey, they're fond of you."

"Just forget it, Mom. Let's just listen to some music, okay?"

For a while, there was little conversation. Sandy was dismayed that things were not going at all as she thought they would. But she bit her tongue and said nothing more. When they were about ten miles from home, Bev asked Ed to turn off the radio.

"What's going on with the College Trust?" Bev asked. "Did you give money to any of the kids Pat and I selected?"

Ed looked back at her in surprise. "Yes, we did, we gave four-year scholarships to three of your choices and four provisional scholarships to another three. Those scholarships will automatically be funded for another year provided the student maintains a 3.4 throughout their freshman year. The pros have it all worked out."

Sandy smiled. "You remember that boy with the bad arm? The one whose dad worked at Pepperdine in maintenance? He got a four-year scholarship."

Bev grew animated. "Wally Blakely. That kid was super smart."

"That's right." Sandy was startled by Bev's change. In a blink, her daughter slipped into her old persona.

Bev was now talking rapidly. "Pat said you guys opened up offices in Santa Monica and hired some people to run the charity. Is that right?"

Ed checked the mirror and caught her eye. "That's right. Santa Monica had some nice office space available and it's only 25 minutes away, so I rented a suite on the second floor, furnished it, and then we hired some really good people to do the day-to-day work. There's a lot more to giving money away than I had thought."

"I go down there two or three times a week," Sandy said. "If you like, you can come along and I'll show you around and you can get a better idea of just what we are doing. It's pretty exciting when you think about the number of people we'll eventually be able to help."

"Yeah, I could do that." Bev gave her mother a tentative smile. "I'm going to need something to do. I can't just sit around all day, can I?"

"You can do whatever you like, but keeping busy is the best way I know of to stay out of trouble. Remember what we talked about when we strolling down the beach last summer? That hanging out with too much time on my hands and too much money to spend about did me in?"

"I know, Mom." Beverly squeezed Sandy's hand. "That's what got the whole charity thing started."

Ed remarked, "It's possible that something bad can be turned around and become something good." He slowed to turn into the driveway and pulled into the garage. "You two go ahead, I'll get the bags."

Bev quickened her step as she went through the house and on to the patio. She gazed at the sea, kicked off her shoes and walked to the edge of the water. "Ah, this is more like it," she muttered. "This is what I needed. They can't hurt me here." She pulled her cell phone from a pocket and called Pat.

Sandy slipped into bed and snuggled up against Ed. "You awake?" she whispered.

"No, unless you want to talk."

"I do."

Ed rolled onto his side to face her.

"Beverly was so sullen when she first got in the car and then... switcheroo. I never saw her behave like that before."

Ed thought about it. "I'm sure Millstein would be able to explain it. I suspect she may be having guilt problems. She got away while Kevin got killed. I think that is weighing on her and until she recognizes that it was not her fault that Kevin was killed, she'll continue to carry around some guilt. But these are things she can work through if she's motivated. The best we can do is try to prevent her from wallowing in self-pity or whatever the psychological name for it is." Ed rolled onto his back. "She just got here, so let's give her some time, okay?" He looked over at Sandy. "I know it goes against your grain, honey, but let's avoid asking her a lot of questions."

"You're right. We'll leave her alone and let her set the agenda." Sandy planted a kiss on Ed's cheek. "Tomorrow's another day." She fluffed up her pillow and said, "Goodnight."

Ed awoke and got out of bed a little before seven. He washed his face and put on a light-weight robe. He was grinding coffee beans for espresso when he noticed the patio door was open. Beverly was in the ocean, standing knee deep in the water. Not wanting to startle her, he remained quiet as he moved slowly toward her. He stopped in the sand immediately outside the patio wall and stood there, watching. Bev's hands and arms were moving and every few seconds he heard a word or two drifting his way on the light westerly breeze. He distinctly heard her say, "I am so sorry. It never..."

A pang of guilt hit Ed. He was intruding on his daughter's private thoughts. Quickly, he returned to the kitchen. He went about making espresso but was uneasy. Hearing her say, *I am so sorry,* spoke volumes in his imagination. Here was the guilt Ed had mentioned to Sandy. But was Bev truly culpable in Kevin's death? Had she held back some important detail during the police investigation? What unspoken burden was she carrying? He watched her through the open door. Had she taken another step or two into deeper water? He shook off his lethargy and hurried to the patio door, flung it open and walked briskly in her direction. He called, "Bev, Bev!"

She jumped at the sound of his voice and looked back. "Hi, Dad. You going swimming?" She waded toward him. "Better take that robe off first," she added with a grin.

"No, I just saw you standing out here and decided a little wade around in salt water would be invigorating."

"That's what I was thinking, too." She cocked her head. "You been out here very long?"

"No. I was in the kitchen making coffee and saw you and...ah...I thought I'd bring you a cup."

Bev looked at Ed's empty hands. "So, where is it?"

Ed seemed puzzled. "Where's what?"

"The coffee!"

Ed waved his arms in frustration. "I don't know what I'm talking about. Come on. Let's go in the house and I'll make you breakfast." He took her hand and they walked across the sand to the house.

Sandy came into the kitchen just as they walked through the door. She noted wet legs and the water on Ed's robe. The three of them stopped and looked at each other. Sandy spoke first. "You two take a walk on the beach?"

Bev and Ed exchanged looks. Ed said, "Yeah, we took a little stroll. A wave came in and caught us."

Bev nodded. "Can't do that in Poughkeepsie. I love wading in the water. It's–" she glanced at Ed. "It's very soothing."

"Good," Sandy said and gave Bev a kiss. "Now, why don't you two take a seat, read the paper, and drink some coffee while I fix breakfast." Trying not to appear to be scrutinizing, Sandy asked Bev, "How did you sleep, honey?"

"As matter of fact, I had the best sleep I've had in months. I was really tired—that helped, plus the three-hour time difference. Anyway I had a good night."

Ed looked up from the paper and smiled at her. "Let's hope all your nights will be peaceful now that you're home."

Bev asked, "Are you still sailing every day?"

He shook his head. "Not every day and not when it's cold or too windy, but I try to get out there as much as I can. Would you like to go sailing?"

"Sure. Not today—I want to get settled. But maybe later on this week, if the weather's good."

On Wednesday morning, Bev asked Sandy if she could borrow her car. She had an appointment with Dr. Millstein in Santa Barbara at 10:30. Although Sandy offered to drive, Bev insisted that she was fine and could make the trip alone.

"It's no problem." Sandy said that she had things to do in Santa Barbara anyway but in the end, Ed intervened, reminding her that Beverly was totally able to make the drive on her own.

After Bev left, Ed said, "It might drive you crazy, honey, but we need to let Bev do the things she always did. We have to help her rebuild her self-confidence. And this isn't Mexico. She's pretty darn safe here." Sandy reluctantly agreed.

Dr. Millstein greeted Beverly with a warm hug. "Come in and sit in that comfortable chair." Beverly settled into a large leather chair. Dr. Millstein took a notebook from his desk, slid a straight-back chair opposite Bev and sat. He flipped the notebook open to a clean page and began the session.

"It's good to see you again, Beverly." It was his familiar, formal opening.

She murmured, "You, too, Doctor M."

"Although I am sorry that attending Vassar didn't work out as we had hoped," he said, "I understand your reasons for leaving, and I think you made the right decision. Will Rogers—you know who he was? Good. Will Rogers had a saying: *If you find yourself in a hole, stop digging.*"

Bev smiled and Millstein laughed. "Now that you've stopped digging in New York, and now that you are home, you have to stop digging here as well. You have to let what happened in Mexico go. It happened, it was terribly hard on you, but it is over and done with. Nothing that happened can be changed or denied. But," he cautioned, "that doesn't mean you have to let that experience dominate you the rest of your life."

Bev's expression grew shuttered. She shrugged.

"And now you're saying to yourself, *so, what's new?*"

Bev smiled because that was exactly what she was thinking. She had heard the doctor say the same thing in different forms a dozen times or more.

Millstein picked up the thread of his narrative. "What's new this time is something you are about to tell me. Something you overlooked or perhaps hesitated to say in the past. I'll bet you a dollar to a donut that there is more going on in your head than you have told me about. If I am to help you this time, I have to know what that is..." He smiled broadly. "Or I, myself, will have to go see a shrink."

Beverly couldn't resist smiling.

"Listen, Beverly, you may be able to fool your parents and your sister, but you are not fooling me. You want to get back to your pre-Mexico self? You want to shed this thing that is making you crazy and you want to get on with your life? Is this what you want to do?"

"Yes, of course I do."

Millstein leaned forward in his chair and spoke more sternly than usual. "Then no more mucking about." He tapped his pen impatiently on the open page. "What is the one thing you haven't told me? What went on after you were captured that you failed to tell me or anyone else?"

Beverly laid her head back and closed her eyes. She took a deep breath and let it out slowly. "I told Pat and she said I was crazy. Maybe you'll say the same."

Millstein raised his eyebrows but didn't respond. He waited patiently.

"Okay, here's the thing." She blurted out, "I am responsible for Kevin's death." She explored Millstein's expression but it didn't change. "When I first suggested that we go down to Mexico for the weekend, Kevin wasn't exactly thrilled with the idea. In fact, he said he didn't want to go. He wanted to go to the sand dunes or someplace like that where he could race his Jeep around—you know, have fun with the Jeep."

Dr. Millstein did not comment or shift his eyes away. "Yes, go on."

Bev took another deep breath and blew it out between pursed lips. "I didn't want to spend the weekend doing that. I wanted to go someplace romantic and...and..." She squirmed and blushed.

The doctor broke the silence. "You wanted to go someplace romantic and have sex. That was the point of the whole trip. Not chasing around in some stupid Jeep."

Bev's face was now fully red. "Well, yeah, I guess."

"No, there was no guessing. The whole idea was to get Kevin in bed with you so you two could have a great weekend of sex. Look, Beverly, I'm not here to judge you. I'm here to get to the root problem of your anxiety and get you comfortable with it. Yes, you wanted sex. What girl your age doesn't? Let's get past that part of it."

Beverly looked up in alarm.

Millstein softened his tone. "You are not going to convince me that having sex with Kevin is what is bugging you. What I need to know is what happened between you two up to the time Kevin was killed."

In a small voice, Beverly said, "No, I'm sorry, you're right. Sex is not what this is about. What this is about is me demanding him to take me to Ensenada when he didn't want to go. You understand? He didn't want to go to Mexico at all." The words spilled out. "He said it was a bad place with lots of drug deals going down. He said people were getting killed down there all the time and, well, he just didn't want to go to Mexico." Her eyes pled with Millstein for understanding. "But I kept after it. I found the hotel on the internet, I made a reservation, I said I would pay for everything, and I also said that we would have a wonderful weekend, it would be fun and he could play with the Jeep down there." She sighed. "Then I asked him, didn't he want to have sex with me? If he did, then he would agree to go to Ensenada." She closed her eyes and rocked her head sideways. "And you know what happened? We went down there not because he wanted to, but because I offered him something that I knew he couldn't refuse... and I even told him about the different kinds of sex he'd be able to have with me. It was too much, and he finally agreed to go, and because he went, he got killed."

Beverly leaned forward, her voice rising. "You understand? I got him killed. It's simple. He didn't want to go but I made him go and now he's dead. It's no different than if I'd shot him with a gun." Her voice began to tremble and the tears rolled down her cheeks. "There. That's what you wanted to hear and now you've heard it. My nightmares are less and less about Gordo trying to rape me and more and more about Gordo killing Kevin right in front of my eyes and I couldn't do a damn thing to stop it." She took the tissue Millstein offered and dabbed her eyes, then breathless, leaned back against the soft leather and closed her eyes. "There is no way around it," she moaned softly. "If I hadn't pushed him so hard to take me down there, he'd be alive right now."

"Thank you, Beverly," Millstein said quietly. "That admission was an act of pure bravery."

She opened her eyes and looked at him, astonished.

"I know it was very hard for you to summon up the courage to say that," Millstein said, "but now that you have, we can stop fiddling around and go to work."

She shook her head. "I know you're one of the best, Doctor M., but not even you...not even God can bring Kevin back."

"Yes. That's the bad news. The good news is, we can and we will bring <u>you</u> back."

Chapter 31

Beverly drove south on the 101 thinking about her session with Dr. Millstein. She had asked him what he meant by "now we can get to work." He told her that would find a way to fix the problem, now that he knew what the problem was.

She thought, *Really? To really fix the problem he'd have to bring Kevin back to life and there's no way he's going to do that. So what's he going to do? He'll sit me down in that leather chair for an hour or so three times a week and try to convince me that what happened wasn't my fault at all. Sure, Kevin could have said no and not gone down there but what Millstein doesn't know is the shit I gave Kevin. Maybe I should have told him about showing Kevin that porn site on my computer. We must have watched it for an hour. Kevin was so stoked he could hardly stand it. And I kept asking him, would you like to try that, how about that? He was all over me but I held him off. I'll let you do it, but not here where Pat can hear us. When we get to the hotel...we'll start off with a hot bath and we'll wash each other, then in bed...no hurry. We'll take it slow...all night, all the cool stuff but we can't do that here. But in Ensenada we're on our own. We can do whatever we want. I can't believe you wouldn't want to.*

Hell, he didn't have a chance!

So, Dr. Millstein, you think you can magically undo all of that crap I laid on him and make me a happy ending?

Beverly rubbed her lips with the back of her hand. The blast of a horn startled her. She looked in the mirror and saw a car on her tail. Her eyes went to the speedometer—she was only going twenty-five miles an hour. She carefully worked her way into the right lane and took the first off ramp she came to, then a right turn, and another right into a strip mall parking lot. She pulled into a parking space, turned off the engine and got out of the car. *Geeze, I got to stop thinking about all this stuff before a get into a wreck.*

She looked around and realized she was in Ventura not very far from the Channel Islands Marina where Ed kept his boat. She took out her phone, tapped the map icon, got a route to the Marina and headed in that direction. Along the way, she stopped at a restaurant where she and Ed had lunched during the summer. She parked the car behind the building and walked around to the entrance in front and was surprised to see her dad's Aston-Martin.

Ed was sitting at the counter. She walked up behind him and said, "Excuse me, sir. Is the seat next to you taken?"

Her father spun around and his eyes lit up. "It is now! Where the heck did you come from and how did you know I was here of all places?"

"I didn't know. Just dumb luck, I guess."

"Well, c'mon and sit down. You want lunch?"

"Sure."

Ed beckoned to the waitress.

"Hey, Cindy, you remember my daughter Beverly? She went sailing with me quite a lot last summer."

Cindy gave Bev the once-over and said, "Well, seems like your daughter had really pretty red hair." She looked again. "You must be the twin sister, right?"

Bev smiled. "No, I'm the redhead. Thought I'd try being a brunette for a while."

Cindy laughed. "Well, honey, how's that workin' out for ya?"

"Not as good as I thought it would. I'm gonna let it go back to red." Bev looked up at the large menu board. "I'll have a barbeque beef sandwich and milk."

"Comes with fries, but you can have potato salad or chips instead."

"Make it fries, thanks." To Ed she said, "Been out on the boat yet?"

"I was just messing around, cleaning it up, but I was thinking of taking it out after lunch. You want to go?"

"Sure, but in these clothes?"

"I think there's some stuff of yours or Pat's on board that you can wear or we can stop at one of the shops and get you an outfit."

"I'd better call Mom and tell her what's going on or she'll get worried I wrecked her car or something." She pulled out her cell phone and made the call. Sandy told her to be careful and she would see her at dinner.

Bev's lunch arrived and while she was eating, she gave Ed a thumbnail sketch of what went on at Millstein's office, although she left out the part about enticing Kevin to go with her.

Out on the water, a fair wind was blowing. They put out a lot of sail and soon the boat was skipping over the water at a brisk pace. At the helm, Bev was doing a fine job of keeping the line. Ed did the deck work. They made an efficient team. Admiring his daughter's skills, Ed suggested that maybe next spring they could try a little racing.

Back in Malibu, Sandy was waiting when they entered the house. Sandy gave Ed a quick kiss and Bev received a long hug. Sandy said, "Gosh, darling, you look great. Your cheeks are all red, your hair is a mess, and what in the world are you wearing? You must have had a wonderful time this afternoon."

"I did. It was great getting back on the water. I love it! Dad and I were talking about maybe trying some racing next spring. I'd love to do that, I mean, that's what like every sailor dreams about—the big race!"

"Sounds as if you've found your vocation in life. The America's Cup, first female skipper." Sandy gave Bev a smart salute and both of them broke down laughing. "Okay, get cleaned up. Mrs. Weir has another great dinner on the stove." She looked at her watch. "We'll eat in an hour."

Beverly's days were busy days. She spent them sailing with Ed or working with Sandy at the Noble Charitable Trust offices in Santa Monica. She loved what the Trust was doing, and as time went on, she became more and more involved in the day-to-day activity. For the most part, the busy pace kept her mind active and interested, leaving little time to dwell on Mexico. When she went to bed at night—usually after midnight as she had become addicted to watching the late, late shows—Jimmy Fallon and Craig Ferguson—she was ready for sleep.

The horror shows she dreamt continued but at an abated frequency. Her visits with Dr. Millstein now included her relating stories about sailing or the work being done by the Trust and how she was becoming more involved with it. Dr. Millstein encouraged her to relate current events but he also cunningly injected snippets that suggested that she seemed to be releasing some events of the past. When Beverly realized what he had done, she would often become hostile. She would say, "I see what you just did. Well, you're wrong! What I am doing now with my life, enjoyable as it might be, doesn't change one thing about Mexico. I am responsible for Kevin's death and I've told you why a million times. I am never going to forget it or change my mind about it...I got him killed!"

When Beverly exploded like this, Dr. Millstein would respond, "Okay, I get it. I have always gotten it. But I'm still going to ask you the same question again and again until you answer it with conviction. Are you going to let Kevin's death destroy your life when you know that you have the power to stop that from happening? If your answer is yes, then why waste your time and money seeing me? If your answer is no, then live with what happened in the past but don't embrace it." He waited. "And your answer is?"

Beverly jumped up and glared at him. Then she screamed, "I don't know!" She snatched her purse off the table and stormed out of the office.

Dr. Millstein looked after her, shaking his head. "Ah, that girl. She's making me meshugge." He walked to the window and watched Beverly get into her car and drive off. "She's either going to get over it on her own or she'll quit fighting it and..." He wouldn't allow himself to finish the thought.

Pat flew home on the Wednesday before Thanksgiving for a short break before classes resumed the following Tuesday. Ed had made the first-class flight arrangements almost a month earlier in spite of Pat's remonstrations regarding the outrageous cost for such a short visit. Of course, Bev was the prime motivator. She was desperate to spend time with her twin, even if that time was just a few days. Besides, she thought, *what's a few thousand dollars to a man who is a multi-millionaire?* What she actually said to Ed and Sandy was, "A few days with Pat will be much better therapy than a month with Dr. Millstein."

Bev and Pat were inseparable from the time Pat got off of the airplane until she boarded again five days later. They went shopping in Santa Barbara, they went with Sandy to the Trust offices and they lunched at Rusty's Surf Ranch on the Santa Monica

Pier. The whole family spent a full day on the boat and that evening enjoyed a catered dinner aboard.

Thanksgiving Day featured an over-the-top meal prepared by Mrs. Weir. During the meal, Pat declared that she was leaving Vassar at the end of the next term and transferring to Pepperdine right there in Malibu. She added that she planned to live at home while attending school. She turned to Bev and said, "Now, tell them your news."

All eyes focused on Beverly. "I'm going to go back to school with Pat—at Pepperdine and major in psychology with a minor in business so I can do a better job with the Trust."

Sandy said, "Oh, darling, that's wonderful!"

Bev added, "They say that most psychologists get into that field because they themselves are screwed up and are trying to figure out how to get back to normal. I guess I'm as screwed up as any of them so—"

Ed laughed. "They also say that you can't begin solving a problem until you acknowledge that you have one."

Straight-faced, Bev replied, "For sure, I've got one and it sucks. I've just got to figure out what to do about it."

Later, the four of them sat at the breakfast room table and did something they had not done since leaving Arizona. They played Monopoly.

"Your sister had a great idea for your Christmas present. Want to hear it?" Ed asked.

"Sure, unless it's supposed to be a secret," Bev replied.

"It doesn't have to be. Pat said you need a car and so you and I are going Christmas shopping for one this morning. Want to do that?"

They took off in the Aston-Martin and drove south to Santa Monica, where they stopped at an Infiniti dealership on Santa Monica Boulevard. The new 2009 models were on display and after looking at dozens of them, Beverly liked the G-37 Sport. A salesman had been shadowing them since he first saw the Aston-Martin arrive. He approached.

"Would you like to take a test drive?" he asked.

"Yes," Beverly replied. Opening the door of the G-37, she said, "I'd like to try this one."

The salesman went into the office and came back with the keys. He pulled the car out, got out and held the door for Bev. The salesman got in the passenger seat and Bev drove. Five minutes into the drive Bev said, "This is really nice."

Back at the dealership Bev got out of the car with a big grin. Ed said to the salesman, "How much do you want for it?" The salesman told him and Ed said, "Knock off $2,500 and I'll write the check."

"Ahh, I'll have to talk to my manager."

"Sure, talk to him. But be sure to tell him I don't want to hear counter offers. This is the only offer...your one and only chance to sell me this car."

"Yes, sir. I'll tell him." Fifteen minutes later the salesman came back. "I had to work very hard to get him to agree. He said there would be hardly any profit in it, but you've got a deal. Come inside and we'll get the paperwork done."

Beverly later told her dad, "That was pretty amazing how you did that, got them to sell the car for $2,500 less. Very cool, Dad."

"Honey, if I'd have asked for twice that, there would have been some haggling, but they would probably have sold me the car. The moral is, that just because you have a lot of money, doesn't mean you don't try to drive a hard bargain whenever you can."

During the weeks leading up to Christmas, Ed, Sandy and Beverly spent most of their days at the offices of the Noble Charitable Trust. Ed had his group of advisors fly in from Phoenix for a two day strategy meeting with the Trust Board of Directors.

Beverly's job was to contact families who were potential recipients and evaluate their needs and then make specific recommendations for gifts. It was an important job and she handled it well. One of the staff who worked with Bev was a twenty-two year old recent graduate with a bachelor's degree in Social Sciences from Miami University, in Oxford, Ohio. His name was Brett Peterson. He was tall, good looking with bright blue eyes and unkempt wavy black hair. His taste in clothing ran from sloppy to laughable. But he was a bright kid, a wiz with computers and his soft speaking voice made it necessary to listen very carefully. It was a ploy, of course, but it worked very well.

They had been working together for three days when Beverly asked Brett if he would like to have lunch.

"What? With you?"

"Yes, with me. Anything wrong with that? It's just lunch! I hate to eat alone."

"Okay, that'd be cool. Thanks. Ah, when would you want to do it?"

Bev looked at her watch. "Today. Meet me in the lobby at 12:30."

Brett was waiting when Bev stepped out of the elevator. "Ah, good, you're here," she said. She pushed through the lobby door and briskly walked to her car, Brett following. Arriving at her car, she pressed the key button and unlocked the doors. She looked across the roof at Brett. "Go ahead, get in." She backed out of the parking space, drove out of the lot to Santa Monica Boulevard.

Brett asked, "Are you going to tell me where we are going?"

"To a place one of the girls told me about. It's off of Santa Monica on Lincoln. I've got it punched in on my GPS."

Brett said nothing, just nodded. Looking around the interior, he noted, "Nice car. Smells new."

"It is new. My dad got it for me for Christmas."

Under his breath, Brett said, "Imagine that!"

Bev looked at him for a moment. "What did you say?"

"Ah, I don't know... 'that's nice'...it was nice he got you the car."

Noting that Brett wasn't going to engage her in conversation, Bev turned on the radio. Guns N Roses playing *IRS* blared out of the multi-speaker, high-end audio. Brett immediately began nodding in tempo with the music. Bev looked at him. *Was he lip-synching?*

"You like Guns?"

"Yeah, they're great. I play a lot of their stuff."

"That's interesting." She saw the sign, Bay Cities Italian Deli and Bakery. "Oh, here's our place." She turned in and parked.

The deli was very busy and they had to wait for a table. Once seated, they scanned the menu. Bev looked across the table at Brett. "Now, don't be looking at the prices. This is my treat so order anything you want, okay?"

Brett raised his eyes and smiled. "Okay, if you say so, but I'm perfectly—"

"I know, I know. But like I said, I invited you for lunch so I'm paying. So, don't hold back. Get whatever you want." She scanned the menu, decided on a salad topped with crab meat, then turned to the wine list.

A waitress came over. Bev ordered, the salad plus a glass of white wine. Brett ordered an Italian meatball sandwich and a Budweiser.

Bev looked at Brett for long moment. "So, what's your story? I'm sure you have an interesting one."

Brett grimaced. "It's probably not that interesting, but since you're buying lunch, you deserve an answer."

Beverly's face showed surprise and Brett took note of it.

"I come from a small town in northeast Ohio. My father is a detective and my mother teaches math and science at the high school. I have one brother, three years older than me. He's a ski instructor in the winter and teaches water sports and mountain climbing in the summer. He's a big-time biker, motorcycles and bicycles. He's married to a cool girl who has a very good job."

He paused as the waitress brought them utensils and napkins. "I first majored in music but in my second year I met some people who got me interested in, you know, the kind of stuff I'm doing now. I was going with a girl for about four years but, I don't know, we just ran out of steam or something. Anyway, that's been over for a while now. So, when this job came along I thought, well, this could be interesting. Your father was there when I did the interview with Mr. Jankowski."

The food arrived, and Brett took a couple of bites and then resumed. "After the interview, your father and I talked and he seemed real nice, sort of a down-to-earth kind of guy which I didn't expect from a millionaire. But after checking him out on Google and learning how he became rich, that explained some things." Brett spread his hands, palms up and added, "And, that's about it. Not very exciting, like I said."

"Well, thank you for sharing your bio with me." Bev laid her fork on the plate. "Here's my deal; I need somebody to do things with. Go to dinner, maybe a movie once in a while, or just to talk to." She thought about what she should say next. "Not too long ago I went through a very, ah—"

Brett offered, "Traumatic time?"

Bev's head snapped up. "Why'd you say that?"

"Because when I was Googling your father, I also read about you being held hostage in Mexico and about your boyfriend being killed. I would call that a major traumatic experience."

Beverly stared at Brett. She could feel the tears forming and she raised her napkin to her face. "I'm sorry," she mumbled through the paper. She dabbed her eyes and lowered the napkin. "It looks like there's no way to get away from Mexico, no matter where I go. I was at Vassar and even there everybody bugged me about it until I had to run away." She dropped her chin to her chest and a huge sigh escaped. "I'm sorry, Brett," she said, raising her head and looking at him.

"No, I'm sorry for bringing it up. I didn't mean to tap a hot button. Obviously what happened is still very much with you and I can understand how any mention of it would set you off. Believe me, it won't happen again. But if at some time you do want to talk about it, I'm a good listener."

Bev allowed herself a small laugh, "So is my shrink...a very good listener." They sat silently for several minutes. Bev finished her wine and saw that Brett had finished his meal. She said, "Would you like anything else?"

Brett said, "No, thank you. That was plenty."

"Then maybe we better get back." Bev stood, picked up her purse and the guest check, which she handed to the cashier along with her credit card.

There was very little conversation on the way back to the office except for Brett's saying, "I'd like to buy you lunch next time." He looked at her. "Do you think there'll be a next time?"

"Sure. There'll be a next time and you can pick the place."

That evening, Bev got into her bed and thought about the events of the day. She liked Brett. Sure, he was a little different but then again, she reasoned, so was she. Anyway, he was someone to talk to and without Pat close at hand, she felt like she needed someone besides her parents and Dr. Millstein, someone to just chat with—someone with whom she could just chill.

She opened the nightstand drawer and found the card Missy, the cabin attendant, had given her. She punched in the number and voice mail came on the line. "Hi, Missy. This is Beverly, the college girl you talked to on a flight to LA. I'd like to talk to you sometime if you'd be okay with it. If not, it's okay. I'll understand. Thanks." She left her cell phone number and hung up.

Bev awoke to her ringtone. The sun was streaming through the window blinds. Bleary-eyed, she picked up the cellphone and croaked, "Hello."

It was Missy. "I hope I didn't wake you."

Bev looked at the clock, 8:12. "No. That's fine. Thanks for calling me back."

"How are you doing and what have you been doing since you got home?"

Bev gave Missy a synopsis of her activities with a special emphasis on her working with the Trust and how much pleasure it gave her to be helping struggling families, especially at Christmas time.

"That sounds great. Good for you and your parents for doing it. I certainly can imagine what a good feeling you get helping people with their problems."

"I do love what we're doing." Bev pulled back the covers and sat up on the edge of the bed.

Missy said, "Now, tell me, when you called last night, what was it you wanted to talk about?"

Bev cleared her throat and tried to put her thoughts together. "Well, I've been thinking about what we talked about on the plane and I just need to get another opinion—No, that's not right, it's like, geeze, now I don't know what the hell I'm talking about." She stood up and began pacing as she listened.

Missy said, "Hey, just slow down. I'm thinking you want to talk about the kidnapping and what happened to your boyfriend."

"Well, kinda...yes, I do. I talk about it with my shrink all the time and with my sister and they keep saying it's not my fault Kevin was killed but I know it was. If I hadn't made him go down there, he'd still be alive, right?"

"I suppose. But that's a big 'if.' But okay, let's say that it is your fault. Let's say you are responsible for his death. Since you're convinced, it must be so. Let's just think about it. What are your choices? You are responsible for killing a human being. That is unacceptable and you believe you must pay some sort of price. You are miserable living with this burden. What can you do? How about this idea? Just end it all and that will be that!"

Bev gasped, "Wait. You're talking like suicide?" She sat back down.

Missy snapped back, "That's right. What, are you going to tell me that you haven't thought about it? You don't need to answer that. But let me continue because this might not be the only scenario. Suicide is one option but are there others? You say no, what's done is done and can't be undone. But can it? Let me suggest an alternative course of action. You ready?"

"Yes."

"You are a very fortunate girl. You have a millionaire father who enjoys giving money away to people who need it. And you are right in there with him doing the same. Many years from now you are going to be in charge of that charity and you are going to continue your parents' legacy by helping folks in need. You with me so far?"

"Yes, I get it."

"Alright. To sum up, your choices are to die, thereby helping no one. In fact you will be causing serious grief to a lot of people who then may think they failed you and are the cause of your death or—are you paying attention?"

"Yes."

"Or you stop dwelling on the one life that you couldn't save and concentrate on the potentially thousands of lives that you can save."

Beverly was sobbing. "Oh, Missy, I don't know what to say."

"I know what your answer will be because I made the same decision twenty years ago. My guess is that you'll make the right decision too."

"Can you come and see me sometime. I live in Malibu..."

"Yes, I know and sure, after the holidays, I'll pay you a visit, okay?"

"That'd be great." Bev found herself smiling. "Thanks so much for talking to me. You helped me a lot—really! Thanks again. Goodbye."

Beverly lay back on her pillow and thought about what had just happened. *How simple. Why didn't I see it before? If I die, who benefits from it? Just me. If I live, no telling how many lives I may be able to help.*

She closed her eyes. "Okay, Kevin," she whispered. "I'm sorry I killed you. There's nothing I can do about it now except make up for it by helping people stay alive." She opened her eyes and added, "It's time for me to say Goodbye."

Chapter 32

Christmas vacation at Vassar began on December 21 and Pat came home the following day. She found a changed Beverly who was no longer dwelling on what happened in Mexico. Instead, her twin was bubbling over with enthusiasm for the good works the Noble Charitable Trust was accomplishing.

Bev couldn't wait to show her what they were doing for Christmas and introduce her to the new members of the staff.

"Nice wheels!" Pat exclaimed as she and Bev headed for Santa Monica on Tuesday morning. "Santa Claus must have come to your house a little early."

"Yep, he showed up with this car and said, 'Have you been a good little girl?' And I said, 'Why, hell yes, I've been good—too damn good, as a matter of fact.' And he said, 'What you need are some hot wheels and a good lookin' boy to go with it.' And I said, 'Damn right, Santa.' And he said, 'Well, little girl, I'll see to it that you get both.'"

Pat punched Bev on the arm. "Cut the crap, will ya? I happen to know Dad took my suggestion—that's right, *my* suggestion, and got you the car and I don't know anything about any good looking boy. Is there one?"

"There is and you're gonna meet him when we get to the office."

"Where was he when I came at Thanksgiving?"

Bev thought back. "Probably visiting his family for the holiday. I didn't really know him then. We've just been to lunch a couple

267

of times but he's an interesting kind of guy—different, you know what I mean, and—"

Pat cut in, "No, I don't know what you mean. How is he different?"

"What I meant was, he's way different than Kevin, for example." Bev surprised herself by saying the name but she let it go and went on. "He's older, twenty-two, college grad, from a small town in Ohio and very quiet." She shrugged. "He's just different. Anyway you'll meet him soon enough and you'll see what I mean. Now tell me about this guy you've been dating. How's that going?"

Pat talked about Wes Blanchard, a senior at Columbia. She liked him a lot. She confided that she and Wes hand "done it" several times and she giggled when she talked about what a good lover he was.

"Wow!" Bev exclaimed. "So, where do you think it's going? I mean, after you leave school."

"He'll graduate and go home to Chicago for the summer." Pat frowned. "He's going to MIT in the fall to get a Masters in engineering. So, our deal is probably going nowhere. But for now..." She let the sentence hang and gave Bev a wicked look that made them both laugh.

They arrived at the building and entered the lobby. Bev returned the receptionists wave with one of her own. "That's Cass, she's new." Bev said as they rode the elevator to the second floor.

Sandy stood by the bathroom door watching Ed shave. "You know tomorrow is Christmas Eve. Don't you think we should decorate the tree before Christmas?" The ten foot high Colorado blue spruce, for which they had paid an obscenely high price, was standing bare in the living room.

Ed took another swipe at his face and replied, "We'll get on it this evening." He cleaned up his neck, rinsed the razor, washed the remaining lather off of his face and reached for a towel. "I already got Bev the car for Christmas."

Sandy laughed. "Tell her it's her Christmas for the next hundred years."

Ed hung the towel. "No, I'll give her a card that says, 'Your present is in the garage—enjoy it!' And for Pat, I got her a really nice cashmere sweater."

"Good for you. I hope you got one for me as well." She cocked her head and gave him a questioning look. "Did you?"

Ed walked to his closet. Over his shoulder he remarked, "No, I'm getting you a dozen roses just so you don't forget what I want for Christmas."

Driving to Santa Monica they talked about the great change that seemed to have suddenly come over Beverly. "Do you think we should ask her, how come the dramatic turn-around?"

Sandy replied, "No. She'll tell us about it when she's ready. Besides, Dr. Millstein said this might be a temporary state of euphoria and we shouldn't be surprised if she goes back to her on and off depression."

Ed shook his head. "Hmm. That's not very encouraging. Although, I think when Pat comes home this spring, she'll help keep Bev on track. I know that when Bev's on the boat, she's happy and not thinking about—"

Sandy cut in, "And working at the office seems to keep her engrossed and happy. I'll tell you something else. She is darn good. That girl is going to make a difference—already has made a difference in the lives of a lot of people. You should hear her talking to them!"

"I have a hunch she'll end up running the Trust," Ed said. "Oh, I almost forgot, I brought home a bunch of hundred dollar bills to give to the people who work for us at home. Did you give them out?"

"Yes. I gave the housekeepers two-hundred each, Mrs. Weir, five hundred, the gardeners, pool guy, newspaper carrier, mailman and the guy that washes our cars a hundred each. Let's see, did I forget anyone?"

Ed thought for a moment. "What about the couple that washes the windows and the girl who brings the fresh flowers and, ah, let's see, who else?"

Sandy added, "The butcher, the baker, the candlestick maker."

"For sure. And don't forget the checkers, stock boys and clerks at Ralph's." Ed pondered the implications of it. "God almighty! It's crazy. The three of us live in that house...just the three of us and we have an army of people serving us like we are royalty? Something is definitely wrong here. Didn't we decide way back when we won the lottery that we were going to live on...what was it?"

"Three hundred a year?" Sandy said.

"That's right. Three hundred thousand. You remember, how we thought that would be living high off the hog? That was about three times what you and I were earning back then."

Sandy sighed. "I know, but at least we're doing good things now with the money. We started getting crazy but we eventually reined it in and now with the Trust, we're helping a lot people." She thought about it. "Of course, we could sell this house and scale back on all the services but what would that prove?"

"It would prove that we're not idiots like most people who win lotteries."

Pat, Bev, Brett and another young man from the office, Andy Durak, who was working part time during the holidays, were having lunch at the Bay Cities Deli. Andy, a twenty-one year old Valley native and former liberal arts major, had graduated from UCLA the previous June. Unlike Brett, he was an outgoing, somewhat effusive sort of guy who garnered friends wherever he went. Amongst the office staff, Andy was a favorite.

"What kind of music do you like, Andy?" Bev asked.

"I like all of it, although the big bands of the thirties and forties are what I listen to most. The music is so cool, the musicians are the best and those old-time arrangements just knock me out." He looked around the table. "Sorry, didn't mean to get carried away."

Brett said, "I know exactly what you're talking about. Those guys were real musicians."

Pat asked Andy, "Where do you live?"

"I rent a little guest house in Lynwood. It's off the 105 north of Compton."

Pat said, "We should all go over there and listen to his stuff. Who knows? He might even have some beer in his frig. As for the music, I don't know about that."

Bev held up her hand. "Not to change the subject, but do you know that by tonight, the Trust will have given two million dollars in cash to over one thousand families and individuals plus another three million to various charitable organizations? That's right. Five mil! How cool is that?"

The others at the table broke out in spontaneous applause causing the patrons to look around to see who was having a birthday party.

Ed tapped his fork against the water glass. All conversation ceased as Sandy and the twins turned their attention to him. "Ladies, your attention, please. After dinner we will assemble in the living room and commence operation *Decorate Tree*. After that is successfully accomplished, we will spend the next hour singing traditional Christmas carols, followed by your choice of hot chocolate with a marshmallow or a hot whiskey toddy. We will suspend the twenty-one year drinking age law for this one special occasion, noting that you are going to be twenty next March which is only a year away from being twenty-one so—"

"Stop already," Beverly insisted. "I'll take the toddy."

"So will I," Pat declared.

Sandy added, "I'll take the hot chocolate since I'm the only one old enough and smart enough to have one."

In less than two hours the tree was decorated to the satisfaction of everyone and as they sat on the floor admiring their handiwork and sipping their drinks, Beverly said, "You know, this may turn out to be my best Christmas ever. I've got my family here with me." She sighed happily. "And by the way, thank all of you for being so supportive all these months." She got up and put her arms around Ed. "And Dad, I know what hell you went through working so hard to get me out of there in one piece." She moved to Sandy and hugged her. "Mom, it was a nightmare for you but you held it together and were there for me when I came home." She looked over at Pat who was sitting across from her. "You're more than my twin sister, you're my very best friend and I love you more than anything in this world." Tears welled up in her eyes. She looked at each of them and saw tears in their eyes as well. Through the tears she was able to manage, "I love you all. Merry Christmas."

The next morning, after opening their presents, the family enjoyed a breakfast of waffles and country sausage along with a multitude of side dishes and pastries prepared by Mrs. Weir, who insisted on coming to work Christmas morning to prepare and serve a holiday breakfast. "It's the least I can do for you," she told Sandy, "after all you have done for me all year. So let's not argue about it please. Your Christmas breakfast will be my present to you and Mr. Ed and the girls."

Later, Sandy put together a nice picnic lunch and the family headed up the coast to the Channel Islands Marina where *Pilcher* was berthed. By eleven o'clock they were motoring out of the harbor and preparing to put up sail. Everyone had a job on deck and they turned to. A light, four knot wind and the sixty-eight degree temperature made for a pleasant, though not particularly exciting sail. Ed tried to spice it up by constant maneuvering, changing course from a beat to a following wind, and that required the crew to make constant adjustments to sail. At last, after hearing protests, Ed settled down to a steady course and set the autopilot.

They sat in the cockpit munching Doritos, drinking Mrs. Weir's home-made Meyer lemonade and chatting about nothing in particular until Pat mentioned Bev's interest in Brett Peterson.

"I wouldn't have thought he'd be your type," Sandy said. "He does good work at the office and he's very bright but not exactly your typical bubbly, bouncy boy."

"That's true enough. But bubbly, bouncy?" Bev laughed. "No. He's pretty quiet and you're right, he's really smart. Like intellectual smart. I just think he's an interesting kind of guy, that's all." She shifted her gaze from Sandy to Pat. "Now, this guy Andy that we had lunch with, he's totally different, like he's the exact opposite of Brett."

Pat added, "Yeah, he's smart like Brett but he loves to talk. He'll talk your arm off but he's not stuck up or anything like that. He's just a nice guy with an outgoing personality and I like him. He's very cool."

Bev jumped in. "Get this—he loves that old-timey band music. He said his grandfather used to play in a swing band and he got Andy hooked on it."

"He names all these old musicians," Pat added. "I mean he like knows the names of every musician in the band and what instruments they play and like that. It's weird in a way 'cause we've never even heard of these guys but he talks about 'em like they were still alive. It's weird—"

Sandy said, "My dad, your grandfather, had those records when I was a kid growing up. I remember a lot of those songs and the bands too. Benny Goodman, Tommy Dorsey, Artie Shaw, Woody Herman..."

Ed joined in, "Duke Ellington, Charlie Barnett, Lionel Hampton. Louis Armstrong..."

Pat held up her hands. "Hey, you know what's weird? Those are all regular names of people...anymore bands have names like, Pink, Buckcherry, New Kids on the Block, Pussycat Dolls, Paramore..."

Tiring of that subject, Ed and Bev talked about looking forward to the sailing season next spring and asked Pat if she'd be interested in joining them. Pat was ambivalent about sailing. She said she certainly enjoyed going sailing once in a while but didn't think she'd want to spend a summer doing it. Abruptly switching topics, she asked Ed. "What should I do with the car when I leave school next May? Should I drive it home?"

"That's up to you. Personally, I think you'd be better off to just sell it, ship your stuff and fly home. You can buy another car here."

"Or," Pat volunteered, "you can buy me a new one for my twentieth birthday, only wait 'til I get home so I can pick it out myself like Bev did."

Ed looked at Sandy who just rolled her eyes and said, "No comment."

Chapter 33

New Year's Eve 2009 in Malibu was, as Sandy later put it, "insane." She and the family had been invited to no less than a dozen parties at neighboring beachfront homes. Actually, some were open house parties and invitations had been sent to practically every near neighbor. The Nobles had received a few invitations in previous years but other than making a brief appearance to say "Happy New Year," they never stayed. Ed and Sandy felt totally out of their element in a gathering where conversations never seemed to vary from investment yields, exotic travel, and the newest toys and their price tags. These definitely were not people with whom they felt comfortable.

There were a number of movie and TV personalities who had homes near theirs but "ordinary" people like Ed and Sandy were typically not invited to their parties. What was different this New Year's Eve was that the entire Noble family had taken on an aura of celebrity because of Beverly's kidnapping. The intense media coverage when the Nobles returned from Mexico guaranteed that their beach-front neighbors as well as the general population of Malibu now knew who Edward and Sandy Noble were and how they became millionaires.

The girls made certain they would not be involved with the local festivities. They arranged dates well in advance with Brett and Andy, promising them that it would not cost them a cent. "You won't have to do a thing," the girls told them. "We'll handle everything. All you have to do is get to the Island Hotel in Newport Beach Wednesday afternoon. Bring some dress-up clothes." Pat also recited a list of other clothing they might want to include as they would be spending the night and possibly New Year's Day in Newport Beach. The boys willingly accepted.

Andy had a question. "So, we're going to stay over at the hotel with you guys?"

Bev fielded the question. "We reserved a two-bedroom suite. Each room has two queen size beds. You will be spending the night at the hotel, and yes, it will be in our suite. I'm not saying you guys are going to sleep with us," she continued soberly. "That is something proper Vassar ladies would never do—share a bed with a man unless they are married."

Pat added, "That's right. Neither of us is a ho, but it's New Year's Eve. Who knows what could happen?" She laughed aloud. "You're not afraid, are you?"

Brett said nothing but Andy said, "I don't know about Brett, but you two scare the shit out of me."

Brett and Andy drove to Newport Beach in Andy's car, arriving a little before four. A quick cell phone call and they were in the hotel elevator going up to suite 1218. Bev and Pat were still in their bikinis and terrycloth robes, having just returned from the pool where they had been lying about in the sunshine since lunchtime.

The four exchanged hugs and token kisses, then the boys were given a brief tour of the suite. In the adjoining bedroom Bev said, "This will be your room so put your stuff in here." She looked at her watch. "Okay, what say we all get cleaned up and dressed?" She paused and cocked her head. "I hope you followed instructions regarding the dress code for tonight."

Brett answered in a very believable English accent, "Yes, Madam Nobel, we did indeed do as you directed. I believe you will find our attire for tonight's event to be most acceptable, not only to you ladies, but to the maître d' where we will be dining."

Andy added, "They do have a maître d' at Denny's, don't they?"

The girls looked at each other then broke down laughing. "Very funny," Pat stammered, "but I'll have to admit that Brett's English accent was a damn good. Where did you pick that up?"

Brett gave her a large smile. "I had an English roommate one semester at college. I found myself talking like him every time we had a conversation. It infuriated him so I kept on doing it. The next semester he found another roommate."

Bev said, "I can sympathize with him for leaving you. Anyway, let's be ready to go around six." She looked at Pat. "Is an hour and a half enough time for you?"

"Sure." Pat addressed the boys. "How about you guys? Is that enough time for you to get ready? I mean, like you'll probably need a half-hour just to tie your tie."

"Very funny," Andy said. "But seriously, I don't know. I have an appointment to get my hair and nails done and that could take a couple hours right there..."

Bev gave Andy a push. "Well, do your best but be ready to go at six. Our dinner reservation is at seven. We'll stop in the lounge and have a drink first."

In his very quiet and constrained voice, Brett asked, "*We* will have a drink? Andy and I are old enough to drink legally but I hope you're not going to ask us to contribute to the delinquency of minors."

Bev gave him a sharp look. "We're not asking you to do anything, and I hope you won't be asking us to *do*," she placed special emphasis, "anything either. When the waiter sees us, he won't be asking any questions about age—trust me."

The girls left the room and closed the door. Andy sat down in a chair while Brett sat opposite on the end of the bed. They looked at each other and smiled. Brett broke the silence. "So what the hell was that all about?"

Andy leaned forward. "I'm not sure but we'd better be careful. Under-age girls, not to mention, daughters of our boss—makes things pretty tricky."

Brett considered the question for a moment. He made a wry face and said, "As far as I'm concerned, I'm not going to initiate anything, if you know what I mean. If they do drink we need to make sure they don't drink too much. The last thing we need is for them to get sloppy."

"For sure! And, I don't have a clue as to what they're thinking about for sleeping arrangements tonight. Do you?"

"Not really. After I learned what Beverly went through down in Mexico—she almost got raped and her boyfriend was killed right in front of her eyes—I wouldn't think she'd be interested in sex or anything to do with a man."

Andy started to undress. "I don't know what her mental condition is but you're probably right. We'll just have to wait and see what happens, but we sure as hell don't want things to get out of control." He headed for the bathroom. "I'm going to take a shower and shave. I'll be done in fifteen—twenty minutes."

Brett lay back on the bed. "Take your time, no hurry." He closed his eyes and thought about the possibility of being in bed with a willing Beverly.

At ten after six the boys, dressed and ready to go, were watching television. A knock on their door, brought Andy to his feet. He opened the door and his jaw virtually dropped. Before him stood not their pals Pat and Bev, but two hardly recognizable and completely stunning women. They were tall (In high heels Pat stood close to six feet, while Bev was just an inch or so shorter). They were impeccably dressed to reveal their alluring contours. Tastefully applied makeup enhanced their natural beauty. After his composure returned Andy's first thought was, *Bev was right. No waiter is going to think this is a nineteen year old girl.*

Bev smiled demurely. "Everything okay, Andy?"

He looked at her and then turned to Pat. "Wow! You girls are, are...Wow!"

Brett adjusted his tie and said, "What he means is..." he mimicked Billy Crystal doing an impression of Ricardo Montalban, *"you look marvelous!* I don't say this very often but, I'm impressed, no kidding."

Pat exclaimed, "And you guys look very well turned out, as they say." She walked up to Andy, bent down, as she was several inches taller than he, and gave him a light kiss on the cheek. "Maybe I shouldn't have worn such high heels," she said through a laugh.

"It's okay," Andy said. "I would have been intimidated if you were only five feet tall. You really do look beautiful...You, too, Bev."

Pat grabbed Andy's hand and led him toward the door. "Okay then. Let's go down and get this party rolling."

Ed in a tuxedo and Sandy in a designer gown arrived at the first party around eight. They were greeted at the door by the hostess, their neighbor Marion. "My husband is still upstairs," she said.

Sandy recognized Marion's gown as an Armani that she had considered buying, but the price tag had struck her as obscene. She looked around and realized they were the first to arrive. "I'm so sorry. It seems we've arrived too early."

"Oh, you know how it is," Marion said with a dismissive wave of her hand. "New Year's Eve parties usually don't get going until a little later. But never mind, dear. Do come in and sit. Actually, I'm glad you did arrive early as it will give us a chance to get better acquainted. One never is able to have any meaningful conversation at these things—just a lot of silly chit-chat." She led them to what Marion called the study, a beautifully appointed room with walls of warm wood and a cheery fireplace alight with gas logs. She turned toward the doorway. "Ah, here's Charles," she said, giving her husband a kiss on the cheek. After introductions were made, Marion suggested glasses of champagne which a uniformed maid dutifully delivered. "I'm disappointed you didn't bring your girls. They're certainly old enough to attend a function such as this, aren't they?"

"I suppose they are—they'll be twenty in a few months." Sandy hastened to add, "However, they had made plans early on to do something with a couple of young men. Obviously, twenty-year-olds have a different concept of what a New Year's Eve party should be."

Charles laughed. "I certainly hope so. Why would they want to be with a bunch of old fogies? I'm sure they made the right decision."

Ed said, "And Pat will have to return to college in a couple of days and those two want to spend the remaining time together. The twins have always been very close."

Marion said, "You said the one girl is going back to school. What about the other?"

"She decided to come home a short time ago. College life was just not working out very well for her. She...ah... she still has some problems, as you can imagine, but she's doing much better and plans to enroll with her sister at Pepperdine this fall. Frankly, we'll love having them at home."

The doorbell rang and Marion jumped up. "If you will excuse me. Charles, please fill their glasses." She hurried out of the room.

Within an hour, the home was filled with people and perfunctory introductions were hastily made, but for Ed and Sandy, it was impossible to remember who was who, let alone their names. Around ten they found Marion and Charles, thanked them for their hospitality and departed.

"Shall we go to another one?" Sandy asked.

Ed held the car door open for her. "I don't know. Do you want to? Practically everyone I talked to wanted to know about Mexico. They were polite about it—you know, they didn't blurt it out first thing—but sooner or later the subject came up." Ed walked around the car and got in. "So, what do say?"

Sandy opened her little clutch purse and pulled out a leather bound note pad. She flipped the pages. "I've got all the invites with addresses written down." She paused at one page. "This one could be interesting from Robert Redford. Of the dozens of movie and TV stars who live around here, he was the only one who sent us an invitation with a hand-written note."

Ed said, "I remember. It was about how he hoped Beverly was doing all right. We collaborated on the thank-you note."

"Yes. And now we're invited to his party. So, do you want to go there?"

After leaving the lounge, the girls and their dates were seated at a table next to a window. The view with all the sparkling lights was dazzling. The waiter arrived. "Would the ladies care for a cocktail this evening?"

Beverly looked up from the drink menu and gave him a gracious smile. "I can't decide between a Sapphire gin or a Purple Rain. Any suggestion?"

"Both are very popular and very good. I think you'll be pleased with either one."

Pat said to Bev, "Let's get one of each and find out which is better." She looked at the waiter. "I'll have the gin one and my sister will try the Purple thingy."

The waiter smiled and turned to Andy. "And you, sir?"

"I'll have a Corona."

"Yes, sir, but may I see some identification please?"

Andy's face flushed momentarily as he reached in a pocket and pulled out his wallet. He removed the driver's license and handed it to the waiter who looked at it briefly and handed it back with a mumbled thank-you.

Brett pulled out his driver's license. "Here," he said, handing the license to the waiter, "I'll save you the trouble of asking."

Now it was the waiter's turn to feel embarrassed. "That won't be necessary, sir. And you wish to have...?"

Brett scanned the drink menu. "I'll try a mojito, please."

The waiter departed and Bev put her hand over her mouth and softly said, "And you were worried about me and Pat? The waiter in the lounge didn't ask our ages either. I told you there wouldn't be a problem. Beautiful, tall women in designer dresses are rarely asked their age."

Pat scowled at Bev. "Hey, don't get bitchy. Andy has a youngish face. I'll bet when he's forty waiters will still want to see some ID."

The drinks arrived and the four of them toasted one another then turned their attention to the large menus.

Bev noticed Brett's expression. "Remember, it's like I told you before, do not be concerned with the price of things, okay? You and Andy are our guests. Think of it as a Christmas bonus."

Brett ran his eyes up and down the menu. He said to Bev, "Okay, you're the boss."

Pat gave the waiter her order then added, "And I'll have a glass of a nice chardonnay."

Bev ordered and after scanning the wine list, said, "Bring a bottle of Rhone Valley Condrieu, the Andre Perret, and cancel the chardonnay."

Brett decided on steak and Andy said he'd have the same.

Bev winked at Pat. "Okay, we got through that part of it. Now, everybody relax 'cause this is going to be a super-good dinner."

And it was. Andy raved about his steak—the best he'd ever had. Brett agreed.

They finished off the bottle of wine and the girls asked to see the drinks menu again, to see what sort of after-dinner drink sounded appetizing. Brett suggested they cool the drinking for now, have some coffee and take a walk around the grounds to help settle the huge meal. Bev called for the check. She looked at it and smiled. She laid her credit card on the silver tray and handed it to the waiter. She looked up and saw that Brett and Andy were staring at her.

"What? Yes, it's a big number but it's New Year's Eve." When the waiter brought back her card with the bill, she added a twenty percent tip, signed it, put the card in her purse and said, "Okay, let's take that walk."

On the way out, Bev and Pat stopped at the ladies room. Inside, Pat asked, "How much was the bill?"

"A little over five-hundred with the tip."

"Geeze, what's Mom gonna say when she sees that?"

"I don't know. Two nights for our suite will be like twelve hundred. But she doesn't pay the bills herself any more. The bills go to some guy who pays them. Since it's my credit card, he'll probably call me and ask if the hotel bill is correct and I'll tell him yes and that will be that." She stood at a sink watching Pat's reflection in the mirror.

Pat said, "I guess, it's all a part of being super-rich, right? We have different values than other people."

Bev's face showed surprise. "Really? We have different values? What are you talking about?"

Pat's tone was sharp. "Let it go, Bev. If our lifestyle is a problem, remember you're part of it." She turned and walked out to the hallway where the boys were waiting. Bev arrived a minute later. Pat welcomed her with a smile. "Okay, let's take a walk and then let's find a club and party on!"

After leaving Redford's party, Ed and Sandy stopped briefly at two more houses and decided that they had had enough of champagne, mind-numbing conversation and thick, noisy crowds. The attendant brought Ed's car around and after leaving yet another five dollar tip, they drove home.

"Let's not do this next year, okay?" Ed said, pulling his tie loose. "I couldn't tell you the name of one person I met tonight—well, maybe Charles, the guy at the first house."

"I can remember a few more than that but I get the point."

"The point is, there is no point to it. I'm a grocer and you're an office manager. The only thing we have in common with most of these people is money." His lips tightened. "Which is to say, we have nothing that matters in common and that's why about the only thing they wanted to talk about was Mexico, the one subject I didn't want to talk about. I really get it how it bugs the girls."

Sandy gave his hand a little squeeze. "Oh, come on. It wasn't all that bad. Just to see those houses..."

"And those women with their one-of-a-kind designer dresses. Man!" Ed whistled. "The jewelry some of those gals were wearing was worth more than our house."

Sandy said, "Several people praised us for giving money away. I don't know how they even knew about that."

"There've been some articles about it in the papers."

Sandy was draping her wrap on a satin hanger and tucking it into the foyer closet. She turned to him in surprise. "Really? I never saw them."

"You know, out here everybody seems to know everybody's business. I'm beginning to think we should move someplace where the people are more like us." Ed led the way to their bedroom. "Sometimes I just feel like I'd like to go bowling or play pool and have beer at a local bar like I used to in Peoria. At least with the people there, you knew what the hell they were talking about."

Sandy kicked off her shoes, stood on her toes and put her arms around Ed's neck. "Are you going to give me a New Year's kiss?"

"I kissed you at midnight at whatchamacallit's house. I noticed that quite a few men wanted to kiss you, too." He laughed. "That was pretty funny when that one guy moved in to kiss you and you started sneezing and blowing your nose."

"It worked, didn't it?"

"Yeah, it sure did."

She looked up and gazed at him. "Well, I'm not sneezing now."

Ed gave her a long, luxurious kiss, his tongue engaging hers. He held her at arm's length and scanned her from head to toe. "In case I forgot to tell you, you were without a doubt the prettiest girl of the entire evening. That's a fantastic dress you have on. In fact, the whole picture is just perfection." He took her in his arms and whispered in her ear, "I love you, you know that?"

"Yes, I do know that, and you know I love you—a lot. You're a good guy and a damn good father and maybe even a damn good lover."

"Maybe? If you have some doubts, come on, get out of those clothes. This New Year's celebration is not anywhere near over yet."

Chapter 34

A few minutes after 2:00, the twins and their dates managed to fit the card key into the slot and get the door to their suite open. In spite of their best intentions, the boys couldn't keep a lid on the girls' drinking and they, too, eventually found themselves matching the girls drink for drink.

Both girls, as if by some silent signal, kicked off their shoes and fell crosswise on one of the beds. They were giggling and chatting in whispers while keeping an eye on the boys.

Bev propped herself up. "So, what do you want to do now?" She laughed loudly as did Pat, who added, "As if we didn't know what you'd like to do."

Andy looked at Brett, who stepped back from the bed and slumped into an over-stuffed chair. A moment later he sat up straight and gazed at Bev. "And what is it you think we'd like to do?"

Bev's reply was lazy and laced with humor. "I'm not going to answer that. That's a stupid question."

Pat said, "Hey, take it easy. Let's not get pissy, okay?"

Andy moved to defuse the tension. "Would anyone want to share a joint with me?"

"You got weed?" Bev asked.

"Yeah, enough for a couple of joints."

"Well, bring it on, bring it on," Bev said eagerly. To Pat she said, "C'mon, let's get out of these clothes." Her voice deliberately sultry, "Let's slip into something more comfortable."

The twins helped each other slip out of their dresses. Pat, in bra and skimpy panties, saw Andy staring as she posed with hands on hips. Her eyes dancing, she asked, "Like what you see?"

Andy nodded. "I sure do."

Pat pulled a robe from the closet. "If you want to see more," she said as she wrapped the luxurious terry around herself, "better go get that grass and share a joint with me."

Andy quickly walked toward the adjoining room, answering her over his shoulder, "Sharing is what I'm all about. Don't you know that?" Pat tightened the robe and followed him.

Bev, wearing nothing but a short slip, asked Brett if he'd ever smoked grass.

Brett willed himself to look at her face. "I've tried it a couple of times, but I certainly don't make a habit of it. What about you?"

"I haven't used it since I came home from school—wouldn't know where to get it. At Vassar, Pat and I would share a joint once in a while." She picked her dress off the floor and turned toward him.

Brett caught himself wondering if he knew another woman who could be so graceful while nearly nude—and fairly inebriated— at the same time. He swallowed and tried to sound normal. "Did you start in high school?"

"No, hell no." She tossed the dress over a chair. "We both started when we were at UC Santa Barbara. Of course, darn near everybody used." She walked over and sat on his lap. Her breasts were just under his chin. She put an arm around his neck, bent down and kissed him on the mouth. His response was restrained. She pulled back and asked, pouting, "That's the best you can do?"

Brett didn't answer right away. He just looked into her eyes. Realizing it made her uncomfortable, he said in his quiet voice, "Look, you're pretty drunk and you've already said you want some of Andy's smoke. You'll get high and then you just might end up doing things that maybe you wouldn't ordinarily do. You're my boss' daughter. I really like my job and I'm not going to do anything that could screw that up."

Bev started to speak but Brett put his finger on her mouth.

"I know what you're thinking, so let me just say, yes, I'd love to have sex with you, and yes, I'm sure it would be great. But until we know each other a little better, I'm thinking we should just cool it for now."

The sound of laughter drifted in from the other room. Bev jumped off of Brett's lap and stalked into the other bedroom. Brett slumped back quietly thinking, *So much for New Year's Eve. Happy New Year.*

Pat and Andy were sitting cross-legged on the floor. Pat held up the joint and said to Beverly, "Hey, sit with us and have a toke."

Andy flipped his lighter and held the flame to the joint.

Bev took a long drag and held her breath then slowly let it out. She smiled at Pat. "That's the first hit I've had since I came home."

Pat nodded. "Wait a minute before you take another."

"Yeah," Andy said. "That's Black Mo. This shit is pretty potent."

Pat giggled. "You aren't kidding. I think I'm getting high already." Pat looked around. "What did you do with Brett?"

"He's in the other room, being all righteous and..." Bev shrugged.

"What do ya mean?"

"I wanted to play around and he turned it off. Got all holy on me. Said we should take our time. I mean, that sucks. Who the hell has time, for Christ' sake? I had all kinds of time in Mexico—"

"No, don't talk like that." Pat blinked a few times to clear her head. "No more about Mexico." She stood up and took Bev's hand and pulled her up. She looked down and said, "C'mon Andy, let's go cheer up Brett."

Andy got up and laid the joint on the soap dish he'd brought from the bathroom.

Bev waved her arm at Andy. "No, bring that with you. What Brett needs is some smoke."

The three of them found Brett still sitting in the chair where Bev had left him.

Andy gave Brett a slap on the shoulder. "Come on, buddy. What's the problem? It's New Year's Eve—no, it's New Year's day—it's 2009." He held out the joint. "Here, take a hit on this joy stick and get with the program."

Brett looked at the others' faces and realized he was definitely being a mood killer. "Fire it up," he said as he pulled the joint from Andy's fingers and put it between his lips. He took a hit and then another. His eyes watered and he coughed. He passed the stick to Beverly who took another hit and passed it on to Pat.

Andy held the roach carefully and took a drag. He pinched the lit end and laid it on the marble topped table next to the chair.

"Anybody feeling high?" Brett asked. All hands went up and the group broke out in uninhibited laughter. Brett ran his tongue over his lips and asked Andy, "What the hell kind of pot is that, man?"

Andy chuckled, gave Brett a large smile and held up his hands. "Primo, right?"

Brett turned around and scooped up Bev in a giant bear hug.

Bev mumbled, "So, now what do you think?"

"What do I think?" Brett kissed her extravagantly. "Party on, man, party on."

A bright light shining on her closed eyes woke up Beverly. She raised her head and saw the sun streaming in a window on the other side of the room. She let her head fall back on the pillow. She was cold. She rose up on her elbows and reached for a blanket and saw that she was still in her slip and lying on top of the bedspread. Bev rolled her head to the left. Brett was sleeping in the other bed. He was clothed except for his pants and shoes. She noted his red plaid boxer shorts. Her eyes slowly scanned the room. Several table and floor lamps were on and a large silver tray with the remnants of sandwiches and condiments lay on the floor near the TV.

She wanted to go back to sleep but her mouth was so dry she could barely swallow. Easing out of bed, she walked a cockeyed line to the bathroom and filled a plastic cup with water. She held the water in her mouth to ease the dryness then spit it out and took a drink. Sitting on the toilet, she tried to reconstruct last night's events. She remembered most of what happened up to the time they started smoking weed. What happened after that was fuzzy. Did she have sex with Brett? She didn't think so but couldn't be sure.

Bev flushed the toilet, washed her hands and splashed cold water on her face. She looked in the mirror and quickly turned away. It wasn't a pretty sight. She walked back into the bedroom, got a robe from the closet and went to the adjoining bedroom where she saw Pat and Andy asleep on one of the beds. The lower halves of their bodies were partially covered by the sheet and blanket. Bev reached over and pulled the covers up to their necks and left, almost tripping over the crumpled bedspread on the floor.

She made her way back to her bed, pulled down the bedspread, got under the covers and promptly fell asleep. When she next awoke, she saw Brett sitting in front of the TV with the sound off. He had a coffee mug in his hand and was watching a football game. Bev looked at her watch. It was twenty after two. "Wow, that must have been some night we had!"

Brett got up and walked to the bedside. Looking down at her disheveled hair and puffy eyes, he remarked, "Yeah, it sure looks like it." He smiled briefly and asked, "How you doing?"

She swallowed a couple of times, cleared her throat and replied, "Okay, I guess." She glanced around the room. "Did you clean it up?"

"Yeah, then I called room service to bring up some coffee and take the trolley from last night away." He walked to a table where a coffee thermos and some cups stood next to a basket of assorted pastries and breads. "Get up and have coffee and something to eat."

Bev eased out of bed. She was still wearing the robe. She went into the bathroom and came out a ten minutes later fresh from a shower, her hair still wet.

"That any better?" she asked.

"A little." He poured some coffee and when she was seated at the table, handed her the basket of rolls. She drank the coffee, refilled her cup and ate a croissant. Then she covered her mouth and tried to stifle a burp. "Sorry. That just popped out." She stood and said, "Man, I'm hungry."

Brett was watching the game on TV. "You're hungry? So am I. Get dressed and we'll go get something to eat."

"Okay." Bev walked to the other room and looked in. "Where are Pat and Andy?"

"I don't know. They left a little while ago. They asked if I wanted to go with them but I told them I'd wait for you. Wasn't that nice of me?"

"Yes, it was." She walked up to him and put her arms around him. "If I ask you something, will you promise to give me an honest answer?"

Brett kissed her forehead. "I'm pretty sure I know the question but I'm not so sure I know the answer. I know when I woke up I was in one bed and you were in the other which doesn't prove anything but..."

Bev held him at arm's length. "Let's just cut to the chase, okay? Did we have sex last night?"

Brett murmured, "Honestly, I don't know. Maybe, but if we did, I sure as hell don't remember anything about it—but then again, I don't remember much of anything after we started smoking the second pill. What did he call that weed?"

Bev dropped her arms and said, "Black something. That stuff was strong!"

"No kidding. I've never had a high like that before. That was some very serious weed."

Pat and Andy were sitting by the pool chatting, their dirty brunch plates still on the table. Pat pulled the ringing cell phone from her purse and looked at the I.D. "Hi, Mom. Happy New Year."

"And happy New Year to you, darling. How was your date last night?"

"Fine." She winked at Andy across the table. "Did you guys have a good time partying with the rich and famous?"

Sandy said, "It was okay. Not that exciting but Dad and I had a good time. So where are you now?"

"Andy and I are sitting out by the pool."

"What is Beverly doing? I called her a while ago but didn't get an answer. Is she okay?"

"Sure, she's fine."

"Hold on. Dad wants to say hi."

"Hi, honey. Happy New Year."

"Hi, Dad. Happy New Year to you, too."

"Tell me about last night. What did you do?"

Pat gave Ed a sanitized run down on last night's activity with particular emphasis on what a great dinner they had. She said that they visited a couple of clubs that were very crowded and noisy and came back to the hotel a little after midnight, watched a movie on TV and went to bed. "The boys had their own room, of course," she hastily added.

Ed's laugh was genuine. "Of course they did. The question is, did they actually use it?" Another chuckle from Ed as he added, "Just kidding, honey. I know you two were good little girls. Ouch! Your mother just punched me."

Sandy came on the line and said, "Patty, when you see Beverly, ask her to call home, okay?"

"Sure."

"So, what's the plan for today? Are you coming home? Bev said something about you two staying over tonight. Are the boys staying, too?"

"No, they're going home today, probably this afternoon." A waiter came by and picked up the dirty dishes.

"Will there be anything else I can get you?" he asked.

"No thanks. Just bring me the check." Andy said.

"I'll have Bev call you as soon as I see her. Love you. Bye."

Andy asked, "Did your dad say something about where Brett and I slept last night?"

Pat laughed. "Of course he did but you heard what I said."

"You said the boys had their own room, that's all."

"Look, my dad's not square. I'm sure he thinks we all did it last night but he was very cool about it. He asked if you guys actually used your room last night and truthfully you did. Right?"

"We used the hell out of it as I recall although I got to admit, I don't recall that much of what happened after we started hitting the nail. What about you? Did we do it? I'm not sure."

"I had my panties on this morning when I woke up so..."

Andy laughed and quickly covered his mouth with his hand. Under his breath he said, "Okay, let's leave it that as far as we know, you're still a virgin."

Pat laughed out loud, then, regaining her composure, said, "That works for me."

"Feeling better?" Brett asked.

Bev dabbed her mouth with the napkin and returned it to her lap. "Much better. Whew. It's a good thing New Year's Eve only happens once a year." She folded her hands and laid them on the table, leaned forward and in a soft voice said, "I think I could learn to like you but you're going to have to learn how to loosen up a little."

"Loosen up? I thought I was pretty damn loose last night."

"Sure you were. But it took a load of grass to get you there."

"Well, I'm a serious kind a guy. Haven't you figured that out by now? Basically, I'm a nerd that somehow lucked out and got himself a date with a beautiful, intelligent and ridiculously rich girl. How many nerds does that happen to?"

Bev laughed. "You're not a nerd. Just because you are serious about your job, and crazy good with computers and tech stuff, doesn't mean you're a nerd. Anyway, I like you. I want to spend more time with you and get to know you better and I want you to get to know me better. I know my head's fucked up and maybe someday I'll tell you about what happened to me and Kevin down in Mexico so you'll understand why I act the way I sometimes do. You know what I mean?" She raised her head and gave Brett a questioning look. "Do you want to continue this relationship or do I make you..." she paused, searching for the proper word, "uncomfortable or put off, something like that?"

"I guess at times you do, but I think I understand where you're coming from." Brett took a drink of water and fiddled with his napkin. Then he focused on her again and said, "The thing that sort of holds me back from going all out with you is the disparity in our situations. It's a big deal for me."

"You mean the money, don't you?" She frowned. "It shouldn't matter—"

He cut her off impatiently. "Of course it does. You are the daughter of a millionaire who apparently lets you live the millionaire lifestyle, at least as far as I can tell, there are no restrictions or restraint on what you spend. Well, I can't keep up with that, no way."

"Nobody is asking you to," she made quotation marks with her fingers, "'keep up.' Hey, I can scale back if it makes you uncomfortable and do stuff with you that doesn't cost a lot of money if that's what you want. But why? It isn't like my dad had to work hard to earn the money. He won it in a damn lottery. One day we were an ordinary family living normal lives like everyone else and the next day, bam! We were millionaires. We tried not to let all the money change our lives but it did—we couldn't help it. We're giving away millions of dollars every year, as you well know." Bev stopped speaking, spread her arms and said, "So, does that mean we, you and I, can't find a way to deal with it?"

Her phone rang. She looked at it. "It's Pat."

"Go ahead and take it."

Bev stood and walked a short distance. "Hi Patty. What's up?"

The waiter approached the table and handed the bill to Brett who took some money from his pocket and paid it.

Bev watched and smiled. She said to Pat, "I just stuck Brett with the bill for lunch. I'm sure that will make him happy."

"Why, was he not happy?"

"No, he's fine. I'll tell you about it later."

"Andy wants to know if Brett is ready to leave."

"I don't know but we're coming back to the room in a few minutes."

Pat said, "Okay. Oh, Mom wants you to call her. Better do that now. Bye."

Bev walked back to Brett, waiting at the table. "Andy wants to leave pretty soon." She walked behind his chair and put her arms around him. "I saw you pay the waiter so thank you very much for lunch."

After the boys left, Pat and Bev spent the remainder of the afternoon people-watching at the pool. A waiter arrived at their chairs. He pointed to two young men sitting on the opposite side of pool and said, "Those gentlemen would like to buy you ladies a drink. What would you like?"

Without consulting Pat, Bev replied with a giggle, "Thank them, but tell them we had quite enough last night."

Pat nodded. "You're quite right about that." The waiter walked off to deliver the message. "Well," Pat asked, "do we want to do a tell-all about what happened last night?"

Bev laid back in the lounge chair, closed her eyes and said, "Not really."

"Oh," Pat said, surprised by Bev's reluctance to *tell all.* "Well, then, what do you want to do about dinner?"

Bev considered the question. "I don't care, except let's not eat here. Let's go someplace that's not too expensive."

Chapter 35

On January fifth, the family drove Pat to the airport to board a plane to New York. Classes at Vassar were scheduled to resume the following day. While Ed and Sandy hated to see her leave, Beverly was most affected by her twin's departure. She felt secure and in control when Pat was around but after Pat left for school, she became anxious, unsure of herself and frequently depressed.

When she was at the office working with Brett on a Trust project or when they had lunch or late afternoon drinks, their conversations were cordial but, from Bev's perspective, unsatisfying. The brief period of intimacy that was theirs at Newport Beach had somehow evaporated. She enjoyed being with him and wanted the relationship to move forward and she felt confident that Brett had feelings for her as well. Sadly, she knew what was happening; it was the money thing. What could she do about it? How could she convince Brett that they could have a relationship in spite of his qualms about what he called "their economic disparity?" The answer was obvious. She must somehow detach herself from the family wealth. And she must discuss it with him.

After the February board meeting adjourned, Beverly and Brett remained in the conference room. Brett, reorganizing a folder, looked toward the end of the table and asked her, "So, how did I do?" It was about the presentation he had made. Beverly had an idea for a new charitable project. She had worked it all out and then asked Brett to present it to the board. More at home with data and computer codes than with speaking, he was reluctant at first but she convinced him to do it, which he did and did well.

Bev gathered up her papers. Smiling broadly she said, "You did great. See, I told you you'd be better than me and I was right. You had their attention all the way. I'm proud of you."

As they both headed for the conference room door, Brett stopped her to give her a peck on the cheek. "Thanks, but most of that was your idea. I didn't do that much."

She looked at him intently. "You know that is the first time you've kissed me since New Year's Day?"

"Should I not have?" He swept his arm around the room. "I mean here at work?"

"No, I meant, oh never mind." She walked out of the room.

She left Brett wondering what had just happened. He was well aware that she had feelings for him, as he did for her, but he couldn't see any way that it could work. The simple fact was that they lived in two totally different worlds and he could not contemplate a situation where those worlds could come together and be compatible. Nothing had changed since New Year's Day. He wished things could be different, but unless he could—he smiled ruefully at this thought—win a lottery, what was the point? She needed to hook up with someone who traveled in her world.

Meanwhile, he wondered if remaining at the Noble Charitable Trust was a good idea. Maybe he should leave and work elsewhere. The trouble was, he really liked his job and wanted to stay, maybe someday become one of the executives. That would be ideal. If he were an executive making a big salary, then being with Beverly might work. He brightened at the thought. But his smile dimmed as he reasoned that even the top guy doesn't make *that* much money.

Nonetheless, he and Beverly could still enjoy working together with a lunch once in a while—or could they? He had been thinking about asking her out to dinner but kept putting it off. Going to lunch was okay but a dinner date? Probably not a good idea. Maybe she'll find someone else. That would be good. Or would it? He had a momentary flash of some guy in bed with Bev. He was surprised that the thought made him angry. He wanted to be that guy.

It was a sunny morning and warm for the time of year. Bev, Ed and Sandy were finishing breakfast. Bev said, "How about we all go sailing? It looks like it's going to be a beautiful day."

Ed looked up from the newspaper. "Sure. How about you, Pilcher? You up for a sail on your namesake?"

"I was going to go to the office today but there's nothing earth-shaking going on. So, okay, why not?"

"Good!" Beverly said, looking at her watch. "It's almost eight. Shall we leave, say, in a half-hour?" She didn't wait for an answer but went running up the stairs to her room.

Sandy picked up the dirty dishes. Ed folded the paper, tossed it in the wastebasket and came up beside her. He said, "She looks a little brighter today." He paused then decided to say what was on his mind. "I think she's been a little depressed recently. Have you noticed it?"

"Actually, I have." Sandy turned the faucet off and gave Ed her full attention. "I think it started shortly after Pat left. I asked her several times if there was anything she wanted to talk about but she kept insisting she was fine, even though she also admitted that she missed having Pat around. Of course you know how it is with those two."

"Yeah, well, maybe being out on the water will cheer her up and maybe we can coax some information out of her about what's wrong." Ed finished his coffee, rinsed out the cup and put it in the dishwasher. "She saw Dr. Millstein yesterday. Did she tell you anything about her visit?"

"All she told me was that it went fine. I tried to get her to tell me more but she said there was nothing more to tell that was interesting. I don't think it's a good idea to press her for details of her sessions so I don't."

For an hour or so they all enjoyed the pleasure of manually sailing the boat, then Bev asked Ed to shorten sail and turn on the autopilot. She called to Sandy who was on the deck and asked her to come down to the cockpit.

Sandy dropped into the cockpit. "What's up?"

"Have a seat Mom and you too, Dad. I want to talk to you guys about something." Sandy and Ed sat together on the port side bench. Bev pulled up a deck chair opposite. "Okay, here's the deal: when I was at Dr. Millstein's I told him about a problem I was having that I felt was, you know, interfering with my recovery. He told me I should discuss it with you and so..." A deep breath of sea air seemed to fortify her. "Here we are."

Ed and Sandy exchanged looks.

Bev took another deep breath. "Okay. Here goes. As you know, I have been working with Brett Peterson the past few months. He's a real nice—"

"Smart as hell," Ed broke in. Sandy frowned at him for interrupting.

Bev nodded. "And a serious kind of guy. Other than at New Year's, we haven't been dating or anything but we've had a bunch of lunches together. Anyway, I really like him." She paused and gave them a questioning look. "You think he's a good guy, too, don't you?"

Ed nodded and Sandy said, "Sure, honey. He's a very nice boy, which is why we had no qualms about you spending time with him New Year's Eve. So, you like him. Why wouldn't you? He's smart and darn good looking to boot. But I take it you're having a problem…" Sandy let a question hang in the air.

"Not with him. I'm not having a problem with him; it's the other way around. He's like having a problem with me."

Her parents looked astonished. "What the—" Ed started, but Sandy shushed him and nodded for Beverly to continue.

She gave them a recap of the conversation she and Brett had about their economic disparity. She elaborated, "See, I paid for everything for him and for Pat's date. It was expensive. The dinner was over five hundred bucks and the suite for two nights was like twelve hundred."

"Holy smokes," Ed exclaimed. "That's a hell of a lot of money to blow over a dinner and a hotel room."

Sandy said, "Okay, Ed, you can discuss it with Beverly some other time." She turned to Bev. "Go on with what you were saying, honey."

"No, Dad's right. It was totally insane. I agree and it won't happen again. But that's exactly the point I want to make now. This is what Brett was talking about. He was appalled by the cost of the dinner. He said I lived in a different world, not just me but all rich people. He said we have no future together because he can't live in my world. It's not only that he can't afford to—he doesn't even want to." Bev looked down at her hands clasped on her lap. "To tell you the truth, I don't think I want to live this way anymore, either. It's unreal. It's crazy and nothing like the life we used to have. If you think back to before the lottery and the way things were then, you just have to know that we were happier and more grounded in reality than we are now." She looked up at them, her eyes pleading for their understanding.

Sandy and Ed exchanged a little smile, then Sandy, her hand in Ed's, told Beverly, "Dad was talking about that very thing when we came home New Year's Eve." She turned to him. "Do you remember what you said about the people we met that night? You said we had nothing in common with them except having lots of money. You remember?"

"Of course, I remember." He looked at Beverly. "I said something about how the jewelry the women had on was worth more than our house."

"Yes, but tell Bev what else you said."

"What? I don't remember any...Oh, wait a minute. I said I wished we were back in Arizona where—"

Sandy finished for him. "You said you thought we should move someplace where the people are more like us. And then you said, you'd just like to go bowling and have a beer at some bar with people you could just talk to who would know what you were talking about. Am I right?"

"Pretty close. And I'll tell you something else, both of you." He leaned forward. "I've been thinking more and more about doing just that. Getting the hell away from all this—well, not this boat, I love this boat—but away from Malibu and everything that goes with it."

Beverly jumped out of her chair and threw her arms around Ed's neck. "That's exactly what I was going to tell you I wanted us to do. Get out of this crazy lifestyle before we're ruined forever."

During the sail back to the marina, they found themselves bubbling with excitement. It was a bizarre scene—the three of them discussing ways and means of becoming un-rich. After securing the boat in its slip, they continued the conversation in the car, eagerly planning the steps they could take to get back to living as they had before winning the lottery. By the time they reached home they had a rough idea of a plan. As soon as they got in the house, Beverly got a pad and they sat down at the breakfast table. Beverly wrote down the key points.

1. Buy a smaller home in one of the little towns in southwest LA (near the water?).
2. Sell the Malibu home with most of the furnishings.
3. Sell the Aston-Martin and buy a pickup. (Ed's idea)
4. Keep the boat but move it to a marina near new home. (Ed's idea)
5. Keep Trust office in Santa Monica.
6. Bev and Pat live at home. Both work at Trust part time and go to UCLA. B & P get modest disbursements for living and school expenses from their education trusts. (Doubt that Pat will go for that. Bev's comment)
7. Sandy will work full time (more or less) as office manager of the Charitable Trust with a reasonable salary (Don't think that's legal. Ed's comment)
8. Ed will continue as Chairman of the Board. He will try to get a job as a supermarket manager. (Ed's idea) (That won't happen. Sandy's comment)
9. Ed could turn over most of the money that has not been previously designated for some other purpose, to the Trust (have to consult with advisors. Ed's comment)
10. Live on a budget of $300,000/yr. as originally agreed. (Sandy's comment)

Beverly looked up from the page. "Anything else you can think of?"

Her parents exchanged glances. Sandy said, "I think that covers it. Of course before it's finalized, we can modify or change it as we go along. Plus, we need to get input from our financial committee as dad said. And we'd better talk to Pat, too."

Ed said, "I think we have a good start with what you have there." He tapped the legal pad with a finger. "And we definitely want to talk to the guys about the financial aspects, tax problems and that kind of thing." He suddenly broke into laughter. "You know what's going to happen when we tell them about all this, don't you?"

Beverly said, "They're going to think I'm not the only one in the family who needs to see a shrink." She began to laugh and soon all three of them were laughing. "Of course," she blurted out, "they'll be right. We *are* crazy!"

Sandy called Pat that evening to tell her what the plan was. Both Ed and Beverly were on extension phones listening in and adding their comments.

When Bev read her the list of things they thought they might do, Pat's reaction didn't really surprise them. "What are you people smoking? Why in the world would you want to do that?"

"Because it will get us out of this phony life and back to reality," Ed said.

"Well, you don't have to give all the money away to do that. Just because we're rich doesn't mean we have to act like it. You can be as conservative and natural as you want. You can still give millions of dollars away like you've been doing. Hey, if you're feeling guilty about being rich, give more of it away. The point is…oh, hell. What is the point?"

Beverly said, "Look, Patty, normal everyday people—you know, people like we used to be, they feel different about us because we are different and it's the money that makes us different."

Pat fired back, "What you mean is that Brett thinks you're different. Come on, isn't that what this is about? Hey, you can be a normal working girl if you want. Just because we have money doesn't mean you have to use it."

Ed jumped in, "Listen, Pat, I feel the same way as Bev. This has nothing to do with Beverly and her boyfriend—"

Bev raised her voice several decibels. "He's not my boyfriend, he's—"

Now Ed's voice was elevated. "As I was saying, your mother and I want to get away from Malibu and all that goes with it and live the life we used to live back in—"

Sandy joined the fray. "Okay, okay. Everybody quiet down and let's not get into a shouting match." She lowered her voice. "Here's the way it is, Patty—we think this plan is going to make us, as a family and as individuals, more responsible, more realistic, and by that I mean, more down to earth and happier. You and Beverly both have your trusts for your education, but also as I recall, each of you has a million dollars that has been invested and probably worth quite a bit more now. So the reality is, you both will be relatively well off. What you do with that money is your business. You can live it up or spend it wisely or give it away. That's up to you."

Pat replied, "Okay. Whatever. But here's the thing, I like the freedom that money gives me. I enjoy being able to do what I want, spend what I want and not have to worry about it. You know!"

"All right, then," Ed said. "Nothing is going to happen in the next month or so. It could take six months to accomplish it. Hell, I don't know what all the legal and technical aspects will be. But Patty, you'll have plenty of time to think about what it is you really want to do. I can always give you more, a lot more before this plan goes into effect. Don't worry about it. When you come home in May, we'll have plenty of time to work on the details."

Sandy added, "Is that alright, honey? We won't do anything until after you come home and we've all had a chance to think about it and talk it over."

Patty said, "Listen you guys, I don't want you to think I'm like being a greedy bitch or something. This is a big deal and once it's done you may not be able undo it. So let's give this a real good thinking through." Her voice held a distinct chill.

"Patty?" Bev broke in. "Are you mad at me about this? I don't want anything to—"

"Hey, this is just kind of a shock, that's all. I'm sorry if I said anything to upset you. I didn't mean to. But you and I have always been straight up with each other and please, please let's keep it that way, okay? I love you and want you to be happy and I'll be a hundred percent behind you, whatever you do. But..."

"I know, I know. Don't worry, we all want it to work for each of us, right? I'll talk to you soon."

Ed and Sandy said goodbye in unison and the call ended. Ed looked at the other two and remarked, "I'm not going to do anything about this for a while. Maybe we got carried away and Pat could be the one who's thinking straight."

"You're not changing you mind about doing this, are you?" Bev asked.

"No, but you always have to remember—there's more than one way to skin a cat."

Chapter 36

True to his word, Ed did nothing to further advance the scheme. Even when he met with his financial committee, he refrained from mentioning it. Frankly, the appeal of the plan was losing significance except for the basic element—to change their lifestyle, leave the big house in Malibu and try to recapture the life they had before September 2005. The exact steps to making that happen had become more elusive.

This particular night, Ed and Sandy were in bed. Ed had been watching TV and listening through earphones so not to disturb Sandy, who happened to be reading a story about a couple who had won millions of dollars in a local lottery and within three years had somehow managed to become penniless. Sandy lowered the book and said something. Ed removed his earphones.

"Sorry, what did you say?"

"I said, there but for the grace of God go us. These people I'm reading about won a lottery, something like twelve million dollars and blew it all away in a few years. That could have been our story."

Ed scoffed, "No, it couldn't. We had a good plan right from the start. The fact is we have more money right now than the eighty-eight million we won. So, no way could that be our story."

"I said *could* have been. It could have been if we hadn't been wise enough to know how to handle it." She put the book on the bedside table and switched off her reading lamp. She rolled onto her side and looked at him. "I think we've done a pretty good job of not going crazy with all the money, don't you think?"

"We've had our moments of craziness." He couldn't help chuckling, albeit somewhat ruefully. "Like this house for example..."

"And your fancy-shmancy convertible and your sailboat and your daughters' colleges and condo and—"

Ed cut in with a smile. "Easy does it, Pilcher. They're *Our* daughters. How about your designer dresses and shoes? Not to mention the clothes you bought for the twins that didn't exactly come off the rack at Walmart. Oh, and let's not forget your fresh flowers twice a week, your full time cook, the housekeepers and—"

Sandy couldn't hold back a guffaw. "Fine! The point has been made and then some. Sure that was extravagant but—you know how it's been. After all, it's a fact—we are rich! However we're certainly not like the people in that dumb story. By and large, I think we've spent money wisely but probably not frugally. When you have millions, there is no need to be frugal." She winked at him. "Although you do need to be sensible."

Ed swept a lock of hair behind Sandy's ear. "See, that's what I love about you. You always manage to put things in their proper perspective."

"Is that what I just did?"

"Yes, darling, that's what you did." He kissed her on the lips. "So, you know what I'm going to do tomorrow?"

"No," Sandy replied, "but I'm sure you're about to tell me."

Ed propped his head up with his hand and said, "I'm going to sell the Aston Martin. A couple guys said they would like to buy it. And then I'll buy a pickup."

"That's a good idea." Sandy rolled on to her back to gaze at the ceiling in thought. Meanwhile, I'm thinking of calling a realtor and putting this house up for sale."

"Whoa. We told Patty we would wait till she comes home before we did anything drastic," Ed said.

"Putting the house on the market doesn't mean it's going to sell right away. Houses like these take time to sell. So I think we should to go ahead and list it."

"For how much?"

"I don't know. What do you think we should ask?"

Ed considered it. "Well, we paid four-seven and the furniture and stuff was a half a mil or more so maybe we should ask five or five-five. You probably should ask a realtor."

"You know what else we should do?" Sandy said. "We should start looking around for a house that's not too far from the UCLA campus and our office in Santa Monica."

"Hey, slow down."

"Look, even Patty seemed alright with our letting the house go. And all I'm saying is we start looking. Even if we buy something, chances are we wouldn't move in until we sold this house. We need something by the time the girls start school this fall. I don't want them commuting every day from here."

Ed turned out the bedside lamp. "Once again, you're right. We'll take a drive tomorrow and check out some neighborhoods and see what's out there."

Beverly opened the picnic basket she had brought from home and set the contents on her desk. She laid out plastic plates, utensils, cups, and paper napkins. She looked up as Brett came through the door.

"What's all this?" He surveyed the array as he dropped into the visitor chair. "Not going out?"

"We have cold chicken, potato salad, some fresh veggies, and Mrs. Weir's famous blueberry pie. There's home-made lemonade in the Thermos." Bev could not have been more pleased with herself. "Go ahead, help yourself."

"Looks good," he said as he picked up a chicken leg and bit into it. "It *is* good. Very good. That lady knows how to cook." He took another bite and filled his plate with salad and a few raw string beans. "So, does your mother ever cook or does Mrs. Weir fix all the meals?"

"Of course she cooks. My mother is a damn good cook. Mrs. Weir just does dinner and not every night." She gave him a mock-frown. "You need to remember that up until my dad won that lottery, we were just regular folks living in a little subdivision in Peoria, Arizona. Remember—I told you about us. My dad was a supermarket manager and my mother was an office manager."

Brett held up both hands in surrender. "I'm sorry, I didn't mean to get you all defensive. I was just curious, that's all." He gave her a disarming smile.

"Hey—I've got nothing to defend. We got rich because my dad happened to buy a ticket with the winning numbers. The point is, we are not really a part of that super-rich culture."

"I understand. You're just like the rest of us except you happen to have a lot of money but other than that—" He stopped to spear a slice of tomato.

"No, no other than that. We *are* just like most everyone else." She put her fork on the plate. "In the near future, I can tell you that we will be just like everyone else in every way. You know why?"

"I have no idea."

"We've decided to move out of Malibu and get a place in some nice family neighborhood and give all the money to the Trust and live like we used to. My dad and mother will get regular jobs and they'll live off of what they make. So, no more fancy cars. No more spending money like we used to. All of that stuff is over. Pat and I are going to UCLA and we'll be on a strict budget." She gave Brett a look that conveyed, *how do you like that!*

She sat back and folded her arms over her chest.

Brett, dumbfounded, stared at Bev for a long time without speaking.

Bev dropped her arms on to the desk and said, "Well? No comment?"

Brett shook his head. "Ah, not really." He thought for a moment. "Well, yes. Maybe I do have a comment."

"Let's hear it."

His response was abnormally loud. "Are you people crazy? What in the hell are you thinking? You're going to give all those millions of dollars away and live like us common folk? Sorry, but I think that's the dumbest thing I've ever heard."

It was Beverly's turn to be dumbfounded. She yelled, "Why is it dumb? We think it's...it's noble." She had to laugh in spite of herself. "I know. A pun. Sorry."

Brett couldn't resist a chuckle. "I know what you meant and I'm sure the concept of it is to be admired—millionaire gives all his money away so he can resume former mediocre lifestyle."

"Hold it. There was nothing mediocre about our former lifestyle. It was just fine."

Brett picked up his fork and scooped up some potato salad. He kept her in his sights as he chewed. "Damn, this is really tasty." He swallowed and said, "Okay, your old lifestyle was fine. You can still live like that if you want, without getting rid of the money. Your folks can go to work and earn wages like the rest of us if they want, without getting rid of the money." He picked up a chicken wing and was about to take a bite when he had another thought. "Wait a minute. Is this about you and me and—"

Bev cut in, "And the money disparity thing? Could be. You told me that we live in two different worlds. Okay, if we do then why can't I leave my world and move into yours? I want to be a part of your life. What's so complicated about that? The world I came from and plan to return to is your world." She sat back and waited.

"Beverly," he said. "Just what the hell is this really about?"

"It's about closing the divide between us. It's about pointing out that I am really—bank account aside—the same as you. Same values. Same interests. I want you to see that. Look," she almost begged, "what do you see here? Fancy food? Pricey restaurant? And here we are enjoying ourselves just the same."

"It really *is* good food," Brett said, warming up to her speech.

"Damn right. So," she asked with a distinct twinkle, "are you going to invite me out to dinner and have like a regular date? Are you going to take me to your place and spend the night with me? Because if I was you, I'd quit screwing around and ask me out right now."

Brett's eyes crinkled, his mouth broadened into a wide smile and a low laugh escaped his lips. "You are something. Okay, you win." He stood and went to her. He was going to say, "Beverly, I'd like you to have dinner with me and afterward—" Instead, he had another idea that he hoped would give her a laugh. He got down on one knee and in a somber voice said, "Dear Beverly. Even though I'm not fit to bask in the glow of your beauty and even though my humble station in life precludes much of what I long for, I nonetheless fearlessly ask you to accompany me to a place where food and drink are served and there to sup with me. Afterward, I shall bed thee with most care and concern for your comfort and caress thee in such a way as to remove all inhibitions. So, how say you to this proposition?"

At first, Beverly was speechless. Then she broke out in gay laughter but in a moment, tears trickled down her cheeks. She reached for a napkin and patted her eyes. Holding his face with both hands, she purred, "That was beautiful. Thank you. And I eagerly accept your kind offer of dinner and sex." A warm smile blossomed as she whispered, "Especially the sex."

Pat had occasionally been dating Wesley Blanchard before she came home for Christmas vacation. However, when she returned to Vassar in January, she and Blanchard began going out every weekend. Blanchard had a 2008 Ford Shelby GT and he would brag that he could make the seventy-five mile drive from Columbia to Vassar in a little over an hour. He rarely mentioned the number of speeding tickets he received en route.

Blanchard, she learned, came from a substantial family who owned a large home in Clarendon Hills, a prestigious Chicago suburb. He had one older sister who was studying law at Harvard. Wes would graduate from Columbia with a degree in engineering at the end of May and he planned to continue his education at MIT in Cambridge. Pat hadn't told him that she would be leaving Vassar at the end of the term. As she told Bev during one of their marathon phone conversations, she "didn't want to screw things up."

On a Saturday evening, Pat and Wes had dinner with cocktails and a great bottle of wine at a lovely restaurant in the city. Pat got a glimpse of the bill—funny how the cost of things never seemed to be a matter of concern to Wes. On several occasions she virtually pleaded with him to allow her to pay for their dinner but Wes thanked her politely and refused the offer. This evening, when the waiter presented the check, Pat made a grab for it but Wes beat her to it.

"Pat, for gosh sake, stop doing that, will you please? Just call me old-fashioned."

"I know," Pat replied, "but it just doesn't seem right that you always end up getting stuck with the bill. After all, this isn't like the 1950s. Women like to pay their share sometimes."

"I know your family is wealthy. I know all about the lottery thing. Hell, after your sister was grabbed down in Mexico, your family's life history was all over TV and—"

"Yeah, that was miserable."

Wes nodded. "That was a bad deal, no two ways about it " He pushed back his chair. "Want to hit the clubs?"

"I don't know. Do you?" Pat replied.

"Want an honest answer?"

"Sure."

"Let's run over to my place, smoke a little weed, get high—not too high—and get in bed. Sunday morning we'll get some breakfast, pick up a copy of the *Times*, get back in bed and read the whole damn paper."

Pat gave him a shove. "You gotta be kidding, right?"

"What? No."

"You and me are gonna get in bed and read? I don't think so. But good luck anyway."

Pat and Bev were on the phone again. Bev told Pat, "Mom and Dad are thinking about listing the house for sale. Dad told her to wait until they find another home they want to buy. So I don't know, but I'd say they are totally serious about making the move."

"It's their decision to make, you know. Besides, it's what you want as well, so you should be happy about it." There was an edge to Pat's tone.

Bev said, "I am happy about it but I'm not so sure you are, at least that's the vibe I'm getting from you."

"You're right. I'm not. I've said so right along. I think it's crazy to leave that house and blow off all that money, but it's their money, not ours, and they should be able to do what they want. I mean the moving and all, I guess that's fine if that's what they want to do, but all the other bullshit, I'm not down with that."

Bev changed the subject, and asked about Wes. Pat, as always, told her everything that happened on every date, from soup to sex. "I really like this guy—a lot, you know? But he's going home to Chicago and I'm going to California and theoretically I'm going to UCLA this fall while he's clean across the country in Cambridge. That sucks."

Bev asked cautiously, "What do you mean, theoretically? We're already enrolled."

Pat, after much prodding from Bev, finally got to the meat of it. "What I guess I'm saying is that, maybe I should stay at Vassar for another year and see if this thing with Wes is going anywhere."

"What are you talking about? Now, you're the one who's talking crazy. So you have had some good sex with the guy. Good for you, but that's not love, for God's sake. And if it is love, okay, fine, then it should be able to survive a little separation."

"If we weren't going to the poorhouse," Pat declared sarcastically, "then I could fly to Massachusetts every now and then and see him, but under the new rules that would be impossible, wouldn't it?"

Pat was sorry she said it. She realized Bev would take it as a major breach—perhaps their first ever. She knew Bev was counting on her being with her at home, at school, everywhere, just like in the past. But now some boy had managed to take her place..

Pat didn't want to leave Bev in that frame of mind. "Listen, baby, I'm just like, you know, talking. I would never do anything that would upset you or make you have bad feelings toward me. You know that, right? We're just talking. If a choice would ever be about you or some guy, you know it would be you. You're my twin. We're like one person and that's the way I want it to be."

Bev's reply was barely audible. "You scare me, Patty. Something has changed. You have changed. It's not just about your Wes. No, something in your thinking has changed. All I ask is that you think of the big picture. It's your life but the decisions you make now could affect you for the rest of it."

"I know. Don't worry. We'll figure it all out. I won't let you down, I promise. Now, I've gotta go to bed, it's after 2 a.m. here. Okay? So goodnight. Give my love to Mom and Dad and to Brett. He's a nice guy and I'm tickled you two are finally working it out. I love you. Bye."

"Bye, Patty, I love you too."

Late that night, Sandy burst into Bev's room. Bev was thrashing about and screaming, "Get off of me, get off of me."

Sandy wrapped her arm about Bev and rocked her. "It's okay, darling. You're okay, you're home in your own bed." When the thrashing continued, Sandy shook Bev firmly and commanded, "Wake up, Beverly. WAKE UP!"

Bev's eyes sprung open. She stared at her mother, blinked a few times and took several deep breaths. When she had calmed down a bit, she whispered, "I'm afraid we're going to lose Patty."

Chapter 37

After attending a brief staff meeting at the Trust office in Santa Monica, Ed and Sandy took a drive to see some of the better neighborhoods and possibly find a home for sale. A Santa Monica location would be ideal for the girls as the UCLA campus was about five miles away. They cruised around for an hour through many lovely areas with wide, tree lined streets and attractive homes. They drove down Montana Avenue with its tall palms and tidy grass lawns. Montana Avenue ended at Fifth Street.

"Which way? Right or left?" Ed asked.

Sandy craned her head around looking both ways and said, "Let's take a right. This looks nice."

Ed made the turn and immediately stopped. "Hey, look at that house, the yellow one across the street. It's got a realtor's sign."

Ed parked in the shade of an enormous sycamore. "Let's take a look around." The two-storey house was a little larger than the houses on either side and had a small lawn in front, nestled in pleasant, mature landscaping. A white wood fence ran parallel to the sidewalk and just behind the fence were thick bushes.

Sandy pulled the phone from her purse and called the advertised number. The phone was answered by a woman who introduced herself as Ruth Krasner. Her office was just minutes away, she told Sandy, and if they would wait, she would be happy to show them the home. Fifteen minutes later, Ms. Krasner drove up in a Cadillac SUV.

Escorting them up to the door, Ms. Krasner said, "We're in luck. Mrs. Goodwin is home and she said we could come in and have a look around."

The agent toured Ed and Sandy through the home, pointing out, in realtor fashion, all the wonderful and unique features. Sandy was impressed with the layout and the quality and how very clean and tidy everything was. Then, gaining permission from the owner, Ed and Sandy walked around the home again by themselves, only this time they scrutinized things more critically. On the second floor, Ed said, "Four good size bedrooms, excellent bathrooms and a nice office up here. Downstairs has everything we need and it looks like they've taken good care of the place." He ran a hand over a gleaming wainscot and turned to Sandy. "Do you like it?"

"It's very nice," she said. "I could live in this house."

"I'm sure you could. The question is, do you want to?"

Sandy cocked her head and flashed a smile. "You're going to buy it, aren't you?"

"We'll see."

They found Ms. Krasner and the owner in the kitchen. Ed asked, "How much are you asking for the place?"

Krasner replied, "It was listed at $449,000 but the Goodwins have lowered the price because of the recession to $399,000, which makes it quite a bargain, don't you think?"

Ed said, "A bargain? I don't know about that. How many square feet of living area?"

Krasner looked at the listing sheet. "3,600."

"We really didn't want to sell the home," Mrs. Goodwin said, "but this recession has hit us hard. My husband got laid off a couple months ago and there's no way we can afford to make the mortgage payments now."

Sandy felt sorry for her. "What sort of job did Mr. Goodwin have?"

"It was a fine job. He was the CFO of Bidwell-Collins, a manufacturing company that makes parts for GM cars and trucks. It's really sad, you know. They've let half their work force go."

"Oh, my," Sandy said. "I'm so sorry."

Ed asked her, "Would you mind telling me how much you folks still owe on house?"

Mrs. Goodwin looked at Krasner. "Should I...?"

"That's up to you," the agent answered, "Although I don't think it will do any harm to tell him."

"Very well," Mrs. Goodwin said. "I believe we owe close to four hundred fifty thousand—we just bought it a couple years ago."

Ed thought a moment, looked at Sandy, who nodded. "Okay, here's our offer: We'll pay $470,000 cash if Ruth will agree to take no more than a $20,000 commission." He turned to Ruth. "Would you be willing to do that?"

She gave the Nobles a large smile. "Of course I would. That is so generous of you, Mr. Noble."

Mrs. Goodwin sat in a chair, covered her face with her hands and began to cry. Then she looked up at Sandy. "Why would you do that? You don't even know me. You want to pay me more than I'm asking? Nobody does that."

"We do." Sandy touched Mrs. Goodwin's cheek gently. "This is what we do, help folks out who are having a hard time."

Ed took the realtor aside, handed her his card and said, "Write up the offer and check it over to make sure it's right, then fax it to me."

Ruth looked at the card. "Yes, Mr. Noble. I'll take care of everything right away."

On the drive back to Malibu, Sandy said, "Goodness, that was an unexpected event. That woman was overwhelmed, especially when you said she and her husband could stay there rent free until they found a place."

"Like you told her, Pilcher, this is what we do." To Ed's way of thinking, the first step of their plan was coming along very nicely.

Spring vacation at Vassar began on Friday, March 6, and Pat flew home the following day. That Sunday the twins belatedly—but together—celebrated their twentieth birthdays. Bev had organized the whole thing. She invited the six full-time Trust staff, plus some of her and Pat's closest friends from both high school and UCSB. She had also invited, Missy, the flight attendant who'd been so helpful.

Most of the guests had arrived and were clustered in small groups chatting, laughing and having a good time. Ed was talking to some of the kids when the doorbell rang. He excused himself and hurried to the door.

"I'm Melissa Dembinski," she said as they shook hands. "I'm a friend of Beverly. Are you her father?"

"Yes, I'm Ed Noble. Come on in. Bev's told us about meeting you—you're the stewardess, right?"

Missy laughed. "Well, that was what they called it when I started decades ago but now I'm a flight attendant. Different title, same job."

Sandy came into the hallway and saw Missy with Ed. "I know exactly who you are," she said, extending her hand. "Beverly has told us about you. We certainly appreciate what you've done to help her." She gave Missy a warm smile. "Do you mind if I give you a hug?"

"I'd love a hug." Releasing Sandy, Missy said, "I can sure see where Beverly gets her good looks and her height."

They led Missy out to the patio where Bev and Pat were chatting with a cluster of girls. As soon as Bev saw Missy, she grabbed Pat's hand and broke away from the group. Missy, with arms wide apart, was ready to receive Bev's hug.

Pat shook Missy's hand and said, "I can see you're a little confused. We're twins but we obviously don't look anything alike."

"I guess I assumed you would be similar but what a delight to find that you two each have your own special look."

Her hand in Missy's, Bev introduced her to every guest, including Brett Peterson.

After Bev excused herself to get Missy a drink, Brett and Missy asked each other the usual questions, except, unlike most mind-numbing party conversations, Missy found herself listening with great interest to everything Brett said.

"Your friend here seems a likeable kind of guy," Missy said to Bev when she returned.

Bev turned to Brett and winked. "He is a likeable guy...very likeable." She gave Brett a warm smile. Then she caught sight of Mrs. Weir, Sandy and Ed bringing platters of food. "Ah, here's our dinner." She stood and whistled loudly. "Come on, everyone, it's time to eat."

After all the other guests had departed, Beverly and Missy sat on the couch in Ed's office holding hands. Missy broke the peaceful silence. "You're a much different person than the girl I first saw on the airplane. Looks like you made it through the dark and are out in the light now. Am I right?"

"Maybe...well, maybe not the bright light but yes, I'm like a long way from where I was when I left Mexico."

"I'm just guessing, but your friend, Brett—is he responsible for that?"

Beverly smiled briefly and gave Missy's hand a squeeze. "Partially. But you were the one who first put me on the right track."

Missy gave her a hug. "That's sweet of you to say, but you know that you and only you have the power to change yourself." She leaned back and scanned the room, her eyes alighting on a large framed picture of Ed, Sandy and the twins. "And your family, they are a big part of it, too, I'm sure. They're lovely people."

"I know, I've got a great family." Bev went on to tell Missy about how the family was changing their lifestyle, moving away from Malibu and getting back to the way they used to be before the money.

"How...interesting," Missy said. "I'm inclined to ask again, if Brett had anything to do with that."

Beverly was taken aback. "What? I'm sorry, I mean, how did you come up with that?"

"I guess it's a vibe I got from Brett when we were talking earlier. It doesn't matter. What does matter is that you're okay and hopefully things will even get better for you." Missy looked at her watch. "It's getting late, I'd better get going. But I want you to remember that any time you want to talk about anything at all, please call me."

"I will."

Beverly walked Missy out to her car. Missy got in, opened the window and said, "I love you. Take care."

"I love you, too. Be careful driving home. Bye."

The family had one conversation after another about how best to return to their former lifestyle. Pat had to be back at school by March 22 and by the time she left, they had discussed the subject until all four of them were tired of it. Sandy told the girls that they planned to move into the new home before school started in the fall so the girls wouldn't have to commute from Malibu. Whenever the subject of going to UCLA came up, Pat became ambivalent. It was all about Wesley Blanchard. She hated the idea of him being in Cambridge while she was a continent away. She had seriously considered remaining at Vassar but by this time, the deadline to make any changes had passed. The reality was she was enrolled for the fall semester at UCLA and if she was going to continue her education that was where she was going.

Bev and Pat had a long talk the night before Pat returned to school, especially about Pat's relationship with Wes. Pat couldn't say enough about what a great guy he was. She confided that she thought she was really in love with him. She became excited just talking about the great sex they were having. "Honest to God, Bev, I'm not kidding—it's killer sex!"

"Okay, I believe you," Bev said, "but great sex isn't great love. You know what I mean? It's part of it but it's not like all of it. That's why so many marriages end up in divorce. Once they have to deal with everyday life—children, job, all those things—good sex isn't enough."

"I know, I know." Pat put up a hand to stop Bev's lecture. "But I think it's more than sex with me and Wes. I think we're falling in love."

"Maybe you are, but all I'm saying is don't let it get in your way of planning for the life you really want. Look at Mom and Dad. See, there's a couple in love. They're the best of friends, they respect each other and they're people who you know will always be there for you." She squeezed Pat's hand. "That's the kind of love you want and that's what I definitely want for you. For me, too. And we shouldn't settle for less."

"How's it with you and Brett? You think that's going anywhere? Do you want it to?"

"Am I in love with Brett? No, I'm not but I think in time it could develop into love. He's a damn good lover. I've no complaints in that department. But Brett isn't like Wes, at least from what you've told me about him. No, he's cautious and very cerebral. He's not a guy who will jump in bed with a girl just because she's available. I think he's looking for more than a quick lay. But if he finds the right girl, I think he'd stick with her and make it work no matter what."

Pat said, "So are you the right girl?"

Bev replied, "I don't know but I'm going to stay with it and see where it goes. He's helped me a lot and well, I'm grateful for that. Plus," she added with a smile, "the benefits are pretty darn good."

Waiting at La Guardia for her luggage, Pat called Wes who was parked outside ready to pick her up. "Hi, honey. I'll be out as soon as I get my bags." She caught sight of the dark blue cases sliding down the conveyor to the carousel. "Ah, here they come now." Pat grabbed the two suitcases and wheeled them out to the pick-up curb. She saw Wes at the wheel of his Mustang and waved.

He bounded over and Pat threw her arms around him and they kissed and kissed again.

"Damn girl, it's good to see you," he murmured. He would have held her longer, but a traffic cop whistled for them to get moving. Laughing, they ran to the car, tossed the suitcases in the trunk and took off. Wes said, "I'll give you two options."

"What? Two options? What are you talking about?"

Wes glanced her way and smiled. "The options are, we drive to Vassar. That will take about an hour and a half which is too long. The second option is much faster. We go down this road about another mile to a motel where I have a room. That will only take five minutes. Which option do you prefer?"

Pat leaned over and kissed his cheek. "That is so genius. It tells me you can't wait an hour and a half to get into me."

"You got that right. I can't wait, and something tells me, neither can you, so it's option two, what a surprise. Here's the motel." He pulled into the drive, drove past the office portico and parked in front of room 110. "Here we are."

"You son of a gun," Pat exclaimed. "You sure know how to take care of a girl!" They pulled the suitcases from the trunk and went inside. Pat kicked the door closed then threw her arms around Wes and kissed him long and hard. "Okay, I'm going to take a hot shower and then..."

"In order to conserve water," Wes said, "would you mind if I join you?

Pat kissed him fiercely. "I would mind if you didn't."

"I can't believe it," Sandy said, recounting a visit that morning from potential buyers. "They walked through the house with Norma—actually they spent quite a long time looking around—and then they sat down in the living room and asked me a bunch of questions, then they got up and walked outside to the beach, and then they thanked me for my time and left." Norma Stern, the Nobles' listing agent, had obviously done a good job of showing the house.

"What did they think of the place? Did they say?" Ed asked.

"Norma said they were interested. We talked for a while and then she left. About an hour later, she called and said they'd made an offer."

"No kidding? How much?"

"The listing price is five-million-nine—remember that was Norma's idea. Their offer is for five-five, which is what we hoped to get so..." She grinned.

Ed laughed out loud. "So it's a no-brainer, unless there are some weird stipulations."

"Norma said it was a really clean offer. No contingencies. Just the usual inspections and we know—" She looked around at the immaculate space. "We know the house will pass with flying colors."

Ed used his cell phone to calculate the commission. Okay, call her back and tell her it's a deal. We'll need a month to get out of here and get the other house ready, so tell her to set the closing around the middle of April."

Ed sold his Aston-Martin to his lawyer friend, Aaron Feldman, and bought a top-of-the-line Chevrolet Silverado crew cab pickup. He drove his new truck home and happily displayed all its bells and whistles to Sandy. "Now, this is what us common folk drive. This vehicle has utility; I can haul stuff around in it."

Sandy gave the gleaming white truck an admiring glance and said, "Of course you can, sweetheart. That's been our problem ever since you came home with that stupid convertible. You couldn't haul stuff in it and God knows we had stuff that needed to be hauled."

Ed gave her hug. "Are you making fun of me and this wonderful machine? Well, when we start moving our *stuff* to the new house, you'll see how useful this pickup can be."

Chapter 38

On April 14 the moving van pulled up to the Malibu house. The movers loaded up the furniture and personal belongings that were not included with the sale and took them to the Nobles' new home in Santa Monica.

Ed and Sandy had furnished the new place without the aid of, as Sandy put it, "snooty interior decorators like Keisha Burkhardt." All of their purchases were made at local stores that Ed said, "didn't cost an arm and a leg." Furnishing and decorating their new home was a fun project for the three of them. Going from store to store, looking for the best values, actually being out there *shopping* was something they hadn't done—hadn't needed to do—for four years. They talked about doing some of the interior painting themselves but after doing one bedroom, they decided some things were far better handled by professionals.

On Thursday, April 16, the Nobles moved in the house on Montana Avenue. The next day, Ed and Sandy went to the title company office for the closing of their Malibu home. When all the papers had been signed and the deal completed, Sandy confided to Ed, "I have to say that Malibu was fun while it lasted, most of it anyway, but I'm not sorry to say goodbye. I'll miss having the ocean at my back door. I'll miss Mrs. Weir and her wonderful meals. I'll miss the housekeeper and her girls and the gardeners and the gal that used to bring the flowers. But I won't miss living there, not really. I'm looking forward to getting back to the kind of married life we had in Arizona so, all in all, I know we're doing the right thing."

That evening, sitting around the little table in the kitchen, with a dinner made by Sandy, Ed said, "Before we dig in, let's do something we don't often do. Let's say grace, okay?" They joined hands as Ed said, "Dear Lord, thank you for this meal and for the people who grew or raised it. Thank you for giving us the wisdom to do good works with the money we won and to finally realize what is truly important in our lives." Ed looked at Beverly, then Sandy and smiled. "We pray this move will be the beginning of a new life for each of us and our daughter Patricia, who will be joining us soon. In Jesus' name we pray, amen."

Beverly said, "Amen. Thank you, Daddy. That was really nice. And thank you and Mom for being there for me when I so desperately needed you." Her voice got a little choked up. "And for all the things you've done for Patty and me and for the hundreds of people you've helped." She looked down and could feel a flush coming over her face.

Sandy came to her and hugged her. "Don't be embarrassed, darling. That was a beautiful sentiment. Dad and I appreciate it and you."

"Amen to that, too," Ed said. "Now, let's enjoy our first dinner in our new home."

Pat and Wes were also about to have dinner. It was Saturday evening and they were at an intimate table at Watawa Sushi, a highly recommended Japanese restaurant in Queens. Wes had driven up to Vassar on Friday afternoon, slept with Pat that night and the two of them had gone back to Wes' apartment in the city on Saturday morning. They saw the movie *17 Again* in the afternoon, then went back to the apartment, made love, showered, dressed and drove to Queens.

Waiting for the first course, they sipped the exotic cocktails their server had suggested. Pat gazed starry-eyed at Wes, thinking, *oh my God, this boy is too much. Is this love or what? It's gotta be love—it's too beautiful not to be.* Aloud she asked, "You didn't say anything about the movie. Didn't you like it?"

"Yeah, it was good...not the best flick I ever saw but it was okay."

"I thought Zac Efron and Matthew Perry were good but I'll tell you something, that Leslie Mann is one cool chick, right? I'll bet we'll be seeing a lot more of her."

Pat said, "I don't know about her but I'll bet you'll be seeing a lot of me before this night is over."

Wes chuckled. "I certainly hope so." He set his drink down and leaned toward her. "Seriously, I want you to know that even though we are going to be apart after school is over, I'm not giving up on you—that is, if you don't want me to."

Pat quickly replied, "No, I don't want this to end, you know that." She lowered her voice. "This isn't just about the sex. I hope you know that by now."

"I do know that," Wes said earnestly. "I, well, I have strong feelings for you. I've never been so, I don't know, so..."

"Smitten?"

Wes couldn't help laughing. "Smitten. Geeze, where'd you come up with that word?"

Pat cracked a smile. "The dictionary. Look it up."

"I know what it means. Okay, I'm smitten by you. There, are you satisfied? But the point is, I can't spend the whole damn summer thinking about you and not seeing you. So what do you think about this idea? When we've finished our exams, we'll drive to my house in Clarendon Hills, that's near Chicago, and you'll meet my family and maybe some friends and after that—"

Pat held up a hand. "Wait a minute. What are you saying? You want me to meet your family? Why?"

Wes bit his lower lip and sucked in air. "I don't know—maybe because you're my girlfriend and I'm proud of you and you're beautiful and–" Wes threw up his hands. "Come on! I just want to, that's why. What's wrong with that?"

Pat didn't know how to respond. She got a respite when the server placed tiny bowls of Miso soup in front of them. For a long moment, she studied a piece of mushroom floating on the surface. She looked at Wes intensely. "What's wrong with that? Nothing is wrong. It's just, well, you caught me by surprise. I just wasn't prepared for that kind of invitation." She picked up a spoon and tasted the soup. "Mmmm, very good." Holding the spoon like a pointer, she said, "Okay, I'll do it. I just hope your folks don't kick my ass clean to California when they find out their darling boy is sharing a bed with some goofy blonde."

Wes nearly blew soup across the table. "Whaaat? No! They're not going to know that. Are you kidding? You'll be sleeping in a guest room, not with me. My family is totally straight, in fact super straight. Jesus! They'd be shocked if they thought you and I were having sex in their home."

Pat's laughter was spontaneous and loud enough to cause some patrons to glance at her. "I'm sorry," she gasped. "You're kidding, right?"

"No I'm not," he said emphatically.

"Really? Well, I sure wouldn't want to disappoint them."

Pat refrained from seeing Wes the week before and during final exams in May. She wanted to do well and she studied hard. Her mid-term GPA was 3.4 and she wanted to end the year with a 3.5 or higher. But throughout the run-up to the finals she couldn't keep him completely at bay. He would call her just to say, "Hey, how ya doing?" But those calls could last up to an hour and then Pat would be up till two or three in the morning trying to make up for lost time. During finals week, he honored her request not to call, but then she became anxious to hear his voice. The exams were hard, very hard, but in the end, she felt she did okay.

With finals over, she and Wes planned their trip to Clarendon Hills. Wes checked on towing Pat's car with his Mustang and found out it couldn't be done. He called car shippers who told him the cost would be around thirteen hundred dollars. The mileage from New York to LA, he learned was twenty-eight hundred miles. At a low thirty-five cents per mile, the cost to drive the car to California would be around a thousand dollars.

"What the hell," Pat said, "I'll just drive it, that way I can pack all my stuff in the car and not have to ship anything."

"Okay then, if that's what you want to do. It's a hell of a lot of driving. The trip to Chicago isn't too bad...about eight hundred miles. I've driven it in twelve hours but we could cut in a half and stop overnight someplace. The Chicago to LA part will be a couple thousand miles. If we drive around six hundred miles a day..." He pulled up Google, and said, "It says it will take 29 hours. You really want to do that?"

"You'd drive with me?" Pat brightened as a thought hit her. "Suppose we make a regular road trip of it? A vacation trip. We could stop different places and do some sightseeing, maybe spend a day or two in Vegas, stop at some national parks—it'd be fun!"

Pat explained the plan to her parents. "You don't mind me bringing Wes home to meet you guys, do you?"

Sandy fielded the question. "No, honey, but what's this all about? This sounds like a serious relationship. Is it?"

"I guess you could say that. I think I'm in love with him and I'm sure he loves me. But we're not talking like marriage, at least not until I've graduated and he gets his master's degree."

Ed was listening on an extension. "Pat, as far as I'm concerned, it's fine if you want him to come here for a visit, but thinking about this long range, how's it going to work? He'll be back east, you'll be here. Your chances for seeing each other are zero except maybe during school breaks."

"I know, Daddy, but who knows how this will end up? Maybe this will be like a test."

"All right then, but you have to promise us that you will call us every day during the trip. And Patty, I mean every day. I don't intend to go through another Mexican adventure."

Pat laughed. "Geeze Mom, we'll be nowhere near Mexico."

"You know what I mean. So, you'll call us every day while you're on the road?"

Pat stopped laughing when she recognized the near-panic in Sandy's voice. "Yes, Mom, I promise."

Ed added, "And no drinking and driving, right?"

"Okay, okay." Pat's exasperation was clear. "We don't drive drunk! In fact, I've never seen him drunk. Wes is a smart guy and sensible. You'll see."

The call ended and Ed joined Sandy downstairs in the kitchen where she was sitting at the table, still holding the phone. She looked up and said, "Well, what do you think about that?"

"You know what I think about it. The reality is there is nothing we can do about it one way or another. She's twenty years old, she has money, she can do what she wants. She's a good kid who is not inclined to make stupid decisions. So, I think she'll be alright."

Sandy let a long sigh escape through pursed lips. "I hope so."

Pat's stay in the Blanchard home was pleasant enough. Both of Wes' parents were very considerate and accommodating. They were, however, displeased at the prospect of Wes leaving for California so soon after coming home, in spite of his assurances that he would be back in a few weeks. Pat stayed a week before she and Wes left for California.

They drove to St. Louis in a little over four hours and then continued on toward Oklahoma City, stopping overnight in Henrietta. Pat called home. The next day they got into New Mexico where they took a little detour to Santa Fe, did some sightseeing and spent the night. Pat called home. The seven-hour drive the next day brought them to Phoenix. Pat wanted Wes to see where she used to live and they drove to her former home in Peoria.

Over dinner, they discussed whether they should head to LA or take a few more days and go to Vegas and have a look around. They opted for Vegas. Pat called home and told Sandy the plan. Sandy wanted them to come straight home from Phoenix. She lost that argument, so she cautioned Pat to be careful and not do any gambling.

At the start of the trip, Pat insisted that they would share all the expenses equally for food, gas, lodging—everything. And so they did. Driving on I-15 near the outskirts of Las Vegas, Wes spotted a Holiday Inn Express. He took the off ramp and swung on to the frontage road.

Pat had been napping but woke up when Wes made the turn. She looked around and said, "What's going on? Where are you going?"

"I'm going to that Holiday Inn over there. I thought we'd stay here instead of downtown. It'll be much cheaper."

"No, I don't want to stay here," Pat complained. "We need to stay where the action is. What's the point of coming to Vegas if we're going to stay out in the sticks? I was thinking Mandalay Bay or New York, New York, someplace like that down on the strip." She picked up the map and scanned it. "This place is miles from the strip. Get back on the 15. It'll take us downtown."

Wes parked in the motel lot and turned off the engine. He swiveled to face Pat. "Listen, we've already spent a ton of money and if we go to one of the big hotels, you know it's going to cost a couple hundred or more a night just for the room."

Pat's reply had an edge. "Okay, I get it. So, let's say our stay in Vegas will be my treat. How's that? After all, I'm the one who wanted to come here." She immediately saw his expression change.

With clipped words that surprised her, he barked, "No, we're not playing that game. We've never done that before and we're not doing it now."

"Done what? Pay for things? I've bought dinner and other things too. What the hell is wrong with that?"

He got right in her face. "You listen to me. You know exactly what we agreed to before we started this trip. We would share expenses equally. No exceptions. I'm telling you I don't want to blow five hundred or a thousand bucks on a couple days in Vegas."

Now Pat became aggressive. "If that's so, why the hell didn't you say so before we left Phoenix?"

Wes backed off. "I suppose I should have said something but I thought we could have fun here without going crazy."

Pat put her head back against the seat and took several deep breaths. She spoke slowly and quietly, "This is our first fight. I never thought we'd fight about anything, but of course, that's stupid. I suppose it was inevitable that the money thing would get between us. Your parents are obviously well off but that doesn't mean you are."

"That's right. I don't have millions like you."

"It's always the fucking money that screws things up, isn't it? My folks and sister have already figured it out. They sold the house on the beach in Malibu, my dad sold his Aston-Martin, they're gonna live like we used to before the lottery. I didn't want to do it. I like the money. I love the fancy clothes, the hot cars, the ability to spend money without even thinking about it. Like now. I can afford to drop a couple thou in Vegas—no problem." She rolled her head to the left and gazed at Wes. "My sister almost lost a very good guy because he said she lived in a different world and there was no way he could live that way. So she changed her world to more like the world we lived in back in Peoria. And my folks did the same. And now, she and Brett, her boyfriend, have a solid relationship."

Wes remained quiet looking straight ahead. After a while he turned to her. "I'm sorry, Pat. I guess we let things move too fast without understanding the reality of our relationship. Too much good sex and you end up thinking with the wrong organ. Maybe it's time we put our brains in charge."

Pat leaned into him. "Thinking with the wrong organ. That's good." She smiled. "Okay, go ahead and check in. We'll go someplace for dinner, maybe drive around the strip just to see what it's like and tomorrow we'll head to LA."

Chapter 39

Beverly finished her morning run and entered the house through the back door. "I'll have to admit it's not as much fun as running down the beach and ending it with a swim in the ocean but it's exercise anyway," she commented as she entered the kitchen.

Ed was standing in front of the stove, frying bacon. "Yeah, I know what you mean," he said without turning around. "It's the difference between driving a Chevy pickup and an Aston-Martin—that isn't quite as much fun either." He turned and smiled. "Anyway, you got some exercise and that's the important thing."

Bev went to the refrigerator and pulled out a bottle of orange juice. Pouring a glass full, she said, "It was okay, but like I said, you know." She gathered up some silverware and a couple of coffee cups and placed them on the table. "While you're at it, make some bacon for me, would you? What else are you having?"

"I was going to make some scrambled eggs with green chilies. You want some?"

"Sure. I'll make toast." She pulled a couple of slices of rye bread from the loaf and dropped them into the toaster. "Where's Mom?"

"She wanted to get some work done at the office this morning and be back home before Pat and her boyfriend arrive."

"Every time Patty and I talk, she spends most of it yakking about Wes. I hope he's half as good as she says he is." The toast popped up, Bev got some jam out of the refrigerator and took it and the toast to the table. Ed brought the plates of bacon and eggs plus a pot of coffee and the two of them sat down to eat.

Bev asked, "Are we still going sailing?"

"If you want to. We can take off right after breakfast."

Marina del Rey, where Ed now had his boat, was only five miles from their home. The boat was in a slip off of Palawan Way near Mother's Beach. In some ways, Ed considered this his sailing home, since it was at this marina that he and Sandy had first taken sailing lessons.

He parked the pickup, Bev grabbed the picnic basket with the food, and they walked down the pier. As they were getting things shipshape for motoring out of the harbor, Ed said, "You should bring Brett down here sometime and take him sailing. I'll bet he'd enjoy it. Pat and her boyfriend, too."

She stared at him. "What do you mean? I should take them sailing without you?"

"Sure, why not? You handle this boat as well as I do. You've become a first-class sailor. What's the matter? Don't you think you could do it?"

"I guess so. Wouldn't you worry I'd wreck the *Pilcher*?"

Ed started the engine and let it idle. "If I was worried, would I have said you could do it? Tell ya what. I'll crew today and you run the show. Let's see how you do."

Beverly jumped out on the dock and stood by ready to cast off when Ed gave the word.

Ed yelled, "Okay. Let go bow line." Bev pulled the knot and Ed reeled it in. "Let go stern." Bev undid the line and jumped into the cockpit. Ed stepped away from the helm and said, "Go ahead. Take her out."

She hesitated for a moment then took the wheel, advanced the throttle and backed out of the slip. As soon as the bow cleared the slip, she turned hard to port and used the bow thrusters to assist the turn. Lined up in the alley between the docked boats, she increased power.

"Good job," Ed said as Bev piloted the boat out of the marina into open water. "Okay, skipper," Ed yelled, "Let's roll out some sail."

Pat and Wes left the Holiday Inn Express at 7:30, stopped at a Denny's for breakfast, then got back on the I-15. They stopped in Victorville for gas and a snack then continued on to Santa Monica.

Pat used her cell phone GPS. "This will be interesting," she said. "I've never seen this house. They say it's very nice but after Malibu and our house on the beach..." She let the end of that thought evaporate.

Wes said, "I'm sure it's very nice." After a brief pause, he added, "After all, they didn't go broke. You said they just decided to scale down. I have to tell ya, I think that was a very cool move. Did you ever hear of anyone who won millions in a lottery ever do anything like that?"

"No, but we don't know what other winners have done...well, we do know about the ones who went crazy and spent it all in a few years, but I'm sure some winners were smart and have done alright. Anyway, I know my family has handled it pretty good." Pat was silent for a while. "Our charitable trust has given millions away and it looks like they'll be doing even more with the recession getting worse and so many people out of work."

Wes nodded. "You should be proud of your folks. You know, it takes courage and dedication and smarts to resist the temptations of being super rich. Anyway, I'm anxious to meet them and your twin sister, who you say doesn't look anything like you." He glanced in her direction with a sly grin. "In other words, she must be the pretty one."

Pat punched his arm.

"Hey, take it easy. I'll find out soon enough." Wes stopped at a traffic light. "Okay, here's Fifth. Now, which way?"

Sandy looked at her watch. "Gee, I better get going," she said to Brett. "Pat and her boyfriend should be getting to the house pretty soon." Sandy began to organize the paperwork she and Brett had been working on.

"You go ahead," Brett said, as he reached to take the papers from her hand. "I'll take care of it."

"Okay, thanks." She picked up her purse, took out her car keys and said, "Don't forget you're having dinner with us tonight. Come over around five-thirty."

"I'll be there. I'm kind of anxious to see what Pat's super-hero is all about."

Sandy chuckled. "Me too. See you later."

When Sandy got home, she saw a car parked in front. Just as she pulled in her driveway, the two front doors of the other car opened and Pat and Wes got out. Sandy pulled the key, got out of the car and ran into the arms of her daughter. "Have you been waiting long?" she asked.

"No, we just got here a few minutes ago. I called your office and Brett said you were on your way." Pat turned toward Wes, "Come, meet my mom."

Wes walked toward them to shake Sandy's hand. "I'm very pleased to meet you, Mrs. Noble." He gave Sandy a large smile. "You know, based on what Pat told me about you, I could have picked you out of a crowd."

Sandy laughed and said to Pat, "No doubt about it. Your friend sure knows how to score points." To Wes, she added, "And Pat's description of you was very accurate." To Pat she said, "Get your stuff and come on in." She looked in the car and said, "Oh, perhaps not all that, just what you need for now. You can unload the rest later."

"Where's Dad and Bev?" Pat wanted to know.

"They're sailing. They should be home by five." Sandy unlocked the front door and they went inside.

Pat dropped her suitcase in the foyer. "Excuse me for a minute. I'm just going to take a quick look around."

Sandy smiled at the young man. "Are you hungry?" she asked as she led the way into the kitchen. "I can fix you a snack to tide you over till dinner."

"I'm fine, thanks, ma'am. Well, maybe something to drink."

"How about a beer?"

"Awesome."

Pat came bouncing into the kitchen. "Hey, Mom, not bad. I like it."

"Did you notice the one bedroom that's not furnished? That's yours. We thought you would want to pick out the furniture and decorate it yourself. Wasn't that thoughtful of us? Actually, it was your sister's idea. Meanwhile, you guys can use the guest bedroom." Sandy couldn't help but smile. "There's just one bed. You don't mind sharing it, do you?"

Pat looked at Wes and the two broke into laughter. Pat said, "We can do that, although we've been using separate rooms on the trip here. But since it's all you have, I guess we'll have to make do." Her tone grew honeyed. "You don't mind do you, Wes?"

His face took on a pink glow. "Boy oh boy, that's a conversation you will never hear at my house."

Pat added, "He's right. We actually did sleep in separate rooms."

Bev started the engine after the sails had been stowed. "Shall I take it in?"

Ed stepped into the cockpit and stood next to her at the helm. "Of course but, keep a sharp eye."

"A sharp eye?" Bev said in a pirate's accent. "Aye aye, Cap'n, a sharp eye it is."

Bev piloted the boat skillfully to their slip, made the turn, backed to get lined up and then inched forward. Ed jumped out with the bow line. Bev reversed the engine for a few seconds and the boat stopped as if it had brakes. Ed grabbed the stern line and tied it down. He jumped on board as Bev shut down the engine.

"That was great, honey," he said, wrapping her in a bear hug. "If you want to bring Brett out and go sailing by yourselves, I hereby grant you a license to do it." He released her, stepped back and said, "No kidding, you put her in there like a champ." He checked his watch. "Now, we'd better get a move on and get home. Your sister and her boyfriend must be there by now."

When Ed and Bev entered the house, Pat came running up to throw her arms around Bev and give her a big kiss on the cheek. Then she took hold of Bev by the shoulders and held her at arm's length. "Damn girl, you be lookin' good. Man, that salt air must do wonders—it even turned your hair back to red."

Ed watched this playful scene with amusement for a moment. "Hey, Patricia, what am I, the invisible man?"

"Oh, Daddy. No, you're the extremely visible man," Pat said as she returned his hug. "You are and always will be the best father in America."

Sandy appeared with Wes in tow, and Pat made the introductions.

Ed was chatting with Wes in the library while the girls were busy in the kitchen preparing dinner. The doorbell rang and Ed yelled toward the kitchen, "I'll get it," but Bev beat him to the door.

She flung it open to greet Brett, who stood holding a bottle of red wine in one hand and a dozen red roses in the other. "May I come in, please? I was invited by the lady of the house who—"

Bev cut him off with a lavish kiss.

Ed took the bottle of wine, examined the label and said, "Thank you. That wasn't necessary but since you brought it and it's really a very good wine, we should drink it."

Brett kissed Bev and in his quiet voice said, "These roses are for you. Your Dad told me that roses bring luck.

Ed smiled. "That's right, my boy. Come on, I'll give you a beer and you can meet the famous Wes."

Pat came out of the kitchen, gave Brett a hug saying, "Looking good! Bev must be taking good care of you, hmmm?" She turned to Ed. "What did you do with Wes, Daddy? I want to introduce them."

"He's in the library passed out drunk."

"Very funny," Pat said.

Bev excused herself and returned to the kitchen while Pat more or less dragged Brett to the library. "This is Bev's friend, Brett," she said to Wes.

Wes stood and shook hands. "How ya doing?"

Pat said, "I'm going back to the kitchen. You kids remember, no fighting, okay?"

Ed said, "Well, I guess I'll leave you boys to get acquainted while I run upstairs and grab a shower. See you later."

Over the next half-hour Brett and Wes exchanged brief bios. Wes was full of questions about the Nobles but Brett, true to his nature, was not especially forthcoming. He gave Wes the briefest of answers—just enough to satisfy Wes' curiosity—and steered the discussion to the work of the Trust, which he obviously was passionate about.

Ed found the boys where he had left them. Their conversation stopped when he walked in. "Don't let me interrupt you," he said. "I just wanted to fix a drink." As Ed made a martini, he stood at the bar listening to Wes who was asking Brett what he thought would happen with the recession worsening

"Dinner's ready," came a call from the dining room.

"Better not keep them waiting," Ed said. "It's okay. Bring your drinks. You can finish them at the table before we get into Brett's bottle of wine."

Chapter 40

Wes was like a kid on a merry-go-round during his stay with the Nobles and he didn't want to get off. This was his first visit to California and he was overwhelmed with it. His life in the mid-west and in the east didn't prepare him for the extravagance and excess he encountered in greater Los Angeles. Pat showed him everything she could pack into a short week, and she packed a lot in—Rodeo Drive to Marine World and everything in between.

Pat and Wes went sailing with Beverly who was surprised to see what a good sailor Wes was. He explained that they had a Catalina 350 and since they were kids, he and his sister had spent a lot of time on various sailboats his dad had owned.

Bev told Pat that if for only his sailing skills, he was a keeper.

"Oh, but he has many other skills," Pat said with a grin.

"Hey!" Wes said. "Put a lid on that."

"I'll bet he does." Bev laughed at her sister's blush. "You're not going all modest are you, Patty?"

After returning to the dock, the three of them went to Mermaids, a restaurant just a short walk from *Pilcher's* berth. They had drinks and calamari while waiting for Brett, who joined them after work.

The two couples went to dinner several evenings. Although disappointed, Sandy gracefully accepted not having them eat at home every night—the twins obviously wanted the guys to get to know one another without parents around. One night, Ed and

Sandy took all of them to dinner at Michael's on Third Street. Brett and Wes couldn't stop raving about that meal.

By the time a week had passed, Ed and Sandy had a chance to understand, to some degree, who Wes Blanchard was and they concluded that Pat had indeed made a good choice. Brett too, formed a positive opinion of Wes and enjoyed hanging out with him.

Wes would have loved to continue his stay for another week—for that matter, all summer—but his parents pressed him to come home. The reality was, he did have an engineering internship waiting for him and so, he told Pat, he needed to leave Sunday morning. While she hated the thought of him going, she knew she shouldn't make it difficult for him.

Pat and Wes left the house Saturday morning after breakfast and drove to the U.C.L.A., parked the car and strolled hand in hand looking at the buildings and taking in the feel of the huge campus. Wes said, "I'm glad we're doing this. When I'm in Cambridge and I think of you, I can picture in my mind where you'll be and what you'll be seeing as you walk around."

"Will that make you happy or sad?" Pat asked.

"I don't know." He stopped and brought his face close to hers. "I do know I'll be wishing I was here with you." They walked silently for several minutes when Wes said, "You know, maybe I'll take my second year right here. They've got a damn good engineering department and—"

"And we'd be together. That would be awesome! Do you think we will still feel this way after being apart?"

Wes turned to her and drew her close. "I don't know about you, but I will."

The twins and Sandy planned a special dinner for Wes his last night with them. Ed wanted to barbeque steaks but he was overruled.

"Don't worry," Sandy told him. "The girls and I have got it covered. It'll be excellent."

While the three ladies were putting the final touches on what they were calling "The Bon Voyage" dinner, Ed and the two boys were in the library where Ed was introducing them to *The Martini.* "The secret to a really good martini," he was telling them, "is getting the proportions right and, of course, using a good gin like Sapphire, or if it's a vodka martini, then Belvedere or my favorite, Chopin." He poured the vodka into a large ice-filled shaker and added several squirts of dry vermouth. He gave the mixture a vigorous shake, put a jalapeño stuffed olive in each of three stemmed cocktail glasses and poured. "And that's how it's done."

Brett laughed. "That's it? Some vodka and a dash of vermouth? What's the big deal? I thought you were going to show us some highly crafted concoction."

Wes added, "I have to agree. No offense, but it's like vodka, vermouth and an olive." He took a sip and sputtered. "Wow! Hey, how 'bout this. Cheers, Mr. N."

They clinked glasses and said, "Cheers," just as Bev arrived to announce that dinner was on the table. As they walked to the dining room, Wes whispered to Brett, "Did you like that martini?"

Brett gave him a wry look. "Are you kidding? I hated it."

The ladies of the house had outdone themselves and prepared, at least to their way of thinking, exactly what their men would like. The centerpiece was Prime rib of beef au jus.

"That was an excellent meal, Mrs. Noble," Wes exclaimed.

Brett added, "I'll second that." He looked admiringly at Sandy. "I've had dinners at your house in Malibu that Mrs. Weir made and they were fantastic. But really, this was as good as anything of hers and everybody used to say she was the best cook around."

Sandy grinned. "That's sweet of you, Brett, but I'm no match for Mrs. Weir. Furthermore, the girls had a big part in preparing the meal, so you boys should thank them as well."

Wes stood and, clearly tongue-in-cheek, said, "Thank you, Miss Beverly. Thank you, Miss Patricia. That dinner sure was keen. I don't know about Brett, but if I was ever to marry some girl, I'd sure want her to be as good a cook as you two are." He took a little bow and sat down. The others at the table applauded and laughed. Wes stood and bowed again, holding his hands up as if to quiet the accolade.

Brett looked up at him and shook his head. *Give me a break* was written all over his face.

After commanding their mother to stay seated, the girls cleared the table. Bev returned from the kitchen with a stack of desert plates. Pat was carrying a cherry pie.

Wes asked Pat, "Did you make that?"

"You're kidding, right?"

They lingered at the table drinking coffee and chatting, everyone quizzing Wes on his reactions to southern California, what he thought of the UCLA campus, his plans for the rest of the summer.

After fielding questions to everyone's satisfaction, he looked around the table. "I just want to say that I'm very glad that I got to meet all of you," he said sincerely. "Especially you, Bev. Pat talks about you all the time. Your relationship really is something special. I've got a sister and we're close but it's nothing like you two. Anyway, now that I've met you I can understand why Pat loves and admires you so much."

Bev smiled at him, feeling suddenly a little shy.

"As for you folks," he looked at Ed then turned his gaze to the opposite end of the table where Sandy sat, "of course I saw the stories in the papers and on TV when Bev was being held in Mexico. Heck, everybody did. When I met Pat at school, she never said anything about it but some of her girlfriends told me who she was and naturally, I was curious so I checked it out on Google."

Bev sucked in air and straightened in her chair.

Wes looked at her reassuringly. "No, I'm not dredging that up. The point is," he continued, "I just want you all to know how much I respect what you have done, what you are doing with your winnings. It seems to me that starting your charity would have been enough, but making this big change, going from that rad life in Malibu to this, say, more conventional life was a big step but obviously one you were willing to take. I can't say for sure, but I'm guessing part of your motivation was to insure that your daughters didn't end up being air heads and dopers like some of the wealthy girls I know."

"Here, here," Pat couldn't resist chirping.

He gave Pat a smile. "Anyway, I don't know what's going to happen with Pat and me. We're going to be far apart for long periods of time and I don't know how that'll work. But whatever happens I just want you to know it's been a privilege for me to have her as a girlfriend and to have been able to meet all of you." Wes looked around the table, cleared his throat and sat down."

All eyes lingered on him for a long moment. There wasn't a sound until Sandy spoke. "That was a lovely tribute, Wes. Thank you so much for putting words to it. Ed and I have always hoped our daughters would make good choices in their relationships. We don't know you that well, but I think I speak for everyone when I tell you that we believe Patty has made an excellent choice and we hope your relationship flourishes." Sandy turned from Wes and looked at Pat who was wiping tears away with her napkin. Sandy smiled at her. Pat returned her smile with a tremulous one of her own.

Ed spoke up. "I agree. Of course, I always agree with my wife. It's the only sensible thing to do." He paused as giggles and chuckles abated. "We appreciate your kind and thoughtful words. I just want you to know that if during your school breaks you'd like to pay us a visit, and by us I really mean Pat, I'll see to it that an airline ticket is provided." Ed cleared his throat. "I'm not trying to bribe you—"

"Daddy!" Pat broke in.

"I'm just trying to help my daughter enjoy life and I guess you might be a big part of that enjoyment."

More laughter broke the tension and everyone started talking at once. Brett looked around the table than tapped a spoon against his wine glass. Immediately, conversation ceased and all eyes turned toward him.

"Since speeches seem to be on the menu this evening, I would be remiss if I didn't offer one as well." He paused as everyone at the table waited expectantly. "I know what I'm about to say may cause some consternation in view of the recent decisions made by this family. Nonetheless, I really have no alternative other than to confess that while I was leaving the office recently, Cass, the receptionist in the lobby, asked me if I had bought any raffle tickets and I said no, I never buy them. She told me it wasn't a big lottery like the one you won," he glanced at Ed, "but it was in the millions. Now, most of you know how I feel about lotteries. The odds of millions to one are enough to keep me from spending money on it. So, I can't explain why I bought ten tickets. Maybe I just felt lucky after bringing Bev those roses the other night."

Bev was the only one to speak. "Are you kidding me? You actually bought lottery tickets?"

There was a general buzz around the table.

"That's right. I bought the tickets. I knew that was stupid." A rueful little smile played across his face as he looked at Beverly.

Then he took a deep breath and continued, "But I didn't feel stupid when I found out that I and two other people had the winning numbers."

The table erupted. "You won? You gotta be kidding! What the hell!"

Ed jumped up and yelled, "Quit the fooling around, Brett! You didn't win any lottery."

Brett face broke into a huge smile. "I know it's crazy but, honest, Ed, I won the damn thing. I expect after taxes I'll end up with around three million or so. It's nothing like what you won but it's better than a poke in the eye."

Mayhem ensued as Beverly jumped up and threw her arms around him. Everyone was talking at once. Brett held up his hands and yelled, "Hey, take it easy. I've something else I need to say."

The room became still. Brett drew Beverly to his side, turned to her and whispered, "I love you." Then in response to the question hovering in the air, he said, "I know you want to know the first thing I'm going to buy with my new-found wealth. Well, I'm not going to *buy* anything. The first thing I'm going to do is ask this beautiful red-headed girl to marry me."

Beverly melted into his arms. Brett held her tightly. He looked deeply into her eyes. "Do you think you might say yes?"

Her radiant smile told him everything he needed to know.

Brett turned his attention back to the table and in a firm, and for him, quite strong voice, said, "And the next thing I'm going to do..." He paused and looked into the face of each person in turn, a twinkle in his eye. "And next..." He stopped to heave a theatrical sigh. "I suppose I'm going to have to buy a house in Malibu."

In bed that night, Sandy asked Ed, "Can you believe he won a lottery? What are the chances of that?"

Ed laughed. "Pretty damn slim. It defies logic and yet, I know there have been a number of people who have won twice. One guy won three lotteries."

Sandy thought about it and said, "For a person who is so reserved and serious, the Malibu thing was pretty funny."

Ed grinned. "And slipping in that marriage proposal—that was clever."

They remained quiet for a while. Each with their thoughts.

Finally, Sandy said, "Anyway, that was some remarkable evening."

To which Ed replied, "One of the best."

"One of the best? Which evening then was the very best?"

Ed didn't have to think about it. "The evening you and I got married."

Epilogue

It was just another day. Nothing special about it. Ed stood up, stretched, then put the report he was reading in its folder and placed it in the file cabinet, satisfied that the Noble Charitable Trust was, indeed, doing a good job. Time to go home. He took his black leather jacket off the hook, slipped it on, closed the office door and walked to the elevator. He stepped out into the lobby and walked toward the exit, waving to the receptionist as he went by.

"Hey, Mr. Noble," the woman called after him. "Did you buy some tickets for the Powerball? It's the last day. The drawing's tonight."

His hand on the door lever, he turned. "No, I didn't, Cass, but thanks for reminding me."

The receptionist said, "It's a big one—something like $300,000,000. I bought ten tickets."

Ed's eyebrows lifted. "No kidding, ten tickets. How 'bout that?"

"You should pick some up on your way home. You never know," she said with a grin. "You might get lucky."

Ed smiled and replied, "That's what I'm afraid of. I might get lucky."

He pushed the door open and walked out to his pickup.

On the way home he spotted a florist shop and stopped. "I'd like a dozen long stem red roses please," he told the clerk.

"I do have some long stems. They're five dollars apiece, sir. Do you still want them?"

"That's okay." Ed smiled. "I can afford to splurge once in a while."

Roses in hand, Ed walked back to his pickup, a spring in his step. "Don't have a Powerball ticket," he muttered, "but I've got these roses. I think I'll get lucky tonight."

-END-